Roots Run Deep

N.S. Nichols

For My Family
Thank you for keeping me deeply rooted.

In Memory of My Cousin Tisha
*You inspired me in so many ways. I am a better person for knowing you. Thank
you for the love and friendship you offered me my whole life.
Forever in my heart.*

CHAPTER ONE

Orange, yellow, and burgundy decorated the rolling landscape. My favorite time of the year held hostage by the worst time in my life. Yellow buses lined the front of the building beside a parking lot full of vehicles. Teens filtered through the parking lot, on the sidewalks, and along the steps. When the car pulled to a stop, two girls appeared in the side view mirror. My hand froze on the door handle as the knots in my stomach tightened. Mom's voice broke the silence.

"It's gonna be great. New school, new town. Lots of new friends."

Mom and her incessant need for positivity. My eyes shot to her beaming face, and I involuntarily gave her a smile.

"I know," I said begrudgingly.

"Zinn, it's not that bad," Mom assured as she threw me a look of frustration. "We're just one county away from our old home."

Not that bad? I moved away from all my friends to my rival school, and she has the nerve to say it's not that bad.

"I know." I let out a sigh as I reluctantly opened the door and slid out of the car.

Mom cleared her throat. "Bug?"

My eyes shot to her.

"Love you."

"Love you too," I replied, then closed the door.

With the chaotic crowd surrounding me, I cradled a notebook against my chest as I stood frozen. The flip-flopping of my stomach urged me to look over my shoulder to see Mom's smiling face. Taking a deep breath, I took the dreaded first step and climbed the stairs to walk through the front doors. Navigating through the crowd of students, the hush of chatter followed me down the hall. Turning right, I finally arrived at the school's main office and opened the door. The grey-haired secretary from registration last week smiled warmly at me, explaining it would be a moment before she could assist me. The waiting area consisted of three chairs that of course happened to be occupied, so I moved toward the empty wall when a throat cleared. A deep voice sounded, and my chest tightened involuntarily.

"Here ya go!"

A statuesque boy with dark hair rose from a seat, smiled, and casually leaned against the wall next to the vacant chair. Heat filling my cheeks, I slinked into the chair. The warmth of the seat comforted me. Realizing I'd said nothing to this guy, I immediately straightened myself.

"Uh, thanks," I blurted awkwardly.

His eyes danced as he gave a nod. "Welcome."

The office door opened, and noise from the hallway spilled into the room. "Savvy, you done yet?"

"Nope," he replied.

Savvy? I thought. *Interesting name.* In the hallway stood a curly haired boy with his back to the office door. Facing him, a stunning platinum-haired girl, who looked like she'd just stepped off the runway, batted her voluminous lashes as she pouted her lips at him. All of a sudden, her eyes darted my way. Then the platinum princess grabbed hold of the muscular, curly haired guy's hand and pulled him down the hall.

"Later, Savvy," said the curly haired boy.

"Later, Bear," replied Savvy.

Then the door closed, muffling the noises in the hallway.

The secretary motioned and the red-haired girl seated next to me walked toward the counter. My eyes darted toward Savvy again. He made no movement toward the seat. I exhaled as I relaxed the grip on my notebook.

Within a couple of minutes, a door on the left opened and a short, pudgy man stepped out. "Mr. Sullivan," he summoned.

The statuesque boy pushed himself off the wall, and his green eyes twinkled as he smiled at me. "See you later."

I sheepishly smiled back as he walked past me and followed the man into the office.

As the clock changed to 7:52 a.m., the bell rang. I squirmed in the chair, stretching to see the grey-haired woman sitting behind the counter. She had the phone against her ear as she typed away at the computer. *Ugh! I'm gonna be late for my first class.* Another minute ticked away on the clock, then another and another. Five minutes remained until the final bell, and a scurry of teens hurried down the hall. I closed my eyes and leaned my head on the wall.

"Zinnia Danthes?"

My eyes shot open. "Yes, ma'am."

The secretary stood at the counter with some papers in her hand. I picked up my backpack and walked over to her.

As I reached the counter, she rattled instructions. "Your schedule, locker assignment, combination, parking pass, and school ID." She scanned the desk and concluded, "That's it."

"Um, okay. Thank you."

Turning her back to me, she replied, "You're welcome, dear." She turned to face someone else and said, "Shannon, I need you to show this new student to her class." The girl didn't respond, only shook her head in confusion. "Oh my, you're not Shannon! Emily, I'm so sorry! I'm just so flustered this morning. Have you seen Shannon?"

Emily shook her head side to side.

"Wonderful. She's late again. Are you still working on Mr. Howard's files?" Emily nodded and the secretary let out a sigh. "Well, I can't take you from that." Facing me, she said, "Dear, I'm sorry. Give me a minute to find someone to help you."

The secretary walked toward a room on the left, then turned her head when the pudgy man's office door opened. Savvy stepped out of the room. Relief came to the secretary's face.

"Savage, could I borrow you for a few minutes to help Zinnia? This is her first day."

"Yes, ma'am. Happy to."

"Thanks so much, dear." Looking at me, she said, "Savage will show you to your first class."

"Yes, ma'am," I said, not disappointed to see him again.

She smiled warmly. "Welcome to Bargeston, dear."

Savage walked to the door and smiled. "Ready?"

I nodded as I fiddled with my papers and placed my backpack on my shoulder. His muscular arm pulled the door handle as he motioned toward the doorway with his free hand. I smiled at him. "Thanks."

Outside the office he turned left and walked a few steps, then broke the silence. "So, it's Zinnia, right?"

"Zinn, actually. Zinn Danthes."

With a slight smile, he gave a nod. "Hmm, interesting. I'm Savage."

My teeth scraped across my bottom lip.

"Well, Zinn, where do I need to get you to?"

Handing him my schedule, our hands lightly touched as he took the paper. I quickly drew back my hand. Warmth immediately filled my cheeks, and no doubt redness filled my face. His gaze dropped to my schedule.

"Hmm, econ for first period, and it looks like we've got English together."

The bell was about to ring, but instead of rushing me to econ, he decided to study my schedule. He didn't flinch with the sound of the final bell. I let out a sigh to signal I'd heard the bell, and Savage looked at me, unruffled. My teeth slid over the corner of my mouth as I fidgeted with the strap of my backpack.

"No worries. You got Coach Bowman."

Raising an eyebrow, I gave him a questioning look.

"He's drinking his coffee for another ten minutes." He motioned with his head to the hall on the left. "Your class is this way."

As we walked to econ, Savage pointed out this wing, that hallway, a classroom here and one over there. The overload of information created chaos and confusion, causing me even more stress.

"You a junior?"

Nodding, he then explained something about lockers. Trying my best to make note of all his directions, I didn't notice our pace had slowed until we stopped at a door.

"So here you are," he said, smiling.

The gold flecks in his green eyes mesmerized me. He cleared his throat and made eye contact as calmness and kindness radiated from him.

Breaking the too-long gaze, I ungracefully fumbled with the pocket on my backpack as I reached for my water, a total cringeworthy move. "Uh, thanks for the help."

"My pleasure, Zinn." He opened the classroom door and handed me the schedule. The sudden hush as the students noticed me—the "new girl"—making my entrance made my stomach tense. I grabbed the paper from his hand and stepped into the room.

"What can I do for you?" asked the large man wearing shorts, a knit shirt, and a baseball cap embossed with the school's mascot—the Bobcats. He looked at his watch and placed his cup on the desk.

"Um, I'm Zinn Danthes. It's my first day." I handed him my schedule.

Nodding, he took the paper. "Oh yeah! They told me I was getting a new student today. Well, find a desk and we'll get started soon." He picked up his cup and took a sip as he propped his feet on the large wooden desk.

In the back of the room, there sat an empty desk behind a guy with curly chestnut-colored hair surrounded by two others just like him—cocky. *That's the last place I want to sit.* Every other row was full, and that one empty desk surrounded by the hotshot squad appeared to be my only choice. *Great!* I took a deep breath and maneuvered my way down the row of cackling, arrogant boys. I'd nearly reached the empty seat when an arm extended in front of me.

"And who are you?" the chestnut-haired boy asked.

"Um, Zinn. Can I please get by?"

"Yeah, Zinn, you can get by. But answer one question," he said with a smug grin.

"Fine." I sighed.

"Was your dad a boxer?"

"What?" I shook my head in confusion.

"Was your dad a boxer?" he repeated with emphasis. "Cause, dang, you're a knockout!" Quiet chuckles ensued from the other boys, which only boosted his overinflated ego.

Raising my eyebrow, I replied with sarcasm, "Yeah! And I got his gnarly left hook."

Snickering, the boy lowered his arm. I stepped past him and slid into the seat.

"So, Zinn, huh?" He turned around and put out his hand. "I'm Drew."

Obligingly, I shook it and gave a partial smile.

"What brings you to the fine halls of Bargeston?"

"Moved from Kowinville." Totally disinterested in this conversation, I unzipped my backpack and kept my eyes down, hoping he would take the hint.

"Kowinville, huh?" Keeping his eyes on me, he said, "Boys, we got a Raven in our midst. Moans ensued from the cluster of boys surrounding Drew. I rolled my eyes and shuffled through my backpack.

"How you likin' it so far?"

"Honestly, not very much right now." Feeling my phone, I pulled it from the bag and checked my texts.

"C'mon, Zinn, you should be happy."

I raised my eyebrow. I would regret the decision, but I couldn't seem to stop myself. "Oh, why's that?"

"You're in Bobcat country now." Raising his hand to the boy seated across from him, he received the expected high-five and smacked back. With a smirk he added, "And a girl like you has her pick of the litter."

Propping my elbow on the desk and resting my chin on my fist, I coolly responded, "Good to know, 'cause I eat bobcats for breakfast."

He gave me a mischievous grin and winked as if I were a noble adversary. "Okay, Zinn, I catch what you're throwing." His brash annoyance almost concealed the innocence in his eyes; their sea of blue sent shivers down my spine.

"Quiet!" Coach Bowman interjected.

Immediately, I sat up and put my attention on the words of the teacher.

"Stock exchange day." The coach snapped his fingers, and a boy on the front row jumped up and walked over to him, ready to receive the stack of papers. "Check your stocks and turn this in by the bell."

Students resumed talking with each other as they casually passed the stack. Several pulled out phones as they looked at their stocks.

Handing me a paper, Drew stared. "I'm here if you need me," he said, then winked.

The glint in his eyes intrigued me, but I coyly replied, "I think I can manage."

The paper showed no instructions, only a chart that gave no explanation to what should be filled in it, leaving me completely confused. Around the room, everyone else worked with complete ease on the assignment. Shaking my head, I closed my eyes. *I can't believe I have to do this.* After inhaling a deep breath, I stretched out my arm and tapped Drew on the shoulder. Immediately turning to me, Drew's face had an anticipative expression.

"So, you do need me?"

"Uh, no!" I said emphatically. "What I need is to understand this assignment."

Suddenly, his suspicious look transformed into sweetness. I boldly asked several questions about the assignment, and Drew patiently answered everything. After we finished discussing stocks and investments, something I was forced into caring about strictly for the duration of the class, we continued talking. Drew seemed pretty chatty—for a guy. He talked about school, football, and the local hangouts. He asked me about why I moved here. Then came questions about my family, which always caused that familiar lump to form in my throat.

"Um, well, my dad passed away."

"Wow, I'm sorry," Drew said.

I expressed the obligatory words of gratitude and returned to the assignment. Avoiding that awkward hesitation that always followed the mention of my deceased father, I scribbled an answer to the stock market increase on the paper.

"So were you close to your dad?" Drew said, peering at me.

Did he just ask about my dad? That almost never happens.

"Yeah, we were close."

"When did it happen?"

"Almost two years ago." Tears formed in my eyes, so I gritted my teeth, hoping it would somehow stop them. Instead, puddles formed, causing one eye to release a tear from its corner. "Sorry." I quickly wiped it away.

"Don't be sorry. You miss your dad. That's normal. Besides, I'm the one who needs to apologize."

"For what?"

"That stupid line about your dad being a boxer."

"Yeah, that was pretty stupid, but funny too. No need to apologize. Honestly, I did get my dad's gnarly left hook."

Drew's smile broke into a laugh. "I'll look out for that then."

As we kept talking, Drew's captivating blue eyes peeked out from underneath the chestnut curls across his forehead. His sweet, boyish face contradicted his forced, cocky bravado. In the corner, I saw two girls huddled together. The blonde one feverishly typing on her phone narrowed her eyes at me and then muttered something to the brunette. Drew's voice pulled me back into our conversation.

"Friday's game . . . You coming?"

"Um, not sure. Supposed to go out with my friend Sam."

"Out with Sam, huh? Interesting. So tell me about this Sam guy."

"This Sam guy has been my best friend since third grade. And Sam is technically Samantha," I clarified.

"Samantha, huh? Even more interesting." He gave me a wink, implying he was glad to know Sam was a girl.

A smile formed on his lips as he rattled off something, but my attention gravitated toward the two girls. As they glared at me, they whispered to each other. I quickly returned to Drew, trying my best to diminish the shattering effects on my self-esteem by the mean-girl duo.

"Coach!" came a deep voice from the center of the room.

A boy sat a couple of rows from me displaying a panic-filled face. A loud snicker came from one of the girls in the corner, drawing my attention. The panicked boy rambled something to the coach that filtered through the room.

"My stock crashed today! I lost all my money."

"Anyone gonna bailout Malone?" Hands flew into the air, then the teacher said, "Bear, take it."

The two girls with their stares caused a sick feeling in my stomach. I waved Drew off as he mumbled something and walked away. Without thinking I said, "Yeah, okay."

The brunette gave me a smug look as she cocked one eyebrow. Quickly, my gaze shot away. The tightening in the pit of my stomach was followed by another wave of nausea. I closed my eyes and took a deep breath, then resumed the classwork.

As I worked on the assignment, the wanna-be divas continued to glare at me, which perpetuated my nausea. I put my head down and focused on my work. Within a matter of minutes, I had completed the few questions.

Feeling the stares of the two girls, I took some deep breaths. Looking for a momentary distraction, I opened the spiral-bound journal and flipped to my latest song. The pencil flipped between my fingers as I softly hummed the melody. Inspiration hit, and I scribbled a line.

Drew's voice interrupted my writing. "Miss me?"

Turning my head toward him, I raised an eyebrow. "Not yet. Maybe leave again and I will."

"Ouch." He grabbed his chest. "That hurt."

He laughed lightly as he turned forward in his seat and I went back to my writing. Within a few minutes he turned sideways to continue whatever awkward conversation he'd begun.

"Zinn?"

"Yeah," I said, not taking attention away from the lyrics.

"You know how they say *nothing lasts forever?*"

"What?"

Drew repeated himself, so I offered a generic reply. "Uh, I guess."

"Zinn, would you be my nothing?" He stared into my eyes.

Rolling my eyes, I smirked at him. "That's very bad."

"Yeah, but it made you smile a little." He winked at me, clearly not ready to stop the banter. Suddenly, his eyes fell to my notebook. His head twisted around as his eyes scanned the page. He mumbled some of the words, then said, "You write songs?"

I shrugged my shoulders. "I guess."

"You guess?" He gave me a smirky smile with questioning eyes. "This is music notation with lyrics, a hook, and a cool bridge. I would say it's a song."

"Hold up. You know music?"

He nodded his head up and down, leaving me at a loss for words. His casual charm seemed to push past my defenses. "Don't seem the type?"

"It is surprising."

"Well, I'm no musical genius like you, obviously, but . . ." With a mischievous glint in his eyes, he replied, "I will say I am full of surprises."

My first impression of Drew was totally wrong. The more he talked, the more he surprised me—in a good way. He was proving himself to be more than a cocky football player vying for the center of attention. Entranced with his words, the bell sounded—sooner than I expected—unfortunately ending our conversation.

Walking out of class, Drew put his dry wit on full display. "Catch you later, Zinn. Oh, by the way, you religious?"

Shrugging, I said, "Uh, yeah, why?"

"Because you're the answer to all my prayers."

Pleased with his joke, he held back a laugh and gave me an *I can't help it* look while placing his hand over his heart.

I bit the corner of my mouth to keep from smiling, unsuccessfully. "Bye, Drew."

"Bye, Zinn." He took his hand off his heart, offered a casual salute, then walked opposite me down the hallway.

As I walked away from Drew, the two girls from econ traipsed ahead of me. The brunette flaunted her perfect catwalk. The blonde's feeble attempt couldn't compete with her friend, but it didn't keep her from trying. The captivating duo, who were obviously starved for attention, succeeded at their mission of turning the heads of all the guys. The girls' heads turned, too, intrigued, probably wondering how they could be more like them.

What a joke.

Students filtering into the hallway didn't seem to pay attention to the unknown face in the crowd—mine. According to my schedule, I needed to find West Hall. The sign showed it was the next left. I fought against the mass of teens like a fish swimming upstream. I battled through lip-locked couples, guys rough-housing, and girls congregating to exchange makeup and gossip. Turning into West Hall, someone collided into my back, pushing me forward. Everything moved in slow-motion as I reached the point of no return. Falling on my face became inevitable. I instinctively braced my hands to lessen the impact but collided with a muscular chest instead.

"Woah! Easy does it."

Hands gently eased me back to a standing position and in front of me stood Savage. "You okay?" he asked.

"Yeah, um, just embarrassed."

"Hmm, no worries. The stumble wasn't even noticed." Smiling sweetly, he released my arm.

Stumble? I was pushed! Not wanting to play the victim since no one in the crowd showed any recognition of what just happened, I took the high road. "Uh, well, thanks for the help."

Savage smiled. "Where you headed?"

"History. Mr. Wilson . . . Room 210?"

"Mind if I walk with you?"

"Okay," I said nervously.

Even though our walk remained relatively quiet, it did provide comfort. As we approached room 210, sitting alone in an empty class-room for the next five minutes sunk my heart. Readying myself to say goodbye to Savage, he stopped a few feet shy of the classroom door, leaned his back on the wall, and asked me another question. The hall began emptying as the two-minute bell rang. Savage pressed himself off the wall and walked me to the door.

"I'd better go. Thanks for the walk."

"You're welcome," I said, feeling silly he thanked me for walking *me* to class.

"Hmm, see ya." He threw up his hand and walked back the very direction we had come, then casually strolled down the hallway. He turned back around, and his eyes locked on mine as he flashed a smile. Giving him a quick smile in return, I stepped into the classroom.

I walked to the teacher's desk and handed him my registration slip. The man introduced himself as Mr. Wilson and pointed me to an empty seat. As soon as I settled in my seat, my "first day of school" nightmare came true as he handed out a quiz.

The girl next to me tapped her nails on the desk. As my skin began to crawl, I combatted the annoyance by squirming in my seat. *Is this what misophonia is? Or is the stress of the quiz just making me overly sensitive?* Mr. Wilson sat behind his desk, keeping his brow furrowed as his eyes scanned the class. The tick of the clock taunted me. With three questions answered and ten minutes left in class, I would be lucky to get five completed. *Five out of twenty. That's fantastic.* My phone buzzing, the clock ticking, or the tapping of the nails—I didn't know which was worse.

Since I'd left Sam in the middle of our text conversation this morning, she was the likely culprit of the incessant buzz. Honestly, taking the quiz gave me a break from having to listen to Sam go on and on about Bryce. As much as I loved Sam, she couldn't or wouldn't take the hint that I didn't want to talk about Bryce. It still hurt too much.

With the ring of the bell, I grabbed the test paper with only six questions answered and set it in the basket on the teacher's desk. I slipped out the door and headed down the hall. Turning right toward the east wing placed me in the path of a group of guys leaning on the wall. *Great, just my luck. I'm going to have to walk past them.* I took a deep breath and casually strolled by.

"There she is!" one of the boys said.

"Yo! New girl." A superb-looking guy with dark, wavy hair and piercing dark-brown eyes gave me a quick nod paired with a cocky grin. "What's your name?"

"Um, me?" I pointed to myself.

"You're new and a girl, right?"

I nodded nervously.

"So what's your name?" The gutsy guy pushed himself off the wall and took on an alpha stance.

"Uh, Zinn." I swallowed the lump that had formed in my throat.

The other guys still propped up on display snickered. The self-assured character certainly stood out from the other boys as he casually strutted over to me.

"Hi, Zinn." Moving closer to me as he spoke, my pulse quickened. I simply nodded my head in response. He leaned toward me with an air of familiarity I was not expecting, placed his lips close to my ear, and softly said, "Name's Dawson. You have amazing eyes, by the way."

Heat filled my cheeks. "Uh, thanks." What else could I say?

Casually shrugging his shoulders, he added, "Just wanting you to feel welcome."

My eyes widened. A chuckle came from the other guys. *Is this some kind of game or bet? Who can talk to the new girl first?* The group looked on eagerly as they awaited my response. Dawson raised a brow as his lips formed a slight grin. "See you later, Zinn."

I clenched my backpack straps, nodded at Dawson, and resumed my walk to trig. Moving on past them, one of them said, "Yo, dawg! She's definitely top rung. New contender?"

"Maybe," Dawson said.

Top rung? What does that mean? Their attention and comments made me self-conscious and confused, as if I'd unknowingly been interviewed for something. But for what?

When I came to the classroom door, Dawson and the other alpha guys pushed off the wall and headed toward me. *Are they in my class?* Dawson's eyes bore into mine as he passed me. He gave me a flirtatious smirk before slipping into the classroom across from mine. I stepped into trig with two of the alpha guys behind me. *Great, another hour filled with anxiety-fueled distraction.*

I went through the new-student routine, walked with forced confidence past the girls who sent me haughty glances, and found my seat. Yet another room full of inquisitive teens. No one seemed interested in talking to me—only staring at me like I was on exhibit. I pulled out my phone and read over Sam's text. Just as I predicted: she talked about Bryce. With no desire to discuss him anymore, I texted her that I would talk to her later.

CHAPTER TWO

As much as I hated trig, class went by pretty fast. When I left the room, the books weighing down my backpack motivated me to finally search out my locker. Fumbling through the front pocket of the backpack, I found the paper with my locker assignment. The lockers trailed down both sides of the hall. About a third of the way down on the right appeared locker 117. I let out a sigh, grabbed the lock, and turned the dial. When the dial came to the last number, I pulled it firmly, but nothing happened. I double-checked the combination and landed on each number precisely, gave another pull, but still nothing. Frustrated, I started to try again when I felt a tap on my shoulder.

"Need some help?" Drew leaned on the locker next to mine and shot me a big grin.

"Absolutely." I handed him the paper with the combination scribbled on it.

His nimble fingers spun the dial, he gave a quick pull to release lock and . . . the metal door opened. "There you go, ma'am."

"You're a prince." I placed my books in the locker. "Thanks a bunch."

A mischievous grin formed across his face. "You could say I'm your knight in shining armor."

"I could." I slung my backpack over my shoulder and looked at him expressionless. "But I won't."

He laughed in understanding, which I appreciated. "Where you headed?"

"English. Room 134."

"Walk you?"

"I guess it's better than walking alone." He deserved a smirk over a smile from me at this point, to keep my guard up, so I offered one and headed with him down the hall. Falling into step with me, he laughed as he shot back with a witty comment. The playful repartee ensued as we made our way to my class.

Drew's towering physique made my petite frame feel even smaller. As we walked together, eyes shot our way as whispers ensued. Drew either didn't notice or didn't care. He smiled and gave a heads-up to people as we passed. Enjoying his flirtatious banter, our competition in quick-wittedness entertained me. His comebacks required some cunning retaliation on my part. Overall, the lighthearted conversation made for a quick walk to my class. With a few minutes left until the bell rang, we arrived at the door to my English class.

"Well that went way too fast," Drew said as he leaned on the wall.

His serious tone stumped me. He seemed disappointed to go, which made me smile.

"Um, I should get in there."

Drew pushed off the wall and gave me a look that implied he was prepping for another witty remark. "By the way, thanks for the gift."

"What gift?"

"For the smile. Been wearing it since you gave it to me."

My smiled widened and I gave a slight chuckle.

"See ya, Zinn." Drew winked, then dashed down the hall as the bell rang.

A middle-aged woman sat behind a wooden desk in my English class. I walked over to her and held out my registration slip. She smiled and introduced herself as Mrs. Hart. Handing me a spiral notebook, she explained about the daily journal entry. As she gave me the English book, she pointed to a seat in the back near the window. "That's your assigned seat. Welcome to class, Zinnia."

"Thank you." I walked to the desk and settled into my seat. The clock on the wall showed three minutes before the bell. I grabbed my phone and sent a reply to Sam's text.

Me: Hey Sammy, school's okay.
no surprise, she's been after him since fresh yr
Sam: Jasmine's such trash
Me: doesn't matter he ended it he's a free agent now
Sam: just give him time
Me: Idk, may be 4 the best
Sam: no way…trust me, he'll call
Me: whatev…gotta go…class starting

Jasmine had always been a point of contention for Bryce and me. No doubt he loved the attention she was giving him now. Fighting the tears spilling out of my eyes proved pointless, so I let them stream down my cheeks. Lowering my head, I shuffled through my backpack to avoid eye contact with anyone.

"Zinn, how are you?"

My eyes shot up and there sat Savage, right next to me.

"Um, good." I returned to my backpack as I tried my best to rid my face of any tears. When I faced him again, he smiled.

"Heard you met Bear."

"Met Bear?" *What is he talking about?* "I didn't meet a bear."

"Drew Behr. Econ?"

Drew is Bear? The same guy outside the office door this morning with the platinum-blonde girl? How did I miss that? Coach Bowman even said the name Bear.

"Uh, yeah, I met him. Didn't realize he was called Bear."

"It's what he's called on the field," Savage clarified.

So, the platinum-blonde and Drew are a thing. No wonder we got all the stares walking the hall together. He has a girlfriend. My pulse quickened. *Is that why I got the evil eye from those girls in econ? They're probably friends with the platinum princess. Great, now I had a real-life* Mean Girls *scenario going on.* Heat rose in my face and I sighed. *Drew really had some nerve. I can't believe I was so stupid.*

"Okay, class, we're starting biography writing today." The teacher acknowledged the moans from the class. "I know, I know! Not your favorite. Instead of a historical figure, you're going to write about someone you know personally." Several hands raised, but the teacher ignored them as she passed out the papers. "It's due in six weeks. Details are on the assignment sheet. Partners will be chosen at random. When you finish your journal entry, see me for your partner's name."

Quickly finishing the day's journal entry, I slipped out of my desk chair. With the long line at Mrs. Hart's desk, I retreated and sat back down, too impatient to stand there doing nothing. I grabbed my journal and started writing. My hand couldn't write fast enough as all the emotions from the day poured out. Thoughts about my new school, Bryce, and Drew—aka Bear—filled the page. Savage cleared his throat and shot me back to reality.

"Sorry. Um, we're together."

My eyes widened.

"I mean, for the assignment," he said nervously. "We're partners."

"Yeah, uh, that's cool."

What is the assignment? The paper peeked out from under my notebook and I picked it up. "This thing? What is it again?"

"The biography thing," he said, confusion filling his face.

"Guess I'm a little lost."

"Hmm, no worries." His eyes softened as he stared at me.

I gulped and then clarified the information on the paper. "So, this assignment? We have to do some interviews and a paper?"

"Hmm, it's not so bad."

I shrugged my shoulders. "I guess."

"You free Saturday?"

Did I hear that right? His green eyes peered back at me as he waited for my response. I replied awkwardly, "Sorry?"

"Saturday? Wanna work on the assignment?"

"Uh, well," I stammered. "Um, I'm busy Saturday." *I'm one beat off with this conversation. Of course, he was talking about the assignment. Why would he ask me if I'm free otherwise?*

He scribbled on some paper and handed it to me. "Text me later and we'll go from there."

Taking the slip of paper from his hand, I laid it on the desk. *Should I give him my number too?* His eyes still on me, I fidgeted in my seat, then scribbled down my number and handed him the paper.

"Here ya go!"

"Hmm." He smiled and slipped the paper in his pocket.

The teacher dismissed for lunch and the class filtered out of the room into the hallway. I grabbed my backpack and followed everyone out the door.

"Know where you're going?" Savage said from behind me.

"Not really." I turned and looked at him. "Just following the crowd."

"Hmm, could be trouble."

"Yeah, I guess it could." I was being sarcastic but playful.

"How 'bout I show you?"

"Thanks." The color rose to my cheeks.

As we walked the hall, whispers came from the crowd. The upside-down flip of my stomach made me feel nauseous. *Could walking with Savage cause me trouble too?* No flirting came from him, so that was good. Hopefully, this innocent walk wouldn't carry a risk of establishing another group of enemies on my first day.

"How's classes?" Savage asked.

"Decent."

"Hmm, cool."

Savage and I walked wordlessly to the cafeteria. I wasn't used to someone so quiet. Weirdly, I didn't feel the need to say anything. I think this experience was a first for me. Whenever there was silence, it tended to make me nervous, but with him it didn't bother me.

As we turned the corner, the noise from the cafeteria grew louder. Seconds later, walking toward me came none other than Drew. *Or should I say Bear since that's how he's known?* I cringed as he gave me a friendly smile. *He really has some nerve.*

"Savvy!" he said jovially. "Aren't you the lucky guy."

"Bear," Savage coolly replied.

"Hey, Zinn, how's it going?"

I said nothing.

"Uh, Zinn, you okay?"

I clenched my jaw and forced a reply. "I'm fine." I looked at Savage. "Thanks for showing me the way. I'll see you later." I walked away from the two of them and headed toward the noise. Drew's voice filtered to me. "Dude, she okay?"

Savage's voice trailed away as the noise from the cafeteria increased. A line leading into what I assumed was the cafeteria prompted me to fall into it. A few minutes passed when someone yelled, "Yo! Savvy!"

Savage came around the corner alone. I exhaled. He spoke to someone and then fell into the line several people behind me. I grabbed a tray, chose a suspicious-looking pasta dish and a waxy apple from the underwhelming options, then paid. I stepped into a crowded dining room and there was not one familiar face among the numerous round tables. *Wonderful! A cafeteria full of people and I recognize no one. Ugh, this is all Drew's fault. If I hadn't seen him, then I wouldn't have stormed off from Savage. Now I'm stuck eating alone. Pshh! My first day keeps getting better and better.*

Outside were several empty picnic tables, so I navigated through the mass of bodies and exited the dining room and found an empty table next to some potted plants that could use a sip of my water. The sunshine felt remarkable as I basked in its brightness. A couple of minutes passed, then the warmth of the sun disappeared.

"Enjoying the sunshine?" Savage stood over me with a grin and soft eyes.

"Uh . . ." I fumbled with words as I straightened myself in the seat. "Yeah, just getting my daily dose of vitamin D."

Savage settled into the seat across from me and kept his gaze fixated on me. His intensity made me squirm in my seat. Picking up my fork, I pushed the food around on the plate. His twinkling, attentive eyes stared at me.

"How're classes?"

"They're okay," I said.

"What about econ?" Savage's eyes narrowed as he waited for my response.

"Good, I guess. Didn't really do much."

"Hmm." Savage, not taking his eyes off me, consumed his lunch.

I tried my best to avoid his stare, but it seemed impossible since his eyes stayed locked on mine. *Has this guy even blinked?* My leg began to shake. The staring caused enough stress, but the silence became unbearable. *Is he going to say anything? Where's that big black hole to disappear into when you need it?*

Clearing his throat, he said, "How'd you like Coach B?"

"He was fine."

"Hmm."

The silence returned in full-force and hung awkwardly in the air, but at least Savage's eyes weren't boring into me anymore. I could handle our silences but not paired with his stares. He busied himself by wolfing down his pizza and fries while I nibbled at the pasta dish. When he started on the chocolate cake, he broke the silence.

"Meet anyone else in econ?"

"Not sure. I talked to some people."

Savage showed no reaction to that response. As a matter of fact, Savage hadn't shown much reaction to anything. He kept a pretty straight face through this whole conversation. I couldn't get a read on him at all. *What is with all the questions about econ? Something to do with Drew, maybe?*

"I sat behind Drew. He helped me with the assignment."

With this information now out, he shifted in his seat.

Aha! His interest piqued. I was right. He is fishing for information about Drew. He nodded and looked like he might speak, then cleared his throat and paused for a brief moment, then Savage decided to continue. "Sounds like Bear. Always ready to help."

I nodded. Savage's poker face had returned and offered no other clue. *So he needs another nibble.* "Yeah, he was eager to help."

"Hmm."

That's it? Nothing else? My questions still lingered, eating away at me, and I blurted out, "Is there something you wanna ask me?"

"Hmm, not really."

"Not really?" The sarcasm dripped from each syllable.

"Well, your mood . . . Um, it kinda changed."

Unable to make eye contact for the first time, this calm and collected guy seemed uncomfortable in his seat as he abruptly shifted positions.

"Um, well, I mean . . . when . . . uh—"

"When we saw Drew?" I interrupted.

He only offered a casual nod. *Great, he's leaving me to do the talking.* I grabbed my juice and took a drink. *Who is this guy? Why is he criticizing my mood? If he knew how Drew or Bear or whatever his name is flirted with me, would he be so inclined to question my mood?* I shoved another bite of over baked pasta in my mouth to refrain from blurting out the thoughts swirling through my head.

"Sorry I upset you," Savage spoke timidly.

I let out a sigh. "I'm not upset. It's just with being new here, I prefer to keep a low profile."

"Low profile?" He gave me an inquisitive look. "Bear don't seem low profile?"

"*Hmph!* Definitely not."

"Hmm."

"I've got econ with the guy. That's it. Nothing more to say." Realizing my sternness, I softened my tone. "And if you don't mind, I'd prefer not to talk about Drew anymore."

Thankfully, Savage obliged my request. He inquired about my move with some questions thrown in about my old school, Kowinville High. I avoided mentioning anything about Bryce. We discussed the English assignment and made plans to work on it. Overall, lunch was good—at least once the topic of Drew got dropped.

Walking back to class, Drew's girlfriend, the platinum-blonde, stood huddled with the girls from my econ class. Call them what you want—Pink Ladies, Heathers, or Plastics—I had them pegged exactly right, and the platinum princess was the apparent ringleader. As I got closer, the three of them glared at me, but the girlfriend gave me the most disdainful stare down, her eyes piercing me like daggers. When her eyes shot from me to Savage, her look instantly changed. She flashed him a flawless smile as she flirtatiously waved. Savage paid little attention to the vixenish display.

"Savage Sullivan? Aren't you even gonna speak to me?"

"Hello, Sierra," Savage replied.

The platinum-blonde sashayed over to Savage and linked her arm in his, simulating a coy expression. "That's more like it." Immediately, she began bombarding him with compliments. The alluring looks, kittenish giggles, and flirty touches didn't falter Savage's collected presence. The attempts of the platinum princess had failed; Savage remained unfazed.

Unwilling to accept defeat, she remained haughty and turned toward me. "You're the new girl?"

I nodded in agreement.

"Doing pretty good for your first day."

"I'm sorry," I said.

"Meeting all the right people. I'm Sierra, by the way. Looks like Savage here wasn't going to introduce me." Turning her attention back to Savage, she continued. "Of course, Savage, it's just like you to be so sweet and take in strays."

"Excuse me?" I blurted.

Sierra attempted a look of innocence. "Oh, that came out wrong. It's just when we were kids, Savage was always rescuing some hurt animal. Weren't you, Savage?"

"Hmm." Savage remained subdued but gave a short nod and a shoulder shrug.

Sierra returned to the other two girls. She gave me a condescending smirk, signifying I was no threat to her. The other two cronies followed suit behind her with their own smug looks. My feeble attempt at intimidation had no effect on the testy triune. They brushed me off dismissively as they went about their routine of drawing the attention of the testosterone dominant.

The eventfulness of the day had taken its toll on me. Learning Drew played me felt bad enough, but entering enemy camp . . . that part did me in. I had borrowed enough trouble for one day. Now I needed to keep my head down and stay far away from Drew, his girlfriend, and her cronies.

CHAPTER THREE

"Bug, I'm so sorry!" Mom called out the open window of her grey car.

"No big, Mom. It's fine." I got into the car and she rattled off her excuse for being late. I didn't care enough to process what she said because of the text from Sam updating me on the Kowinville gossip. My gut told me to change the subject with Sam, but something in me just couldn't. Instead, I replied, which only invited Sam to feed me even more juicy details. Big mistake! Sam filled me in on the specifics of Jasmine's pursuit of Bryce. A sick feeling came over me, so I slipped the phone under my leg. The puffy white clouds filled the blue sky as I softly hummed along with the car radio.

When Mom's cell rang, her phone conversation replaced the music. I grabbed my earbuds and shoved them into my ears. Every song on my playlists reminded me of Bryce. *Ugh, why can't I get him out of my mind?* The only time I hadn't thought about Bryce today was when I talked with Drew. *Ugh, Drew!* I opened my phone to the latest trending videos, hoping to push away any thoughts of Bryce Waters and Drew Behr.

When we got home, I headed upstairs to shut myself off from everything and everyone—except Oreo, who perked up when I entered my room. I tossed my backpack on the chair as Oreo stared at me with his sweet puppy dog eyes. He pawed at me to pet him, so I ruffled his floppy ears as I sat on the edge of the bed. The unpacked boxes lay scattered throughout my room. I rolled my eyes at the work ahead of me.

"They won't unpack themselves, boy," I said to Oreo as I stood from the bed and grabbed the closest box. The box had no label, so I opened it. It contained a bunch of random items—mostly knick-knacks, candles, a couple of books, and a white envelope with Sam's trademark *Z* written on it. Obviously, one of the boxes Sam helped pack, which explained the lack of label and mix-matched items.

Within minutes, the items from the box filled my shelves. I tore open the envelope from Sam. It contained a stack of pictures from our last day at the lake. That was the best day. Sam and I laughed so much. Flipping through the pics, I found my favorite one of us. As usual, she looked beautiful with her sleek, smooth chocolate-brown hair and brown eyes. Beside her I felt like an ugly duckling with my curly auburn hair and pale skin. But still, I liked the pic. I slid it under the ribbon on the photo board, then quickly flipped through the rest of the pictures, tossing on my desk the ones I wanted for my board. As I flipped to the next picture, I paused. It was of Bryce with his arms wrapped around me, kissing me on the cheek. The tears blurred my vision as I put the picture back in the envelope and shoved it into my desk drawer. Just then, my phone vibrated on the desk. Glancing at the screen, a notification popped up: *da_Bear requested to follow you.*

"Who is that?" I said aloud. Clicking on the notification, a page appeared with pictures of Drew Behr. With my thumb hovering over the decline button, I hit the sleep button instead and threw my phone on the bed.

"Mom, do you know where my grey hoodie is?" I yelled.

"Check the laundry basket in my room!" she answered from downstairs.

Walking to her room, I fumbled through the basket of clean clothes and found the hoodie. Slinking it over my head and shoulders, the nuzzling warmth hugged me. Returning to my room, I removed my AirPods from the case and shoved them in my ears. Grabbing the phone, I bounded down the stairs.

"Going for a walk!" I yelled as I opened the door.

Stepping outside, the cool air filled my lungs and cleared my head. Ready to blast the music, I opened my phone and saw Drew's page. The screen was plastered with pics of him playing football. *So typical! Of course his page would be a shrine to himself.* As much as I wanted to not look at his account, I scrolled anyway. Several pictures were of him with an older man. Some were hunting pictures; others were the two of them on a fishing boat. Then I saw the picture of him with some puppies with the caption, "Bargeston Animal Shelter. The best thing about volunteering is all the Puppy Love!" My heart melted. *No, Zinn! Steer clear of Drew Behr.* Shaking my head, I closed the app and opened the music.

Scrolling through the playlist, I exhaled deeply as the song began to play. It chilled me as it pumped into my brain. Each step became more rhythmic as I sang along. Mrs. Fritz walking her poodle, Dody, Mr. White trimming his hedges, and the two little Baker boys playing catch prevented me from being completely overtaken by the melody.

The song's description of an attention-grabber brought to mind images of Drew. His flirtatious demeanor and nice-guy routine made me grit my teeth. He was adorable and he knew it. I almost fell for his game, but not anymore. *Ugh, Drew Behr has some nerve, boldly flirting with me when he has a girlfriend!* The more I thought of him the angrier I got. I turned up the music to put Drew out of my mind.

As I returned to the house, the red, pink, and orange light kissing the tops of the trees with the disappearance of the sun reminded me of the sunsets over the lake. My friends and I had spent summer break swimming, lounging on the shoreline, sitting around the bonfire at dusk, and watching the stars fill the sky. The entire summer had been perfect, and I had hoped it would never end, but it did. It came to an abrupt end the moment I told Bryce I was moving. The best summer of my life ended with the worst day of my life. *A day I wish I could forget for sure.* My plan of telling him about the move at his favorite place to avoid the bad scene didn't work; instead, it caused a huge blowup and Bryce breaking up with me. That day was the last time he spoke to me.

The next week at school, Bryce ignored me every time he saw me until my last day of school. That day, he actually had me hoping things weren't over for us. I remember walking through the lot and seeing Bryce leaning on the hood of his car with his eyes locked on me. He had been ignoring me for days, yet now he seemed possessed, a guy who wanted his girl back. *Why the attention today, my last day here? Does he want to work things out? Maybe he realizes that me moving away doesn't have to change anything.* Hoping his eyes would soften, I smiled at him. His stare changed to an anger-filled glare, and it gave me chills. He hopped off the car and got in the driver's seat, squealing his tires as he sped out of the parking lot. My heart sank. He'd left for good, and that was it—the last time I saw Bryce.

As the sun set behind the trees and the darkness increased, I went inside and let thoughts of Bryce drift away with the daylight.

The next morning as I stood on the sidewalk, my shoulders sank. Avoiding econ was not an option. My only options were to arrive earlier or later. *Which will it be?* The crowd offered no solace in any of the faces until I saw Haley from chorus. The bubbly blonde smiled as she motioned me over to her. *My arrival time dilemma has been solved. I'll be arriving later and hopefully avoid any interaction with Drew.*

The walk wasn't nearly long enough. Five minutes gave me more time than I wanted, but I'd lingered as long as I could. Rounding the corner, there he stood, and my stomach sank. He walked toward me. I only had one escape. With a quick dart, I disappeared into the girls' bathroom. My situation weighed on me. I could no longer delay the inevitable. I took a moment to rehearse what I wanted to say, repeating it quietly in the stall. Taking a deep breath, I walked out of the bathroom and into the hall. Drew pushed off the wall and fell into step with me.

"Hey, Zinn."

"Hello." I stared straight ahead and quickly entered the classroom. Drew stayed on my heels. I sat down, and he slid into his chair, never once taking his eyes off me—or so it seemed.

"Are you mad at me?"

"I don't need any drama, okay?" I gave him an unfriendly side glance.

"Drama?"

"I don't play games, and I don't want to be played," I retorted sharply.

Drew squinted his eyes and slightly shook his head. "Um, Zinn, I'm really confused. Can you tell me what you're talking about?"

"The tall blonde is who I'm talking about."

"Tall blonde? What tall blonde?"

I slowly rolled my eyes to emphasize my disgust with him. "Hmph! Figures."

"Zinn, what's going on? Yesterday we had fun."

"Fun, really?" *He really thinks I'm so naïve or stupid—or both. Total jerk.* I inhaled deeply, trying to calm myself while also trying to find the right words to let this loser know where I stood. "As for yesterday and that so-called fun, let's leave that in the past," I said sharply with a curt smile. The satisfying retort deflated quickly when Drew's blue eyes grayed.

"Um, okay. If that's what you want." His shoulders slouched and his face turned downward, making him appear totally defeated.

"That's what I want," I replied quickly so I could keep my guilt from backpedaling my defiant stance.

He turned around and didn't say another word to me. During class, his friends cracked jokes, and he only offered half-hearted laughs in response. I busied myself at my desk, but his eyes were piercing through me, and I hated that. *Don't even look at him. It will only cause problems.* If I gave him even an inch, his charming nature would drag me back into that addictive flirtation whirlwind. *Nope, better to ignore him totally.* Besides, I certainly didn't need the Bobbsey Twins in the corner reporting back to their Queen Bee.

Finally, class came to an end, and I escaped out the door as quickly as I could. With that confrontation done, I let myself breathe a little easier as I walked to my next class.

During English, the fresh air blew through the open window, carrying with it some distant laughter from the courtyard. The lesson on technical writing and citing sources couldn't compete with the tempting sunshine. I envied the teens enjoying their momentary freedom from the oppressive lecturers that held us hostage for most of the school day.

Huddled in groups throughout the courtyard, several students lounged in the grass while others sat at the tables scattered throughout the area. One thing they all had in common was the phone that appeared to be tethered to each of them. Except for a group of guys over in the grassy clearing, they laughed while tossing a football. The boy holding the ball and ready to make a pass, yelled, "Bear! Go long!"

My eyes shot over to Drew and his long, graceful strides. Effortlessly and with immense speed, he ran. His tall, muscular physique floated across the courtyard as he attempted to retrieve an impossible catch. With ease, Drew sprung into the air, snatching the dreadfully overthrown pass. He took off in a sprint, slinging past one guy on his right, darting past another on his left. He spiked the ball to the ground as his run came to a halt. Laughing with the other guys, he looked toward the building and came to my window. When our eyes met, the brightness of his face dimmed. His smile was gone. Fighting to break the trance of his heart-wrenching gaze, the smile returned as he threw up his hand. I quickly shifted my gaze to Mrs. Hart in the classroom.

When Mrs. Hart finished the lesson, she dismissed us for lunch. Savage and I left the room and headed toward the cafeteria.

"So, no practice for me today. Wanna work on English?" Savage said.

"Yeah, if my mom can pick me up later."

"I can take you home."

I shrugged. "Okay, thanks."

Savage gave a quick nod and kept his words to a minimum, but not in a rude way. He actually exuded kindness coupled with an upbeat steadiness. He intrigued me for sure. The crowd filled the hallway outside the cafeteria, but Savage and I managed to easily find a place in line. Many in the crowd spoke to Savage while I got inundated with stares, which I did my best to ignore.

"Savvy, come over here, would ya?" a voice boomed among a crowd of boys.

"Hmm, later?"

"You can go. Don't feel like you have to babysit me."

"Hmm, I don't, Zinn." He smiled as he handed me a tray while allowing me to walk in front of him.

Placing a salad and juice on my tray, I took a plate of lasagna from the plump lady behind the counter.

"How are you, Mrs. Smithson?" Savage asked.

She smiled as she grabbed a plate and spooned an extra-large scoop of lasagna on it. Obviously favoring this boy, she then spooned heaping servings of vegetables onto a separate plate and gave both to him. Taking the items, Savage looked at her sincerely and said, "Thanks."

She grinned, and a slight color came to her cheeks. "We want you strong for the big game."

He smiled. "Yes, ma'am."

Swiping our cards, we entered the noisy cafeteria. As Savage led us through the hormone-filled crowd of rowdy teenagers, he mentioned going outside, and I eagerly agreed. Thankful to leave the noise behind, I stepped through the door Savage held open.

The crispness of the air provided a pleasant contrast to the warmth of the sun. I took a deep breath. The smell of the leaves and ripe persimmons comforted me while the cooler temperatures exhilarated me. Another breath pulled me deeper into the blissful moment until a girl squealed in laughter. Savage, still standing there, just looked at me.

"Sorry. Just enjoying the moment," I said sheepishly.

"No worries." Savage set his tray on the table closest to us. "Here good?"

I nodded as I sat down and placed the tray of food down. Savage seated himself across from me. Battling with opening the juice bottle, he cleared his throat and held out his hand. I smiled at him and twisted the cap even harder. With the pop of the metal lid, I nodded and smirked at him. He gave a nod and slight smile.

"How're classes?" Savage asked.

"Good."

"Hmm. How's econ?"

"Fine," I said a little standoffishly.

"Hmm."

My brow slanted in strong disapproval. "I don't wanna talk about econ."

"Okay, we won't talk about econ." Savage's eyes bore into me as he casually said, "Seen Bear today?" His phrasing didn't match the intensity of his eyes. The relaxed tone contradicted the seriousness of his stare.

"Saw him this morning," I replied, shoving a forkful of lasagna in my mouth.

"Hmm."

His green eyes shifted in color slightly, which made him appear overly concerned, and he opened his mouth as if he wanted to say something, then stopped. His eyes became electric green as he stared, but we continued on in silence. Taking another bite of food, I waited for his words, but still nothing came.

Laying down the fork, I glared at him. "Something you wanna say?"

"Just thinking."

"About?"

"You being new here."

"Yeah, so?"

"You don't know many people," he said casually, while those entrancing eyes remained steady on mine.

Where is Savage going with this? I pushed the food around, trying to come up with a response to my lack of friends. Nothing came to mind. He didn't break his stare. *How can he say nothing?*

"Okay . . . And your point is?" I blurted.

Savage's composure remained intact. "No point. It's just an observation."

"Observation of what?"

"Hmm, well, being new," he said in an even-keeled tone. "Hard making friends, I'd think."

Savage wasn't gonna let this go. As much as I didn't want to, I was going to have to talk about Drew. "Is this about Drew?"

"Is it? I didn't mention him."

"Look, Savage, I get it. You and Drew are friends. I totally respect that. Just respect that I don't want to talk about him, okay?"

"Hmm." He nodded, then said, "Okay."

My mouth twisted. "Can we please change the subject?"

"Whatever you want."

The conversation changed to light chitchat. Savage's attentiveness calmed me. I blabbered about my old school and my best friend, Sam. Talking about Sam made Bryce come to mind, but I quickly pushed thoughts of him out of my head. Bryce was the last thing I wanted to talk about or even think about. As I rattled on more about Sam, Savage listened intently. People trickling in and out of the doors never drew Savage's attention away from me. His cool demeanor and controlled presence comforted me. Quite the opposite of Bryce, who had a brash, raging personality.

Ugh! Why does Bryce keep coming to my mind? He's certainly not thinking about me, not with Jasmine throwing herself at him. He loved the attention she gave him, even while we were dating. The one time I mentioned her blatant flirting, he laughed and called me stupid. Shaking my head to get the image out of my mind, Savage gave me a puzzled look.

"You okay?"

"Yeah, I'm fine," I responded. His smile couldn't shade the concern in his eyes. "Just memories." I offered a smile in return, but it wasn't genuine.

"Hmm," Savage said.

Savage was easy to talk to, but I certainly didn't want to share anything about Bryce. That whole thing still hurt way too much. The best thing for me to do would be to keep my mind off Bryce. So that meant not talking about him, no matter how much I wanted to do exactly that.

After school, I made my way through the crowd and to the front entrance. Savage stood by himself, leaning against the wall while the crowd filtered past him, drawing the attention of those walking by. His muscular build, towering height, and chiseled face naturally turned all the girls' heads, but something more than his physical stature drew people to him. He had a presence of humble confidence. He acknowledged everyone who spoke to him with a genuine reaction, even if it was just a head nod. You saw in his eyes that he noticed *you*. And not just the popular people. He gave the same level of attention to each and every person who acknowledged him. He even paid attention to people who didn't care, like me on the first day of school.

When his eyes caught mine, he maneuvered through the crowd and met me. "Ready?"

"Yep," I said.

Savage pushed open the door, allowing me to walk through it as he followed. He pointed to the left and we sifted through the crowd on the sidewalk. As we walked to his car, he weirdly stayed beside me all the way to the passenger's door. When he opened it, my mouth dropped. *Is he for real? No guy I know opens the car door for a girl.* I smiled nervously as I slipped into the seat and told him thanks. He gave a nod of respect, like he always did.

Walking around the front of the car, Drew walked toward him, and they talked for a minute. Drew held out his hand. Savage's hand slid across Drew's palm, then they bumped fists. *Guy greeting.* I rolled my eyes, mostly because he did this with Drew. Before Drew turned away, he cut his eyes to me and smiled. Piercing my lips, I immediately turned the opposite direction.

Savage opened the door and slid into the seat. He didn't say anything as he started the car. Once he'd pulled onto the road he asked, "You up for Jack's?"

"I'm new here, so wherever is fine with me."

Savage gave a low chuckle as he kept his eyes on the road.

Jack's looked like a dive, but a cool one with its red door and blinking neon sign. The excitement of somewhere new had me almost giddy. Savage parked and we got out of the car. Through the windows I could see that high school kids packed the restaurant. Inside, we found a table in the corner away from most of the crowd. After ordering food, we got to talking. Even though I had every intention of working on the assignment, I rattled off something about Bryce. *Why am I talking about Bryce? I want to forget about him, but here I am talking about him with a guy I barely know.*

For some reason, talking to Savage came easy. He listened and didn't offer any judgments or opinions. Plus, he never once interrupted me. He made me comfortable enough to share things about Bryce I've never shared with anyone else.

"I miss Bryce, but being out of the relationship is kinda like . . ." I paused, then hesitantly concluded, "A breather."

"How so?" Savage said with quizzical eyes.

"I don't know. Things just feel easier, like I don't have to walk on eggshells now." I gasped softly. *Did I really just say that?* "Please don't think Bryce is this horrible guy, 'cause he's not. He was actually a really sweet boyfriend."

"Hmm." He offered his trademark response, which I kind of liked. It sort of gave him space to listen and think. Even though I didn't really know him, I did know his presence calmed me.

I paused to catch my breath. *Why am I defending someone who was so cruel to me? Shouldn't I hate Bryce for what he did?* No matter how bad he hurt me, I couldn't ever hate him. Then I rambled some more. "Like, he was totally great with the grand gestures. Any time we had a fight, he would go over the top, trying to make me feel better."

Savage stared at me with somber eyes and said nothing. My stomach tightened while that little voice inside screamed, *Would you shut up already?* But I didn't. Instead, I continued talking about Bryce as if a faucet had sprung a leak. I shared things about Bryce that I didn't even know I felt. With this word explosion now in full force, it had me realizing that the breakup with Bryce was a relief.

Savage dropped me home shortly after six o'clock. Waving as he pulled out the driveway, I went inside and walked upstairs. As I entered the room, Oreo nuzzled my leg. Swooping him in my arms, I sat on the bed, pulled out my phone, and finally answered all the texts I'd ignored. Of course, Sam had sent me a half-dozen messages. I had a text from a number I didn't recognize. *Oh, it's Haley. She wants me to go shopping with her. Ugh. What do I say?* I debated on how to reply.

Haley had been super sweet when I met her in chorus, actually going out of her way to talk to me. The other girls, though, had been pretty frigid. She impressed me when she introduced herself, totally ignoring the glares of the ice queens coming my direction. She even told me to not pay attention to the unwelcome committee that gave me the freeze-out, which made me laugh. As nice and funny as she was,

I didn't know if I had the energy to do the whole teen-girl shopping scene. Besides, it wasn't really my type of thing anyway.

I typed no, then deleted it. I held the phone in my hand, unsure how to respond, when I heard a knock on my door.

"Hey, Zinn, you hungry?" Mom came into my room.

"No, I'm good. I already ate." As I continued to read over the texts, Mom sat at the end of my bed. Oreo crawled over and she rubbed his ears.

"So, who was the guy that brought you home?"

"Savage. He's in my English class."

"I see. So are you making any other friends?"

I shrugged my shoulders. "I don't know. There's this girl in chorus, Haley. She just texted and asked if I wanted to go shopping tomorrow."

"Sounds fun. You gonna go?" Mom asked.

My look of indifference didn't faze her, so she stared right back at me. "I don't know. You know I'm not a shopper, Mom."

"Yeah, but it might be fun. You know, have some girl time."

"Maybe."

Mom walked over to me and kissed my forehead. "I think it would be good for you. Just my opinion."

"I'll think about it."

"Well, I'm gonna go soak in a hot tub. If you need me . . . Well, don't need me for at least half an hour," she said with a laugh.

"Okay, Mom. Enjoy!"

She left my room and Oreo curled up beside me. "What do you think, Oreo?" He nuzzled his nose against my hand. "I guess you're right." I responded to Haley's text.

Me: Sounds fun. I'd love 2

Haley: Yay! Let's go to the Shoppes then grab some food

Me: Sounds like a plan.

Haley: I need help picking an outfit. Ryan asked me out for Friday night. 🙂

Me: Cool! Date shopping. Thanks for the invite!

CHAPTER FOUR

Haley drove to the small downtown area near the square and pulled into in a parking spot on the side of the road. People were scattered on the sidewalks, entering and exiting the different buildings. This part of town would make anyone appreciate the small town of Bargeston with its quaint coffee shops, boutiques, vintage buildings, and beautifully landscaped sidewalks.

Haley excitedly discussed her plan to check out a particular shop first and then a new boutique she'd heard about until she accomplished her goal of finding just the right attire for her first date with Ryan. As we moseyed along the sidewalk, she blabbered about people at school. Haley was definitely in the know about Bargeston, and she didn't hesitate to let me in on all the goings-on. I paid little attention to the chatter since I didn't really know many of the people she talked about, but she didn't seem to register my disinterest.

In the store, she quickly shuffled through the rack, pulling anything that had a semblance of blue or green in it. With a pile of clothes draped over her arms, she headed toward the dressing room. After she'd tried on at least a dozen outfits, she scrounged through the clothes hanging in the dressing room and decided on the second outfit she'd tried on. As we made our way to the cashier, she got sidelined by the jewelry. She spent the next thirty minutes looking for just the right bracelet and earrings to make her new attire flawless.

Finally, after two hours of shopping, Haley said she was famished, so we headed to the Mexican restaurant to curb her craving for chips and queso. Immediately seated, we ordered our drinks. Most of the people in the restaurant were families with a few couples scattered throughout, and a group of women sitting in the bar area who looked to be enjoying a night out without husbands or kids. When the server returned with our drinks, we ordered and Haley resumed sharing her excitement about her upcoming date.

Some Bargeston football players walked into the restaurant. The one leading the group was Dawson, the guy I met on my first day. Malone from econ was with him, but the other three I didn't know. As they walked past our table, one of them stopped beside Haley.

"Haley, you're looking good." He leaned closer to her and whispered, "Where you been hiding?" Haley sat up straight and kept her face on me the whole time.

"Still sore, huh," the boy said as he backed away. "Oh well, everybody hurts sometimes." Snickers ensued from the group of guys except from Dawson. He stayed cool and showed no reaction while keeping his eyes locked on me. I forced my eyes away from his stare and turned it onto Haley. Anger filled her face. When they moved to their table and out of earshot, I had to get the scoop.

"Who was that?"

Haley let out a sigh and rolled her eyes. "That's Tristan Jackson. Total jerk. We went out a couple of times. Then this post about me on The Boneyard happened."

"The Boneyard?" I questioned her with my eyes as much as my words.

"The Bobcat Boneyard. It's this stupid blog started by some guys on the football team." Haley narrowed her eyes at me and leaned in closer. "It's the guys' stats page. The posts are Gossip Girlesque with coded names. Like they're fooling anyone. I mean, Tristan Jackson's alter ego is Thriller," she rattled. "It's all stupid and immature."

Haley told me about The Boneyard and the Tristan situation. She and Tristan had English together last year and were kind of chatting it up. He asked her out, and after the date came the made-up post about her. She revealed how it pretty much ruined her reputation and emotional state that semester.

Haley wiped under her eyes. "Oh crud, did I smudge my eyeliner?"

I shook my head no, then glanced over to the table of guys. Dawson was looking at me with a cocky grin, then nodded. I quickly brought my attention back to Haley, who hadn't quit jabbering about the Tristan ordeal.

Grabbing a chip and shoving it in the cheese dip, she said, "Let's change the subject. I hate thinking about all that."

Shifting the talk to Ryan and the upcoming date, Haley's bright-green eyes sparkled as she shared all the details of how Ryan asked her out. She talked so fast as she relived the moment right before my eyes. She gushed when she described what he wore and what he said. This girl didn't let anything slip past her. Haley's excitement had me almost giddy myself, and before I knew it, she'd drawn me into a discussion about hair, makeup, and outfits. It was the stereotypical teenage girl conversation, and one I didn't typically have, but with Haley, I didn't mind it.

Haley took me home a little past nine o'clock. When I came in, Mom and Grandma were watching TV. Immediately, Mom asked about my afternoon with Haley. I told them both about the shopping and shared details about Haley's energy, liveliness, and talkativeness. Mom hung on my every word. Even with no smile on her face, the joy over-flowed from her. She had been right about going out with Haley. It was good for me. Sometimes it really irked me how Mom knew better than I did what I needed.

I shared all that came to my mind. When a lull came, Mom had just the right questions to pull out more information. She attentively listened as Grandma drifted in and out of sleep. Oreo lightly snored in the corner. When I finished and Mom had no more questions, I headed to my room. Oreo roused and followed me up the steps. In my bedroom I changed into my pj's, then climbed under the covers. Instantly, Oreo snuggled beside me. I reached for my phone on the nightstand and opened Google, then typed "Bobcat Boneyard." One site matched the name and I clicked on it. A stealthy looking bobcat with the words "The Bobcat Boneyard" headed the page. The menu read "Bobcat Happenings, Saturday Scoreboards, and News from the Den." I found some posts about Thriller and came across one that could be about Haley:

It appears the paparazzi's been busy this weekend. The little shutterbug obviously got up close and personal with the one and only Thriller. From what we can tell, it was a thrill for them both. Now there's a new contender on the scoreboard.

Haley was right: the site is stupid. The posts featured the bragging rights of these imbecilic guys and were full of sexual innuendos. More posts were like the one about Haley. The page went back a couple of years, tallying in the hundreds. The Saturday Scoreboard posts included twelve names, but of course the names were coded, like Haley had said. Thriller being Tristan Jackson was the only one I knew since Haley had told me that one. All the names had some points except for one—Grizzly. Scanning through the posts, Grizzly didn't have any posts except for a few from two years ago. All the other names showed up regularly. *Who is Grizzly?* I shook my head, then closed my phone and set it on the nightstand and pulled the covers over me. Rolling to my side, I closed my eyes, waiting for sleep to overtake me.

Tossing and turning, I leaned over and checked the time. It read 1:45 a.m. I grabbed my phone and pulled up The Boneyard page. Scrolling to the posts about Grizzly, I read them all. The posts included a couple of mentions of him hunting, and one described him stalking and pouncing. The last post said that Grizzly had pounced and was headed into the cave. Was Drew Grizzly? I threw the phone on the floor, pulled the covers over my head, and prayed for sleep.

The sound of a mower woke me. Fumbling around the floor, my hand grazed the cool metal. I picked it up and opened it. *Who mows the yard*

at 8:47 on a Saturday morning? Moaning, I rolled out of bed and headed to the bathroom. Smoothing out the tangles in my hair, I grabbed a band and twisted my frizzy hair into a messy bun. After brushing my teeth and washing my face, I went downstairs.

Mom and Grandma sat at the kitchen table. Mom's eyes were on the computer while Grandma studied her sudoku. Both had the same focus and concentration. Though they shared many of the same mannerisms, their biggest commonality was that they looked almost identical. Me, on the other hand? Well, I looked just like my dad. I had his auburn hair and fair complexion. My pale, freckled skin contrasted the olive tones of my mom and grandmother.

"Morning, Zinnia Rose." Grandma smiled as she sipped from her cup.

"Morning, Grandma." Oreo plodded over to me and stayed at my feet.

"There's bacon and French toast on the stove," Mom said, not taking her eyes off the computer.

"Coffee?" I walked to the stove, snatched a piece of bacon, and shoved it in my mouth.

"In the pot." Mom nodded, still focused on her screen.

Taking a mug from the cabinet, I grabbed the pot of coffee and poured some into the mug, topping it with some cream and sugar. As I walked over to the table, I grabbed another piece of bacon and took a bite. I sat in the chair beside Grandma, sipping the hot beverage, enjoying the warmth trickling down my throat.

Outside, the sun shone in a clear-blue sky as the trees gently swayed in the wind. The sparse leaves on the branches made the distant mountain skyline look drab and grey, especially against the bright-blue sky. In just a matter of days, the array of colors had disappeared and leaves now littered the yards.

"Got any plans today, Zinnia Rose?"

"Um, I don't know. Not really."

"Sure is a pretty day. You should get outside." *Grandma's guilt rearing its ugly head again.* Since moving here and me having to transfer schools, Grandma had taken it upon herself to try and make me happy about being here. *I have been in a mood since the move. Grandma didn't necessarily want us to move here and be uprooted any more than I wanted to. I really need to do better.*

"Maybe I will get out today." I smiled, trying to appease her and remove some of her regret. Directing attention toward Mom, I said, "Unless I could borrow the car and go see Sam?"

"Sorry, Zinn. Can't today. I've got to show a house in Cookeville." She kept her focus on the screen as her finger moved across the touchpad of her laptop. "But I got a commission check, so we can finally get the car fixed." Her gaze finally moved to me and she smiled.

"So I can use Grandma's car?"

"You can use it til I get released from the doctor," Grandma said.

I jumped up from the chair and wrapped my arms around Grandma, then gave Mom a hug. "I'm gonna go call Sam."

When I got to my room, I called her. It went straight to voicemail. In a few minutes Sam texted that she was with her dad and would call me later. I sent her a reply and then texted Haley.

Me: How'd the date go?
Haley: It was so perfect! Ryan is so sweet!
Me: Can't wait to hear all about it
Haley: Busy with the fam now…meet later?
Me: Sounds good
Haley: How bout the park?
Me: Sure, time?
Haley: 3ish?
Me: cu then

With a few hours to kill, I spent some time unpacking my boxes. The clock read 1:15 p.m. when I went to shower. Returning to my room, I unwrapped the towel from my head and let my wet hair fall to my shoulders and ran a comb through the smooth strands. Flipping my head over, I scrunched the long tresses to make it curlier. Predicting that at three o'clock it would still be pretty warm out, I walked to my closet and chose a green T-shirt and grey leggings. I grabbed my backpack and headed out the door by 2:15.

I allowed myself time to get to the park early so I could spend time writing. I entered the park from the footpath off the main road, which led me past an open area. Some guys from Bargeston were huddled together while another group positioned themselves in a defensive line formation: football, obviously a pickup game. That familiar chestnut hair stood above most in the group. As I moved closer, Drew smiled and then waved. I continued walking without giving the wave any recognition.

It was about 2:35 when I settled at a picnic table in a wooded area away from the crowd. Retrieving my journal and pen from my backpack, I placed my phone on the table so I would be sure and get Haley's text when she arrived. I started writing and, as usual, found myself caught up in the moment. My phone buzzed on the table, jerking me out of the storyline that had drawn me in. Reading the text that Haley would be late, I went back to writing. The words poured on the page.

That moment of darkness comes so fast
Creating havoc from thoughts of past.
Split-second it's real; I've been swallowed
Suddenly feel completely hollow.
The fear consumes me; I lose myself
Like I've fallen under a spell.
Overtaken by the emptiness
Making me feel nothing but useless.
That moment, the cost when I get so lost.

A few minutes later another text popped up and I replied.

Haley: Ugh! Sorry can't come. Stuck watching kid brother. How about tomorrow?
Me: It's fine. Tomorrow's out.
gotta study☹
Haley: Sorry again. Another time
Me: No big. Getting some writing done
Haley: Call you later and tell you all the deets!

Not wanting to lose the momentum I had on the story, my attention went back to the words and I continued to write pages and pages.
A light breeze caused me to shiver as the darkness crept in. *How long
have I been here?* My phone showed 6:45 p.m. As I closed my journal,
some male voices and boisterous laughter came from behind me.
Hurrying to get my things together, my backpack fell off the table and
spilled onto the ground. I quickly scooped up my water bottle, keys,
lotion, aspirin, and hair scrunchy and shoved them into the backpack.
Scrounging to retrieve the small items left on the ground, my hand
raked the gravel and felt the squishiness of Ooshi—my soft, plastic toy
fish—Chapstick, and some bubble gum. As the voices got closer, my
heart raced. Finally, I had everything back in the backpack, and I
turned to leave. My heart sank as three twenty-something guys stood
in front of me, giving off a bad vibe.

"Well, well! Who do we have here?" A tall, boozed-up guy wearing a
Bargeston ball cap staggered toward me. "What's your name,
beautiful?"

"Um, I was just leaving." I stepped to the side of him but had my
way blocked by a red-headed guy with scraggly facial hair. Stepping to
the other side, my way got blocked by a stocky bearded guy. The
wasted trio chuckled as the tall one inched himself closer to me.

"Woah, there. No reason to run off."

Gripping my backpack tightly to my chest, I backed up and the
metal bench of the picnic table hit the back of my leg.

"Hey, it's okay." Moving even closer to me, the drunk guy dangled
two beers attached to a plastic six-pack ring from his finger. The
stench of alcohol flowed from his breath as he leaned toward me,
pressing me against the bench. Turning my head to try and bring relief
from the nauseating smell, he shoved an open can of beer into my face.
"Thought you might wanna have a drink with us?"

Slapping his hand, the can slipped and fell to the ground. Cool
liquid splattered on my leg. While laughing loudly in my face, he said,
"Ooh, boys! She's a fiery one." Pulling another can from the plastic
ring, he tossed the remaining can to the stocky guy on his left.

Cutting my eyes at him, I replied, "My friend is waiting in his car. I
was just getting my stuff."

"You sure 'bout that? 'Cause I didn't see any car."

"Uh, could I please get by? He's waiting on me."

"I don't think so. Besides, you haven't had a drink yet." Offering the can to me, he smirked. "Now don't be wasting this one." He chuckled and his friends bolstered his brazenness with their laughter. The guy's hand grazed my cheek, and I turned away from him. He slipped his hand around my neck and pulled me toward him. Extending my arms, I tried my hardest to push him away from me. My fighting only seemed to boost his efforts. My hands were growing weaker as I pressed against his heaviness which only made him laugh as he continued to push his weight harder against me. Suddenly, something rustled in the trees and bushes behind me, followed by a low growl.

"What was that?" The red-haired guy looked around frantically.

The rustling grew louder, then something shot out from the wooded area. The three guys scattered in different directions as a large, hairy creature pounced toward them. My heart raced, and I froze for a brief moment. The darkness prevented me from seeing anything, and the fierce growls from the unknown creature rattled me. I ran as fast as I could toward the parking lot.

When I reached the end of the path, the parking lot had emptied. I ran down the hill near the lake and slowed my pace when I reached the crowd. Tears rolled down my cheeks. Breathing hard, I came near a couple with two kids. The woman looked at me in worry and fear and tapped her husband. She took a step toward me.

"Sweetie, you okay?" Tears came pouring out of my eyes. She put her arm around me. "You need help?"

"Um, I don't." Exhaling, I couldn't find any words. The woman spoke calmly as she guided me to a bench.

"Hey, Zinn!" a male voice yelled from a distance.

CHAPTER FIVE

"Thank you, but I'm fine." I smiled at the woman. She nodded and said goodbye as she headed toward her husband and children. I let out a sigh of relief as she left me. Drew came running down the hillside. *Someone I know. I don't even care that it's Drew Behr.*

"Zinn, how you doin'?"

"I'm okay," I replied while pawing through my backpack for my phone. "Crud, where is it?" My breathing became shallow.

"Where's what?"

"My phone!" My vision blurred as tears formed in my eyes. Tossing my backpack upside down, the contents fell to the ground—again. I sat down and fumbled through everything.

Drew knelt and starting rifling through it with me. "I'm sure it's here somewhere."

"No!" I yelled. "It's at the table."

"Okay! Then you can just go get it."

"No! I can't. I won't."

"It's okay, Zinn. I'll get it for you. Just tell me where it is." Drew's gentle eyes had a calming effect on me. My fast-paced breathing finally began to slow.

"Um, I don't know. I can't explain to you where it is. It was my first time at this park," I said.

"Okay, well, how about you show me? Would that work?" Drew smiled as he picked up the items from the ground and handed them to me. With the contents returned to my backpack, Drew held out his hand. I took it and he helped me to my feet.

"It's just over there," I said as I pointed to the wooded area on the hillside. Drew chatted as we walked the paved road. The lights shone on us as we made our way across the parking lot. Drew's hair was tousled, and his shirt dirtied, overstretched, and ripped. When his eyes caught mine, he smiled.

"Football got kinda intense."

When we came to the path leading to the area where I had been sitting, I stopped and shuffled my feet as we came to the end of the asphalt. Drew pulled out his phone and lit the path with it. I inhaled and exhaled a few times. Drew's hand touched my fingers, and I let his hand engulf mine. I stepped onto the path and proceeded toward the table.

As we moved closer, my mouth started watering. I paused and bent over. Drew put his hand on my back. "Zinn, you okay?"

"Uh, yeah, just skipped lunch."

I straightened my back, returning myself to a standing position. Drew folded my hand in his. The light shone on the disturbed ground where the three guys scrambled as that creature jumped at them. Even though no trees rustled and nothing lingered nearby, my body still pressed against Drew's arm. Thankfully, my phone was still on the table—that was an unexpected mercy. Drew extended his long arm and picked it up. "Here you go. Found your phone."

"Thanks." Staying close to his side, I took the phone and hit the home button, but it remained black. Tears formed again, and I heard the crack in my voice. "It's dead." My breathing increased.

"No problem. Mine's in my truck. You can use it."

"Thanks. That'd be great."

"I'm parked near the lake."

Walking closely beside him, I tucked behind him slightly as we walked the trail out of the wooded area toward the lake. With the moon shining behind us, the light on Drew's back spotlighted his chestnut curls even more. A memory of Sierra pulling him down the hall flashed in my mind. I quickly released his hand and took a sidestep, increasing the space between us. His eyes gave a look of disappointment. I let my eyes trail to the lake, avoiding additional eye contact with him.

His truck was across the park, so we had a bit of a walk. He tried to interest me in light chitchat, but I replied with one-word statements and kept my view on the water. When we arrived at a red truck, he opened the door to the passenger side and handed me his phone.

"Thanks," I said, still trying to act nonchalant, then called Mom's number. There was no answer. Tapping my foot, I shook my head. *I can't believe this is happening.* I handed Drew back his phone. "She didn't answer."

"No worries. I can give you a lift." He smiled and his blue eyes danced with interest.

"It's not that far. I can walk," I said matter-of-factly. "But thanks for your help."

"I'll take you."

Take me home? No way, no how. I'm already on Sierra's hit list. I am not about to fuel that fire anymore.

"Zinn, you're not walking home. Just get in." His eyes pleaded. "Please."

"Um, I'm fine. Like I said, it's not that far."

"It's dark and your phone's dead. Not really a good idea for you to walk home with what happened earlier."

I squinted my eyes at him. "What do you mean with what happened earlier?"

He got wide-eyed, then cleared his throat. "I mean, obviously something scared you."

How did he know something scared me? Did he see something? No way! He was playing football on the other side of the park, so why would he say that? Maybe the fact that I was so rattled about losing my phone or how tightly I held his hand? I didn't exactly hide my paranoia well.

Heat filled my cheeks.

"Let me take you home, okay?" Drew asked.

"Do you mind if I call my mom again?"

Drew nodded and gave me an adorable smile as he held out the phone. When I took it from his hand, my fingers lightly grazed his calloused hand and I quickly pulled away. I tried Mom again but no luck. The phone rang and rang as my eyes darted to Drew. He smiled, and I immediately dropped my gaze to the ground. *He has a girlfriend, which means he's off limits—no matter how nice or how cute he is, and he is very cute.* Those broad shoulders and muscular biceps would cause any girl to look twice. The chestnut curls that fell across his forehead were more than adorable. But those blue eyes . . . Well, they got to me. They were mesmerizing and captivating and made my heart skip a beat.

"Still no answer," I said awkwardly.

He smirked and cut his eyes to the passenger's seat.

"You're not gonna let this go?"

Drew shook his head with sternness as a hint of a smile formed on his lips.

My mouth twisted and I let out a sigh. "Okay, in five minutes if there's no answer, then you can take me home."

"I accept those terms as long as you get in the truck first. It's cold."

I nodded my head in agreement and climbed into the truck seat. He shut the door and walked around the front of the truck while I called Mom again.

As Drew opened the door, I ended the call. "Still no answer."

"Looks like I'm taking you home." Drew climbed into the driver's seat and started the truck.

"It's not been five minutes yet," I said matter-of-factly.

"True, but it's more like four now," he said with a wink.

I pierced my lips to prevent a smile. *How do I get out of this predicament?* "You wouldn't possibly have a phone charger, would you?"

He pulled the cord from the console, and I plugged it into my phone. *Maybe if I charge my phone enough, I can finagle my way out of this ride home.*

He smirked, then offered a smile, likely picking up on my overcautiousness with him. Then he laughed lightly. "Just so you know, your phone being charged won't make a difference. I'm not letting you walk home alone. I'll follow you in my truck if I have too."

Chill bumps ran across my arms. He had read my thoughts. This whole thing was a mistake. *Why did I agree to let him take me home? Keeping my distance was my plan. Now I'm sitting in Drew's truck with three minutes until I have to surrender to the fate of letting him give me a ride.* As I called Mom again, I prayed for her to answer. Instead, it went straight to voicemail. *Not a good sign. This means she's likely dealing with a client, so giving her three more minutes held little promise.* I handed Drew his phone and he flashed an optimistic smile.

He increased the volume of the stereo. I let my head fall to the headrest. My shoulders softened into the seat as the music surrounded me. I sang, only allowing a whisper to escape from my mouth.

"You know this song?" Drew questioned.

I nodded. "Yeah, 'Where I First Found You'—great song."

His eyes lit up. "Hmph, you know Forest Blakk? I'm impressed."

I gave him a slight shoulder shrug and a smirky grin, then relaxed back in the seat and allowed myself to be consumed by the soulful, haunting voice coming through the speakers.

"Zinn, can I ask you a question?"

"I suppose."

"Why don't you talk to me anymore?"

"We're talking right now?"

Drew sighed. "You know what I mean." His eyes pierced through me.

"Because you have a girlfriend!" I said flatly.

"What?" Drew had a confused look on his face.

The same Drew Behr from my first day of school finally made a reappearance. *A week later and he thinks I don't know he has a girlfriend. Or does he think I'm the type of girl who would be a side piece?* "The blonde," I said bluntly.

"What blonde?"

He sat there and pretended he didn't know who I was talking about. My cheeks filled with heat, so I inhaled deeply. When I released the breath, I gave him a blank stare. "The platinum-blonde . . . Sierra."

"Sierra? She is not my girlfriend."

He really thinks I'm stupid. "I saw you two." My anger popped out the words with more harshness than I intended.

"What are you talking about? Saw what?"

I narrowed my eyes at him to let him know my annoyance with his denial. "Saw you holding hands with her."

He gave me a questioning look. "What?" He shook his head defiantly. "Never happened."

Now it was my turn with the defiance. "Yes, it did. My first day at school, I was in the office. The door opened, and you yelled something to Savage. Sierra glared at me and then took your hand and you two headed down the hall."

"I headed down the hall with Sierra?" For a moment he paused, then a light bulb turned on, and he shot out the words, "Oh yeah."

Now he's finally admitting the truth.

Drew glanced at me with concern. "Zinn, we weren't holding hands. She wanted my history notes. What you saw was her dragging me down the hall."

I scraped my teeth over my bottom lip, somewhat embarrassed that I had this wrong, then my annoyance returned. "Well then, why did Jordan and Riley say you and Sierra were dating?"

He closed his eyes and took a deep breath. When he opened his eyes, they flashed with anger. "Jordan and Riley told you Sierra and I are dating?"

"Well, not directly, but I heard them talking about you and her going out."

His jaw clenched as his hands grabbed the steering wheel. My eyes widened. He took a deep breath, then his blue eyes softened. "So that's why you stopped talking to me?"

"Yeah," I whispered.

A sweetness appeared in his eyes, and he shook his head ever so slightly. "I promise I don't have a girlfriend. I am not dating Sierra or anyone else for that matter."

A lump formed in my throat as the embarrassment returned. "Oh, I guess I should apologize for being so cold to you."

"It's okay. Let's just forget it." Drew lightly chuckled. "You really believed Jordan and Riley?"

I nodded and he began to laugh. I fidgeted in my seat as I waited for the laughter to stop. As soon as he appeared close to stopping, he would start to say something, and the laughter would return. After a couple of minutes, I had grown quite agitated. Finally, his boisterous laughter lessened.

"I'm glad you find this so funny."

"Oh, I do." Drew pierced his mouth with his teeth, trying to conceal more laughter. Crossing my arms, I rolled my eyes. "Zinn, I'm sorry, it's just—" Drew began laughing again, and I huffed loudly, signaling my annoyance. "Okay, okay. I'll stop laughing."

"You wanna tell me what's so funny about all of this?"

"I don't know. It's just a bunch of . . . Well, it's just funny. I hope you know now that you can't really trust Jordan and Riley. I'm pretty sure they wanted to make you think me and Sierra were dating."

"Oh, thanks for telling me that now. But it's not that far-fetched thinking you and Sierra were a thing. She's gorgeous and you're, um—" I stopped myself from saying anything more. With the color flooding my cheeks, I was very grateful for the darkness.

"I'm what?"

"Nothing," I quickly blurted.

His eyes narrowed as he smirked. "You're not gonna tell me?"

I pierced my lips and shook my head side to side.

"Bet I can guess it."

I shrugged my shoulders, indicating I was up for the challenge and would not be defeated.

"Okay, then. If I guess it, you have to tell me if I'm right or not."

Immediately, I gulped while trying my best to maintain my cool. Drew paused, obviously trying to get a read on me. Keeping myself completely composed, I wasn't about to let him know I was a bundle of nerves.

"You think I'm too tall?"

He narrowed his eyes and looked intently at me, studying me for a moment. I kept my face expressionless and said nothing.

"Hmm, not it." Another brief pause, then he gave a sly look. "You think I'm mysterious?"

Squinting my eyes at him, I shrugged my shoulders.

"You think I'm . . ." His eyes narrowed again as he paused. I held my breath and slowly blinked. "You think I'm a Spanish goat herder?"

Clicking my tongue, I nodded in agreement. "Totally."

Drew asked me questions and told me some about himself. We got so caught up in conversation that my phone had over a fifty percent charge.

"Oh, wow! I didn't realize it has been so long. I'm so sorry."

"I'm not." His eyes danced as he smiled flirtatiously.

I nervously cleared my throat as I returned with what had to be an awkward smile. The call to Mom went straight to voicemail—again. I let out a sigh as I pressed End Call. *Why isn't Mom answering? I hope everything's okay.* The heaviness of my chest prompted me to take a deep breath. *Everything's fine. She probably misplaced her phone again.* I offered Drew a smile. "She's still not answering."

"So I'll take you home?"

"I guess so."

We left the park and headed to my house. When the truck rounded the corner, I saw Mom's car in the drive and sighed softly. Drew parked the car and then walked me to door. I pushed my way in and dropped my backpack on the floor, motioning for Drew to follow me.

"Mom?" I hollered.

"Upstairs!" she called back. Within a few seconds, she popped her head out of her bedroom door. "Have fun with Haley?" She crested the top of the steps. "Oh, you have someone with you?"

"Yeah, this is Drew. He gave me a ride home."

"I see." She smiled as she walked down the steps.

"Hi, Mrs. Danthes. It's nice to meet you."

"Nice to meet you, Drew. I was just about to heat up some food. Wanna join us?"

"Thanks, but I was hoping maybe Zinn would grab some food with me." His eyes darted to me and gave me a questioning look.

I shrugged my shoulders, fighting the smile forming on my face. Drew looked back at Mom and added, "If that's okay?"

I leaned out of Drew's sight and nodded my head at Mom with wide eyes. That smirky grin formed across her mouth. "Yeah, that's fine. It was just leftovers anyway since Grandma's at bridge."

"Cool, I won't be late." I wrapped my arms around her neck and whispered in her ear, "Thanks."

"Have fun and be safe. Drew, nice to meet you."

"Yes, ma'am. Nice meeting you."

We left my house and walked down the driveway, the moonlight shining bright in the night sky. As we approached his truck, a halo of light illuminated it. Drew smiled as he looked at me. This felt safe. Normal. I couldn't believe how wrong I had been about him. *Why had I been so quick to judge Drew? Oh yeah! Jordan and Riley.*

I cleared my throat. "So, Jordan and Riley . . . Why the drama of trying to make me think you and Sierra were a thing?"

Drew shook his head. "Can't really say. Let's not think about them. I don't wanna spoil a perfectly good night, okay?"

When we arrived at The Slice, the parking lot was full. Clusters of teens stood outside by their cars, and others were standing in pairs along the sidewalk. Inside the restaurant was an even larger crowd. Most tables were full. Drew pointed to one in the back corner, and we nudged through the crowd to claim it. He easily maneuvered around the horde of bodies while I floundered behind him. Obstacles seemed to jump into my path. On one side of the restaurant, a group of girls huddled around two tables they were shoving together. On the other side, a guy flanked by two girls side-stepped into my path. As Drew got closer to the table and farther away from me, the right side appeared to be the most advantageous path. As I navigated my way around the tables, a guy pushing out his chair rammed into me. Stumbling, I lost my balance and pushed into someone else. "Woah, chill!" he called out.

"Uh, sorry," I said as I turned around to face the person that I'd just knocked over. Glaring at me was Dawson. His eyes softened when he saw me, then he gave me a smile. "Hey, new girl."

"Um, hey. I'm really sorry about that. Someone was getting up—" Fumbling with my explanation, Dawson slowly moved his head from left to right as he shushed me. Startled by his response, I immediately stopped talking as my eyes widened and I gulped. His eyes cut to the guys across from him and then back to me.

"It's all good, new girl."

"Um, thanks."

His eyes locked on me and I saw a mischievous grin appear. "You can bump into me anytime."

"Zinn!" Drew stood beside me with his hand on my elbow. "I got us a table."

I nodded to Drew. "Uh, yeah. Okay!"

"Feeling a little territorial, Bear?" Dawson said patronizingly.

Drew's eyes darted to Dawson. "Zinn, it's just over here." Drew directed me away from Dawson and led me through the crowd. Sniggering came from the guys standing with Dawson.

"Yo, Zinn!" Dawson said loudly enough to quiet the noisy restaurant. Several eyes shot in my direction. My heart immediately sank and my pulse quickened. He cocked his brow and stared at me with unwavering confidence. "Hit me up sometime."

Stunned, I just stood there while the crowd stayed silent. Drew's blue eyes filled me with confusion as they had become somewhat gray. Obviously irritated by Dawson, his brow furrowed and his jaw clenched. Anger dripped from him, but his eyes looked empty and sad. Motioning his head toward the empty table, he forced out a smile. "I'm starving! Let's order."

Finally, the noise level resumed while my heartbeat decreased. As we settled at the table, nothing was said about Dawson, which took me by surprise. Instead, Drew had a staring contest with Dawson. Neither of them flinched until our server came. Eventually, the stares broke, and Drew's joviality returned once we ordered our food. After that, Drew's talkative self reappeared.

He and I discussed everything from school to music to his love of fishing and being outdoors. I shared about my writing and playing guitar. Then I talked some about my mom and dad. Just as Drew started to tell me about his family, my phone buzzed. Mom texted, asking when I would be home. "It's nine forty-five. Wow, I didn't realize it was so late."

"Better get you home. Don't wanna get on your mom's bad side 'cause I kept her daughter out too late." Drew winked to keep the vibe light, then we got up from the table and headed toward the door.

As Drew walked behind me, I did my best to fight through the crowd. My petite frame offered little help in getting me through the mass of bodies without staggering. I had just about given up when Drew placed his hands on my waist. Then, stepping in front of me, he slipped his hand into mine and led me to the exit.

As we passed through the door, I saw Jasmine draped on some Bargeston football player whose name I didn't know. *What is she doing here?* Water filled my mouth, the kind that precedes nausea, as she moved closer to me. She eyed me pretentiously, then flashed Drew a warm smile. Drew didn't respond to her as we walked to his truck. He opened the passenger door and I climbed into the seat. Jasmine stared daggers at me. *It's just like her to flirt with Bryce all week and then be out with another guy on the weekend.* The heat rushed to my face, but I took a deep breath to calm down. She entered the restaurant and got lost in the crowd. The driver's door opened, and Drew tucked himself inside, free from the eyes of judgement.

"Are you tired?" he asked.

"No, not really."

"Are you sure?"

"Yeah, why?"

"Because you've been running through my mind all day."

With my hand, I slapped his rock-hard bicep and grinned at him. Drew started the truck and headed toward my house. Enjoying the drive with more conversation, the ride felt too quick. I didn't want to leave his truck. Drew walked me to the door and we said our goodbyes. He stepped off the porch and headed to his truck, then he looked back to me and smile broadly. "Hope you have a good night, Zinn. Thanks for a great day."

I waited on the porch as his truck pulled out of the driveway. Opening my front door, I stepped into the living room and spent a few minutes babbling to Mom, replaying the day's events. I settled in my bedroom for the night and turned on some music and lowered the volume, not wanting to disturb the rest of the house.

Finally comfy in my pajamas, I plopped on my bed and checked my texts.

Haley: Drew Behr? Deets please!

Me: What do you mean?

Haley: Heard you and Drew went out?

Me: NO! Who said I went out with Drew? Saw him at park. Phone died. Used his charger.

Haley: What else?

Me: What do you mean what else?

Haley: I heard you were at The Slice with him

Me: Yeah, we went and got some food, so what?

Haley: So you WERE at The Slice with him?

Me: Yeah, but it was nothing

Haley: It wasn't nothing. This is big!

Me: Trust me, just getting some food. Nothing more!!!

Haley: I'm not so sure

Me: Well I am!

Haley: I think Drew was making a statement

Me: There was no statement

Hey I gotta go. Tired. TTYL

CHAPTER SIX

On Monday, Haley came pounding down the steps when I got out of the car. "Zinn, everyone's still talking about you and Drew."

"What? Why?"

Haley's mouth dropped, and she stood there staring at me. "Because you were at The Slice."

"I already told you it was nothing. We just got some food."

Haley's lips smacked as she chewed her gum and we walked into the building. She told me that it was all around school that Drew and I had gone out over the weekend.

"This is ridiculous. We didn't go out. Me and Drew just got some food. That's it."

Haley stopped and looked at me, completely dumbfounded. "Just food?"

"Yes, just food."

"And the hand-holding? Explain that!"

I stood silent. Without flinching, she repeated herself. "What about the hand-holding?"

I shook my head in total disbelief. "How do you know about that?"

She gave a slight shrug as we fell back into step and navigated the crowded hall. Haley proceeded to explain the rumor-mill pathway of information that provided all the juicy tidbits of information that she had been privy too. Annoyed by her play-by-play of my time at The Slice with Drew, my head began to ache. *This is why I detest being the center of school gossip.*

"Even if we had gone out—" I halted my words when Haley's eyes widened. "Not that we did! But even if we had, what is the big deal?"

"Because it's Drew."

I exhaled and rolled my eyes. *Like I need a reminder of how popular he is.* "Okay, but that doesn't explain all this talk."

"You do know Drew hasn't gone out with anyone since freshmen year, right?"

I shook my head, signifying I wasn't aware of that fact.

"Zinn, taking you to The Slice on a Saturday night was Drew's way of making a statement."

This time I stopped walking and gave a questioning look. "Seriously?"

I had a hard time believing Haley. Drew had in no way hinted anything about this being a date. "Haley, I really don't think so. It was just a ride and pizza."

"I promise you, Drew was making a statement. Everyone knows what going to The Slice on Saturday night means."

Not sure what this all meant, the whole Drew event played over in my head. Haley didn't notice my distraction and kept clamoring on about the whole incident with Drew and telling me what people were saying. Her head bobbed as she chatted away about all the talk that eventually transitioned to the other happenings of the weekend—who went out with whom and who broke up with whom. The typical high school drama spilled from Haley's mouth.

Interrupting, I said, "Oh, Haley, I forgot to tell you about what happened at the park."

My details about the incident with the drunk guys mesmerized Haley. Wide-eyed, she said, "Oh geez, Zinn. What did you do?"

"Nothing. I couldn't do anything. I was trapped, but then . . ." I hesitated to say the words but decided to go for it. "Something big and hairy jumped out from the woods. And then I took off running."

"Oh wow, Zinn! I bet it was the Beast."

"The Beast? What are you talking about?"

"You know, the Beast of Bargeston." She gave me that *duh* look.

Just then, Dawson and his group moved past us. "Haley, you're really telling the new girl all about that ridiculous, glorified Big Foot?" Tristan butted in.

Haley cut her eyes to him very slowly. The look of disgust gushing from her caused his cocky grin to grow bigger. "Hey, new girl! Come over here. I'll tell you some things. Ain't that right, Haley?"

Haley shot Tristan a scowl. Boisterous laughter came from the group, except from Dawson. His steely eyes caused the hairs on the back of my neck to stand. "Yo, Jacks! Let's go," he said sternly.

Tristan slowly backed away, not taking his eyes off either of us. Haley dragged me away, but I couldn't break my gaze, the tension leaving only when they got out of sight.

"Ugh, Tristan Jackson turns my stomach," Haley grumbled, flustered by the whole incident. "He and that whole stupid crew." As Haley complained about Tristan, my mind mulled on Dawson and him basically calling off Tristan. As disgusting as the whole incident was, Dawson had me intrigued. I wasn't sure why, but I would almost say he impressed me.

"Zinn, when you get to chorus, you should ask Jake about the Beast."

"Haley, I don't even know what I saw or what this Beast thing is?"

Again, with a *duh* expression and slightly annoyed tone, she said, "The Beast is a local legend. People say he lives in the woods and is part man and part animal. Ask Jake. He knows about all of it. Supposedly, he saw the Beast when he was a kid. He even has a whole website about the legend and sightings and stuff. I'm not saying I believe in the Beast, but this legend is not taken lightly in this town. Honestly, if I saw what you saw, I might believe."

Haley had me intrigued. Talking to Jake might be an idea.

Haley's bubbly self finally returned, and now she quizzed me about the guys who had harassed me. "So, like, what else happened with the three guys?"

"I don't know. I ran away and didn't look back. Then this woman approached me, and that's when Drew ran up."

"Wait . . . What? You didn't say anything about this until now. Drew was there?"

I told Haley the rest of what happened at the park as we walked to class. Thankfully, the bell rang, so I didn't have time to tell her about Drew and me talking in his truck. She wouldn't leave it alone if she knew what he'd said that night. Better for that information to stay with me. I didn't need Haley's contagious optimism about Drew. It wasn't a luxury I would allow myself. If Drew "didn't date," then I wouldn't let myself think about him in that way. I was just glad Drew and I were friends.

I arrived at econ a couple of minutes before the bell. As usual, Coach Bowman sipped his coffee and read the paper, unconcerned with starting class anytime soon, which was fine with me. I would use that time to write. Since I had a new song to work on, I pulled out my journal and flipped to the lyrics I'd begun days earlier. As I jotted some phrases, Drew walked into class.

"Mornin', Zinn."

"Hey, Drew." I offered a smile. Drew gave a head nod and slid into his chair. He said nothing else—didn't even mention Saturday at all. No goofy lines or dry jokes. Nothing. He talked to Malone, so it wasn't that he felt antisocial. He just didn't want to talk to me! I fought the tears building in my eyes. Haley's optimism had gotten to me. I had let myself hope that Saturday meant something. Sadly, Coach starting class didn't drown out the thought that played on repeat: *Drew doesn't want to give me the time of day*.

When the bell rang, Drew chatted with Kyle, the boy in front of him. I walked past the two of them without saying a word and headed to the door. Drew, pausing the conversation with Kyle, said, "See you, Zinn." Then his eyes narrowed as he said something to Kyle and grabbed his books.

Quickly, I shot out the door and wove myself into a crowd of people in the hall, then entered the bathroom. I splashed water on my face and looked into the mirror—it was beet red. Unsure if the redness was due to embarrassment or anger, I panicked when the water didn't relieve the crimson staining my cheeks.

I rolled my eyes as I stared at my reflection. *Saturday night meant nothing. Drew was being a nice guy and that's all. Haley and her excitement, ugh.* My fingers brushed the hair out of my face. *Drew would never be interested in a girl like me. What am I thinking anyway?* I gathered my backpack and pushed open the door. It had only been a little over a month since my breakup with Bryce, and the truth was guys needed to remain off limits, at least for a while. *Keep it together, Zinn. Being friends is all I will offer or expect.*

Drew's cold shoulder kept eating at me. When I entered English, Savage was already in his seat and shot me a smile. "Hey, how was your weekend?"

"Fine," I replied coolly.

Placing my things on my desk, I opened my notebook and copied the topic from the board. Savage didn't press for additional information. I busied myself with the journal entry.

My mood slightly better, I asked Savage about some school stuff but didn't mention the weekend since I didn't want to hear or talk about Drew. Actually, I didn't even want to think about Drew.

Savage leaned over to me. "Zinn, you free Tuesday or Thursday?"

My breath left me as I tried to regain my composure. "I'm sorry, what?"

"Tuesday or Thursday, I thought we could work on the paper."

"Oh yeah, of course. I'm good with either."

"So tomorrow? The Slice around seven?"

"Uh, yeah, that works."

"Cool."

What would Haley say about this? A Tuesday meet-up at The Slice? Is Tuesday the same big deal as Saturday? No, Savage said we could work on the paper, so it was just a study thing. Great, Haley had me reading into everything.

Mrs. Hart started class as soon as the bell rang. As usual, class flew by, and it was time for lunch. While Savage and I walked to the cafeteria, he received a few invites from people who wanted to eat lunch with him. *Must be nice to be in high demand.* He declined each invite and stayed with me. We eventually made our way outside to the picnic tables.

We gravitated toward the familiar table that had been our lunch spot last week. Savage had few words to say, which was a nice change of pace. Eventually, he quieted, and I began my typical rattling. Savage was attentive with his standard response of a nod and smile and the occasional, "Hmm." Talks with Savage consisted of me doing most of the talking. It was weird having someone so interested in what I had to say. We finished lunch and headed back to class. Dawson appeared to be lying in wait, his dark eyes following us, then he walked our way.

"Savvy, what up?"

"Dawson," Savage replied.

"Wondering if I could see your notes from chem lab?"

"Yeah, I'll get 'em to you later."

"Kinda need 'em now, bud."

"Yeah, okay." Savage looked at me apologetically as he left.

"Appreciate it, Savvy," Dawson replied, turning toward me. "So Zinn, how you like Bargeston?"

"I guess it's okay. I mean, I'm still getting used to it."

He smiled with extreme cockiness, then he inched closer to me as he spoke. "Maybe you'd like it better if you got to know some other people."

His deep-brown eyes pierced into me, and I gulped.

"I'm not so scary, new girl. No matter what you hear." He gave off an air of nonchalance, like he couldn't care less about me, yet he definitely had an unexplainable fascination with me. *What in the world would make this guy look my way?*

My mouth went dry as I stumbled with finding words. "Um, I, um—"

"Other people might open up a whole new world for you."

Feeling heat come to my cheeks, I gave a partial smile. Dawson's eyes flickered and he opened his mouth ready to say something when a throat cleared.

"Dawson, I think this is what you wanted." Savage interrupted.

"Thanks, Savvy," Dawson said as he tapped Savage on the shoulder with the notes. "Owe you, bud."

"Hmm." Savage eyed Dawson, eager to move on. "Zinn, you ready?"

Dawson smirked, not taking his eyes off Savage.

"Later, Dawson." Savage placed his hand on my back, urging me to start walking.

"Yep." Dawson's eyes moved to me and he gave a nod. "See you around, Zinn." Then, he walked away.

After a few steps, Savage removed his hand. "So what did Dawson have to say?"

"Um, nothing really. Just asked me how I liked school."

"Hmm," Savage said, looking like he wanted to say more but instead stayed silent.

My phone buzzed and I pulled it from my pocket. A notification popped up on my screen. *DawG_47 wants to follow you.* I clicked the notification, opening the page of Dawson Gregory. Savage's eyes still on me, I slid my phone back into my pocket and rattled something about the English assignment as we walked to class.

Mrs. Hart raised an eyebrow as we settled into our seats. "Now that everyone's here, we can get started." She reviewed for the upcoming test, which provided me with the opportunity to focus on other things: Saturday and the three drunk guys, Drew, The Slice, and the awkward whole thing with Dawson.

When the bell rang, my notes were few, mostly doodles covered the page. I shoved my things into my backpack and slung it on my shoulder. I said goodbye to Savage. His eyes bore into me with that intense look of concern. I gave him a casual smile and headed out the door.

Snap out of this, Zinn. Now Savage is acting weird.

Walking to chemistry, my pensive mood pepped up when I saw Haley and Julie.

"Hey, Jules and I are going to The Slice after school. Wanna go?"

"Um, yeah, if I can get a ride home."

Haley nodded. "Yeah, that's not a problem at all." Haley scanned the crowd, waving and smiling as people walked past.

"Hey, Jules," I said, trying to get her attention.

Julie shyly smiled. "Hey, Zinn." Her eyes darted from me to the ceiling, back to me, and then landed on the floor. Her shyness was overshadowed by Haley's extreme friendliness, which made them an odd couple, but somehow it worked.

"See you in chorus. C'mon, Jules." Haley pulled Julie by the sleeve, and they continued down the hall.

I waved as the two of them walked away. Haley's head bobbed and her hands kept waving as she rattled on to the quiet brunette, who kept her books wrapped in her arms and pressed against her chest. I liked Jules well enough but didn't yet know what made her click.

Facing the hallway on my own, I hoped to get to my next class without being noticed. No such luck . . . Dawson stood with a couple of other guys at the end of the hall. I had to pass them to get to class. I felt weak and unprepared for another encounter with Dawson. *What is his deal? Does he want my attention, or does he want to humiliate me?* I straightened my shoulders and tried to muster a little bit of confidence to continue my walk past them.

"Hey, Zinn." My stomach dropped hearing Dawson's voice. "Where you headed?" Dawson said with a tone of undeserved confidence.

"Um, chemistry." I kept walking, barely acknowledging him.

Pushing off the wall in a macho display, he announced, "Later, boys!" then stepped toward me. "Zinn, wait up. I'm headed that way."

As he caught up to me, we passed Jordan. She stared as we walked past her and immediately got on her phone. A sick feeling hit me as I imagined who and what she was texting. Dawson didn't notice or care. He asked me a few questions that I easily answered, then challenged me with a tougher one. "So how 'bout those digits?"

I stopped in the middle of hallway and he casually laughed. "It's just a number, Zinn."

"Um, uh, I—"

"I'll make it easy," he interrupted. "Just accept my follow and we'll go from there."

"Uh, okay," I said nervously. "I guess so. I mean, yeah, I can do that." *Shut up, Zinn. You sound like a complete idiot.* Immediately, two girls approached and distracted him.

As I stepped away, he said, "Zinn, text later."

I gave an obligatory nod. *Does he actually think I'm gonna text him? Wait, maybe he meant he would text me.* Confused, I shook my head. *Why is Dawson Gregory even talking to me?* His glance turned toward me again, and he flashed that cocky grin. *Oh shoot.* I dropped my eyes and took off toward the door.

Situated at my desk, I pulled out my phone. In a moment of weakness or maybe stupidity, I went to Dawson's page and hit Accept to his follow request. *What's the big deal? It's just a follow.*

Jake sat across the room, so I walked over to him. As his eyes shot to me, he straightened the wire-framed glasses on his face. The round lenses suited his squared jawline. Awkwardly, his eyes darted away from me as he slid his book out from his leather messenger bag.

Why is he so nervous?

"Hey, Jake."

He cleared his throat. "Zinn."

"So, I have a question."

He nodded for me to continue.

"Haley mentioned that you know a lot about the Beast?"

He situated himself in his chair as his eyes scanned the room. Lowering his voice, he said, "Um, yeah, I know some things."

"Well, I . . . You see, I may have seen one. But I'm not sure."

His eyes filled with enthusiasm as he opened his notebook and grabbed a pencil. "When? Where? What time?"

"Um, Saturday. In the park. I guess around dusk, maybe like seven o'clock."

Why am I nervous?

"Were you alone?" Consumed with his note-taking, he didn't take his eyes off the notebook.

"Well, not exactly."

Jake glanced up from his notes.

"Well, as I was leaving, these three guys . . . Well, um, they sorta approached me, I guess you would say. And . . ." Not sure how to explain the rest, I hesitated.

He narrowed his eyes and paused for a moment. "Uh, Zinn, are you okay? They didn't . . . I mean, nothing happened, right?"

My fingers fidgeted as I shook my head, signifying no.

"If this is too much to talk about—"

"No, it's fine. Just ask your questions."

Mr. Cavers walked into the room pushing a cart as the bell rang. Students took the cue to get settled at their stations.

"Can we talk later? After school tomorrow?"

I gave a nod.

"I'll text you." He handed me his phone, and I quickly typed in my number and headed back to my seat just as Mr. Cavers poured something into a beaker. As he shook it, the liquid turned blue, giving him a segue into the lecture on chemical reactions involving oxidation. When class ended, Jake walked toward me.

"Zinn! Was wondering if you noticed the eye color of the Beast?"

"Um, no. Honestly, I barely saw it. Why?"

"Some have described Beasts with intense, brightly colored eyes that seem to glow."

On the walk to chorus, Jake shared more about the Beast, his research, and his website. He explained there'd been reports of the Beast going back for more than a hundred years. The way Jake described the Beast and all his research, he'd no doubt had a personal experience. Maybe his story could give me some answers. At least, I hoped it could.

The Slice wasn't too crowded when we arrived. As usual, Haley dominated the conversation as she rattled on about Ryan. The door opened and Drew entered with some other football players. *Weird! Aren't they supposed to be at practice?* He and his friends found a table when his eyes met mine. He said something to them and walked toward my table.

"I think Drew's coming over here," Haley declared.

I couldn't argue with her. Drew made a straight line to us.

"Hey, girls. What's up?"

Haley smiled. "Not much, Drew. Just hanging out."

"Cool." His eyes scanned the three of us and landed on me. "Mind if I borrow Zinn for a minute?"

"Not at all," Haley said.

"Zinn, you care to step outside?" Drew's cool tone didn't match his pleading eyes.

"I guess I can." Haley gave me that giddy, wide-eyed look.

"Have her back in a minute," he said as he winked at Haley and Julie.

He led me outside, then shoved his hands into his pockets as he cleared his throat. "So, um, I was wondering if you're mad at me?"

"No!"

"You sure? It seems . . . Well, it seems you've been avoiding me all day."

"I don't know what you're talking about. I'm fine," I said emphatically.

"Well, you didn't really talk to me in econ, and then you jetted out of there at the bell. After second period, I waved to you, and it seemed like you saw me but just kept walking."

I stood there. I couldn't think of an excuse, so I blurted out, "It seemed like you preferred it that way." Biting the corner of my mouth, I wished I could take back those words as Drew's face filled with shock.

He let out a sigh. "Well, I sorta thought . . . You see, I figured you didn't really want to talk to me since you ignored my message. So I laid low. And then . . . Well, you didn't talk to me this morning."

"What message?"

"I messaged you on Instagram Saturday night. You never responded."

Opening the app, Drew's message stared me in the face. I shook my head. "Clearly, I've not seen this until now."

"Oh?" He casually leaned on the wall. "Obviously, that's not a good way to get ahold of you?"

"Sorry." Color filled my cheeks. *How did I miss his message?*

"I'm thinking we need to fix that, but there's just one problem."

"Oh? What's the problem?"

"Well, I seem to have lost my number." A mischievous grin came across his face. "Could you help me out and give me yours?"

"Is that really gonna help?" I twisted my mouth to keep the smile from forming.

"Definitely," he said with a big grin. He pulled out his phone, typed something, and handed it to me. "I think you could solve that problem." The screen showed a contact page displaying "Zinn" and a winking emoji.

I typed my number into his phone and handed it back to him. He took the phone and gave me an adorable wink.

"Better return you to your friends," he said. "Or there'll be even more talk." He offered a thoughtful smile.

So he's aware of the talk too. Was Haley right? Was Drew making a statement at The Slice?

Drew walked me to my table. "Ladies, thanks for sparing Zinn for a moment."

Haley gushed. "Not a problem."

"Much thanks. You girls have fun."

Immediately, Haley started quizzing me about what Drew said. My vibrating phone interrupted her questioning. I picked up the phone and didn't even fight the smile when I saw the text from Drew.

Drew: Having fun?

I glanced at him. He looked ready for this covert exchange, so I texted back.

Me: Yeah, you?
Drew: Sure. Thx for replying 😉
Me: YW. Thx for texting
Drew: Text later?
Me: 😊
Drew: 😉 Til then

The quick exchange intrigued Haley and she pressed me for answers. I refrained, and she finally gave up. After we ate, Haley drove the three of us to my house. Grandma Rose, who was sitting on the porch when we pulled into the driveway, perked up. As we got out of the car, Grandma said, "Zinnia Rose, who's your company?"

"These are my friends, Haley and Jules."

"Hello, girls. Y'all have a fun time?"

"Yes, ma'am," they replied, nodding.

"That's good."

I gave Grandma a quick hug. "We're gonna be in my room working on some stuff."

"That's fine. I'm gonna sit here and enjoy this pretty evening," Grandma said.

The girls followed me into the house. We bounced up the stairs and Oreo, barking, met us at my bedroom door. Greeting him, I threw my backpack on the floor. Oreo stayed at my side as he observed the two strangers.

"Sorry 'bout the boxes and the mess. I'm still unpacking," I said.

"This is not messy. You should see my kid brother's room. It looks like a bomb went off." Haley flopped on my bed with her phone in her hand.

"I like your room, Zinn." Julie shuffled to the oversized chair, settling there while befriending Oreo.

"Are you going to the game Friday night? Ryan asked me to come," Haley said, not taking her eyes off her phone.

"Not sure," I replied.

Haley sat up and pleaded with her hands folded in front of her. "Please go. I need to sit with someone. Ryan has to sit with the band. I don't want to go alone."

"Maybe. Jules, what about you?"

"Oh, she never goes to the games." Haley returned to her attention to her phone.

"Jules, you wanna go?"

She shrugged.

"Please, please, go." Haley looked up from her screen toward me.

"I'll see if I can get the car," I said.

"Oh, yay!" Haley jumped off the bed and hugged me.

"Jules, wanna ride with me?" I asked.

"Okay!" Julie smiled sheepishly.

"Oh, I can't wait. This is gonna be so fantastic." Haley pounced over to my closet. "You should so wear this." She flung a pale-green peasant top onto the bed. "Green would make your eyes pop, especially with that gorgeous auburn hair. I'm so jealous." Holding a dark-pink fitted sweater, Haley said, "Jules, this color goes great with your complexion."

Julie blushed. I grabbed the hanger from Haley and hung it in front of Julie. "Wow, it really does. You should try it on."

Julie blushed a deeper red. "I'm okay."

"At least try it on, Jules," Haley interjected.

Julie shrugged her shoulders. I grabbed her hand and led her to the bathroom. "Just try it on."

After a couple of minutes, Julie came into my room. Her pale skin and brunette hair were illuminated by the dark-pink top that slightly hugged her waist. She tugged on the shirt as she stood there. "I think it's too tight."

Haley rolled her eyes. "Jules, it's supposed to fit that way." She grabbed Julie and directed her to the mirror. "See how good you look?"

Jules's reflection showed her awe-filled eyes as color came to her cheeks. "I don't know." She looked at Haley doubtfully.

"Jules, you look fantastic. In fact, you look so good in it, I'm giving it to you."

Julie turned to me and shook her head. "Oh, I can't take this."

"Yes, you can. Looks way better on you than me, and I never wear it. So please, take it."

Julie's eyes narrowed as she gave an uncertain smile. "Thanks." She wrapped her arms around herself and shuffled back to the chair.

"Girls, let's go shopping this week," Haley said, looking in the mirror and holding a blue peasant top in front of her.

"Can't this week. Too much stuff to do," I said.

"How 'bout next week?"

"Yeah, probably."

"Wonderful. Shopping trip with my besties." Haley continued rifling through my closet as she chattered away. Her carefree attitude made me smile. Even going through my lackluster closet full of cardigans, T-shirts, jeans, and some of my dad's flannel shirts, Haley made it into an exciting event. Somehow, the way she combined my simple clothes into new outfits made my wardrobe look quite stylish.

The time ticked by as we talked of clothes, boys, and makeup. Haley looked in the mirror and played with her hair in different styles. Before I knew it, she had braided my hair and given Julie an updo, who shyly looked in the mirror and eventually offered Haley an impressed smile.

"Your hair is so pretty, Jules," I said.

"I'm always telling her she should wear it up, but she never listens. She's so pretty, but she hides behind all that hair."

"It really does look good." I smiled at Julie.

Julie smiled humbly, then returned to my corner chair. Haley rummaged through my very basic makeup basket.

"Oh, we should do a spa day. Manis, pedis, facials. Jules, you could finally get a new do!" Haley exclaimed.

"Um . . ." Julie's eyes filled with fear.

"I've never had a manicure." I flashed my unpolished, short, stubby nails at them. "Where can I get this mess fixed?"

"Oh, Kylie at Luxury Nails. She's the best." Disappointment came across Haley's face. "But that's just a nail place."

"Jules, you okay just getting our nails done?"

Julie nodded at me and smiled as she lowered her eyes.

Haley focused on herself in the mirror as she applied the darkest shade of lip gloss from my collection. "Oh, Jules won't mind. I've tried to talk her into a new do since freshmen year, and it hasn't happened yet."

"Sorry." Julie slouched her shoulders, obviously trying to avoid any disapproving glares.

"It's okay, Jules. You're beautiful no matter what your hairstyle." Haley walked over and draped her arms around Julie. I snapped a pic of them, then Haley grabbed my hand and pulled me into their circle. She took my phone and took a pic of the three of us huddled together.

I had fun being around Haley and Jules, but when I thought about Sam, that feeling was short-lived and quickly overshadowed by sadness.

CHAPTER SEVEN

When the last bell rang for the day, Jake remained in his seat while I talked to Haley and Julie. As the girls said their goodbyes, Jake stood and walked toward me.

"I thought we could talk outside in the courtyard," Jake said, overly aware of the people around us to the point of paranoia.

"Sounds good," I replied.

Jake smiled, but he couldn't hide his nervousness. It was understandable that Jake had his guard up since some of the football players gave him a hard time. Being on the basketball team, he wasn't the typical guy to be the brunt of bullying. His signature look of suspenders and a button-down shirt wasn't the typical attire of a teenage boy, but he had a very stylish, classic look. It certainly didn't make him stand out as one to be picked on.

As we walked toward the doors leading to the courtyard, he kept our pace slow as stragglers rushed past us. We came to a set of double doors and stepped outside. Again, Jake scanned the courtyard as if patrolling the area.

"How 'bout over here?" Jake motioned toward one of the picnic tables away from any other students. I nodded, and we settled on opposites sides of the metal table. Pulling out a notebook and laptop from his leather bag, Jake carefully placed everything on the table. Clicking his mechanical pencil, he readied to take notes.

"You okay to answer more questions?"

"Not sure there's more to add, but yeah, I can."

"Did you hear any noises before you saw the Beast?"

"Um, I think so. Maybe . . . I don't know, like I heard some leaves rustling and a growl. Kinda like a dog or maybe a wild animal. A bear? I really don't know."

"What exactly did you see?"

"Not much. I mean, it all happened so fast, and the creature came from behind me. It was hairy, but not too hairy. I guess you could call it furry. I don't know if that makes sense."

"No, it makes sense." Jake wrote rapidly. "Weird question, but was he wearing anything?" Jake leaned closer to me. "Don't think I'm stupid, okay? But was the Beast wearing clothes?" With his hand, Jake wiped his forehead.

Clothes, is this guy for real? My eyes narrowed as I tried to recall. "I really didn't see the creature fully. Like I said, it came from behind me. Everything happened so fast, and then I just took off running." I shook my head, feeling as if I was no help.

Jake relaxed and nodded. "Gotcha." His eyes scanned the notebook to review my scanty details. "You said you felt scared before the Beast appeared, right?"

"Um, yeah." I squirmed in my seat. "Because the guys were harassing me."

Jake stopped and looked at me. "You still okay to talk about this?"

"Yeah. Just . . . you know, a little unnerving."

Hie eyes expressed sympathy as he paused.

I casually smiled to ease his discomfort, which prompted him to continue with his questions. I answered everything I could and described all the details I recalled. Jake listened intently as he took meticulous notes. He didn't flinch about anything I said, and for most of the details, he had a story to share about another supposed Beast incident. His attention to detail amazed me.

When we were about done, he asked, "Is there anything else that stands out to you?"

"Not really. Just wondering if this sounds like the Beast?"

"Yeah, it does."

"Really? So I'm not crazy?"

"You're not crazy." Jake focused on the paper.

"Haley said the Beast is like part man, part animal. Is that true?"

"Uh, well, that's what people say. The legend states that it originated from some kind of family curse."

"So who's cursed?"

Blake concentrated on his computer but rattled off his knowledge confidently. "That's part of the mystery. There are several stories about the Beast. Some say the Beast originated from a curse put on a man who stole his best friend's girl. That particular Beast would be over a hundreds of years old. Others say the Beast is part of a clan that lives somewhere in the mountains. The clan is rumored to protect the town from some evil flying creature. Stories date back to the eighteen-hundreds. Pretty crazy, right?"

"What's your take on it?"

His eyes shot to me and gave a slight look of paranoia. "Nothing definite, but I do think there's a clan for sure." He paused as he looked around. "I also think the Beast is not his permanent condition."

"Really?"

He looked intently into my eyes. "Never mind. Forget it."

"Jake, what do you mean?"

"I shouldn't have said anything," Jake said as he started to pack up his things. "People think it's stupid."

I touched his arm and he lifted his eyes to me. "I don't. I really wanna know."

He gulped. "I, um . . . Well, I have a theory that it's a man who transforms into the Beast. Actually, I believe there is a family of Beasts."

"A family? Really? What makes you think that?"

"When I was around eight years old, a Beast saved me."

With my eyes, I urged him to tell me more. He gave me a side-eyed glance like he was scoping out whether or not I was trustworthy. He hesitated for a moment, then took a deep breath and continued.

"Well, you see me and a couple of friends were in the woods playing. I lost my footing and started sliding down a slope that led to a cliff's edge. My friends couldn't do anything to help me. As I slid down, I screamed for help and grabbed at anything to hold on to, but I just kept sliding." He described in detail how the Beast saved him from plunging into the roaring creek below and then carried him back up the steep cliff to his friends.

"I'm still confused. Why do you think the Beast is a man?" I asked.

"Because when we were in the woods, I saw a man fishing at the creek below us. I noticed he was wearing a red shirt and jeans." He paused, his eyes pleading with me to believe his story in the way he did. "Well, the Beast was also wearing a red shirt and jeans—tattered though." Pausing, Jake narrowed his eyes suspiciously, like he was studying me, then resumed. "Since my friends couldn't remember, no one believed me, and some of the guys started hounding me about it. Doesn't matter though. I know he was wearing the red shirt 'cause I gripped the fabric in my hand."

That's why he asked the clothes question. I was fascinated as he talked about his research, website, and interviews of anyone who claimed to see the Beast. He let out an exasperated sigh as he rolled his eyes. "I get hassled for my interest in the legend, but I don't care. Discovering as much as I can about the Beast is too important."

Suddenly, Jake lowered his head and fidgeted with his pencil, scribbling something in the notebook. While he was engrossed in writing, a pretty girl with caramel-colored hair approached our table.

"Hey, Jake," the girl said.

"Ashlynn." Jake lifted his eyes. The petite girl sat beside me. "I'm Ashlynn. You're Zinn, right?"

"Yeah," I said, slightly narrowing my eyes.

Her brown eyes softened as she looked at me. She had a familiarity that put me at ease. Jake nervously laughed as Ashlynn chatted with us. Her subtle flirtation with Jake flew over his head. He kept his gaze down as he fumbled with the notebook. Ashlynn directed questions to me, but she kept her eyes on Jake while he nervously shifted in his seat.

Ashlynn broke the awkwardness by holding out a flyer. "Y'all coming to the bonfire next Thursday?"

I shrugged, and Jake fumbled with his notebook. "Um, hadn't planned on it."

The smile left Ashlynn's face. I quickly interjected, for Jake's sake. "Sounds fun."

Ashlynn's smiled returned. "It is! It's after the homecoming parade and everybody stays for it. You'll love it." Ashlynn continued chattering about homecoming week and its events. "Has anyone asked you to homecoming, Zinn?" Ashlynn's gaze darted to Jake, who looked everywhere but at Ashlynn.

"No, but being new I doubt I'll be asked," I shared.

"Oh, someone'll ask you. The status quo is for the guys to wait til after the homecoming court is announced on the Friday before homecoming week. It's rather annoying," she said. Ashlynn continued rambling about the homecoming festivities. Jake said nothing. He just looked around or fiddled with his laptop. Thankfully, Ashlynn's spirited conversation made the awkwardness between them bearable.

After a few minutes, Ashlynn looked at her phone. "Well, I gotta go. Mom's waiting. Nice meeting you, Zinn." She directed her final words to Jake. "See you tomorrow, Jake."

"Um, yeah. See you tomorrow, Ashlynn."

"Bye, Ashlynn," I said.

"Later." She bounced toward the parking lot, and Jake's nervousness subsided. *What was that about? This guy needs some help with the ladies!*

Jake sighed and his eyes met mine, obviously not too shy to talk to me. "Ashlynn seems nice," I said.

"Yeah, she is," Jake responded, looking a bit ruffled.

"She's really pretty too."

Jake fidgeted in his seat. "Um, I hadn't noticed." He looked at me with a raised eyebrow and shrugged his shoulders. "I guess one would say she is."

"She seems pretty interested in you."

"No way. Ashlynn's way out of my league."

"I don't think she sees it that way."

"Trust me. She is. Her grandfather is Nicholas Sullivan." I shrugged my shoulders as I shook my head. His eyes widened. "Sullivan Construction?" I remained silent.

"You're friends with Savage, right?" he asked. "He's a Sullivan."

I casually nodded, trying to hide how self-conscious I now was.

"You do know his family's loaded?"

I shook my head, letting him know this was new information for me. He looked at me in disbelief and the heat rose up my neck.

"The Sullivans are like the 'founding family.' Their roots run deep in this town."

Floored by his statements, I didn't know how to respond. Savage was a descendant of the local founding family? Jake's words *his family's loaded* confused me. *What does he mean by loaded?* Clearly, Jake came from a well-off family, but he saw Savage's family in a different class. My head spun as I tried to comprehend it all. *Savage didn't give off a generational-wealth vibe at all. He acted pretty humble and certainly didn't flaunt coming from money.*

My phone vibrated on the table. "I'd better go. My mom's on her way."

"If you have time another day, do you think you could show me in the park where you saw the Beast?"

"Sure!"

"Great, I'll text you about it."

"Okay." I stood and grabbed my backpack. "See ya, Jake."

"Later," Jake said.

I walked to the front of the building. Settling on the step as I waited for Mom, some voices came from inside the building. I glanced behind and saw Tristan, Malone, and Tyler Davis standing just inside the door. Their voices trailed to the outside. "So, Wolf, you and Madison, huh? She gonna earn you some points on The Boneyard?"

"Maybe. Homecoming's got potential."

"What about you, Malone? You ready to make your Boneyard debut?"

"Naw, not my thing, dude."

Relieved when Mom's car pulled into the parking lot, I jumped up from the steps, happy to put some distance between me and their revolting conversation. Malone not wanting anything to do with that horrendous site made me smile though.

I pounded up the stairs and went into my room, threw my backpack on the chair, and plopped onto my bed. I wanted to review my notes before I had to meet Savage at The Slice, so I opened my laptop to do a Google search for Bargeston. I clicked on the city website and read about the history. It had a short blurb about being founded in 1835 by the Sullivan Brothers: Aaron, Caleb, and Joshua. It didn't offer any other useful information though. I pushed the computer aside and grabbed my phone.

I scrolled through my feed and a picture of Madison Taylor and Tyler Davis came up, which made me sick to my stomach. I pulled my computer back to my lap and went to The Boneyard site. *Big mistake!* Reading it made me feel even worse. Madison seemed like a sweet girl. I doubted she would be hanging out with Tyler if she knew what I'd overheard.

Unsure of what I could do about it, I put on some music and closed my eyes.

"What time are you leaving, Zinn?" Mom's yell from downstairs woke me up.

"About six forty-five," I answered.

"It's six thirty now."

Oh crud. "Okay!" I headed to the bathroom and crinkled my freckled nose as I peered at my reflection. The curls in my hair had become frizzy, and my eyeliner was smudged from lying on my hand.

I washed my face and tried to tame the curly mess of hair. As I put on some eyeliner and mascara, Jake's words played on repeat: *His family is loaded.* What Jake said confused me and even sort of bothered me, like I wasn't good enough for Savage. But Savage had never shown any interest in going out with me, so me being good enough wasn't even a concern. *Savage is rich, but that doesn't change us being friends.*

I finished in the bathroom and went to my room. Oreo perked up from his pillow when I entered. I fed him a treat before I stepped into my closet to change clothes. On the shelf was the green top that Haley found yesterday. Barely see-through, I slipped on a cream camisole to wear underneath. I paired the "new" look with my ripped jeans. In the mirror, I smoothed the crinkles from the top. I had to agree with Haley. This color did look good with my auburn hair. The little moisture I added to my hair relaxed the curls, leaving them soft and bouncy. Satisfied with my outfit, I pulled my flannel jacket off the hook as I left my room.

"I'm leaving!" I called as I picked up the keys from the table by the front door.

"What time will you be home?" Mom asked.

"Not sure. No later than ten o'clock."

"Well, text me when you head home. Be careful."

"I will. Love ya!" I rubbed Oreo's head. "Be back in a bit, buddy. You go to bed." Oreo's dark, sad eyes looked at me. As I opened the door, he slowly turned and walked into the living room.

Pulling out of the driveway, I turned up the volume on the stereo and sang along with the music as I drove to The Slice. When I pulled into the parking lot, it was only half-filled with cars. With five minutes to spare, I covered my lips in my favorite light-pink gloss, then rubbed my lips together to smooth it out.

Some girls passed in front of the car, and Savage waved and pushed himself off the building as he smiled at me.

Opening the door, I grabbed my backpack. "Sorry, I didn't see you."

"Hmm, no worries." Savage opened the restaurant door.

Choosing a booth near the window, he stood until I slid into the seat, then settled across from me. He pulled two menus from behind the napkin dispenser and handed me one. A server arrived and placed some rolled silverware on the table. She smiled at Savage while totally ignoring me.

"Hey, Savage, what can I get you?"

"Hmm. Zinn, you ready?"

The girl's smile disappeared when she directed her eyes toward me. "Do you know what you want?"

"Turkey sub with fries," I said.

"Drink?" the girl asked bluntly.

"Sprite."

With an eye-roll, she turned from me and faced Savage with a beaming smile. "What about you, Savage?"

"Hmm, a sub sounds good. Club with cheese fries."

"So, sub club and cheese fries? And what would you like to drink?" The girl put the pen to her mouth as her eyes locked on Savage.

"Just a Coke."

"I'll get it right to you. And Savage, if you need anything else, let me know."

"Thanks, Bri."

"No problem," she said with a giggle.

Savage seemed unfazed by the attention, but it annoyed me. Even though I saw it at school every day when we walked to lunch, this girl in particular was a bit much to take. *What if this were a date? She doesn't know what we are doing here.* The more I thought about how she acted, the more annoyed I became. When my eyes caught Savage's, heat filled my cheeks. He stared intently at me like he might know what I was thinking. *Oh geez! Does he know Bri has gotten under my skin?* I let out a deep breath and my eyes darted away from his. When my gaze returned, his green eyes were still focused on me. The intensity of his stare made my heart skip a beat. My teeth scraped across my lip, and I tasted the sweetness of the strawberry-flavored gloss. As Savage smiled at me, I shifted in my seat as the color rose to my cheeks again.

Returning with our drinks, the server set them on the table. Annoyed by the flirtatious chatter directed at Savage, I rolled my eyes just as she had done to me. Pulling a straw from the roll of silverware, I placed it in my drink and took a sip, trying to ignore the shameless exhibition. The sweetness of the drink piqued my tastebuds and settled my nerves. My fingers returned the straw to my lips for another drink. Memories erupted of Bryce's flirtiness toward any girl who gave him a second glance. But Savage was not doing that. He was just being polite and kind.

Finally, the seductress server left, and Savage returned his focus to me. I sat there. A guy keeping his composure over such aggressive flirtation, especially when he wasn't on a date, stunned me. When he flashed me that subtle smile, I remembered that Savage was nothing like the average guy. My stomach flip-flopped with his intense yet unthreatening eye-contact. I wasn't used to this from a guy. It was too much for a girl to take!

The only time Savage's eyes looked away was when someone spoke to him. Granted, every few minutes a girl would call his name and try to strike up a conversation. He spoke a few words, then politely ended the conversation and returned his attention back to me. It had become increasingly annoying that so many girls tried to divert his conversation with me. Between the numerous girls who walked past our table and Bri, I was quite irritated. *Why is it bothering me so much?* It happened daily at lunch and when we walked the halls together, but for some reason this moment was really annoying me.

After things settled with the influx of flirtatious girls, we finally got to eat in peace.

"Hey, Zinn, Savage." Ashlynn came up to the table with a bubbly greeting. She smiled big and her eyes lit up. I noticed they were the same shape as Savage's. *No wonder she had a familiarity.* Even though they were a different color, the roundish almond shape was eerily similar.

"Ash, have a seat." Savage slid over and made room for her.

"Aw, thanks. Can't. Just grabbing a pizza for the fam." Ashlynn looked my direction and smiled. "Oh, Zinn! I love your hair. It looks so good."

"Thanks," I said.

"Savage, doesn't Zinn look pretty?" Ashlynn's eyes cut to Savage. His olive skin turned an interesting shade of red.

"Um, yeah." His eyes darted down at the table. *Ha! Finally caught him in a weak moment!*

Ashlynn grinned, obviously noticing Savage's self-consciousness in complimenting me. I fought a smile. This is the first time Savage has lost his composure with me. Ashlynn had embarrassed him!

"Well, I'd better get my order and go. You two have fun," Ashlynn said. "Oh! Savage, it's okay to give a girl a compliment."

"Ash." Savage's brow furrowed, obviously annoyed by her attempt at embarrassing him.

"Wow, I know that tone," Ashlynn shot back. "That's my cue to leave. See you kids later."

Ashlynn waved as she walked away. Savage slightly fidgeted in his seat. "So, you've met my cousin?"

"This afternoon. She's sweet."

"Well, most times she is." His controlled exterior returned. "Ash is right though. You look nice." The intensity of his stare had gone. His gaze shifted from me to the window. Ashlynn poking fun had rattled him.

"Thanks."

Moving his notebook from the seat, Savage laid it on the table. "How 'bout we get to work on English?" Smiling, I pulled out the folder from my backpack. Savage started. "Tell me about your family."

"What do you want to know?"

"Hmm, whatever you wanna tell me."

I rattled off the details about being an only child and only grandchild. I shared about watching my dad get sick and losing him when I was fourteen. I talked about growing up in Kowinville, then about my old school and friends. My friendship with Sam was woven throughout most of what I shared. Finally, I finished with moving to Bargeston.

"Okay, so your favorite memory as a kid?" Savage asked.

"Oh, that's definitely my dad reading me my favorite story. I'd climb in his lap. He would read me the story, then I would beg him to read it again and again."

"So what's the story?" Savage asked.

"Not a story you would know. It's like a fairy tale my great-grandmother made up and told my dad when he was little. He handwrote and illustrated the whole story in this cool leather-bound book."

"Hmm, cool. So what's it about?"

Melting from Savage's interest in a simple memory from my childhood, I couldn't resist sharing.

"It's just a story like most fairy tales: kingdom, brave prince, beautiful girl, forbidden love, queen who is an evil witch. What I loved most about it was the artwork. My dad was an amazing artist. He made Amaryllis just beautiful and Prince Liam so cute. Oh, and my favorite was the stable boy named Jack, who was Prince Liam's best friend."

"Amaryllis, really?"

"Yeah, Amaryllis! Why?"

"Oh, it's just interesting. Unusual name. It's like a flower or something?"

"Um, yeah, I think so," I replied.

"Hmm. So your great-grandmother told your dad the story. Obviously, it made a big enough impression on him that he created this book for you. Anything about the story that's special to you?"

"Not really. I mean I was gaga for Jack and dreamed of being Amaryllis so I could marry him.

"The girl, Amaryllis, ends up with the best friend and not the prince?"

"Um, yeah, like Prince Liam knew Jack really loved her."

"They both loved Amaryllis, but Jack and Amaryllis end up together. So what happened to the prince?" Savage asked.

"You like kids' stories, Savage?" I asked quizzically. "I mean, are you really into fairy tales or something?"

He casually laughed. "Uh, I think you're just a good storyteller."

I laughed in disbelief. "Yeah right, for like a seven-year-old."

"Wow." Savage leaned back from the table.

"Wow? What does that mean?"

"Surprised is all."

"Surprised by what?" I asked.

"Just surprised."

Savage's eyes bored into me. I tried not to laugh, but it was too hard to remain serious while watching him be so serious. Savage maintained his controlled stare. Finally, I broke into laughter, but that didn't derail the penetrating look he gave. Even as a smile formed, his intense stare never wavered. "Enough about me! Your turn to answer questions."

"Hmm, shoot."

"You have any brothers or sisters?" I asked.

"One brother and five sisters."

My mouth dropped. This significant information had totally gone unnoticed by me. He chuckled and nodded. I closed my mouth and inhaled, trying to focus myself. Gathering my composure, I jotted in my notes the number of siblings. "Where do you fall?"

"Second oldest."

"Who are you the closest to?"

"Uh, well, my sister, Sydney. She's only sixteen months older than me."

"No, I mean, who are you the closest to in a connection way? Is it your brother since you're the only two boys?"

"Sean? Well, he's only four." Savage smirked and got lost in thought for a moment. "I'm not sure there's one I'm closer to in that way. I feel close to all of them, but with each one it's different."

As he spoke about each of his siblings, his intense attachment toward all of them became obvious. But it was more than attachment; he had sense of responsibility for each sibling. "I feel like Sarah needs me more, so I guess I'm a little more protective of her."

"Oh, why are you more protective of Sarah?"

"Um, well . . . She's autistic. And kids were pretty mean when she was younger."

I nodded, not sure how to offer my sympathetic understanding except with silence. Being this white knight had an effect on Savage. The little chink in his armor showed he had his own emotional scars. The uneasiness he projected showed even more vulnerability. I figured that was enough transparency for Savage for one day, so I asked him questions about football.

Finishing the interviews, Savage said, "When should we meet again?"

"Whenever works for you."

"Hmm. How about next Tuesday, same time?"

I nodded in agreement and stuffed my things in my backpack. As we got up, Savage grabbed the ticket and went to the counter. I followed behind him, pulling my wallet out of my bag. As I handed him some money, he shook his head.

"I got it."

"Um, thanks. I'll get it next time."

"Hmm, we'll see."

After paying the bill, he walked me to my car and we said our good-byes. I drove home and got there around 9:45 p.m. Oreo met me at the door. I said a few words to Mom and headed upstairs. I dropped my backpack on the bed and collapsed onto it. I looked over the notes from the interview and then recalled how Ashlynn made Savage's face blush. I'd never seen him have a reaction like that. My stomach fluttered thinking about it. For weeks, Savage maintained this dignified, thoughtful exterior. With one statement, Ashlynn broke the façade, and for the first time Savage showed some vulnerability. *It's okay to give a girl a compliment.* Ashlynn had just stepped up a rung on the likeability scale.

CHAPTER EIGHT

Homecoming week had arrived and with it all the frenzy of activities. The homecoming court announcement on Friday had prompted a flood of homecoming proposals on Monday. By Tuesday, the chatter of who was going with whom occupied the conversations. Throughout the day, the rumor mill churned about the latest to be coupled off.

Haley, Jules, and I had made plans to watch the parade together and go to the bonfire. No one had asked me to the dance, which was fine by me, but that didn't sit well with Haley. She'd hatched a plan for us to go as a group. Still, if I didn't get asked, I wouldn't be upset. Enjoying the week's events and the game was enough for me, but Haley wanted us to go to the dance together. Convincing me to go with Ryan's friend Blake had become Haley's mission of the day. Explaining to her that the dance didn't really interest me prompted questions that I didn't want to answer. How do I explain that my associations with homecoming dances were less-than-stellar with the best one being that my date abandoned me at the dance after he left with his ex-girlfriend? I certainly didn't want to elaborate on homecoming with Bryce. That homecoming was more like a nightmare. It started off great, even better than I'd dreamed. It was like the perfect scene from a movie. Then the night changed in an instant. After one of

Bryce's friends commented about me looking good, Bryce's eyes flashed with anger—at me! That was the first time I'd ever seen a threatening look from him. Grabbing my hand, he pulled me to the dance floor. While we danced, he whispered in my ear that I was acting like trash and needed to stop flirting with all his friends.

Later, while getting Bryce some punch, I laughed at something said by a boy at the refreshment table. In a blink, Bryce had me by the arm and pulled me out of the gym. The cup of punch in my hand splashed all over my dress as my feet stumbled while trying to keep up with his pace.

Outside, Bryce took me to the side of the building and shoved me toward the wall. Slamming his hand against the concrete, he screamed horrendous things at me. First, he told me I was acting like a slut, flirting with every guy in the room. He followed that with how awful I was for embarrassing him. Then he ended the night by threatening to end things if I didn't start being a better girlfriend. I trembled as he repeatedly screamed insults at me. I just wanted him to stop, but I stood frozen with no words coming from my mouth. Then my mouth started watering and the forceful expulsion of the few contents of my stomach projected onto the ground. Even me getting sick didn't stop the forcefulness of Bryce's words coming at me. He continued to berate me, saying it was my fault that he was so mad.

As people walked out of the gym, they glanced our way but didn't intervene. I prayed someone would come over to stop the yelling. I just wanted it to stop. But no one did; everyone just kept walking. Eventually, Dylan met us outside and told me to go back inside. He and Bryce remained there, and Sam met me at the door and took me to the restroom.

Sam grabbed some tissues and wiped my eyes. In the mirror, the black streaks down my cheeks and around my eyes startled me. Pink smudges were all around my mouth. Shockingly, there were red streaks on my arm. Sam dampened a towel and gently blotted at them. The red splatter on the bodice of my pale-blue dress led to tears pouring down my cheeks. Sam stopped and wrapped her arms around me.

Finally, the tears stopped. Sam took her shawl and draped it around me to conceal the punch stain. Pulling out her makeup bag, she fixed my face and hair. Sam told me everything was fine and Bryce just needed to blow off some steam. As she smoothed my hair, she smiled and nodded in a way that said she'd keep this a secret. After a few minutes, Sam's phone rang. Dylan said he and Bryce were headed back inside. Shaking my head side to side, Sam took me by the shoulders and reassured me again. Sam always knew what to say to calm my nerves, especially after Bryce and I fought.

By the time Bryce came inside, no one would've known he'd just been screaming at me. He draped his arm around my shoulder, but I pulled away slightly. He pulled me closer while tightening his grip around me. His hand squeezed my arm. I dared not budge from his grip or his side the remainder of the night.

That's a homecoming I wished to forget. I certainly didn't want to explain to Haley the real reason homecoming dances didn't appeal to me. No, letting her concoct her plan seemed the easier path.

By the time I headed to history, she'd already texted me five times, pressuring me to agree with her idea. I admired Haley's determination. When she wanted something, she refused to quit until she got it. While I had admiration for that quality, being the object of her determination became somewhat annoying. Haley meant well, and Blake was a nice guy. The eventuality of my saying yes was inevitable, so I shot her a text that I would go if he asked. Maybe Blake would have more of a backbone than me and refrain from caving into Haley's homecoming fantasy.

Standing at my locker before third period, Haley and Blake came around the corner. Blake having no luck at not succumbing to Haley's demands hit me hard. He looked sheepishly at me as she chatted for a couple of seconds before making her obvious exit. Blake stood there silent for a minute, so I broke the awkwardness and said, "Well, I better get to trig."

"Oh, um, yeah," Blake said. "I'll walk with you."

Blake kept the conversation very neutral, talking mostly about music. I gauged Blake's words cautiously. While I had told Haley this was a friends-only thing, did Blake know that? He seemed pretty at ease as he talked, looking me in the eyes and laughing. He also had no trouble keeping a smile on his face—a friendly, lighthearted smile, not a flirtatious grin. I wasn't even sure Blake did the flirty thing. He was typically quiet when Haley, Jules, and I were around. This was the most talkative I'd ever seen him. I was fairly certain he had been roped into the group date just like me.

When we entered the math wing, he stopped by the window. "So, Haley came up with the idea for us to double with her and Ryan." With his eyes darting all over the place, he bent his head to the side. "If you're not up for it, it's totally okay." Blake cleared his throat and his thumb lightly tapped on his leg. When his eyes caught mine, I smiled. He sighed and a smile shot back at me.

"Sounds like fun," I said.

"Cool! I'll text you later about the plans." He hesitated a moment, then laughed. "Actually, I'm sure Haley will have it all arranged."

"Yeah, likely so."

Blake smiled as his brown eyes danced. "I'll see you later! And Zinn, thanks for saying yes."

"Thanks for asking, Blake."

"Saw you and Haley in the hall. What's got her all excited?" Savage asked.

"She's making plans for us to go dress shopping for homecoming."

"You're going to homecoming?"

I shrugged my shoulders and nodded.

"Hmm. With who?" Savage asked.

"Blake Stevens. He's in the band, and I think he runs cross country too."

"Hmm, Blake, huh?" Savage said through pierced lips.

"What about you? You going?"

"No." He opened his notebook and glanced through it.

Not sure what to say, I got my book from the backpack and placed it on my desk. With a couple of minutes until the final bell, Savage's gaze remained on his notebook as he wrote something. *What's he doing? Is there an assignment due today?* Stretching to see what had his focus, he doodled on a blank page. Clearing my throat, Savage didn't flinch. *Is he ignoring me?*

The final bell ringing took away my opportunity to ask Savage anything about it. With ten minutes to complete my journal entry, I quickly jotted down a few lines to meet the requirement. As I shut my notebook, Savage traced the same square.

"Um, Savage, you okay?"

"What?" His gaze flew over to me like he'd been startled.

"You seem a bit distracted. You've been tracing a square instead of writing the journal entry."

"The bell rang?"

"Yeah, about five minutes ago."

It was so out of character that he flaked out and spaced about his assignments. I cleared my throat and Savage's eye shot my direction.

"Something bothering you?"

"Nope! Gotta do my journal," he said, instantly returning his focus to the notebook. Totally confused by all of that, I let it go for the moment, at least until lunch anyways.

Walking to lunch, we both stayed quiet. As we got our food, we found a table near the window. "Blake's over there." Savage motioned his head to the table where Blake and Ryan sat.

"Yeah, so?" I asked.

"Don't you wanna sit with him?"

What is he talking about? Why would I want to sit with Blake? "No." His statement totally perplexed me. Before I realized it, I popped out, "Why would you say that?"

"Homecoming?" Savage's forceful tone surprised me.

My eyes widened. "Okay." Needing to clarify the dating arrangement with Blake, I continued. "It's just as friends."

Savage gave me a confused, questioning look.

"Did you think it was something more?"

"I didn't think anything," Savage said nonchalantly as he settled at the table.

I seated myself at the table and began to rattle off about Haley's concocted plan of the group date.

"Hmm." Savage returned with a smile.

His normal mood had returned, and he was his attentive self to all my chatter. After explaining all the details of Haley's actions, calmness came over me. I fell into silence while I ate my lunch. Savage had little to say, as usual, but his mood was better. Blake and Ryan waved to us. I waved and Savage gave a head nod and smiled. *Did Savage's weird mood before have anything to do with Blake taking me to homecoming? No, that's stupid. Why would he care if it was a date with Blake?* Maybe he thought the whole homecoming dance was a waste of time. I could see him thinking that since he was so serious and focused about everything. He probably thought I was trivial for going to the dance. Part of me kind of agreed with him, but there was the other part that really dreamed of having that perfect movie-like dance night. No chance of that happening with Blake as my date, but with him and the group it would be fun. Besides, Blake was nice and easygoing—certainly not intense like Bryce. *It may not be the fairy-tale dance, but I'm pretty sure I won't leave in tears or in a ruined dress.*

When we were done with lunch, we headed back to class. English drifted by slowly until finally the bell rang. Savage and I left the room and parted ways. As I walked the hallway leading to my locker, the clamoring crowd overwhelmed me. I fought against the masses to get to my destination.

Ashlynn came running up to me excitedly. "Do you have a homecoming date?"

"Yeah, Blake Stevens asked me."

Narrowing her brow, she replied, "Um, Blake?"

"Yeah, he asked me before English. What about you?"

Ashlynn looked a little disoriented, then she seemed to register what I'd said. She rambled about some invites that she had no interest in saying yes to. "I was really hoping Jake would ask me. I've hinted in a million different ways—and nothing."

"Maybe Jake *will* ask you."

"Likely not. I guess I'll end up saying yes to Mike Taylor."

Ashlynn and I talked until the first bell and then headed to our classes. My conversation with Ashlynn confused me. She asked me if I had a date to homecoming, as if she knew I did. *How could she know?* Ashlynn wasn't really someone I could predict. She reminded me of Savage in that way.

When I arrived to chorus, Haley waited for me at the door. Beaming, she said, "It's all arranged! Me, Ryan, you, Blake, Jules, and Max."

"Wait, Max asked Jules?"

"Oh yeah! He asked her first thing this morning."

"You didn't even tell me."

"Sorry, but convincing you and Blake to go to homecoming consumed me, especially after Blake changed his mind," Haley said.

"What? Changed his mind? He didn't want to ask me?"

"No, I mean kinda. He was gonna ask someone else, but they got asked." She paused and looked intently at me. "It's just as friends, right? You're not into Blake, are you?"

"Oh no. Totally not. Blake's nice, but it's just as friends. I feel bad he didn't get to ask who he wanted. Do you know who it is?"

"No, and he won't tell me. He hasn't even told Ryan."

"Well, either way, I'm excited that Jules is going too. Speaking of Jules, where is she?"

"She left early for some appointment. But she's gonna meet after school to work on the chorus float."

Haley started clamoring about her excitement over the group date and all the plans she had for the week with the parade, bonfire, and the dance. Haley's hopeless romanticism made me smile. Her game plan for the group date had been successful, and I hoped her other plans would not be a disappointment for her. The fact that Blake wanted to take someone else made me feel sad. If he'd rather go with another girl, I didn't wanna be a pity date. *Why go there? This is just as friends.*

CHAPTER NINE

"Don't Stop Believing" by Journey blared out of a speaker, preceded by a black truck pulling a trailer that housed the football team. Savage was seated on the side of the trailer and smiled when his eyes met mine. In the middle of the trailer stood a bunch of guys belting the lyrics. Drew stood front and center with them as he energetically sang. His performance took on another level when he knew I was watching. He dropped to his knees as he sang into a pretend microphone and pointed at me. The heat rushed to my cheeks. The crowded sidewalk observing the homecoming parade got an eyeful with Drew's spectacle. He had finally stopped his larger-than-life singing and was now laughing. Obviously, he enjoyed sending all eyes my way and causing me some embarrassment. He winked at me as the truck moved on, followed by the marching band.

By the end of the parade, the crowd had scattered. Haley, Julie, and I headed inside the building to meet up with the guys in the music wing. As we rounded the corner, about a dozen guys walked toward the main entrance, passing us along the way.

Dawson stepped away from the group. "Yo, Zinn! What's up?"

"Um, not much." Nervous and caught off guard, I stopped. Haley and Julie kept walking, unaware of my anxiety.

Dawson turned his back to Haley and Julie and stepped closer to me. "So, you headed to the bonfire?"

"Um, yeah," I said, almost stuttering he made me so skittish.

"Cool," Dawson said. "Then I'll see you over there."

"Yeah, maybe."

"And maybe you'll finally give me those digits."

Wide-eyed, I nodded slightly. His unwelcome coercion was paired with a sly smile I didn't trust. *Is he really this arrogant, or is he hiding something? Stop overreacting, Zinn.*

"Later, Zinn."

As Dawson stepped away, Haley bounded toward me, shaking her head in confusion. "I didn't know you knew Dawson."

"I don't really." I shook my head side to side.

"If you want my advice—"

"Zinn!" Drew interrupted Haley, walking toward me. "You ignoring me?"

"No! Course not! I didn't see you."

"Yeah, you were otherwise occupied." Drew's gaze moved to the group of guys walking down the hall.

"Jules, let's go." Haley's eyebrows raised, signaling her curiosity as she continued toward to the music wing. "Meet you there, Zinn?"

"Yeah, okay." I waved her off, trying my best to ignore her antics.

"So you were talking to Dawson?"

"Not really. He just asked if I was going to the bonfire."

"Oh yeah?"

"Yeah," I said, getting the vibe Drew might think I preferred Dawson.

"I didn't know y'all were friends."

"Oh, we're definitely not."

Drew set rageful eyes onto Dawson and his group, as if a stare would correct any misbehavior they were conjuring. *What is that about? I'm completely in the dark.* Finally, he broke his glower and his countenance softened when he looked at me.

"Did you enjoy the parade?"

I twisted my mouth and cocked an eyebrow at him to signify it was not the best event I'd been to. He lightly chuckled.

"Where's Blake?"

I shrugged my shoulders. "I've not seen him."

"He joining you for the bonfire?"

"I'm supposed to hang with Haley and Jules."

"Maybe I can hang with you all too?" he said hopefully.

"Um, I guess. I mean, if you want."

"I wouldn't have asked if I didn't want to," Drew said with a wink.

Walking to the grassy area beside the football field, we headed toward the flickering flames in the distance. Music grew louder as we got closer. Drew's lighthearted conversation kept me smiling as we enjoyed the warmth of the bonfire.

"Well, I don't see Haley or Jules."

"Let's get some food while we wait." Drew motioned to the row of tailgates full of food, and we fell into a line. Several people spoke to Drew as we waited our turn. I kept my eyes peeled for Haley or Julie while also looking for Blake. I wasn't sure how he would feel to see me with Drew. Even if we were only going to homecoming as friends, Blake was a guy. And from my experience, guys get jealous.

My eyes scanned a snow cone truck hoping Haley would be there. Unfortunately, Dawson stood a few feet away from the colorful van, leaning against a tailgate with some other guys. His eyes met mine. *Why is he everywhere? And why do I always get caught looking at him when I'm really not?* He nodded and gave a cocky grin. I shyly smiled and then turned to face Drew, who was already glaring at Dawson. Satisfyingly challenged, Dawson cocked his eyebrow and gave a smirk. Drew's clenched jaw said it all. Hopping from the tailgate, Dawson motioned the guys toward the bonfire. As they walked toward the fire, Drew kept his eyes on the group. Obviously, Dawson was not threatened by his look and complied to the challenging stare down. Their scowling expressions made a wave of nausea come over me. The line moved, so I followed suit. Drew delayed a moment, then caught up with me. Dawson gave me another cocky grin as he started talking with a couple of his crew.

"I'm starving," Drew said in his happy-go-lucky tone as he handed me a plate.

"I'm not hungry." I threw my hand up toward the plate.

"Zinn, trust me. You don't wanna miss out on these burgers."

"Fine." I rolled my eyes, prepared to force down a rock of tension called meat. That's how anxiety made me feel—food averse.

"That's more like it." He gave a quick wink.

After we got the food, we made our way through the hoard of teenagers. Haley, Julie, and the boys appeared on the other side of the fire, and we waved at each other. Haley gave me a look and pointed to her phone, then a text came through.

Haley: Sorry left phone in music room…had to go get it

Me: No big. You wanna come over here?

Haley: Yeah…gonna grab some food

Be there in a sec

Coming toward us, Julie walked between Haley and Blake. Max trailed slightly behind Ryan. Watching Blake and Julie interacting, she looked at ease. When they reached us, Blake looked my way and his smile slightly faded. His disappointment was evident. *Is he upset seeing me with Drew?* I swallowed hard, suddenly uncomfortable.

We climbed the hillside and found a spot. Haley carried some blankets in her hand, and I helped her spread them on the ground. She pulled me away from the group and said conspiratorially, "So I found out who Blake wanted to ask, and you're not gonna believe who it is."

"Who?" I eagerly asked.

"Jules!"

"For reals? Jules?"

"Yeah, he told Ryan before the parade, but Jules doesn't know."

"What should I do?"

"I don't know. She's going with Max, but I'm done playing match-maker. I can't believe I didn't see it."

Settling on the blankets, Drew sat beside me. Blake positioned himself between Julie and me. Max sort of stayed on the outside while Ryan and Haley sat cuddled up together. The blare of the music and the roar of the fire intensified the overly excited teens. A large, muscular boy riled up the crowd as he led everyone in chants. The energy of the crowd was intoxicating. We ate and talked until the music lowered and Coach grabbed the bullhorn.

Drew leaned over and whispered to me, "Be back in a bit," then darted down the hillside. As he fell in line with the other football players, Dawson glared at him. Drew either didn't pay him any attention or he didn't care. Coach started rallying the crowd with a prediction of defeat against the opposing team and then began his introduction of the team players. Calling the player positions and name, each guy stepped forward. With even more enthusiasm, he announced his "star players": Tristan Jackson, Colby White, Mike Taylor, Dawson, and Drew. Finally, the coach introduced the star of the night—the quarterback. Coach spotlighted the soon-to-be record-breaker for total passing yards. The team began a low growl that grew in intensity as Coach called out number twenty-five and then loudly yelled, "Savage Sullivan!" From the darkness Savage stepped forward, waved, and slipped in beside Drew. The band tore into the fight song while the cheerleaders did some choreographed routine of kicks, jumps, and hand claps. One girl did a backward somersault, and Ashlynn got hoisted up by three girls, then tossed high as she did a spread-eagle jump before safely landing back in the trio's arms. The crowd went crazy and got even rowdier than before. By the end of the song, the teens settled down as Coach continued the pep talk. When he was done, the players took their dismissal cue, and the cheerleaders led the crowd in several more cheers. Drew headed back up the hill with Savage beside him.

"I found a straggler down there among the misfits," Drew said.

Savage casually nodded in acknowledgment.

"Hey, Savage," I said. Drew settled beside me on the blanket, but Savage didn't budge. With his hands shoved in his pockets, he lacked his normal at-ease presence.

"You wanna sit? There's room right here." I patted the blanket beside me.

"Yeah, Savvy, take a seat." Drew motioned to him. "Won't be long til the fireworks."

"Nah, I'm good. I'll just crowd things."

With plenty of room on the blanket beside me, Savage's refusal to sit surprised me. The others chatted and laughed, but Savage stood even more quiet than normal. I walked over to him.

"So what's this talk about you breaking some record?" I questioned.

"It's nothing."

"Really? Breaking a twenty-five-year record is not nothing."

"Hmm."

Geez, why did I think complimenting him would ease the weirdness? Savage barely talks about himself, let alone his accomplishments.

"You gonna be at the dance?"

"Nope," Savage said.

"Really, 'cause I heard a couple of girls were holding out to see if you'd ask them tonight. Don't you wanna ask someone?"

"I did, but she got asked."

"Who is she?"

"Doesn't matter now."

"Geez, Savage. It's one dance. You can always ask her out another time," I said.

Savage turned to me and became extremely serious. "It won't happen."

With wide eyes, I replied softly, "Okay."

"I'm gonna go." Savage stepped away.

"You don't wanna watch the fireworks?" I asked.

Drew perked up. "Yo, Savvy, festivities ain't done."

"Had enough festivities," Savage said as he kept walking.

Drew jumped up and caught up with Savage. They talked but were too far away for me to hear. Drew motioned him toward the group, tugging on his elbow. Savage shook him off and headed toward the parking lot.

"Couldn't get him to stay, huh?" I asked Drew.

"No changing his mind."

We seated ourselves back on the blanket and took in the night. The sound of the boom and the array of sparkles dancing above my head drew my attention. With the brightness filling the sky, Drew smiled, but sadness shown in his eyes. Was it because of Savage? Another spray of colors brightened the sky, and Drew glanced at me with a smile that now filled his whole face. I smiled back. The fireworks showered the sky, streaking it with a beautiful array of colors.

The fireworks ended with a last round of intense booms. I pulled a blanket from the ground to help clean up and folded it with Drew's help. Haley scooped the other one in her hands and impatiently wadded it into a ball. Max said his goodbyes and walked over to another group headed toward the parking lot.

"It's still early. Anyone wanna go to Jack's?" Haley asked with enthusiasm.

"I could go for some food. Anyone in?" Drew said.

I nodded as I handed Haley the folded blanket.

Julie explained she couldn't go, so she said her goodbyes and headed to the parking lot. Blake quickly interjected, explaining that he had to go, and jogged toward Julie. Watching Julie get the attention of Blake made me happy. She deserved a sweet guy like him.

"Haley, can I get a lift there?" I asked.

"Totally! Ryan, you got room for Zinn?"

"Sure, if she's okay squeezing in the cab?" Ryan said.

"I gotcha, Zinn," Drew chimed in.

Haley gave me a giddy look while nearly erupting from the obvious squeal she kept contained. I pierced my lips and gave her a look, begging her to chill. I told Drew thanks and we walked to his truck.

Drew opened the passenger door, and I climbed into the seat. This felt like a habit now. As he walked around the truck, he waved to a group of boys standing in the row across from his vehicle. Dawson stood in the middle of the group and gave no reaction to Drew's greeting. Instead, Dawson's eyes were on me yet again! *Good grief! Find someone else to intimidate!* Some girls joined the group of guys, and one of them slid her arm around Dawson. She leaned into his ear, which made him look away from me. Drew settled into his seat and turned on the ignition. As the truck drove past the group, Dawson's eyes fixated on me again. *This is getting ridiculous!* Fidgeting in my seat, Drew broke the silence.

"Seems you've got the interest of Dawson."

"Um, doubtful. I barely know him."

Drew took a breath and blew it out, looking serious. "Look, can I offer you some advice?"

"Okay," I said hesitantly.

"Regarding Dawson . . . Um, maybe keep your distance."

"Oh? Why's that?" I asked, having already intuited he was bad news.

"Well, Dawson's known to be . . . intense."

"Intense?"

"Yeah, intense is probably putting it mildly," Drew answered.

I waited for him to explain what that meant, but he said nothing.

"So you and Dawson? What's going on there? You're not friends?" I asked, hoping this would lead him to reveal more.

"Friends? Naw, not now."

"But you *were* friends?" I pried.

"At one time, yeah. I guess, you could say that. But not anymore."

So this vibe I'd gotten from Dawson and Drew is something. Still, why does Drew care if I'm friends with Dawson?

"You're saying I shouldn't be friends with him? Is that right?" I confirmed.

"Friends is not really something Dawson does well," Drew offered, looking uncomfortable.

"Okay, but what does that even mean?"

Drew's eyes narrowed as he looked at me. "It means he doesn't always play nice."

"So he's intense and doesn't play nice?" I repeated, giving him a puzzled look. "It sounds like you're describing what he does on the field."

"Hmm. How Dawson plays on the field equates to his behavior off the field. You catch what I'm saying?"

I let Drew's last statement marinate for the remainder of the ride to Jack's. Unsure what all the mystery was about, his words repeated in my head. *Intense. Doesn't play nice. His behavior off the field . . .* Dawson seemed nice enough, maybe a bit overly attentive at times and somewhat assertive toward me. *What's the real reason Drew thinks I should steer clear of him?* Whatever beef existed between these two guys, he wasn't sharing more about it tonight. For now, I would have to let my curiosity rest.

"Once Upon a Time" was now in full swing. The anticipation of the dance provided more excitement than the game since our team dominated with a score of 55–10. The homecoming show didn't disappoint. When Colby White, the homecoming king, got crowned, he never noticed that two queen crowns were being used. When everyone started laughing, including the queen, Summer Sanders, Colby showed confusion. Summer, obviously the one responsible for the stunt, then let him in on the joke. His overly dramatic curtsy elated the crowd even more, making it appear he took being the brunt of the joke well, or at least he did in public. Being his girlfriend, Summer must have known his embarrassment limits, right?

When the buzzer sounded and the crowds began to disperse, Haley told the guys we'd meet them in the music building hallway. We wanted to have our "girl time" as Haley described it to the guys, which basically meant go to the bathroom and touch up our makeup and talk about the boys.

"Zinn, this color would look really good on you." Haley handed me the blush she'd just dotted on her cheeks.

"You think?" I replied, then turned toward her as if to say, "Go for it!"

Haley touched the brush to my cheek. In the mirror's reflection, her gentle pats brightened my face. Suddenly, images flashed in my mind of last year's homecoming night with Bryce. A wave of sickness came over me as I recalled Sam retouching my makeup, trying to conceal my streaked mascara and tear-stained face.

"Zinn, are you okay?" Haley asked.

"You look really pale," Julie added.

"Yeah, I'm fine." Turning on the faucet, I splashed cold water on my face, ruining all my carefully applied makeup. In that moment of full-blown panic attack mode, I didn't care. I reached for a paper towel, but Julie had one ready. I wet it and placed the floppy brown sheet of industrial paper on the back of my neck to help cool me down.

The girls hovered, asking me over and over if I was okay or if I felt faint. I barely understood what they were saying because my mind was so cloudy, but I offered them a weak thumbs-up, hoping that would satisfy. This feeling would pass soon.

"Maybe I'm just hungry. It's been hours since I ate." I hoped my explanation would deflect their concern. Moments later, Haley handed me a granola bar, and Julie had uncapped a bottle of water, pushing it toward me. As I took a swig of water, Haley's phone rang.

"The guys are waiting for us," Haley said, looking at her phone. You okay to go meet up and dance?" Haley looked worried but didn't know what to do.

"Yeah, let's go," I offered weakly.

"Are you sure?" Julie looked at me with concern.

"It's nothing. I promise I'm good," I reassured.

Haley took hold of my arm and warily led me out of the bathroom.

The guys waited in the hallway. When Ryan saw Haley, a smile lit up his face. *Yeah, he was smitten with her. Good for them.* The giddiness filled her face until she looked at me with some guilt, knowing she'd be leaving me behind for him.

I mouthed, "I'm fine." She smiled and left my side to embrace Ryan. When Blake saw me, he causally smiled, but it was simply a polite gesture. How did I know this? Because seconds later Julie appeared. Let's just say the casual smile Blake gave me was a pittance compared to the wide-eyed, awestruck stare he involuntarily gave Julie. Literally, his mouth dropped open. Yeah, he liked her.

Julie stood beside me. For once, her shyness became secondary to her acceptance of someone's stare. A coy smile filled her face as she looked in Blake's direction. *All it took was the right person for Jules.* Blake's eyes locked on Julie caused me to laugh. My happiness for their new beginning quickly vanished when Max's voice filled the empty space.

"You look nice, Jules."

Blake nervously swallowed and then brought his gaze to meet mine. He walked toward me and politely complimented me. After a short exchange of words, the six of us made our way to the gym. The hallway to the gym had been transformed into something from another place with a twinkle-light-covered archway and a gold sign displaying the words, "Once Upon a Time." Entering the gym, a bright crescent moon hung from the ceiling along with streams of more twinkle lights. Lights and tulle-covered latticework created stunning walls that surrounded white-draped tables. Each table had frosted glass jars filled with mini flickering lights, giving the impression that fireflies were inside. Green ivy trailed around the jars, and place settings of gold chargers graced each seating area. The tables surrounded the white dance floor in the center of the room, and white balloons floated above.

The transformation into the fairy-tale scene made the gymnasium unrecognizable. After taking pictures at the different backdrops and the photo booth, we found a table for six and settled there. Haley snapped more pics of us at the table. Before long, we were on the dance floor, laughing and moving to the music. An hour later, the party was in full swing. The upbeat songs allowed us three couples to cut loose and attempt the latest trending dance moves, leaving everyone exhausted but also exhilarated. The boys showed off some well-rehearsed moves, and the girls responded with cheering and accolades, boosting their egos.

When a slower song played, Blake kindly invited me to dance to a couple of them while Max and Julie returned to the table. Ryan and Haley, on the other hand, reveled in the opportunity to partake in accepted public displays of affection. When yet another slow song began, Blake and I decided to go back to the table with Max and Julie. Max leaned over to Julie and she nodded, then he stood and grabbed his coat from the back of the chair. Something was up.

"I'm heading out!" Max announced.

"You're leaving already?" I questioned.

"Yeah, early morning. It was fun. Thanks, Jules, for being so cool. Later, everyone!" Max slipped on his coat and threw his hand up as he walked out.

"Jules, everything okay? I mean, with Max leaving. Nothing bad happened, did it?"

"Yeah, he had to leave early cause his family's headed out of town tomorrow."

"Do you need a ride home?"

"No, my dad's picking me up in about half an hour," Julie said.

"That's so early. Maybe we could take you home?"

"Yeah, we can take you home," Blake said energetically.

"Really, it's fine." Julie appeared a little embarrassed to suddenly be without a date and admitting her dad was coming to pick her up.

"It's no bother," Blake quickly responded.

"Yeah, Jules, just ride with us. We can all go to The Slice after the dance," I said.

Jules nodded and gave her silent agreement. Blake beamed from ear to ear. I'd now be the one left alone soon, which was fine.

Ryan and Haley returned to the table as the crowd got rowdier with the upbeat music. Lines formed to dance to the next track and Drew stood among them. He caught my eye and winked. As the DJ continued to work the crowd, we remained at our table, talking. The strobe lights changed to a soft stream as a softer melody came through the speakers. Blake leaned to me and whispered in my ear. "You mind if I ask Jules to dance?"

I shook my head and gave him an approving smile. *It was now officially beginning. The date handover.* Blake went over to Julie and sat down, fidgeting with the tablecloth as he worked up the nerve to ask her. Her eyes widened as she looked at me with questioning eyes. I tilted my head and gave her an approving nod. Giving me the sweetest look of appreciation, she took hold of Blake's hand as they followed Ryan and Haley to the dance floor.

I now sat alone, enjoying the music, while my friends enjoyed time on the dance floor. Getting lost in the melody, my eyes closed. Suddenly, I felt a tap on my shoulder.

"Did someone turn on the lights, or did you just smile?" Drew said with an adorable smirk.

"What are you doing over here?"

"Well, I saw your date was otherwise occupied."

"Yeah, well, between you and me, Blake would've preferred to be here with Jules from the very beginning."

"Um, I see. Well, since he is occupied, then he shouldn't mind if I steal you for a dance."

Drew was obviously taking pity on me, so I nodded.

Dancing is better than sitting alone.

He took my hand and led me to the dance floor. Finding our place among the couples, Drew pulled me close to him as I draped my arms around his neck. With his arms around my waist, he whirled me around the floor. I felt like I was almost floating as we glided through the crowd. The love song transitioned into another 1980s angst-filled anthem. Drew kept his grasp on my waist and confidently moved me around the floor. I completely relaxed in Drew's arms, surrendering to his lead as he spun me out and then back into his arms. Catching me off guard when he dipped me, I let out a laugh. Changing to another song with a faster beat didn't stop Drew from holding me in his arms for another frolic.

After about five songs, I told Drew I needed a break. He walked me back to the table where Blake sat next to Julie engrossed in a conversation.

"Got room for one more?" Drew asked.

"Sure," Haley injected eagerly.

"Hmm, I guess we can make room," I said coyly. *Did I just use Savage's line?* I wasn't a *hmm'er.*

"Appreciate the hospitality," Drew said with his mischievous grin.

Drew settled in the chair next to me. Haley immediately grabbed her phone and told us to smile. Drew moved closer to me and rested his arm on the back of my chair. When the light flashed, he put some distance between us, but his arm remained protectively behind me.

We got lost in conversation, then I heard Blake.

"Oh! Uh, Zinn, I'm sorry. I was just talking. Um, you wanna dance?" Blake fumbled with his words, most likely feeling guilty he'd left me unattended. But I wasn't complaining with Drew's attention, even if it was just him feeling sorry for me. *Maybe it wasn't just pity? A girl could dream.*

"Uh, no, I'm good. I think I need to rest a minute," I said.

"Want some punch?" Blake asked.

Giving a nod, he inquired about the rest of the table. When they said yes, a look of panic came across his face. Then Drew stood. "I'll help ya there, Stevens."

As the two of them walked to the refreshment table, Drew had his arm draped around Blake as he spoke to him. Blake nodded and shrugged his shoulders.

When they returned with the drinks, the dance floor was almost empty. The DJ opted for an interactive, upbeat song, which drew many back to the dance floor. When the song blasted through the gym, Drew leaned toward Blake. "Stevens, mind if I borrow your date for another dance?"

"No, dude, go for it!" Blake answered cheerfully.

"Zinn, join me for my favorite dance?" Drew smiled as he held out his hand.

"Your favorite dance?"

"Duh, it's the chicken dance. Who doesn't love the chicken dance?"

"Oh, Zinn, you gotta do it." Haley beamed as she held up her phone.

"Fine, but no pictures," I said sternly to Haley, and she obligingly put down her phone.

"We'll show 'em how this dance is done." Drew took hold of my hand. "And Haley? Remember, no pictures. But a video would be great."

I shot him a look as he pulled me onto the floor. He immediately started to flap his arms. My uncomfortable laughter didn't derail Drew from performing the dance. Rolling my eyes, I conceded to my fate of doing the stupid dance. In no time, other students joined in, and the floor became full again.

Returning to my friends, they energetically flapped their arms too. I just gave them all a smirk as I sat down, only mildly embarrassed. Laughter and chatter filled the air as Haley snapped more pictures. The night was great and had most certainly redeemed homecoming for me.

"Okay, Bobcats, it's that time! Grab that special someone for the last dance!" the DJ announced.

Ryan and Haley immediately stood. Blake nervously looked at me as he opened his mouth to say something. I smiled and motioned my head toward Julie. He smiled and leaned over to her. She nodded and took his hand.

Drew cleared his throat as he stood from the chair. "So, Zinn, how about it? Last dance?"

Without a word, he gently took my hand, engulfing it into his. As we found our place on the dance floor, he placed my hand on his shoulder and wrapped his arms around my waist, pulling me to him. My cheek pressed against his shoulder as we slowly swayed to the music. The ending to this fairy-tale-themed night couldn't be more perfect. The voices of Forest Blakk and Meghan Trainer echoed through the gym. Drew softly sang "If You Love Her" along with the duo, holding me even tighter, making my heart do that flip-flop thing. Totally mesmerized by the words and Drew's voice, I barely noticed when he spoke.

"Hope it's okay, but I told Blake I'd give you a ride home."

"Um, what?" *Blake? Ride home?* I knew I sounded a little confused. "Uh, yeah. That's fine."

"I just thought about how you said he wanted to be here with Jules, so I figured I'd help a guy out," Drew explained.

"Drew Behr, who knew you were such a romantic?"

"Zinn Danthes, there's so much you don't know about me," Drew said as he spun me out of his arms. My breath escaped me for a moment. Spinning me back to face him caused me to exhale. Drew looked intently in my eyes. "Well, who knew?"

"Who knew what?" I asked.

"That I would ever succeed in taking your breath away." Drew grinned.

"Um, well . . . I really didn't—"

"Zinn, just let me have it," Drew interrupted.

"Have what?"

"Hope." Drew's blue eyes twinkled as he let the word linger in the air. He spun me out and then back to him, pulling me in a little closer than before. We stared at each other and moved to the music without speaking. Intoxicated by the moment, he had me questioning things again. Especially as his last word dominated the moment: *hope.*

As the song ended, we left the dance floor. Drew said he needed to say something to one of his friends and would be back in a minute.

Blake came over to me. "Zinn, you good with Bear taking you home?"

"Yeah, it's fine."

"You sure? Don't want you to think I'm bailing on you. But when Bear asked me if I could do him this favor, I just figured—"

"Wait, what?" I interrupted.

"Um, yeah! Bear said he really wanted to take you home."

"He did?"

"Yeah, he did. You good with that?"

"Sure, Blake, totally fine."

Drew, talking to some guy at another table, saw me and winked as a smile lit up his face. This whole night had been like a scene from a movie. That last dance with Drew made it feel even more surreal, and now Blake just told me Drew asked to take me home. Not sure what any of it meant, except that it excited me.

Is it safe to get excited about Drew Behr? He asked me to just let him have hope. What does that even mean?

Drew patted the guy on his shoulder and moved toward me. My heart raced as he approached. That adorable smile made his blue eyes seem animated. I held my breath as he got closer.

"You ready, Zinn?" Drew asked.

Lost in his whole vibe, I froze, unable to answer.

"Hello, Zinn! You still there?"

"Yeah, sorry. Just lost in thought."

"Penny for your thoughts?" he asked.

There's no way I can tell him what I'm thinking. Not til I know for sure how he feels.

"Zinn, hello?" He waved his hand in front of my face.

"Sorry." I shook my head. "It's nothing worth saying."

"Don't sell yourself short. I mean, it has to be worth at least a penny."

I laughed, hoping I could snap back to attention soon. We left the gym and headed to his truck. The lighthearted conversation couldn't distract me from that one word still lingering in the air.

What did Drew hope for? Do I dare let myself hope too?

CHAPTER TEN

Saturday morning, my phone ringing prompted my hand to scrape across the fuzzy carpet until it hit the cool metal. I pressed the side button and thankfully stopped the beeping sound. Just a few seconds later it sounded again. I grabbed the phone and squinted at the screen. It was Sam calling for the fourth time. I accepted the call and said hello. She immediately bombarded me, requesting the details of my sort-of homecoming date with Blake. I gave her the surface details first, then began on the Julie and Blake news feature when her dad called and interrupted us. Promising to call me back in a minute, she said goodbye. Last night's dress crumpled in the chair flashed a memory of Drew holding me in his arms. *Sam's gonna flip when she hears what happened with Drew.*

I dragged myself from the bed and swooped up the dress and shoes. Hanging the dress in the closet, I tossed the shoes in the box on the floor. I changed into leggings and a T-shirt and twisted my hair into a messy bun. *Sam's gonna give me the "I knew it the whole time" spiel. She's probably known I've been crushing on Drew since day one. Wait, have I even told her about Drew?*

I couldn't recall telling Sam anything about Drew except having econ with him. Actually, I didn't really talk about my new friends to

Sam. When we did talk, which was rare, the conversations always gravitated to the happenings at Kowinville. But that made sense because they were my friends, too, and Sam didn't know anyone from Bargeston. Besides, the last thing I wanted to do was make Sam feel like she had been replaced. Still, I wanted to share with Sam all that happened with Drew, so I would tell her as soon as she called back.

Waiting on her call, some unpacked boxes on the floor taunted me. *Two months of procrastination is enough.* I picked up one of the boxes and placed it on my desk, then grabbed my earbuds and shoved them into my ears. Emptying the box, I organized the items on my shelves and decorated my room as the music blared in my ears. The beep from a call made me hit the side of my earbud.

"Hey, Sammy."

"It's not Sam. Z, it's me."

The nausea hit me like waves crashing against rocks. Heat rushed to my face and sweat beaded across my upper lip. I weakly fell into the chair as I tried to form words. Adrenaline pulsed though my body like a fight-or-flight response. Nothing would come out of my mouth.

"Zinn, you there?"

"Uh, yeah. I'm here, sorry."

"So how you doing, Z?"

"Um, good. How are you, Bryce?"

Why is he calling?

"Good," Bryce said. "I miss you."

He misses me? Why now? Just when things were going so great for me, he had to call. Before I could stop them, the words slipped from my mouth. "I've missed you too."

"You have?" Insecure longing weighted his voice.

With a deep breath I cautiously said, "Um, Bryce, do you need something?"

"Well, yeah. I just wanted to see how your new school was. Mainly, I wanted to know how you were."

"It's all good."

"So, are you meeting people?" he asked.

"Yeah, I've met some people." I kept my answers short and barely gave him details.

"Making friends, huh? Any guy friends?"

"Yeah, I've made some friends, and some of them are guys."

"Huh, so you dating anyone?" he asked a little smugly.

And there it was. The real reason behind Bryce's call. *Sam! Ugh. She obviously told him about my date to homecoming.*

"Not really."

After a long pause he said, "Look, Z. I messed up. Breaking up with you was stupid."

I sat quietly as he repeated the same words I'd heard so many times before. How was this time any different?

"Z, I'm sorry about how I treated you. It was a jerk move. I'm not that guy anymore. I've changed. Losing you, uh . . . Well, I guess it made me realize how much you mean to me and how much I love you."

Tears pooled in my eyes as Bryce continued saying how sorry he was.

"Bryce, I . . . Um, I don't know what to say. I mean, a lot has happened."

"I get it, I really do. And you need some time. But I just wanna talk. I really miss you. You know you're the only one who really gets me."

Exhaling, my heart sank because I knew he was right. I did get him.

"Z, can you forgive me? And just . . . I don't know. Can we talk again? It's been really bad for me lately."

"Really bad?" I said in a whisper, not really intending for Bryce to hear.

"Yeah, old man's been on a bender. It's been happening every night this week. I just can't take much more."

"Bryce, I'm sorry." I couldn't fight the tears as they poured from my eyes.

"Z, would it be okay if tonight, maybe . . . You know, I was hoping we could hang out. I really need to talk to someone. I feel like I'm going crazy. I don't know what might happen if I'm at the house tonight."

With a deep breath I said, "I guess we can just hang out and talk. But that's it, just talking, okay?"

"Thanks, Z. I'll pick you up around six. And Z, just so you know, I really am different now."

He seemed too excited, and I needed to rein this in before he got the wrong idea. "Bryce, it's just talking, okay?"

"I know, Z. Just talking. See you at six."

As the call ended, I flopped onto my bed. *Why now?* It's like Bryce had this telepathic connection to me, as if he knew that I'd started to connect with another guy. The two of us talking would lead to him pressuring me into getting back with him. And with Bryce, I'd never been strong enough to refuse him.

Our upcoming "reunion" occupied the rest of my day. My walk with Oreo did little to calm my nerves. I rummaged through my closet after lunch until settling on four potential outfits. I spent the hour trying them on to decide the right one to wear. By four o'clock, I jumped in the shower. The hot water beating down on me provided relief until it ran cold. By 5:15, I stood in front of the mirror and fiddled with my hair. Unhappy with the outfit, I changed into the pink top that Bryce had never seen and hopefully wouldn't criticize. By 5:35, I was ready. Since Bryce never arrived early, I could either wait and worry or find something to do to kill the time. Finding the perfect distraction, I grabbed my guitar. My hands wrapped around the smooth neck and body, and when my fingers touched the strings, it felt like second nature. I strummed the chords and jotted some notes. I continued playing and singing the new lyrics but was interrupted by the doorbell ringing. Checking my phone, it read 5:45. No way that could be Bryce. He never picked me up on time.

"Zinn, it's Bryce!" Mom yelled.

He's early? That's weird. I was disappointed he was here already. Not a good sign on my end.

"Coming!" I placed the guitar back in the case, grabbed my sweater, and went downstairs. Bryce was casually talking to Mom and Grandma as if we'd never broken up. He glanced at me and smiled. My conflicting mood threw me off balance. Was I nervous? Excited? Flat? I couldn't place it.

Bryce wore a green shirt, which he always looked great in. *Did he wear it for me? Probably just a fluke.* My mom, being her chatty self, asked

Bryce about school and football. She also told some funny stories about the move. Bryce listened to her ramble on about whatever came to her mind. One thing Bryce did well was make my mom feel special, which I liked. I let her rattle off for a couple of minutes, then cleared my throat. "Mom, we'd better go."

"Oh yeah! Sorry, I'm just blabbering away. You two have fun. Bryce, it's nice seeing you again."

"Good seeing you too." He gave Mom a hug and it weirded me out. Seeing him repeating a past behavior in a new environment was something I wasn't prepared for. Moving changes people, and I wasn't the same person as when he'd come to see me at my old house. I didn't like that he'd imprinted himself in this home, a place free from any echoes of his memories.

As he drove to the restaurant in Kowinville, low music played. The music streamed from his phone. *That's weird.* Since he didn't care about music that much, he typically listened to the trending songs on the radio. When we dated, he would get annoyed with my playlists, rarely letting me play them in the car. This playlist had some of my favorite songs. *Did he make this playlist? No, he must've picked some random playlist for the drive.*

Bryce told the host we needed a table for two. With a twenty-minute wait ahead of us, I headed out the door because Bryce never waited for a table longer than two minutes. With my hand on the door handle, Bryce walked behind me with a pager in his hand. "You wanna wait outside?"

Almost speechless at this patient version of Bryce, I quietly responded, "Sure."

Bryce is willing to wait for a table?

He smiled. "You like this place, don't you?"

"Yeah," I replied. *Strange that he remembered this detail.*

Waiting on the bench outside, we talked mostly about school and our friends at Kowinville. Then the conversation took a surprising turn. He asked me personal questions about school, my music, and if I'd written any new songs. For once, the conversation didn't revolve around him, his friends, or his complaints about something I'd done to make him mad, which always resulted in a fight.

During dinner, the surprises kept coming. First, he didn't spend the entire time on his phone. Another shocker was he didn't let his eyes follow the girls who walked past our table. Bryce acted different . . . better. This Bryce was the guy I *knew* was under all those layers of pain and abuse.

Maybe Bryce finally realized how good I had been for him?

We got done with dinner around 7:30. Since the drive home only took twenty-five minutes, Bryce wanted to drive and talk. He drove toward the high school, which meant he was headed to the park. He pulled the car near "our spot," got out, and came to my side of the car to help me out. *What is going on? He has never done this.* My mouth almost dropped when he took my hand to walk me to the swings. We pumped our knees, swinging slowly, saying nothing. My feet dragged the ground, intending to stop. The heaviness of the silence made the moment more tense. I wanted to be anywhere but here. Bryce had a motive for coming here, and I wasn't up for the pressure, the drama, or the surprise.

Bryce broke the silence. "Z, I've been thinking a lot about us. Since you've been gone, I've been miserable. My dad's on me all the time, and I have no one to support me."

I hoped and prayed he would end it there.

Please don't ask me . . .

"I know I hurt you. Do you think . . . Well, is there any way . . . ?"

My hope was now lost. He was about to ask me back. I inhaled.

He stopped his swing from moving and grabbed the chains of mine and pulled them toward him. "Do you think there's any way you could give me another chance?"

Are those actual tears in his eyes?

I whispered, "I don't know, Bryce."

"Please, Z! I messed up bad. You're everything to me. It was stupid to blow the relationship apart. I love you so much. I'm miserable without you. I need you." Tears streamed down his face, and he dropped his head in despair.

Gripping the swing as tight as I could, I clinched my teeth and took a deep breath. Instinctively, my left hand reached for Bryce's head. *Don't do it. If you do it, you know what will happen.* I quickly pulled back my hand. But then, like a magnet, my fingers lightly flipped the slight waves of his hair. That was it. He put his arms around me and sunk his face into my shoulder. My arms relaxed into his grip. In that moment, my heart gave in to Bryce and I was drawn back to the flame like a moth.

My stomach was going to rebel if I choked down the plate before me. How come thoughts of Bryce always managed to hijack my appetite and make me nauseous? I pushed the eggs around on my plate with the fork, then looked at the toast. Nope, that wasn't going down either. What was I going to do about Bryce's sudden reappearance in my life? My brain hadn't been fully hijacked. I still knew how this would play out. *Maybe I can walk away from him this time?* I shook my head, knowing I wasn't strong enough to leave Bryce.

Why had he called me? I had finally let my guard down and opened myself to the possibility of someone else—Drew—and then Bryce butted in. I shook my head, hoping to rattle the thoughts of him out and away.

My phone vibrated the table as it buzzed. A text from Bryce flashed on the screen. I opened the text, not knowing how I wanted to respond. Instead of dealing with him, I pushed my chair out from the table and said, "I'm gonna take Oreo for a walk."

"Well, don't be long. We need to leave for church in thirty minutes," Mom said.

"Yes, ma'am! C'mon, Oreo, wanna go outside?"

Oreo stretched his legs and waddled toward me. Heading down the road, my phone buzzed again, taunting me.

Bryce: Morning, beautiful! Thinkin bout you. Can I come over later?

My fingers tapped the sides of my phone. Thankfully, I had to meet

Savage to work on English, but that didn't make saying no to Bryce easy. I needed to choose my words wisely so I didn't make him mad. Flashes of him yelling at me flooded my mind. I shook my head to get rid of the image. I typed the words and quickly hit Send. It was best not to overthink; otherwise, I might hit Delete.

Me: Sorry, can't today… school project due
Bryce: Time? I can come later
Me: Not sure, text you when I'm done
Bryce: Z, I wanna see you!
Me: Idk lots of work. I'll try and hurry
Bryce: What about Thursday?
Me: idk
Bryce: Z, please!
Me: I guess I can
Bryce: Pick you up at 6:30

Opening the calendar on my phone, it hit me. Thursday was the anniversary of my first kiss with Bryce. Was it coincidence that he asked me out for that day? Whether he remembered or not, the fact remained that resisting Bryce had always been hard for me. He had an appealing charm, but with that charm came an extreme intensity. Everything about Bryce brought with it a fiery emotional energy. I wasn't sure I could handle that again. Maybe he had changed. Last night made me hopeful. Maybe things could be better between us. I just needed more time to figure out what was going on with Drew. More time to decide if I wanted Bryce back in my life. With Thursday only four days away, it just didn't give me enough time.

I pulled into the parking lot at The Slice to see Savage waiting out front. We said hello as we walked into the restaurant. He chose the table near the window and, as usual, waited for me to sit before he sat.

"How was homecoming?" Savage asked.

"Um, it was good," I said.

The server approached our table and energetically greeted Savage with a flirty hello. She giggled and spent way too much time taking his simple order and thoroughly reviewing it. Finally, she turned to me. "You want anything?" she said abruptly.

"Just a Sprite," I replied coolly.

With a look of complete disgust, she jotted it down before returning her attention to Savage. Her annoyed tone became instantly bubbly when she spoke to him again. *How dare she!* "I'll get this right to you, Savage."

He smiled and nodded at her. With a quick glare at me, she finally left us alone.

Savage's stony-faced look made me squirm in my seat. "No food?"

"Not hungry."

The glint in his eyes showed his concern, but I didn't care. "What are we working on today?"

"Zinn, what's wrong?"

"Nothing," I said sharply.

Savage's intense green eyes bore into me. With a deep breath I said, "I don't know. Bryce texted me yesterday and then came over. I'm just feeling very stressed about it. And I haven't talked to Drew since the dance. I don't even know what that's all about."

As soon as the words came out of my mouth, it was like the floodgates had been opened. I couldn't say the words fast enough. Savage, in his typical fashion, gave me his full attention and let me fill the air with all the stressors of the last two days. Tears filling my eyes didn't stop the words from coming.

"Take a breath," Savage said calmly.

"I'm sorry to unload all this on you."

"Hmm, you're fine."

I stopped talking when the server brought the drinks and food. As soon as she was out of earshot, my ramblings continued. I didn't know all I said, but it didn't matter. It just poured from me, and it wouldn't stop coming. I grabbed a fry off Savage's plate and started eating while rambling about Bryce and all that happened. Suddenly, I reached for a fry in an almost-empty basket. Over half his fries were gone and I cringed.

"Did I eat those? Savage, I'm so sorry. Let me get another order."

"It's fine. Eat all you want."

"Look, I appreciate you listening to my babbling. I guess I didn't realize how much I needed to talk."

"You're good. Talk as much as you want," Savage said.

How does he always know when I need to talk?

Savage's kind eyes mesmerized me. He really meant it. I could talk all I wanted, and he would listen. Tears filled my eyes and then nervousness followed. *Great, now he's gonna think I'm a blubbering idiot.* I dabbed my eyes with my napkin and worked up my best excuse for the tears. "I forgot to take my allergy pill. Eyes have been watering like crazy."

He gave a firm nod of his head.

Wanting to divert his attention off me, I called the server over and asked for two orders of fries. Then I resumed talking as Savage remained fully invested in listening. After filling his ears with all my drama, a change of topic was warranted. "So you're the new record holder. That's pretty cool."

"Hmm, I guess."

"Well, I think it's impressive!" I exclaimed and shot him a beaming smile.

Shrugging his shoulders, he remained fairly expressionless about his outstanding feat.

"Are you really this humble, or do you just not care?"

A stunned look appeared on Savage's face, and he blushed ever-so-slightly. The reaction surprised me, making me even more intrigued about him.

"So, which is it?"

"Uh, well, I'm not sure. I guess I have bigger things to worry about than a football record for total passing yards," Savage said.

"Like what?"

"Hmm, just things."

I grabbed another fry while Savage stared at me. His eyes gave a pleading look, almost as if he wanted to say something but didn't know how.

"So what are these *things*?"

He shook his head. "Nothing."

Narrowing my eyes, I replied, "I guess being a Sullivan brings with it some pressure?"

He casually shrugged. "You could say that." As much as Savage tried, he couldn't hide the pain in his eyes. That struck a chord. Feeling his uneasiness, I rattled off something else about the game.

My phone buzzed. It was Bryce asking me what time I would be done. The last three hours I'd spent talking to Savage had eaten enough time so that Bryce couldn't come over. But he still wanted to talk, and I couldn't exactly get out of that. Besides, I'd kept Savage long enough and had already taken up his whole evening with my jabbering. Plus, it derailed us from doing any work on the assignment. Even if I wasn't ready for any of Bryce's potential drama, I couldn't avoid it any longer. Also, I needed to figure out what to say to Drew tomorrow. I didn't even know how to start that conversation, but Drew deserved to hear from me.

"Hey, I'd better get home. I've rambled on long enough," I said. "And I've got a lot to think about before seeing Drew tomorrow."

"Don't stress about Bear. He'll be fine," Savage said.

"Maybe, but I do need to talk to him."

"Hmm, it'll all work out."

I said my goodbye and left the restaurant, then got into the car and sent a quick text to Bryce explaining that I just finished and was driving home. He asked me to call him when I got there. As I pulled out of the parking lot, Savage stood near his car while talking on his cell. I waved to him, and he returned one to me.

The quickest way home meant only ten minutes before talking to Bryce. I took the left turn instead, opting to delay that call for another twenty minutes. I increased the volume on the radio, escaping into the music and avoiding my drama for a little longer.

Just as I got home, I received a call from Drew. *I guess I'll deal with him now.* I took a deep breath and accepted the call.

"Hey, Drew."

"Hey, Zinn! How are you?"

"Good."

"Cool, cool. So, um, I had a lot of fun at the dance."

"Yeah, me too."

"Yeah, I'm glad it worked and we sorta got to do the homecoming thing as friends, you know?"

"Friends?"

"Uh, well, yeah. I mean, I wanted to ask you as friends, and it ended up working out that way," Drew said.

"Um, Drew . . . Honestly, I'm confused. This is sorta out of the blue."

"Okay . . . Well, you know, I said some stuff when we were dancing. I just kinda thought maybe it made you feel weird. You know I'm good being friends and waiting. I don't mean waiting. Um, I'm just glad we're friends, okay? That's what I wanted to say."

"Okay. Friends sounds great," I replied with a fake enthusiasm.

"Well, I'd better go. See you tomorrow, Zinn."

"Yeah, see you tomorrow."

I didn't have to worry about Drew anymore, but him just wanting to be friends stung a bit. But I was glad to have the space. If only Bryce would give me some space. That wouldn't be happening, especially with Thursday coming soon. As I walked in the house, I went upstairs and texted Bryce, telling him I didn't feel good and praying he wouldn't call. My phone vibrated.

Bryce: Sorry babe. You rest. Text you tomorrow.

Thankful for the break, I went into the bathroom and turned on the tub's hot water faucet. A long, hot bath would help relieve some of my stress, so I turned on my music and squirted some bubble bath into the stream of water.

Afterward, I went to my room and climbed into bed. As I closed my eyes, I tried to figure out any way to avoid Thursday. After accepting that it was impossible, I prayed the situation with Bryce would work out as easily as it had with Drew. I could at least hope for a little while longer.

CHAPTER ELEVEN

Thursday came before I knew it, and the day flew by. In chorus, my phone vibrated. I slid it out of my pocket to see a text from Bryce.

Bryce: Hey beautiful...can't wait to see you 

I texted a reply and shoved the phone back in my pocket. My mind wandered to a year ago when I had become so entwined with Bryce. The beginning of sophomore year, Bryce and I had been talking for a couple of weeks when I got a call from him one evening. He asked me if I could meet him at the park. That night he told me all about his dad's drinking and the abuse. The sadness on his face as he described in detail the first time his dad hit him was almost more than I could bear. Imagining a little twelve-year-old boy who wanted to protect his mom get backhanded and kicked by his own father made me sick to my stomach. It broke my heart hearing about this horrific life Bryce had been enduring, and I began to cry.

That moment changed everything for Bryce and me as he wiped the tear from my eye and leaned in to kiss me for the first time. From then on it was him and me—together forever, or so I thought. But then everything changed again when I told him about my move to Bargeston and transferring schools.

Our last day at the lake, I'd pulled him away from the group and explained that my mom had decided we needed to move in with my grandma because of the stroke she'd had. His expressionless eyes bore into me as if he was already lost and abandoned. In the next instant, his eyes darkened and became filled with rage. It caused chills to move over me. Then his verbal barrage of obscenities spewed at me and all eyes shot our way. I walked away from the fire and away from him, but he forcefully grabbed my hand and pulled me back into a rage-filled embrace. Terrified by his behavior, tears poured from my eyes. He was begging me to stay one moment, then yelling at how selfish I was the next. His profane words echoed over the water. Overtaken by the nausea, I again tried to distance myself from him. That just made Bryce even angrier, which caused me to heave what little I had in my stomach. After I got myself together, he started in with the apologies. The emotional roller coaster he put me through felt like competing in a ping-pong match strung out on . . . some kind of *something*! Since I'd never done drugs, I could imagine how awful it would be based on this experience I was having with Bryce. One second he was saying he loved me. The next second he dished out cuss-filled rants, telling me how horrible I was. In our last moment together, he let out a primordial scream as he slammed his fist on the hood of his car. He turned to me, gave me the most revolting look, and yelled, "I hate you for this!" Then he got in his car and his tires threw gravel as he pulled away. He hadn't spoken to me since—until he called on Sunday.

The final bell rang and shot me back to reality. The day was over and just three and half hours remained until Bryce would be at my house. Walking out of school, the rowdiness of everyone intensified the headache I'd had all day. It felt like a vice grip squeezed my head and was now traveling to my neck. Opening the aspirin bottle, I popped two in my mouth, grabbed my water bottle, and took a big gulp.

To my dismay, Bryce arrived on time. I wasn't going to complain. The quicker we got the night started, the quicker it could end. But

Bryce probably thought the opposite. The quicker the night started, the longer he could have me. He asked me where we should eat, so I chose the Mexican restaurant. Likely a safe choice since it wasn't really one of the main hangout spots, which meant we had little chance of seeing someone from school.

In the car, the talk centered on him, as usual. I was bored and unimpressed when he went on about how he needed to put on five pounds since the coach wanted him to go up a weight class. He asked if I would make it to the Kowinville wrestling tournament. My evasiveness of committing to his invite didn't bode well with him. His jawline clenched. I held my breath, waiting for the explosion about to ensue from him, but instead he smiled. "Okay, well, at least it's not a no." Bryce started telling me about Dylan hurting his shoulder and being out for the wrestling season. I was fading, and quick.

At the restaurant, we sat in a corner booth. The lack of kids from my school brought some relief, since Bryce wouldn't feel threatened by meeting anyone I knew. Bryce continued bragging about wrestling as he looked at the menu. Finally giving me some attention, he asked me what I was ordering.

"Um, not real hungry. Probably just a taco."

Bryce narrowed his eyes at me. "Z, what's wrong?"

"Nothing, just not real hungry. I had a big lunch."

I hated that he knew when I was stressed, I didn't eat. One time he got so mad at me for it. I could remember the day like it was yesterday and can still recall the anger in his face. Bryce and I had been dating about three months when it happened. We were at school, headed to the second floor. At the bottom of the stairwell, I took the first step, then my head started to swim, and I stumbled.

"What's wrong with you?" he snipped.

"Nothing, just lost my footing."

"Lost your footing?"

"Yeah." My head spinning brought more unsteadiness. I reached for the stair railing and instantly Bryce's eyes filled with rage.

"Did you eat?"

My eyes widened and darted away from him. Slightly shrugging my shoulders, I tried my best to avoid answering his question. A loud breath escaped from his clenched jaw as he exhaled. "You're pissing me off with this stupid diet. Like you really need to lose weight or something. Why are you so dumb?" He pounced up the steps, leaving me standing there by myself.

Sitting in his car after school, a calmer Bryce prompted me to bring up the incident at the stairs. I explained I wasn't dieting but that I hadn't felt like eating since my grandma had been in the hospital. Bryce hugged me and held me in his arms. He took us to the drive-in restaurant and ordered me a strawberry milkshake. It was the first time, and one of the few times, Bryce showed true concern for me.

The server's voice snapped me back to the moment. I ordered a Sprite, hoping it might settle my stomach and the taco. As we waited for the food, a familiar laugh filled the restaurant. I closed my eyes, praying it wasn't him. No such luck. Drew, Savage, Ashlynn, and another girl were being seated three tables from us. As soon as they got settled, Drew spoke.

"Hey, Zinn!"

I waved and smiled. Savage, seated next to the pretty brunette, gave a quick nod. Ashlynn beamed from ear to ear as Drew sat next to her with his arm draped behind her on the seat. *Double date, huh? Obviously, she's moved on from Jake.* The four of them lost in conversation caused my heart to become heavy. Any hope Drew gave me at homecoming was completely gone now.

Bryce scowled and my breathing went shallow. I gulped as I prepared for what he was going to say. *Stupid move, Zinn. Too much eye contact on another guy never bodes well with Bryce.* Bryce's hand balled into a fist as daggers shot from his eyes toward the table of four. His jaw clenched as he peered at them.

Immediately, Bryce's eyes went icy. "Who are they?"

"Some people from school."

"And the guy in the blue shirt?"

I took a deep breath in and said nervously, "Drew. We have econ together."

The intensity in his eyes bore into me as nausea made my stomach roil. I silently prayed Bryce wouldn't say anything—or worse, make a scene in the middle of the restaurant. His eyes softened as he smiled sweetly.

"Zinn, let's just enjoy tonight."

Bryce calming down so easily shocked me. As I sipped my drink, I tried to push down my disappointment of seeing Drew with another girl. I certainly didn't want Bryce to sense it and risk him losing his temper.

When we finished dinner, Bryce said he wanted to leave. Sliding from the booth, Bryce grabbed the check with one hand and with the other took my hand a little too firmly.

He thinks he owns me.

"Later, Zinn." Drew smiled and waved.

With a weak smile, I quickly waved back to him. I hoped Ashlynn didn't get upset. As we fell in the line at the register, Bryce cut his eyes over to Drew as we waited for our turn. Bryce slipped behind me and wrapped his arms around my waist, nuzzling his chin against the side of my face. I took a step up and put some distance between us. Bryce tightened his grip on me and pulled me back to him. Drew pushed himself away from the table. As he stood, Savage placed his hand on Drew's shoulder, returning Drew to his seat. Drew stared at Bryce. I turned to Bryce, releasing from his grip. Bryce's jaw clenched as he stared at Drew.

Boys, ugh! What's with Drew? He's on a date. I cringed at the thought of how Ashlynn might feel. I avoided eye contact with her and felt remorse for the effects Drew's barbaric behavior might have on her.

"Bryce." I touched his arm. He broke the stare and turned to me. The coldness in his eyes remained but his lips forced a fake smile. I was chilled to the bone.

Bryce paid the bill and stepped outside into the cool night air. In the car, he squealed out of the parking lot, forcing me to grip the door handle as he drove down the road.

"Um . . . Bryce! Could you slow down, please?"

"Sorry," he said, pressing the brakes.

The car's pace slowed and my hand relaxed but remained on the door handle. I wasn't quite sure how to react to that since Bryce never obliged my requests for watching his speed. When we dated and I asked him to slow down, the standard was an increase in his speed with even more recklessness.

Now, though, Bryce acted surprisingly different. He paid attention to me, listened to me, and hadn't yelled one time. I couldn't recall any time while we dated when a week went by and he didn't raise his voice and spew venom. Actually, I couldn't recall more than a day going by that he didn't say negative things to me.

Has Bryce really changed? Would this time be different? He seemed to be trying. Maybe I should give him another chance. *Stop! Yes, he's being kinder than ever, but don't be so quick to trust him.*

Bryce lowered the volume on the radio. "Can we go somewhere and talk. You know, somewhere private? Like a park or something?"

"Um, I don't know. The elementary school has a playground."

Why didn't I tell him about the park? It was closer to my house. But too much had happened at that park. Those memories were things I shouldn't be thinking about right now, like Drew. Drew on a date with Ashlynn made my stomach feel hollow. I had to get him off my mind. Bryce smiled at me. He really did seem to be trying.

Maybe I need to give him another chance.

Nausea hit me when Bryce pulled into the school parking lot. We walked a short distance to the bench. He put his arm around me and made the assumption it was okay to pull me closer to him. When he faced me and tilted my chin up, my stomach fluttered, but not in the good way. I couldn't avoid what was coming. His lips pressed against mine. The familiarity of the kiss was nice, in a way. In another way, it felt—*off*.

"Z, I love you. Please give me another chance. Can't you see how much I'm trying?"

"Yeah, Bryce. I do."

"Then why are you waiting? Is there someone else? Is it the guy at the restaurant?"

Of course, it's the guy at the restaurant. But that chance is gone now. "No, Bryce, there's no one else," I replied quickly and with a bit of harshness.

"Then what is it?"

"It's a lot of stuff. The breakup, the move, us! I don't know, Bryce. It's just a lot."

He said nothing for a bit, and a lump formed in my throat as I anticipated what exactly he was thinking now.

Bryce softly caressed my fingertips. "Z, can't you see I've changed?"

"Yeah, Bryce. I see. I already told you!"

He took my hand and kissed it. "Please give me another chance. I promise it'll be different."

Letting out a deep breath, I said, "Will it? Cause you've said that before."

"Zinn, I know I treated you badly, and I'm not gonna do that ever again. I need you in my life."

The sliver moon hanging amongst the starry sky reflected just enough light so that the sadness in Bryce's eyes tugged at my heart. Bryce needing me used to make me feel good. Now his neediness felt like I carried a huge weight on my shoulders. Tolerating him had become a cross to bear. Even with all the thoughts flooding my brain, my head still nodded up and down. Bryce wrapped his arms around me and he whispered, "I love you, Z. I won't mess this up." Then he kissed me again. As his hands started moving down my back, I pushed him away. He tried to pull me back, but I resisted.

"I need to get home."

"Z, c'mon! Just a few more minutes." He pulled me closer with a little more aggression as his hands found their way to my waist.

Rustling sounds came from the woods. Bryce jumped up, peering at the trees. "Did you hear that?"

"It's probably just a dog or something." I said, trying to calm him but more so trying to calm myself.

Bryce forcefully grabbed my hand. "I think I'd better get you home. It is getting late."

Even though the distraction saved me from having to battle more with his insistences, his uneasiness had me on edge. As we headed toward the car, I had the eerie sense that something or someone was watching me. I glanced toward the trees. Something bright and glowing flashed that I could've sworn were eyes. But they disappeared as quickly as they came. Sliding into the passenger's seat, a low growl came from the trees. It was the same growl I heard at the park with the three guys right before that hairy creature pounced from the woods.

Didn't Jake say something about the Beast having eyes that glowed? Could this be the Beast again?

CHAPTER TWELVE

I walked into econ late, but Coach Bowman, still preoccupied with his morning paper and coffee, paid no attention to my tardiness. At my seat, I rested my head on the desk. Drew came in a few minutes after me.

"Hey, Zinn."

I threw up my hand and mumbled, "Hey."

"Zinn, you all right? You're looking a little pale."

Lifting my head, the light made me squint my eyes, and I gave a nod. "Just up late," I replied as I laid my head back down on the desk.

Up late was an understatement. I had barely gotten in the bed when Bryce called me upset while driving to escape his dad's drunken rage. We stayed on the phone until three in the morning. So getting less than four hours of sleep had me exhausted. I closed my eyes and tried to tune out the chatter of the class. I didn't know which felt worse: the exhaustion, the noise, or the hunger pangs from missing breakfast. The growl of my stomach became unbearable, so I fumbled through my backpack for a granola bar. I pulled the bar from the bag, ripped open the wrapper, and tore off a bit. Popping it in my mouth, I chomped on the sweet crunchiness. My phone flashed with a text notification.

Sam: Jasmine found out you and Bryce are back together

Sam: She's telling him some big story about seeing you out with
a guy

Sam: I told Bryce it wasn't true…he's upset…you need to text
him asap

Sick about what I had just read, I tossed the bar in my backpack. *Jasmine spreading lies about me and some guy? This can't be happening! The last time I saw Jasmine was over a month ago at The Slice when she was the one draped all over that guy. She had some nerve.* Then I remembered all about that night. That was the night Drew and I had gone to The Slice after talking in the park. Jasmine wasn't spreading lies; she was telling Bryce the truth. She was telling him about me being out with Drew.

My heart raced as I tried to process it all. *What am I gonna tell Bryce?* My mind flooded with images of him screaming in my face, his fists slamming and punching walls. My head began swimming as my vision went blurry. Bryce would never understand that Drew was just a friend.

Drew turned to me as if he knew something relating to him was on my mind. Tears welled in my eyes. Drew smiled sweetly. I dropped my head. *Bryce will never let me be friends with Drew now.* A wave of nausea hit me, then my head started spinning.

Everything went black.

"Back up!" a raspy male voice barked.

The surface underneath me felt cold and hard. *Where am I? Am I on the floor? What's going on?* I opened my eyes. *Drew?* Coach Bowman came into my view next. "Bear, get back. Zinn! Can you hear me?" *What is going on?* Everyone was huddled around me, staring. I closed my eyes and shook my head, trying to orient myself.

Someone snapped their fingers in my face. "Zinn, can you hear me?"

"Yes," I whispered.

"How many fingers do you see?" Coach asked.

"Two."

"Good," he said.

I tried to lift myself, but Coach Bowman's hands went to my shoulders. "Hold up, now. Let me help you."

He eased me into a seated position as he pressed me for more information about how I felt. He ordered Drew to help get me to the chair. When Drew grabbed my left arm, pain shot through my elbow. I winced.

"Sorry," Drew said. A look of concern covered his face as he and Coach Bowman lifted me from the floor and moved me to the chair.

Coach Bowman kneeled in front of me and studied my eyes. He quizzed me about feeling dizzy and nauseous. I shook my head to assure him I felt fine. He explained something about a hall pass and the nurse's office. I couldn't focus on his words because of all the eyes still looking at me with shock and awe. As Coach B left me, he yelled at the class to move and get to their seats. Drew didn't move but kneeled right beside me. His eyes filled with fear and worry. His hand lightly touched under my eye as he brushed the hair from my face. A sudden rush of pain hit me, and I flinched.

"Sorry," he said. I tried to straighten my elbow as a sharp pain shot through it again. Drew gently grasped my forearm, keeping a slight bend in my elbow. He cradled my arm in his hand. "Don't move it," he said tenderly.

"Bear, help Zinn to the nurse and give her this," Coach Bowman said as he handed a piece of paper to Drew. "Zinn, are you still feeling okay?"

I nodded as Drew eased me from the seat and slid his arm around my waist. He took my right arm as he led me to the door.

"Bear, take it slow and keep an eye on her," Coach instructed.

"Sure thing, Coach," Drew said.

He slowly led me toward the door and called out, "Malone, get the door, huh?"

Keeping me beside him, we entered the hallway. Drew kept me in his grasp as we walked. Slight dizziness returning, I let my head rest on his shoulder.

"Zinn, you . . ."

My face being shaken woke me. "Zinn, you there?" Drew cradled me in his arms and kept saying words that didn't make sense.

"What happened?" I asked.

"You passed out again."

"Again?"

"Yeah," he said.

Heat rushed to my cheeks, and I squirmed in his arms. His firm grip wouldn't allow me to wiggle my way loose. The anger rushed over me as I pushed all my weight against his strong arms. Gently, he tightened his grip, preventing me from accessing my freedom.

"Woah, there. Just take it easy."

"Let go so I can get up."

"Ain't happening, Zinn." Drew stood while scooping me up in his arms. "Two times I've seen you pass out. Before I put you down, I'm getting you to the nurse's office."

"Are you serious?" I asked, feeling pressure in my cheek as I got angrier.

"Calm down. We're almost there."

Drew refused to put me down as he walked to the office. Finally returning me to a standing position outside the office, he opened the door. When we entered the room, he frantically said, "Aunt Kim, Zinn passed out in class and in the hall!"

"Hi, Zinn. I'm Mrs. Stone. Drew, wanna help her onto the table?"

Drew's arm held me around my waist as he led me to the other room and helped me onto the table.

"So, Zinn, did you hit your head?"

"Um, I don't know."

"She fell and hit her face on the chair," Drew informed.

"Okay, you do have some redness and swelling around that eye," the nurse said as she studied the side of my face. "Anything else hurt?"

"She hit her elbow," Drew blurted.

"Okay, Drew. Thanks for the help. I can take it from here," Mrs. Stone said while walking him toward the door.

"Are you sure?"

"Drew, I'm sure. Now go."

Keeping his eyes on me, Drew backed out of the room as Mrs. Stone slowly shut the door.

She finished examining me and secured an ice pack on my elbow by wrapping it with a bandage, then handed me another ice pack. "Hold this on your cheek. I'll be back in a minute."

She opened the door. "Drew, I told you to go back to class."

"I know, but I just couldn't yet. Can I see her?"

"Zinn, you okay if Drew comes in?"

I gave a nod.

"Zinn, I'm gonna call your mom." She looked at Drew. "And *you* are leaving when I get back."

Drew shoved his hands in his front pockets and walked toward me. "You okay?"

I pointed to the ice-packed elbow. "She told me to follow up with my doctor for an X-ray and said I likely have a mild concussion."

"You really gave me a scare. One minute you were saying you were thirsty and wanted a drink of water; the next minute you stood up and fell forward. You hit the corner of the desk before I could get to you."

"All I remember is feeling nauseous and lightheaded."

"I'm so sorry I didn't catch you."

"Drew, this wasn't your fault."

He forced a smile but sadness covered his face, and the brightness of his blue eyes had greyed. "Do you need anything?"

I shook my head. Drew was being so nice. I had no idea how to tell him about Bryce, but even more worrisome was that I didn't know how to tell Bryce about Drew. Better to rip off the Band-Aid quickly, and telling Drew would be the least painful. Besides, he wouldn't want to mess things up with Ashlynn either. I took a deep breath. "So, Drew, I appreciate all the help, but I'm good now. I think you'd better go."

"I'll stay until Aunt Kim comes back," he said.

Just tell him already. "Um, maybe you should go."

Drew looked both confused and anxious. "No, I'm not leaving."

Ugh! Why is he making this so hard?

"Drew, I don't wanna hurt your feelings, but I think it's probably better if you leave."

"Did I do something?"

"No, you've been great. Please don't think you did anything wrong."

"Then what is it?" he pressed.

"It's just that . . . Well, I just think maybe us being friends is . . . Well, it's—"

"Okay, Drew! Time's up. I've let you miss class long enough," Mrs. Stone interrupted.

"Aunt Kim, one more minute. Please?"

"Nope. Time's up. You can talk to Zinn later. She needs to rest until her mom can pick her up."

"Nurse Kim" was not taking no for an answer. Placing her arms on his shoulders, she directed him to the door. As she pushed him away, Drew's eyes were fixated on me. "Zinn, can we talk later?"

"Drew, go on. You can see her later." Mrs. Stone shut the door as he stared at me with heart-wrenching eyes.

Returning to me, she handed me a glass of water and two pills. "Here, sweetie, some pain meds. Your mom's coming to get you, but it's gonna be a few hours. So you're gonna hang out here."

"Yes ma'am," I said.

"You rest some and I'll check on you in a bit." She turned off the light and shut the door.

One eye opening, a cabinet with the CPR instructions on it came into my view. Underneath my arm felt cold and wet. Remembering the ice pack, I pushed the squishy wetness off the table, curled into a ball, and fell back asleep.

"Drew, she's sleeping." The nurse's voice trickled into the room as some light streamed into the darkness. "You can see her later . . ." The voice faded as the darkness returned.

A shooting pain went through my elbow, waking me up fully. A blanket covered me. *Where am I?* In the corner sat Savage, reading a book by his cell phone light. He closed the book and smiled. "Hey."

It all came rushing back to me. Swallowing, I cleared my throat. "What time is it?"

"Ten-twenty."

As I tried to sit up, Savage moved over to me. His strong hands took hold of my arm and helped me to a seated position.

"Good?" He winced as he questioned, clearly indicating his empathetic nature.

Flashing a smile, I hoped it would ease the look of worry on his face.

"Need anything?" he asked.

"The light, please."

Savage walked over to the light switch and flipped it. The brightness filled the room. My hand quickly covered my eyes as they flinched closed. A twinge led my hand to lightly touch the puffy, warm tenderness of my cheek.

"You did a number on that cheek," Savage said.

"So I've heard. How bad is it?"

"Between a marble and a golf ball. Guess it's about the size of a baseball."

With an eye roll I said, "Great, pretty typical." I felt my pockets for my phone.

"Bear brought your stuff. Your phone's been buzzing." Savage grabbed the bag and brought it to me.

"Thanks."

Rummaging through the backpack, I freed the phone from the jumbled mess. Ignoring the home screen with all the notifications, I immediately opened the camera. Holding the phone in front of my face, I lightly touched the huge red knot on my right cheek.

"Gonna be a nice shiner," Savage said.

"I can see that," I said irritably. I closed the camera and tossed the phone beside me. "So why aren't you in class?"

"Football workout. Taking a rest day," he explained.

"You typically hang out in the nurse's office on rest days?"

He gave a slight smile as he leaned on the edge of the table.

"Have you talked to Drew?"

Nodding, he replied, "He's pretty shook up."

"Yeah, I kinda gathered that too. I think he's blaming himself or something."

Savage shrugged his shoulders. He paused and then said, "He really wants to talk to you."

"I know." Do I tell Savage what I couldn't explain to Drew? I wasn't even sure how to explain it in the first place. I didn't want to hurt Drew, but if I was gonna be with Bryce, then I didn't have a choice. I had to stop being friends with Drew. Just thinking about him made me want to cry. "I can't talk to him right now."

"Hmm. He's pretty rattled."

"I can't think about this right now. It's hurting my head."

Savage didn't reply but instead walked to the door. "Aunt Kim, Zinn's awake."

Drew called the nurse Aunt Kim. Does she go by Aunt Kim? But she introduced herself as Mrs. Stone.

"Zinn, how ya feeling, sweetie?" The nurse walked to the sink and washed her hands.

"My head's hurting," I replied.

She flashed a light in my eyes and checked my pupils.

"Yeah. The meds may not be strong enough to dull all the pain. I can give you more in a bit. How's the elbow feeling?"

"Achy."

"Well, your mom should be here after one o'clock. I'll get you some lunch in a bit."

I nodded and she sweetly smiled. "You try and rest." She looked at Savage with a cocked eyebrow. "Though I'm not sure you can with all the visitors you seem to be attracting."

Savage smirked. "I'm about to leave."

"You'd better." She winked at me as she shut the door.

"Guess I'll go."

"Thanks for checking on me," I said, blowing my hair out of my eyes.

He gently brushed the hair out of my eyes that I couldn't. "You rest, 'kay?"

After he left, I pulled out my phone to the blowup of notifications. News of my fall had obviously reached Haley from chorus. She had texted me three times. I quickly read the messages and sent a quick reply. I ignored the couple of texts from Savage. My mom had called and texted me.

> **Mom:** Hey bug, in Nashville with Grandma. Be there as quick as I
> can. Love you. Text me when you get this
> **Me:** Hey Mom. In nurse's office. Don't worry
> See you soon. Love you 😊

When I finished texting Mom, I read my other texts. Sam texted me about our upcoming shopping plans. A flurry of texts from Bryce kept appearing, each message getting more frantic. His persistence and aggression stressed me out.

> **Bryce:** Morning beautiful
> Thanks for the talk last night
> Love you
> **Bryce:** Hey Z! text me back! miss you 🤍 😊
> **Bryce:** Z, have you been out with another guy?
> **Bryce:** Why aren't you texting me???
> Answer me now!!!!!
> **Bryce:** WTH Z! why aren't you texting me???
> Is it true??
> **Bryce:** Tell me who this guy is!!!
> I can't believe you would do this!!!

Wiping the tears, the throb of pain went through my face. The door opened, interrupting my text reply to Bryce. Drew strutted into the room balancing two Styrofoam food containers in one hand. "Hey, you're awake! How you feeling?"

I quickly brushed the back of my hand over my cheeks, trying to dry the tears. I forced a smile and said, "Better, thanks."

"You sure?"

"Yeah, um, just hurting."

He smiled sympathetically. "How about some food?" Slightly dipping his head, he lowered the white square boxes as if displaying a platter of fine delicacies. The forced smile changed over to a shy snicker. Drew, looking impressed with his ability to lighten my mood, spoke in an exaggeratedly proper manner with a poorly executed accent that I wasn't sure was British or Australian. "And which would the lady prefer: hamburger or chicken sandwich?"

Laughing, I just shrugged and flapped my hand, signifying the choice was his.

Pleased with himself, Drew set the boxes on the side table, then hopped on the table, positioning himself close to me. I gulped and quickly slid my phone under my leg, not wanting him to accidentally see in case Bryce fired off another half-dozen texts. Drew glanced at me and his jovialness lessened. "You're getting a nice purple hue there, Danthes."

"Am I?"

"You're gonna have a rocking black eye. Hey, you can tell 'em that your gnarly left hook took care of the other guy."

Slightly laughing, twinges of pain hit my cheek and my hand reactively went to it.

He pouted his lip. "Sorry."

"It's okay."

"Guess I gotta stop making you laugh," he said with concern. "It's a shame, though, cause you're so cute when you laugh."

He really couldn't help himself. The flirtation just oozed from him. His eyes constantly flashed philandering looks, especially that signature wink of his. He even had this cute, silly way of saying things that just made me feel doted on. And, of course, his corny pick up lines, timed just right, lightened the intensity of the tension, keeping me wanting more. With his phenomenal eyes and adorable curls, Drew really was the whole package.

He slid the table in front of me. "Lady's choice."

"I told you to pick, but I guess chicken."

"Good pick. You want a drink?"

"Sure."

Walking out the door, he said, "Aunt Kim, whatcha got to drink?"

"Some Cokes, juice, and water in the fridge."

Drew returned with his hands full of drinks. "I've got the finest selection from the wine cellar. What would the lady prefer?" Holding a juice and lemon-lime soda in his hand, he said, "For a nice pairing with the chicken, I would recommend something in the white family."

I smiled with pierced lips, trying to avoid the anticipated pain. "Sprite is good."

Drew handed me the soda can as he eased himself next to me. He slid the container with *chicken* handwritten in black Sharpie across the table, positioning it in front of me. I lifted the lid to reveal a flimsy piece of lettuce, an under-ripe tomato slice, and a couple of pickles next to a breaded chicken patty shoved in a bun with some unappetizing soggy fries. Ignoring the lettuce and tomato, I topped the sandwich with the pickles, tore off a bite of the sandwich, and placed it in my mouth. I savored the simple combination of the tangy crunch on the juicy white meat. Then, I devoured the rest. Drew looked at me and smiled. My hand flew to my mouth, trying to conceal my very unladylike behavior.

Drew inhaled his sandwich before I had eaten half of mine. He demolished his fries. I slid the container of remaining fries over to him. He smiled, grabbed a handful, and shoved them in his mouth, engulfing the whole batch in a matter of seconds.

The vibrating under my knee was trying hard to get my attention, but I refused to give my phone and Bryce the acknowledgment. I didn't want to deal with him and his overreactions or how I was going to say to Drew we can't be friends. Right now, I wanted to enjoy my lunch in peace.

Drew didn't let the obvious phone tremor on the cushioned table distract him from talking. He rattled off about the upcoming football game, classes, and even reminisced about the homecoming dance, allowing me to avoid the Bryce subject a little longer.

Drew pausing made the knots in my stomach tighten. When his leg shaking jostled the table and he cleared his throat, a wave of uneasiness hit me. *Here we go.*

"Zinn, earlier you said something about us being friends. What was that about?"

"Oh," I said, pretending to dab away crumbs on the seat. *I've avoided it as long as I can.* "Well . . . um." I had no idea how to say this. I swallowed hard and finally forced the words from my mouth. "Don't you think it's better if maybe we stop hanging out?"

Drew gave me a puzzled look. "Why would you say that?"

I bit the corner of my lip and sighed. "Uh, well, I don't want to cause problems."

Looking even more confused, he shook his head. "Problems?"

His questioning eyes pierced deep into me. *How can I tell him we can't be friends when he looks at me with those eyes?* Finally, I blurted, "Us being friends might complicate things."

Drew looked as if he'd been slapped in the face, making me instantly regret the forcefulness of my statement. *I can't let Drew think I'm choosing Bryce over him.*

"Since you're dating someone now, I don't wanna make her jealous."

Drew rolled his eyes as he shook his head and lightly chuckled. "Zinn, where do you come up with this stuff? I told you I'm not dating anyone. When I'm ready to date, you'll definitely know, okay?" His fingers lightly brushed the hair from my face as he smiled sweetly.

I was stunned by the whole moment and remained speechless until the click of the doorknob interrupted the intense moment.

"Hey, Savvy," Drew said as he stood. "It seems our girl's finally on the mend."

"Hmm, good."

"Well, I'd better get to class." Drew walked toward Savage, bumping fists as they passed each other, almost as if they were doing the teenage boy equivalent of the changing of the guards.

"Hey, Drew! Thanks for lunch."

"My pleasure," Drew replied as he gave me a wink. "Oh, Zinn, one question."

"Yeah?"

"Did it hurt?"

"When I passed out and hit my face?"

"No. Did it hurt when you fell from heaven?" He was back, bringing on the corny humor. I started laughing and then flinched from the pain.

"Sorry, last time, I promise. At least until the eye heals," he said jokingly.

I relaxed, knowing things between us were okay . . . for the moment.

"Catch ya later, Savvy. Zinn, try not to swoon next time you see me."

"You promised no more jokes."

"Oh, that's no joke. At least I'm hoping it's not." He tapped the wall a couple of times, signaling a goodbye as he left the room.

"I see my cousin is putting on his usual charm?" Savage said.

"Wait! Cousins? You two are cousins?"

"Yep."

"Well, I feel stupid. Two months and I don't know this? Wait! Is the nurse your aunt?"

Laughing, he said, "Yeah, she's our Aunt Kim. Ashlynn's mom."

"Okay, let me get this straight. You and Drew are cousins, and Ashlynn and Drew are cousins too?"

Savage gave his standard, "Hmm," then gave the affirming nod.

A satisfactory smile came to my lips. As I replayed the event at El Rey's and my misunderstanding in thinking it was a date, the slight bit of embarrassment I felt could not compete with the relief.

Another buzz of my phone brought a twinge of guilt, no doubt Bryce again. With the incessant vibration, I snatched the phone from under my leg. I was right; it was Bryce. Still not ready to deal with him, I sent Sam a quick text, hoping she could handle Bryce for now. I needed time to figure out what to say to Bryce, especially about Drew.

"Sorry. Just texting Sam."

Savage nodded his head, signifying my distraction didn't bother him.

"Just needing her to give Bryce a heads-up about my fall."

"Bryce?" Savage had that intense, questioning look that corresponded with his habitual, one-word questions.

Shame-ridden, I set the phone beside me. I wasn't ready for this conversation either. But ready or not, here it was. I blew out my breath. Savage leaned against the cushioned table beside me, his green eyes probing me for the truth.

"Bryce and I sorta got back together last night."

"Sorta?"

"We went out last night and it just happened. I mean, we do have a history. It was bound to happen, right?"

"Hmm." His eyes narrowed, making me self-conscious. "If you say so." He shrugged his shoulders. No doubt he thought I was making a mistake, but he wouldn't flat-out say it.

What did Savage care if Bryce and I got back together? And what did he mean when he said, "If you say so"? I told him the truth, didn't I? Bryce and I were back together. He stared at me, not saying another word. I rubbed the temples of my head. Savage moved closer to me and cleared his throat.

"Um, so we started reading *A Separate Peace* today." His concerned eyes haunted me. I rattled off some questions about the assignment. The intensity of his eyes remained constant while he answered all the questions I threw at him. The back-and-forth continued until the nurse opened the door.

"Why is it every time I walk in here one of my nephews is bugging this girl?" Kim said. "I know you aren't talking her head off like Drew, but she does need rest."

"Sorry, Aunt Kim. I was telling her about what went on in English today."

"*Hmph*, sure you were. Five minutes, then you're out of here."

"Yes, ma'am," he said.

She went to the sink, filled a small paper cup with some water, then handed me the water and a small white cup holding a couple of pills. "Some meds for the pain."

"Thanks," I said appreciatively. I popped the pills in my mouth and threw back the small amount of water in one gulp, realizing my thirstiness.

She flashed a sweet, comforting smile. "If you need anything, let me know." She cut a scolding eye to Savage. "Do rest if you can. I'll be right outside."

Savage smirked as he pulled a chair beside me. He offered some small talk, and I laid my head on the pillow and shifted onto my side, resting my elbow on my hip. Calmness filled me at the steady cadence of his voice. The conversation didn't require anything of me, unlike Bryce's stressed-filled and emotional conversations. Savage's even-keeled demeanor allowed me to process my thoughts. With Bryce, I struggled with finding the right answer or remaining silent while he screamed at me. With Savage, saying what I wanted or remaining silent was under my control. He didn't expect anything from me, and it felt good.

I rattled off something about Sam and my plans for the weekend. It became Savage's turn to listen. As I talked, I fought with keeping my eyes open until I finally . . .

"Zinn?" Mom's voice and a bright light streamed into the dark room.

Savage was gone and a blanket covered me. Rubbing my eyes, I said, "Mom?"

"Hey, bug."

Immediately, tears came pouring from my eyes.

CHAPTER THIRTEEN

We drove home from the clinic. I fidgeted with the sling on my arm. The scratchiness of the rough cotton fabric that was to be my new accessory for the next week aggravated my neck and arm. I wasn't sure I could deal with the restrictive annoyance for that long. Pulling my phone from my pocket, Mom shook her head. "No, ma'am. You have a concussion. You heard the doctor. No screens for a few days."

I rolled my eyes. "Just gonna text Sam. I've not told her about the concussion."

"I'll call Sam."

"Ugh! Mom, just one text, please?"

"No, Zinn. You heard the doctor. No screens and no stress." She held her hand out. "Now don't argue and give me the phone."

"Fine." I handed her the phone and shifted my body toward the window. My view became blurry. With the back of my hand, I wiped the tears as they spilled from my eyes.

Mom handed me a tissue. "Let's grab some dinner. What do you want?"

"I'm not hungry." I crossed my arms over my chest and stared out the window.

Mom, unfazed by my pouting, pulled into the restaurant parking lot. She opened her door and gave me one more try. "Last chance for input."

"I don't care."

"Okay then, but no complaining." She slipped out of the seat and shut the door. Suddenly, my phone rang. She had left it in the seat. I snatched it up and read the text from Sam and replied as quickly as I could.

> **Sam:** Z, where are you? Did you break anything? Bryce is going crazy
> **Me:** Headed home from doctor…no break
> concussion…check!

My heart raced. Sam was taking forever to reply.

> **Sam:** OMG Z, really?
> **Me:** Yeah, it sucks. Out of commish for a few days
> **Sam:** Talk??

The restaurant door opened and Mom stepped out. I quickly replied.

> **Me:** Dr said no phone til Wednesday ☹
> Gotta go don't text – Mom's got my phone

Deleting the texts, I placed the phone back in the seat. With bags in her hands, Mom opened door. "Got you chicken tenders and mac-n-cheese."

"Smells delish." *You're overdoing it with the cheerfulness. She'll catch on.*

"You're in a better mood."

I smiled sheepishly, giving her my apologetic look. She handed me the bags and gave me a smile. The phone rang again, and I held my breath. Mom looked at the phone. "It's Bryce. I'll call him when we get home."

I let out my breath. I wasn't even gonna ask if I could talk to Bryce because she would say no. Besides, I still didn't know what to say to him. Letting Mom talk to him seemed like the better option. At least I could avoid the stressful conversation that I anticipated.

When we got home, we ate dinner, then I sprawled out on the couch with Oreo curled beside me. The sounds of the TV show Grandma Rose watched couldn't keep me awake as my eyes fought to stay open. The disappearance of the noise from the TV woke me. Mom lounged in the recliner. "Sorry, bug, didn't mean to wake you. Go back to sleep."

"It's okay. Gonna brush my teeth and get in bed."

"Okay, I'll check on you in a minute," Mom said.

I walked up the stairs with Mom following behind me. She went into her room as I entered the bathroom. When I finished, I climbed in the bed. Sleep overtook me almost immediately.

Saturday was nothing but a blur. I stayed in my bed, sleeping, with Oreo cuddled next to me. Every few hours Oreo would omit a low growl when Mom checked on me. Through the night, I got to enjoy undisturbed sleep.

Morning's light beamed through the window. With my good arm, I threw the pillow over my head and fell back asleep. Sometime later, Mom opened the door to let Oreo outside. I fumbled around for my phone and remembered she still had it. Taking a deep breath, I threw the covers off me.

Opening my door, I yelled down the stairs. "Taking a shower!"

"Breakfast will be ready when you get out."

I turned on the hot water, ready to feel revived. Grabbing towels out of the closet, I removed the wrap from my arm and slipped off my gown. Stepping in the shower, the hot water flowed over my achy body. I tried to straighten my elbow, but acute pain shot through it like lightning. I let it sit under the hot water to ease the discomfort. The water pounded on top of my head as the mist sprayed over my face. Enjoying the relaxing hot water too long, the temperature dropped and prompted me to end my moment of tranquility.

I put on some yoga pants and my favorite tee. Grabbing my dad's Vols sweatshirt, I slid it over my shoulders. The oversized sweatshirt cascaded over my body and swallowed me like a big warm hug. Slipping on my pink fuzzy slippers, I grabbed the bandage and sling and went downstairs to the kitchen to find Grandma sitting at the table, sipping her cup of coffee.

"Mornin', Zinnia Rose," Grandma Rose said. "How you feeling?"

"Better." I kissed her on the cheek, something that had become a habit since moving here.

I handed the bandage to Mom, and she rewrapped my arm with skill and ease. *How are moms so good at doing this stuff without doing a stint in medical school?* I slipped the sling over my head and looked around for something to eat.

"There's waffles, fruit, and eggs." Mom handed me a plate. "You want some coffee?"

"Juice, please," I said as I topped a waffle with some blueberries.

Oreo scratched on the back door. I opened it and he toddled inside. Mom handed me the glass and I headed to the living room. Placing my plate and glass on the coffee table, I fell into the couch. Positioning myself, I grabbed the plate and cut into the waffle. Mom followed behind me and sat at the dining room table with her computer.

"Anyone text me?"

She held up my phone as she spoke. "Sam, Haley, Ashlynn, Drew, Savage, and Bryce."

"Can I please text them back?" I turned my head to her.

"Not today," she said, giving me the motherly smirk before she returned to her computer screen.

"Mom, please. I don't have a headache anymore."

The keys clacked away but she remained steadfast in her decision. "Zinn, maybe tomorrow, but only if you rest today and have no headache. Besides, you're not helping yourself by getting upset."

"It's upsetting me not to talk to my friends," I huffed.

"Zinnia Rose, listen to your momma," Grandma said, entering the living room.

"Yes, ma'am." I sighed and turned back to my food.

"Maybe later you can call Sam or Haley," Mom said. "That is, if you rest and don't argue with me."

"I will. I promise."

After I finished eating, I dozed on the couch while Mom softly sang along to the radio. I loved to hear her sing. She had such a beautiful voice—so talented at harmonies. The tension left my shoulders, and I drifted off to sleep as her voice filled the air.

The doorbell ringing caused Oreo to bark. Mom answered the door, then began talking to someone. "She's doing okay. Sleeping right now, but I'll tell her you stopped by when she—"

"I'm awake!" I interrupted.

"Well, she's awake. You wanna come in?"

"Thanks." I recognized Ashlynn's voice. I sat up and smoothed my hair down.

"We won't stay long."

Shoot, Drew is here too. I jumped off the couch and darted through the kitchen to Grandma's bathroom. I looked hideous with my swollen cheek, blackening eye, and frizzy hair. I ran my fingers through it, trying to calm down the curly mess. There was no way to fix the coiled tresses. I took a deep breath. *It doesn't matter. Drew's just a friend. Besides, you have a boyfriend. Bryce!* No doubt Sam's clued him in, and he's probably going even more crazy by now. The one good thing about not having my phone was I didn't have to deal with Bryce yet.

I walked back through the kitchen into the living room. Ashlynn, Drew, and Savage stood in the foyer. I smiled at the three of them. "Hey, y'all."

Drew stepped into the living room with the other two following behind. "How's the patient?" Drew's eyes danced in that playful, lively way that made my heart jump.

"Um, still a little sore."

Ashlynn moved closer and gently wrapped her arms around me. "Oh, Zinn. Even with a black eye you still look great."

Oreo gave a low growl.

"Oreo, quiet!" I quipped.

Ashlynn knelt beside him and rubbed his head. Oreo licked her hand, obviously signaling to me his approval of her. "He's so adorable. I love Cocker Spaniels!" She rubbed his floppy ears and ooed and gooed over him, which he took an instant liking to.

Savage sat a platter on the coffee table. "My mom sent some cookies."

"That's very sweet. Please, tell her thank you," Mom said, looking at the cousin trio. "Make yourself at home."

Expressing thanks, they each found a seat as Mom headed toward the kitchen.

I settled in the recliner, folding one leg under me. The fuzzy pink slipper now prominently displayed, I slid both feet on the floor.

Drew smiled. "Cool slippers."

"Ha! It's the latest fashion on the runway this season," I retorted.

Drew gave a low chuckle, and Ashlynn gave Drew a lighthearted slap. "Leave her alone, Drew."

He gave me a wink as he grabbed his arm. "Ash, not so hard! You're gonna bruise me."

Mom returned with a tray of glasses and set them on the table. "Some milk if you want, or I've got coffee."

"Thanks, Mrs. Danthes," Savage said. "This is fine."

"Please, call me Erica." She smiled and lingered for a moment. "Well, I guess I'll head downstairs to the office. Zinn, if you need me—"

"I know, Mom. I'll be okay," I cut her off, hoping I didn't seem rude. She nodded and left the room.

Drew grabbed a couple of cookies and held one out to me. "Zinn, you want one?"

Ashlynn slapped his hand. "Not one from your grubby hands." She slid the plate of cookies closer to me. I shook my head no. Drew winked at me, then grabbed another cookie and popped it in his mouth. Ashlynn rolled her eyes before looking to me. "Did you get my text about the party?"

"No! Mom took my phone. Doctor says no screens til my headaches are gone. It's a concussion thing."

"So that's why you didn't reply. I was afraid my charm spell had been broken," Drew said with a wink.

"Zinn, that's the worst. I would just die without my phone," Ashlynn said.

"Oh, you would die, Ash. Really? Then please give me your phone."

Drew grabbed at it, but she swatted at his hand as she jerked the phone away from him. Savage remained silent as he looked at his cousins while shaking his head. His eyes shot to me and remained staring as if he were looking for clues. Grabbing a glass, I took a sip.

"Oh, Zinn, your fall is epic," Drew said excitedly, breaking the silence. "The stories are hilarious."

"Bear, I'm sure Zinn doesn't care," Savage jumped in before Drew could say more.

"Oh no, seriously, you gotta hear this." With animation, he shared about overhearing some guys talking about the incident with exaggerated and false details. He explained with limited candor that he physically set the guys straight.

Squirming in the seat, I took another sip of milk. "So how was the game?"

"We won 29–22," Drew answered.

"Oh, Zinn. Savage ran the ball for the points, tying the score," Ashlynn babbled.

"Hey, hey! What about me?" Drew whined.

Ashlynn rolled her eyes toward him. "I was getting to that, you big, whiny baby. You're so needy." Ashlynn directed her attention back to me. "So anyways, we kicked off, and Drew intercepted a pass and ran it for the winning touchdown. Totally mind-blowing. Such a memorable game for my senior night."

Savage sat with his hands folded in his lap. He threw an occasional smile my way whenever Ashlynn and Drew monopolized the conversation, affirming they were the talkers in the family. Ashlynn babbled on about whatever entered her brain, and Drew quipped some wisecrack toward her.

Ashlynn and Drew had personalities that mirrored each other. While Ashlynn and Savage shared obvious physical similarities, such as their almond-shaped eyes, olive skin, and dark hair. They could almost pass for twins. Drew's chestnut curls, blue eyes, and lightly tanned skin differed completely from Ashlynn and Savage.

For Drew and Savage, the differences went beyond their looks; their personalities were polar opposites. Drew's passion, excitement, and liveliness contrasted with Savage's solemn and controlled persona. It was hard to grasp they were such good friends, let alone related. Ashlynn's personality complemented both of them. Her lively silliness became prevalent in Drew's presence while also maintaining the controlled temperament that was so prominent in Savage.

The ramblings of Ashlynn and Drew continued until Savage cleared his throat. "We'd better go and let Zinn rest."

"It's fine, really," I replied.

"Best we go. Want you all better." Drew gave me an understanding look and smiled warmly. "Besides, I've got a paper due tomorrow."

"Thanks for coming. It really means a lot." I followed the cousin trio to the front door.

Ashlynn turned to me as she let out a slight whimper, then dramatically threw her arms around me. "Oh, Zinn, we love you!"

Suddenly, Drew's arms wrapped around the two of us while also pulling Savage into the huddle. Surrounded by these three felt good. Being a part of this circle meant more to me than they would ever know.

The doorbell rang, and it sounded aggressive as if it being pressed too often and too long. I pulled from their embrace and stared at the door, holding my breath, knowing who stood on the other side. Leaving the safety of the group, I went to open it.

Bryce stood there, holding flowers and smiling, then his eyes scanned to my friends standing behind me. His transformation was pronounced, and the others couldn't possibly fail to notice how Bryce's smile quickly faded into a clenched jaw.

"Bryce. I didn't know you were coming."

"Obviously you didn't." Bryce's eyes bore into me.

"Uh, well, I was just now saying bye to my friends." *Please don't cause a scene.* My chest tightened as I waited for his outburst.

Drew stuck out his hand to Bryce. "Hey, I'm Drew."

Bryce leered at Drew and huffed. Then his steely eyes pivoted to me. Mumbling a derogatory word, Bryce whipped around and stepped off the porch.

"Bryce, wait!" I grabbed his arm. *Mistake number one? Don't grab Bryce. You know it makes him even angrier.*

Flinging his arm from my grip didn't slow him down as he stomped to his car. "And to think I felt bad about getting upset with you."

"What are you talking about, Bryce? Upset about what?" All at once he stopped and spun around. "I've been sick worrying about you. Sam gave me this sob story about how you were all alone, but you don't look so alone to me."

"Bryce, please just come inside." *Mistake number two? Don't invite Bryce inside. That is the last thing I want!*

"Why? So you can tell me more lies?" His yelling was getting louder with each exchange.

Trying my best to deescalate him and prevent things from getting even more heated, I softened my tone. "Bryce, I promise I'm telling you the truth."

Bryce gave a sarcastic chuckle. "The only one telling me the truth is Jasmine."

"Jasmine?" I blurted out louder than I intended. "Bryce, you've got it all wrong."

"I'm wrong, really?" He edged closer to my face, threatening me with his eyes. "You think I don't know what's going on?"

"Nothing's going on. These are my friends from school who came to see how I was doing."

Bryce screamed, "Stop lying to me!" as he hurled the flowers across the yard. He leaned in closer, shouting in my face. "I'm not stupid, Zinn!" He took me by surprise when he forcefully grabbed my shoulders, causing pain to shoot through my arm.

In a snap, Drew pushed Bryce off. "Yo, hands off, dude!"

Savage grabbed Drew by the shoulders and pulled him backward. Bryce gave Drew a threatening stare, panting with rage, and said, "Dude, you better just keep backing up. This ain't got nothing to do with you."

Drew shifted his feet slightly forward as he leaned into Bryce. "Dude, it does have something to do with me if your hands go on her again."

"Are you the guy? The one she's been all over?" Bryce rotated to me. "Zinn, you act all innocent, but you're a piece of trash and a real—"

"Ho, buddy! Say one more thing and you'll be spitting teeth," Drew interrupted.

Bryce scowled at Drew. "I ain't your buddy, and I'll say what I want. You wanna throw? I'll throw!" Cracking his knuckles, Bryce inched closer to Drew.

"Let's go, hoss." Drew pressed into Bryce, giving him a warning nudge.

Savage slid in between them and grasped Drew by the shoulders, pushing him back. "Drew, let it go." Drew exhaled deeply and gave an obliging nod to Savage.

Savage peered at Bryce and calmly said, "I think it's time you go."

Bryce released a ragged, angry huff. "Shoulda never trusted such a lying piece of trash and cheater. I can't believe I've wasted all this time on such a screwup. As far as I'm concerned, you can have her, buddy!" Bryce spat out, his self-righteous lies piercing my heart.

"Hmm." Savage reared back, then with full force his fist thrashed into Bryce's chin. Bryce smacked the ground, landing facedown in the dirt. Ashlynn yelled frantically at Savage to calm down. Drew's hand slipped into mine and gently pulled me away from the commotion. Bryce pushed himself off the ground, staggering, and held his jaw while grumbling some crass words. Savage, with his hands clenched, was ready to take another swing or fend off any retaliation.

Bryce spit some blood on the ground, then wiped his mouth. "That's your one time, dude. It won't happen again."

Savage straightened his shoulders and kept his eyes locked on Bryce. "Ready when you are."

Bryce walked to his car and spewed more vulgarities, ending with parting words to me. "Z, don't forget what happened here when you're begging me to take you back, because it ain't happening this time!" Slamming the door, he cranked his car and immediately roared his engine. Whipping backward out of the drive, his tires squealed as he sped down the road.

Drew's arm slid around my shoulders and steered me into the house. "You're shaking. Let's get you inside."

"I'm so sorry about this," I said, overcome by shock. He led me to the couch, where I collapsed.

"Sorry for what?" Drew was stunned by my words. "None of this is your fault."

I shrugged my shoulders, oblivious of how to respond.

Of course, this is my fault. Bryce is mad. Savage is mad. And it's all because of me.

Drew took my hands in his. His bright-blue eyes looked deeply into mine. Kind words fell from his lips as he spoke softly. "Zinn, you have nothing to be sorry for. And you need to know the only one to blame for any of this is that loser Bryce."

Twinges of guilt hit me. "He didn't mean it. He's just stressed."

"Zinn, don't make excuses for that jerk."

Ashlynn stood silent in the foyer, and her eyes caught mine. She entered the room and fell into the chair, all warm smiles, but said nothing.

"Is Savage okay?" I questioned as I pulled back the curtain. He was nowhere to be seen. Apparently, he had left without saying anything.

"Um, yeah, just cooling off, you know?" Ashlynn's eyes cut over to Drew.

"I'll check on him." Drew stood from the couch, hesitating. His eyes studied me as if making sure I seemed okay. Flashing him the obligatory smile, I hoped it would satisfy him. He returned with a smile and headed outside.

"Zinn, you all right? I mean, you're not hurting or anything?" Ashlynn asked.

I shook my head to signify no, then tears pooled in my eyes. Ashlynn moved to the couch and wrapped her arm around my shoulder. She pulled a tissue out of the box nearby and handed it to me. Drying my eyes, I leaned closer to the window. Drew stood in front of Savage, talking. He looked in my direction, then put his arm around Savage. Moments later, they walked out of my sight.

Ashlynn rambled off questions that I halfheartedly answered. She offered me a cookie, which I declined. Then she started flipping through the photo book on the table, quizzing me about my childhood photos. I wanted her to shut up and for Drew and Savage to walk through the door. Ashlynn fired more questions at me that only increased my annoyance.

"What's going on with them? Why aren't they coming inside?"

"You know boys . . . gotta cool down." She smiled, then looked around the room. "Where's Oreo?" Ashlynn called for my dog, and he came waddling in from the sunroom. Ashlynn plopped down on the floor and let Oreo cuddle with her.

I let out a deep breath. Ashlynn's right. Guys do fly off and then need time to calm down, except Savage. He always stayed calm and even-keeled. *Well, expect for decking Bryce.*

Ashlynn began rambling about more lighthearted matters while she loved on Oreo. Finally, the front door opened and Savage and Drew came into the living room. Drew seated himself beside me and grabbed a cookie.

Savage said nothing. His breathing was shallow and he looked somewhat disheveled. I swallowed as uneasiness overcame me. Obviously, he was mad. He looked so uncomfortable. Drew repositioned himself on the couch and popped another cookie in his mouth. "Glad you girls left some cookies." He winked at me. Savage still looked ill at ease and gave no reaction to Drew's words.

"Hey, Zinn! I got an idea." Drew grabbed another cookie. "How 'bout we break you out of this doctor-imposed prison? Think your mom would go for it?"

"Drew." Savage shook his head side to side.

Drew has to be joking. Doesn't he feel all the tension? Obviously, Savage doesn't want to be near me.

Not wavered by Savage's response, Drew asked, "What do you think, Zinn?"

I shrugged my shoulders. "I don't care. I mean, it's whatever they wanna do."

"You heard it. Zinn's good. I'm good. Ashlynn, you and Savage need to get good."

Savage's eyes squinted at Ashlynn. She nodded. "I guess we can let Zinn ask her mom."

"Would you get off me, you goof!" Ashlynn whined as Drew stretched his legs across her lap.

"Bear, lay off Ash," Savage said, shaking his head like he was used to their behavior as if they were siblings.

"Yeah, Bear, listen to Savage," Ashlynn said dramatically, letting some humor leak in.

"Oh, little Ashy Mashy needs rescuing from her mean ole cousin," Drew taunted sarcastically.

"Ew, I hate that stupid name. Like, that's from when I was seven years old. Grow up!" Ashlynn rolled her eyes but then gave in and laughed.

Savage cleared his throat, looked in the rearview mirror, and gave the two a parental stare.

Drew and Ashlynn immediately quieted down, giving Savage older-brother status. The closeness the three of them shared fascinated me. Even as long as I'd known Sam, I didn't have the depth of friendship they had. Maybe it was a cousin thing. I didn't have cousins, and being an only child, this kind of intimacy felt foreign to me.

All three appeared close, but Savage and Drew had an extreme bond that was immeasurable. The two of them seemed to converse silently with one another, as if they were telepathic. The two of them mesmerized me. They looked nothing alike and acted nothing alike, but they had an indescribable bond and a deep connection even with their differences. In effect, they were complete opposites. I'd never known or even seen anything like the connection they shared. It was nothing short of unique and powerful—and I'd only begun to know them! What else was layered within this bond?

Although Savage's quietness stabilized Drew's talkative, animated personality, their interactions with others at the restaurant spotlighted their differences even more. Drew took the lead in the public relations category while Savage appeared to stand at attention, always on guard. Savage smiled as Drew cracked jokes to the cashier while we waited for our food. Drew's hand would touch my shoulder when he talked to me. Savage's eyes pierced me as he listened to anything and everything I said.

Getting our food, we headed to the park and settled at a picnic table near the water. We ate, laughed, and enjoyed the sunshine and cool breeze. When we finished eating, Savage's eyes cut to Drew.

"Ash, how about I show you the right way to skip rocks?" Drew challenged.

"What do you mean, the *right way*? I taught you."

"No way! You can barely throw a rock in the water, let alone skip it," Drew countered as he pounced up from the table with Ashlynn chasing after him, their squabbling having resumed.

The water rippled and pushed some small waves up on the sandy soil closer to the grassy edge. Ashlynn and Drew laughed as they splashed water on each other. Savage's eyes were on me, focused and discerning. I wiggled on my seat.

With suddenness, I uttered, "Are you mad at me?"

"No." The stunned look on his face surprised me. His eyes revealed confusion. "Why would you think that?"

"Because of Bryce?"

"You think I'm mad at you cause of him? Why?"

I wasn't sure what to say. Since the moment Bryce showed up, Savage's behavior had changed. How could he not understand my concern about his anger? "Well, you've been extraordinarily quiet, and you seem uncomfortable with me."

Savage shook his head as a look of concern came across his face. "Hmm, I see."

"What do you see?"

"I'll admit I am uncomfortable, but it's not about you."

My chest tightened. *I was right; he is uncomfortable. But he said it's not about me, so what is it?* My leg started shaking and I swallowed dryly. "So what is it about?"

"Hmm, well, the scene with Bryce. He was pretty rough on you."

Fiddling with the sling, I avoided his eyes. "He was just upset about some stupid gossip."

"Hmm, upset?"

"Savage, don't."

"Don't what?"

My shoulders tightened and I gritted my teeth, then I harshly spluttered, "Don't do that whole contemplation thing where you make me figure out what you are wanting to say! You drive me crazy with that!"

Savage's cool composure didn't waver as he nodded his head. I walked to the water. Drew moved toward me but stopped after a few steps, likely sensing the serious conversation.

A shadow formed beside me as Savage moved closer. "Zinn, I'm sorry."

Stepping in front of me, he stood there with no sense of anger, defensiveness, or irritation. Tears welled in my eyes and flowed freely. Savage said nothing. He needed nothing and had nothing to prove. He was simply there. He wrapped his arms around me and pulled me close. I leaned on his shoulder and cried.

I wiped my eyes and stepped back. "I don't even know why I'm crying. I'm not even sad that it's over with Bryce. If I'm honest, I'm glad Bryce ended it. I'm not even sure why or how we got back together. It was like I had no control over the situation. I felt forced into giving it another try."

"Hmm," Savage said. "It kinda makes sense."

"What makes sense?"

"You feeling no control over the situation. It's pretty obvious that Bryce is . . ." He hesitated to finish the sentence as his eyes narrowed. "Well, he's pretty controlling."

Confused by his statement, I offered the silence for once, and obviously he realized my lack of understanding what his words meant. He cleared his throat and proceeded to elaborate even more. "It just seems like that relationship isn't so healthy for you. The way Bryce jumped to conclusions and grabbed your shoulders, he didn't seem concerned about you at all. But you were overly concerned about him."

Savage floored me. *Overly concerned. Controlling. What did Savage mean?* I took a step back. "What are you saying? Are you implying Bryce controls me?"

Savage's eyes stayed locked on me as he remained silent.

"You think I'm being controlled? Where do you get off, Savage? I'm not being controlled," I said defiantly.

"Zinn, calm down, okay?"

"Don't tell me to calm down." I walked closer to the water and farther away from him. I couldn't wrap my mind around all this. Savage was out of line. He didn't even know Bryce. Bryce did not control me. Okay, sometimes he got jealous. He didn't like me being around other guys. That's how it is when someone loves you. Savage has no idea what he's talking about. *Controlling, pshh. That's stupid.*

Savage met me at the water and stood there saying nothing, as usual. I stayed quiet too. The silence created a space for me to contemplate thoughts of Bryce. He had keep me on edge and nervous most of the time. I always worried about saying the right things to Bryce. I tried my best to never make him mad. When he'd had a bad day, it always stressed me out. Why? Because his bad days became my bad days too. *But that's being in a relationship, right? Or could Savage be right and it is control?*

Savage offered me a somber look with his continued silence. I desperately wanted to justify my relationship with Bryce, to prove that it was not controlling or toxic. But right now, I couldn't.

I walked to the table and sat. Memories of Bryce yelling, grabbing my arm, forcing me into his car hijacked my brain. All the fear and stress came rushing back to me. The constant burden of trying to keep him happy flashed in my mind. *Could Savage be right? Did Bryce control me?* Lightheaded from the rush of thoughts, I rubbed my temples and closed my eyes.

Within a few minutes, Ashlynn sat across the table and Drew sat beside me. He placed an earbud in my ear. "Zinn, listen."

The music engulfed me. I became lost in it. My finger lightly tapped on my forehead as the song played. The piercing voice of the singer heartfully crying out the deep lyrics stabbed me in the heart. A tear slid down my cheek, and my eyes opened to see Drew smiling at me.

"Who is this?" I asked.

"Avett Brothers. A song called 'No Hard Feelings'," Drew said.

I handed the earbud back to him and he smiled even bigger and winked sweetly. "Who thinks they can beat my record of eight skips?"

"Eight skips? You are such a liar! Six at the most," Ashlynn said.

"Oh, sore loser. Fine, Zinn, you'll count, so Ash will shut up and stop being a baby." Drew grabbed my hand and led me to the water.

After skipping rocks, we took a short stroll around the lake. Drew and I, lost in conversation, had gotten some distance ahead of Ashlynn and Savage. A whistle came from Savage. He pointed toward the car. We headed toward him and Ashlynn.

"Better get you home," Savage said. "It's three fifteen."

"Geez, the time flew by."

As we walked to the car, Drew and Ashlynn squabbled about who had more skips. Drew taunted Ashlynn by running backward in front of her as she tried to swat him. Finally, he picked her up and squeezed her in a big hug, then threw her over his shoulder while she kicked her arms and legs.

"Let go of me! You know this makes me mad," Ashlynn said.

"Yes, I do." Drew laughed manically.

He carried her to the car before putting her down. When she was free, she swatted him on the arm. Settling in the car, we rode to my house with the sound of music filling the car.

Mom sat on the front porch reading a book. Meeting us on the sidewalk, she quipped something witty that made Drew and Ashlynn chuckle. I faked a smile since I really wasn't paying attention to her.

Eventually they said their goodbyes. Mom wrapped her arms around me as they pulled out of the driveway. "I like your friends."

I gave her a nod. She opened the door and rambled something about us watching a movie.

"Uh, Mom."

"Yeah, bug."

"Can we talk?"

She nodded. "Sure. Everything okay?"

Tears came pouring out as I unloaded all the events of the day with Bryce.

"I really don't even know how to process it all, especially with what Savage said." Mom's side-eyed glance warned me this conversation had just begun. "What did Savage say?"

"I don't know. He kinda thought Bryce was controlling, and he didn't like the way he talked to me. It was all weird."

The color left Mom's face, and tears pooled in her eyes. "I think Savage is right." Mom took my hands in hers and continued apologizing. "Zinn, I am so sorry. I knew you and Bryce fought a lot, but I didn't realize he was being abusive."

"What do you mean? He never hit me."

"Zinn, this is a lot to deal with, and right now you need to focus on recovering from the fall," Mom said.

My brow furrowed and I shook my head as Mom's arms enveloped me. Finally, I rested my head in her lap as her fingers brushed my hair. I tried to let sleep overtake me, but it wouldn't. Savage and his accusation of Bryce controlling me, Mom throwing out the word abuse—it was too much to process. Neither of them understood. Bryce was the one abused, not me. His dad in his drunken rages hitting him and his mom, now that was abuse! Even if I could admit Bryce controlled me, I would never say he was abusive. *No, Mom had this wrong! Obviously, it's paranoia kicking in from her compulsion to Lifetime movies.* Besides, if Mom knew how bad things were for Bryce at home, she would understand more. That's why he yelled. And everyone knows that *yelling isn't abuse.*

Right?

Mom repositioned herself, and her movements roused me. I sat up and moved my fingers, trying to relieve the numbness. "Sorry, guess I was tired."

Mom brushed her fingers down my hair and smiled in her understanding way. "Bug, you don't have to figure all this out today. There's time for that when you're healed. I promise it will get better. Right now, rest and pray. That's the best thing for us to do." She kissed me on the forehead. I wrapped my arms around her and squeezed her tightly.

CHAPTER FOURTEEN

A weekend of recovery didn't do much for my black eye, bruised cheek, and elbow. And since the headache came back in full force by Monday, Mom said no to me going to school. I spent most of that day sleeping. On Tuesday, she kept me home because I'd slept all day on Monday. Wednesday her excuse was that I hadn't rested enough on Tuesday. On Thursday, she wanted me to stay home, but she did give me my phone for a few hours. She said if I didn't get a headache from that, I could possibly go to school on Friday.

When I got my phone, most of the texts that came in were from Sam or Bryce. A couple came from Haley, and one from Ashlynn, but nothing from Savage or Drew since the weekend. I opened the ones from Haley and sent her an update of my status and sent the same text to Ashlynn.

Sam's texts mostly questioned me about the weekend, including some guilt-inducing statements about Bryce feeling upset and betrayed. *Obviously, she's talked to Bryce.* I fidgeted with the phone, then typed out a reply to Sam but quickly deleted it. *What do I say to her?* After a few minutes, I typed something.

Me: Hey, got my phone for a few hours today. Maybe we can talk later?

I pulled up some music and pressed Play. Within a couple of minutes, the music got interrupted by the ringing of my phone. Readying myself to say hello to Sam, I lost my breath as Bryce's name flashed on the screen. My finger hovered over the answer button. An image of Bryce yelling in my face popped into my head. I tossed my phone beside me. When the ringing stopped, the sound of multiple text notifications followed. I turned the sound off. Then it annoyingly vibrated.

Grabbing my phone to turn it off, Sam's text notification stopped me.

Sam: Talked to your mom. Said I can come Saturday
Me: Yeah, she told me
Sam: So…Bryce told me what happened
Me: OK
Sam: What's going on, Z?
Me: Idk. Bryce got mad
Sam: Bryce said he got attacked
Me: Not true
Sam: Bryce said two guys were in his face. One of them punched him for no reason. Sounds like an attack to me

Ugh, I can't believe Bryce. I threw my phone on the bed and almost immediately it rang. *It's Sam! What do I even say to her?*

With a deep breath, I said, "Hey, Sam."

Her familiar voice brought a wave a nausea with it. She quizzed me about what happened with Bryce. Expecting Sam to understand my side of it was clearly not happening, especially since Bryce had gotten to her. As she kept defending him, my answers began to get vaguer, which sparked further questions. Pain shot through my face as my teeth clenched together. Sam rambled on about how hurt and betrayed Bryce felt.

Without a thought, I blurted, "Sam, stop! Me and Bryce are over!"

"Z, just call Bryce. This can all be fixed."

"No, Sam, it can't be fixed. There's no fixing this."

"Z, that's stupid. Of course, this can be fixed. You and Bryce always work things out. Just talk to him."

"Sam, no. Me and Bryce, we're over. I'm done letting Bryce treat me like this."

"Treating you like what? Bryce loves you."

"Sam, please just try and understand what I mean," I pleaded.

"Just tell me what you mean, 'cause you're not making sense," Sam said in a frustrated tone. My chest got heavy and I took a couple of deep breaths. "Zinn, are you gonna say anything?"

"Remember homecoming?"

"Yeah, why wouldn't I? It was a great night."

A great night! What is she remembering?

"Remember how mad Bryce got?"

"I guess. He got a little mad. So what?"

Sam's really pretending like nothing happened. Am I in the Twilight Zone? I took a deep breath and finished. "Sam, he didn't just get a little mad. He dragged me out of the gym and screamed at me?"

"That's a bit dramatic!"

"Sam, what about all the times he yelled at me? Remember how angry he got over the slightest thing?"

"So Bryce has a temper."

"Sam, just listen to me, please?"

"Listen to what? You're not making any sense. Bryce gets mad and yells. He has a temper. Grow up, Zinn. That's life. Nothing to get all upset about. And certainly not a reason to refuse to talk to him."

Sam defended Bryce. *This can't be real.* Exhaling, I stayed silent as Sam went on about how great Bryce treated me. How worried and sick he felt when he heard about me being hurt. How it upset him when Jasmine told him she saw me out with another guy. Sam went on and on, guilt-tripping me. She didn't even care about what I was saying. Finally, I'd had enough.

"Sam, would you shut up? I just can't hear any more about how Bryce feels," I blurted.

"Wow, Z. You don't even care how Bryce feels?"

"That's not what I said," I replied meekly. "It's just that what you've heard isn't the whole story."

"Then tell me what else I need to know. 'Cause what I know is that Bryce got punched out of nowhere by some guy you've been going out with. And honestly, this whole thing doesn't make you look good."

Sam's words really stung, and I wanted to fire back at her. Instead, I took a deep breath. "Sam, I've been trying to tell you, but you're not listening to me."

"Beause you're not talking about anything except some stuff that happened with you and Bryce over a year ago!" Sam said loudly.

"Well, when Bryce showed up and saw my friends and got mad, he started yelling awful things, and Drew told him to stop."

"Yeah, Bryce said one of them got in the middle of him talking to you." Irritation dripped from Sam's words.

"Sam, Bryce wasn't talking. He was screaming and grabbing my shoulders, paying no attention to the fact that my arm is in a sling by the way. That's why Drew got in the middle."

"Well, that's no reason for someone to punch him. Besides, that's not what Bryce said." Sam's combative tone caught me off guard.

I swallowed down the lump in my throat. "But I'm saying it, Sam."

"Okay, so you're saying it. I just don't know where this is coming from. Maybe it's your new friends. I don't know."

The flippancy of Sam's words flew all over me. "This is not about my new friends. This is about seeing the truth!" I blurted out. Then there was a long a pause. "Sam?"

"What truth?" Finally, Sam was hearing me. Now I could tell Sam everything.

"Well, the truth that Bryce is controlling. And I think it's sorta, maybe, abusive."

"You can't be serious? Bryce, abusive? Zinn, how can you say Bryce is abusive? He's never hit you." Her words stabbed me like a knife. The defiance caused me to shudder.

How could my best friend not know what I'm talking about? What else could I say?

We sat on the phone in silence until she said, "I really don't know what you want me to say. You aren't making any sense. I think Bryce is right. You're acting different. It's like I don't know you anymore."

"Sam, why would you say that? You know me better than anyone."

"Do I, Z?" Sam asked.

My heart sank. I struggled to speak while choking back the tears. "Sam, of course you do. You're my best friend."

"If I'm your best friend, then why didn't you tell me about going out with this guy?"

"Because there was nothing to tell. Drew just gave me a ride."

"Drew is the guy you went out with? You mean the guy at your house was the guy who flirted with you at the restaurant? No wonder Bryce was so mad."

The anger quickly boiled inside me. "He wasn't flirting, and how do you know about the restaurant? I never told you about that."

"Exactly my point. You don't tell me much anymore," Sam said.

I took a deep breath and calmly replied, "Did Bryce tell you about it?"

"Yeah, Bryce told me." Sam's voice cracked. *Why is she so nervous?*

"Why did he tell you?"

"I don't know, Z. I guess he was upset."

"Then why didn't he talk to me? Why didn't you tell me he told you?"

"What does that matter? You just said Bryce hits you, and now you're all upset he told me about some guy flirting with you."

"I never said he hit me."

"Oh, sorry," Sam said sarcastically. "It's just that he's controlling and abusive, right?"

Where was Sam's attitude coming from? She sounded so condescending and hateful.

"Sam, are you really gonna pretend like you didn't see it."

"I'm not pretending. I never saw any abuse. What you are saying doesn't make any sense, Z. Bryce is the one who has been abused. He is not the one abusing. I just can't believe—"

"Wait. Did you say Bryce was abused? How do you know about that?"

"Uh, well," Sam stammered. "I don't know. You told me something about it."

"No, Sam, I never told you."

Sam quickly interjected, "Of course you did. You just don't remember."

Did I tell Sam? No, Bryce had made me promise not to tell anyone because I was the only person he could tell that to. Did he tell Sam? Did he lie to me?

"Did Bryce tell you about being abused?"

"No!" Sam said defiantly.

Why is she getting so angry? Her quick reaction made me even more suspicious.

"Calm down, Sam."

"I am calm, Zinn. I just don't like being accused of something."

What am I accusing her of? "I didn't accuse you of anything. I just asked a question."

"And I answered it." Sam paused for a moment. "Look, Z, I gotta go."

"Sam, please don't be mad. I'm sorry."

"I'm not mad. I just gotta go."

"Okay then, I'll see you Saturday?"

"Yeah, Saturday. Bye."

When I hung up the phone, I collapsed on my bed. *How did Sam know about Bryce's abuse? Had I forgotten about telling her that?* My head now aching, I needed some meds. *Getting some meds would give Mom another reason to keep me home tomorrow, so that's not an option.* I slid the earbuds in my ears and hit Play, praying music could bring some relief from the stress and aches.

Since I managed to conceal the headache from Mom, she let me return to school on Friday. As I walked through the doorway, eyes shot in my direction. Struck with a tightening in my stomach, I turned around and exited. Hurrying down the steps onto the sidewalk, I pulled out my phone to call Mom to come back and get me.

"Zinn, finally you've returned," Drew said, quickly coming toward me. He swooped me into his arms, gently squeezing me while avoiding my injured arm. He spun me around, making me slightly dizzy.

"Yeah, I've returned."

"Somebody's gonna have to call the cops," Drew said.

"Huh?"

His smile changed to that playful grin. "'Cause you need to be arrested for looking that good!" His boyish smile returned when he winked.

We headed through the crowd and went inside. Drew's jovial conversation relaxed me and lessened the stress of the staring eyes. A familiar squeal silenced Drew, then Haley happily bounced up to us.

"Zinn, you're back! I've missed you so much. How are you feeling? How's the elbow? You're finally out of the sling. You must be so relieved. The sling would've been a pain for Bargeston Day. Aren't you psyched it's next week?" Haley rambled on and on, barely giving me time to respond to anything.

I interjected when I could get a word in. "Haley, what's Bargeston Day?"

"Oh, duh, totally forget you have that new-girl thing. Bargeston Day is the fall festival. It's so much fun. You have to come. Tell her she has to come, Drew," Haley chattered on.

Drew gave me a serious look with a tone to match. "Zinn, you have to come. Haley said so."

"Ugh, Drew, stop," Haley said. "Zinn, it won't be the same without you. It's such a blast! Isn't it, Drew?"

"Well, it—"

"Oh, never mind, you're no help," Haley interrupted. "Just say you'll come, please?"

"Maybe," I replied.

"Yay!" Haley's giddy excitement overtook her. She suddenly swallowed me in her arms. "So glad you're back." She finished with her goodbye and bounded down the hall.

"So, Bargeston Day. Is it as great as Haley says?" I asked.

"I'm not sure anything's as great as Haley says," Drew answered with a laugh. "But Bargeston Day is fun. You should consider going."

"Okay, I'll consider it."

"Well, you think you'd consider going with me?" Drew gave me a hopeful smile.

"I'll consider it."

"Good, at least I'm a consideration."

Heat filled my cheeks. *Did Drew just ask me out? He said consider.* Dissecting his words generated more questions. *What did consider mean? Is it a friends thing or a real date?* My over-analyzation created more stress in me. Drew meant we'd go as friends, just like homecoming.

Walking into econ brought a lot of stares. Coach B looked up from his paper when I entered. "Zinn, you're back! Good to know." Once he acknowledged me, he immediately returned to his paper.

Everyone had something to say to me, that is everyone except Jordan and Riley. They just scowled at me. When I sat down at my desk, Drew started talking and allowed me to keep my eyes off the mean-girls duo.

When Coach B finished his coffee, he announced worksheets were due Monday. Then he directed Malone to hit the lights and pointed a remote to the television. I tapped Drew on the shoulder. "Wanna fill me in here?"

"We're finishing up *The Pursuit of Happyness* and have to answer some questions." Drew held a worksheet in his hand.

"Great."

"Yeah, no worries. I'll help you."

Since it was the middle of the movie and I was lost, I worked on a new song. It wasn't long until the movie ended and light filled the room. I winced slightly. Drew turned to face me and caught me with one eye closed. He gave a wink and smiled. "So let's get these questions answered."

"I'll do it later after I watch the movie."

"Okay! Maybe this weekend we can watch it together and I can help you with the assignment."

"Yeah, but it'll have to be Sunday. Sam's coming over sometime Saturday."

"Cool, it's a date then," Drew said with his smiling eyes.

A date. Is it a date? Great, more questions. First Bargeston Day, and now he throws out the word *date. Does Drew think this is a date? Of course not, he just said that.* Drew made it very clear after homecoming that we were only friends. Besides, things with Bryce had just ended, and I was still reeling from the idea of being in such a toxic relationship. No matter how much I liked Drew, I needed time—time to heal, time to understand how things got so bad with Bryce, time to trust myself again. Even if Drew liked me, there was no way he wanted to deal with all my baggage. My head began to hurt. Finally, the bell rang, and I slid my notebook in my backpack and walked toward the door.

Typically, after econ Drew and I parted ways with him heading left as I traveled right. But today he turned right and walked with me toward the history wing. Whispers filled the hall as we passed the crowds of teens. Drew's voice became background noise as the soft whispers became murmurs and then murmurs became mumbles. My head started swimming and my breathing went shallow. As my pace slowed, Drew put his arm around me and moved me closer to the wall.

"Zinn, hey, look at me. It's okay."

I swallowed deep and said, "I know, it's just—"

"It's nothing. Just breathe."

Drew's tranquil blue eyes and calming words did the trick; my breathing returned to normal. The voices in the hallway became background noise. The serenity of Drew's eyes remained until I smiled, then his jovial eyes appeared.

"Let's get you to class."

Continuing down the hall, the whispers had pretty much disappeared. When we arrived at my classroom, Drew smiled and gave a nod. "Catch you later."

"Sure," I said as I put one foot into the classroom "Hey, Drew?"

"Yeah."

"Thanks."

"My pleasure." He gave a humble nod.

He walked backward, putting distance between us while keeping his gaze locked on me until he was out of sight.

After history, Mr. Wilson called me to his desk to explain my makeup assignments. I stepped in the hallway to Savage leaning against the wall. His mouth turned upward into a smile when his eyes met mine. Pushing off the wall, he smoothly meandered between the crowd over to me.

"You're back," Savage said.

"I'm back!"

"Good! How's the arm?"

"Getting better."

Savage smiled and we headed down the hall. The chatter of the crowd maintained its normal ambience. I fell right into my normal conversational style with Savage. No matter the amount of time I spent with him, it always provided me a moment of lucidity. His attentive listening allowed me to not only talk but also to hear myself. The arrival to trig class came sooner than I wanted. He left me at the door and continued down the hall. As he turned right at the corner, he looked back, smiled, and threw up his hand. I waved and then entered the classroom.

When the drudgery of trig came to an end, I flung my backpack over my shoulder and scrambled out of the room. Coming out of the door to the crowded hallway, I tiptoed to extend my view. The chestnut curls slightly towered above the mass of bodies. Maneuvering through the crowd, Drew smiled. "Hey, you!"

"Hey, I wondered if you'd forgotten."

"No way. It's been a lonely walk to south hall this week."

"Well, I'll make sure to not fall again and miss another week of school. That way you don't get lonely walking to fourth period."

"Please don't," Drew said.

I chuckled lightly. We walked the short distance to English, then Drew lingered at the door talking to me. The warning bell didn't stop his rambling. With a couple of minutes until the final bell, he said goodbye and made a dash down the hall. I walked into the class and Mrs. Hart greeted me. She motioned me to her desk to discuss my make-up work. She finished just as the bell rang and I went to my seat. Savage was late, which never happened.

I tapped my fingers on the desktop as Mrs. Hart gave directions for the journal assignment. As the time crept to five after, still no

Savage. I sighed and grabbed my pen to write my journal entry. Mrs. Hart began some explanation about our next assignment, and the door opened. Savage walked in and handed a slip to Mrs. Hart, then made his way to his desk. When he got to his seat, I leaned over and whispered, "You had me scared."

"Oh?" he said.

"You're late."

"Guidance counselor."

"Well, I'm glad you made it. Lunch wouldn't be the same," I said.

"Hmm, I can relate."

Mrs. Hart looked in our direction and gave us a stern nod. I swallowed and straightened in my chair. Within a few minutes, Mrs. Hart started lecturing on *Hamlet*. Shakespeare's great tragedy could not maintain my attention. No, the busyness of the courtyard held my attention instead. A day of sunshine always drew the students outside for lunch. Among the crowd of teens, Drew stood among a group of guys. Animated as he talked, the guys around him were drawn into whatever story he told. Chuckles broke out on the faces of the listening crowd, giving Drew a look of satisfaction.

Drew's entertaining nature made others gravitate toward him. It was hard to believe he didn't have a girlfriend, but then Haley said he hadn't dated anyone since freshmen year. His question about Bargeston Day and the plans for studying on Sunday became clear to me. He had way too much confidence to be passive about asking a girl out on a date. And I couldn't forget his post-homecoming conversation about just wanting to be friends. The whole Bargeston Day was a friend thing, no doubt. But that last dance perplexed me. He asked me to give him hope.

Hope for what, exactly?

At lunch, Savage fell into his regular role of listening. Blathering about my week of recovery, the discussion turned to Bryce. Unloading about how Bryce yelled at me, called me names, blamed me for anything that went wrong, and scared me changed Savage's expression. His relaxed face turned into a furrowed brow that darkened his eyes.

"I'm sorry. You don't wanna hear this," I said.

His eyes softened. "It's fine, Zinn."

"I guess I didn't realize how bad it was with his moods, temper fits, and yelling. I kept making excuses for him and truly thought his behavior was my fault. How stupid is that?"

"It's not stupid," Savage emphasized. "You couldn't see it 'cause you were in it. Don't be so hard on yourself. It happens."

"You know, when I told Mom about it, she said it was abuse. I even blurted that word out to Sam, which didn't go well. I can admit that Bryce treated me bad and was controlling, but I'm not sure I can accept the whole *abuse* label. Regardless of what it is, I feel stupid now."

A sickening feeling came over me. I shuffled the food on my plate, but it made me want to hurl. I pushed the tray to the side and sipped on my drink. The coolness of the liquid trickled down my throat, and the sugary syrup and carbonation eased the nausea.

Savage cleared his throat. "Zinn, you're not the only person who has gotten caught up in a bad relationship." Sadness filled Savage's face. "I don't talk about it 'cause it's no one's business, but it happened to my sister, Sydney."

"Really?" I questioned with a whisper.

Savage nodded. His obvious discomfort didn't derail him from sharing with me about his sister and her situation. Savage's eyes filled with disdain as he told the details of all his sister endured. What he described sounded eerily similar to how Bryce treated me. When he said the words *verbal abuse*, a lump formed in my throat. A sickening wave of panic went through me as he explained about finding out she'd been hit by her then boyfriend. When he finished, I just sat there.

"I thought telling you her story could help you understand you're not alone," Savage said.

I slowly nodded my head as I absorbed all he said.

For the remainder of lunch, Savage and I sat in silence. I was thankful for his quiet nature since I couldn't stop comparing Sydney's situation with my relationship with Bryce. Sydney had been hit; Bryce never hit me. He just yelled at me, but Savage did say Sydney's abuse started with yelling. If I was completely honest with myself, his yelling did scare me—a lot. Sometimes it was so bad I wondered if he might hit me. After hearing all Savage had to say, I felt almost convinced that, given time, Bryce *would* have hit me.

When English ended, I collected my things, said goodbye to Savage, and headed out the door. In the hallway, Julie came out of her classroom and chatted with me for a minute. When we finished talking, I headed to chemistry when a tall figure fell into step with me.

"Um, whatcha doin', Drew?" I said.

"Walking. What about you?"

"Your class isn't this way."

"I found a shortcut."

"A shortcut on the opposite side of the school?"

"Yep, saves me a ton of time." He smirked proudly.

My panicked moment from this morning obviously rattled Drew, and telling him to stop worrying about me would do no good. Best to embrace his irrational need to walk with me and just enjoy being with him.

When we came to the science wing, Drew walked me to the door. As people from class greeted me, he winked and waved as he left. The group flooded me with questions about what happened, how I fell, and all the other details. We shifted into the classroom and the frenzy settled down as the final bell rang.

With class almost finished, I cleaned the beakers at the sink while chatting with a couple of girls. Mr. Cavers reminded us to wipe our tables, so I grabbed a paper towel and returned to my work area. With the bell ringing, I quickly wiped the table.

"Hey, Zinn. Glad you're back."

"Thanks, Jake."

Jake looked around and then shifted himself closer to me. "Um, you think we could get together and talk again? I found some stuff that you might wanna check out."

I nodded energetically as I tossed my backpack over my shoulder. "Sure. Just text me. By the way, your website is pretty cool."

"Thanks," he replied as his eyes fell to the floor. We chatted some more as we walked out of class.

When we hit the doorway, Drew stood in the hall. Jake nodded at Drew and said, "Zinn, I'll see you in chorus."

"Drew, why are you standing in the hallway?"

"Because I'm not standing in the classroom?" he answered with a grin.

Bumping into his shoulder, I scowled at him. "You wanna tell me why I've had a personal escort after every class?"

"A personal escort, really?" Drew said.

"You're not here to walk me to chorus?"

"You've got chorus next? That's so weird. I was just about to head that way to talk to the band director about being in marching band next year." Drew's mischievous grin reappeared.

"Oh, you were? What about football?"

"Oh, I can do both," Drew said.

"Really? What instrument, Drew?"

Drew looked at me expressionless and said, straight-faced, "The nose flute." My laughter and Drew's smirk ended my questioning. "Now can we go? The band awaits my great nasally talent."

Laughing as we headed to the music wing, the phone vibrated in my pocket. I had a text.

Sam: Sorry, can't come tomorrow

Her text with no explanation sucker-punched me in the stomach. I fought the tears and shoved the phone in my pocket. As we walked the route to chorus, Drew chatted on about something, but Sam's text had me consumed.

"Zinn, don't you think so?"

"I'm sorry, what?"

"Did you hear anything I said?"

"Um, yeah! You said . . ." I had nothing to offer. "I'm sorry, what did you say?"

A look of concern came over Drew's face. "What's wrong?"

"Yeah, I just spaced a minute." I tried to say it nonchalantly, but Drew wasn't buying it.

"Zinn, what's wrong?"

"This text I got from Sam. She's being weird."

Voicing it out loud made it difficult to fight back tears. Within just a few words, the battle was lost as the tears came spilling from my eyes. I rattled about the text, which then led to the phone call with Sam. I cried even more as I explained how she didn't believe what I said about Bryce. When the bell rang, I wiped my eyes and expressed my apologies for making him late.

Drew took my hand. "C'mon."

"Drew, we've got class."

"Forget class. Let's get out of here."

I followed him out the side door to the quad. We snuck through the quad and slipped out into the parking lot, then got into his truck.

"Drew, where exactly are we going?" I asked as he drove out of the school's parking lot.

"I don't know. Where exactly do you wanna go?"

"Okay, then what is your plan?"

"No plan, just thought we'd drive," he said casually.

"Just drive? Drive where?"

He shrugged his shoulders and flashed me a big grin. The mischievous glint danced through his eyes. Arguing with him would have been pointless.

I shook my head and agreed. "Okay, drive, then."

For the next hour we rode around town listening to music. Drew's idea of skipping class did the trick. The stress of the Sam situation was gone. Somehow, Drew knew exactly what I needed.

CHAPTER FIFTEEN

Drew: Hey! You wanna come over and watch The Pursuit of Happyness today?
Me: I could do that
Drew: Pick you up around 1??
Me: Sounds great!
Drew: cool 😜 see you at 1
Me: 🙂

Within a couple of minutes the phone rang and Sam's name flashed across the screen. My stomach tightened and my heart dropped. Building up the courage, I finally answered. "Hey, Sam."

"Hey, Z. Sorry I bailed on our plans for today. Actually, I can hang out after all."

"Uh, well, I sorta made plans for one o'clock, so . . . ." I bit the corner of my bottom lip.

Please don't ask me about it.

"That's perfect because I need to be home around one thirty. I can leave now and be there around ten thirty."

"Um, okay. I guess I can do that."

"Awesome! See you soon."

What is going on? It's not like Sam to make last-minute plans. Maybe she feels bad about canceling and wants to smooth things over.

When Sam arrived, she talked with Mom and Grandma for a bit, then we went upstairs. She told me about all my friends at Kowinville, but she never mentioned Bryce. I was glad 'cause I had no desire to talk about him.

"Hey, I'm hungry. Wanna go grab some food?" Sam asked.

"Uh, okay."

Sam headed out the door. "Any good Mexican restaurants around here?"

"Yeah, there's El Rey's."

On the way to the restaurant, Drew texted.

Drew: Hey, I'm in town.

Can swing by at 12:30 and get you

Me: I'm with Sam.

We're headed to El Rey's

Drew: Cool. Want me to pick you up there?

Me: That should work. About 1?

Drew: See you then 😊

Sam energetically sang along with Queen's "Bohemian Rhapsody." I took a deep breath and said, "So, Drew is helping me with the make-up work for econ. He's in town so he's gonna pick me up at the restaurant." Sam cut her eyes to me and then forced a smile. "Do you wanna meet him? I can tell him to come early."

"No!" she blurted. "Uh, not today. Maybe some other time." She flashed a big grin and giggled awkwardly. "It's Sam and Z time today."

The cloudy sky and threat of rain didn't deter Sam from insisting we sit on the patio, which I found odd because Sam wasn't one who enjoyed being outside much. After ordering our food, we chatted a bit, but the tension was unbelievable. I'd never been so uncomfortable with Sam.

Finally, I said, "Sam, is something wrong?"

"No, Z, of course not." She forced a smile.

The question didn't seem to ease any of the tension. While I tried to carry on a conversation, Sam remained occupied with her cell. Even when the food came, she kept checking the phone every couple of minutes. What was going on that she couldn't take her eyes off that screen? I mean, Sam wasn't known for her politeness with the phone, but this was out of her ordinary for sure. Plus, she was so quiet. Normally, she would've been updating me on all the gossip.

We finished eating and had about half an hour before Sam would leave, but rather than talk to me, she texted someone. Finally, I asked, "We still got some time to kill. Wanna go over to the Shoppes?"

"Um . . ." Again, Sam looked at her phone. "I'd rather just keep talking."

Keep talking! What talking? She'd barely said ten words to me.

Fixated on her phone, she said, "How 'bout some dessert? You know you can't resist a churro."

With Sam's fingers feverishly texting, she didn't even bother to notice I didn't respond, obviously waiting for the reply from whomever she kept texting. *This is unbelievable!*

Sam suddenly looked at me. "Z, don't be mad, okay?"

Finally, she realized her rudeness. I exhaled. "I'm not mad, Sam."

"Um, well, please don't get mad."

Sam had lost me now. Narrowing my eyes, I stared at her suspiciously.

"He had to see you."

"Who had to see me, Sam?" I blurted out, knowing full well who he was. My hand gripped the arm of the chair. I closed my eyes and took a deep breath. "Sam, please tell me you didn't."

"Z, he just wants to talk. He feels really bad. He said he overreacted about the whole thing."

"Sam, no!" Immediately, a wave of nausea hit me and my pulse quickened. "How could you do this?" I pushed away from the table. "I'm not talking to him. I'm leaving."

"Z, don't be ridiculous. Besides, he's already here." Sam motioned her head to the parking lot.

Behind me, Bryce climbed out of his car. As he walked toward us, nausea hit me again. Taking a deep breath, I turned to Sam. "I'm not staying. You can deal with him."

"Please, Zinn, he only wants a minute. Please, just one minute."

Sam hadn't really given me much choice. I was stuck. As he got closer, the knot in my tummy tightened. "Sam, please do not leave. Stay right here, please."

Sam's nod assured me she understood.

Bryce opened the patio gate and walked toward our table. His cocky swagger was replaced with a look of chagrin. A nervous smile came across his face as his eyes met mine. Those eyes always got me. Eyes filled with hurt, regret, and shame stared at me like they had so many times before. But this time something deeper stared back at me, and it wasn't hurt, regret, or shame. No, annoyance, frustration, and anger loomed behind the disguise he wore so well.

"Hey, Z," he said softly.

"Bryce."

"Sam, give us a minute?" Bryce nodded to Sam.

"Um, I-I . . ." Sam stuttered as her eyes darted between Bryce and me.

Letting out a nervous breath, I said, "I want Sam to stay."

Bryce's brow furrowed. "Zinn, don't be difficult. I wanna talk to you alone."

"Zinn, maybe I should go?" Sam pushed her chair back and stood.

My pulse began to race and heat filled my cheeks. I pushed myself from the table and stood. "If Sam leaves then I leave."

The flash of anger in Bryce's eyes made me weak in the knees.

"Z, you're being stupid. Sam, leave!"

"I'm not stupid, Bryce," I mumbled.

"Z!" Bryce's voice boomed. He loudly sighed as his jaw clenched, then his voice lowered. "I came here to talk to you, to work this out."

"Bryce, there's nothing to work out. Please, just leave," I pleaded.

"I'm not leaving 'til you talk to me." His eyes blazed with anger.

He thinks I'll do whatever he says.

Shaking my head, the anger grew inside me. "What do you want to say, Bryce?"

The color left Bryce's face. He gawked at me and said nothing, then he cleared his throat. "Well, I don't know why you're doing this—not talking to me, not giving me a chance."

My moment of bravery began to waver, and the shakiness in my voice proved it. "Bryce, I can't do this anymore."

"You can't do what anymore?"

"Us," I said softly.

"Zinn, I'm here saying I'm sorry, so you need to get past this."

"Bryce. It's over. Please just accept that." I walked away from the table and headed toward the gate. Bryce rushed to block my path.

"No, Zinn, it's not over!"

My heart raced and my breath went shallow. I summoned the strength to speak. "Please, get out of my way."

"Not until you listen." Bryce grabbed my wrist as anger flashed through his eyes. I twisted my wrist to try and break free of his grip, but his hand tightened around it.

"Bryce, please let go."

Bryce got in my face and yelled, "No, you're gonna listen to me!"

Tears streamed down my face, and my voice cracked as I spoke louder. "Bryce, let go of my wrist."

"You heard what she said. Now let her go." Drew stood at his truck, but in a blink, he bolted across the parking lot, leaping over the gate.

Bryce's jaw clenched as his eyes bore into Drew. "This has nothing to do with you."

"If you're bothering Zinn, then it's got something to do with me."

"Zinn's fine!" Bryce yelled. "Tell him, Zinn."

"Please, Bryce, you're hurting me," I said.

Drew grabbed Bryce's forearm. "You wanna grab someone, then grab me."

"Fine!" As Bryce flung my wrist down, a sharp pain radiated through my injured elbow.

He jerked his arm trying to release Drew's grip but had no success. Drew pressed into Bryce's face. "You ever put your hands on her again, it'll be the last time you ever do anything."

"Yo, dude, we can take care of this right now," Bryce challenged.

"Let's go!" Drew released his arm and headed toward the gate with Bryce right on his heals as they hit the parking lot.

"Drew, don't! Let's just go." I trailed behind them, trying my best to stop the fight before the first punch.

"Zinn, shut up!" Bryce yelled. "This is between me and him now."

"I warned you, dude." Drew shook his head and plowed into Bryce, taking him to the ground.

"Drew!" I yelled.

Sam yelled at me as if I were to protect Bryce. "Zinn, get him off Bryce!"

While they wrestled, I screamed for them to stop. Drew had Bryce pinned to the ground. Bryce twisted his legs to get out of the pin, but it proved unsuccessful as Drew's arms tightened around him. Bryce freed one arm and elbowed Drew in the face, but Drew didn't budge. He kept his grip tight around Bryce. As they continued to battle it out, someone came running out of the restaurant.

"Get out of here. I'm calling the police."

"Drew, please! They're calling the police," I pleaded.

Drew then looked at me and released his grip. He jumped up and quickly faced Bryce. Bryce positioned himself on all fours, exhausted. After some deep breaths, he finally got on his feet but remained bent over. Spitting blood and wiping his mouth, he straightened himself and looked at me. "You happy now?"

My mouth dropped but no words came. Was he blaming me for this? Tears welled in my eyes.

Sam ran over to Bryce. "Bryce, let's just go." Her glance focused on me and she shook her head. The disapproving look stabbed me in the heart. She saw me as the one at fault and not Bryce. Even after all that, she still didn't see it. She leaned closer to him and whispered something I couldn't hear.

"Back off, Sam. I'm not done with Zinn." Bryce wiped blood from his mouth as he straightened himself.

"Dude, trust me, you're done with Zinn," Drew replied. "And if you ever come near her again, I'll end you."

"Drew, let's go, please?" I lightly touched his hand. Engulfing my hand in his, he led me toward his truck.

"Zinn, this ain't over!" Bryce yelled.

I stopped and turned to Bryce. "Bryce, it is over!"

Drew put his arm around my shoulders protectively. "Keep walking, Zinn. Don't look back. Just keep moving forward."

Bryce continued his rant at me. "You don't decide when this is over. I'm not done with you."

Sam's voice intermingled with his as she begged Bryce to leave. I climbed in the truck and settled in the seat. Bryce's intense stare sent shivers down my spine. Drew got in the truck and drove down the road. Even when we were a few miles away, Bryce's stare still haunted me.

"Zinn, talk to me, please."

Tears streamed down my face as Drew lightly touched my hand. I fumbled to find words. *How could Sam do that to me? How could Bryce do that to me?* Drew pulled off the road, then his arms wrapped around me. His spicy, musky scent took my breath away. His eyes so full of warmth enchanted me as he pulled me closer to him. He gently wiped a tear from my eye and smiled warmly. "He doesn't deserve your tears."

I swallowed and blurted out nervously, "How's your lip?"

"Don't worry about it."

"I think we need to do something about it." I softly touched the swollen, busted spot on his bottom lip.

"Aw, it's fine."

"Your lip is not fine. It's bloody and busted." I motioned to the convenience store. "Pull in there."

"Trust me. It's nothing."

"Don't argue with me."

He nodded and drove over to the convenience store, and I jumped out of the truck. "I'll be right back." As I got to the door, Drew was beside me. "I don't need your help."

"I know." He smirked.

After paying the cashier, I pulled Drew by the hand back to the truck. Sitting in the truck, I wetted a paper towel and slightly lifted his chin so I could tend to his lip. Drew's enchanting blue eyes caused goosebumps to rush over me. "This may hurt some." With his eyes fixated on me, I lightly dabbed the swollen, bloody lip. He didn't flinch or react. He just gazed into my eyes as I kept cleaning the blood and dirt from his face. "You're a very good patient."

"You're a great nurse," he said. "My own personal Florence Nightingale."

As the color rushed to my cheeks, I busied myself with the gauze. Fumbling as I removed the gauze from the package, Drew touched my hand. "Let me help." Another rush of color filled my cheeks. He smiled as he handed me the gauze. I swallowed and nodded slightly.

Dabbing some peroxide on the gauze, I finished cleaning the lip. "All done."

"Thanks," he said in a breathy whisper. He brushed a strand of hair out of my eyes. His breathing was steady as his fingers lightly touched my arm. "How's your elbow?"

I tried to form words but was caught up in his enchanting aura. Eventually, I uttered, "It's fine."

He smiled and then shifted his weight and moved himself closer to me, his face slowly inching to mine. Suddenly, a loud honk caused him to jerk his head. He had a rattled look as he shook his head. Realizing it wasn't anything more than an irritated car passing by, he said, "So, um, you hungry?"

"I just ate, so not really."

"Yeah. Stupid question. Sorry. How about the movie? You still good for it?"

"I think it's better if I go home."

"Whatever the lady wants," Drew said as he winked.

He drove to my house and walked me to the door. Hugging me goodbye, he said, "You need anything, just call me. Okay?"

"I think you've done enough." I lightly touched his lip.

"Aw, this is nothing. Experienced much worse."

"Still, I'm sorry you got hurt. But I'm really glad you showed up when you did."

"Me too." He lightly brushed hair from my face. My heart skipped as his hand grazed my cheek. His blue eyes made my stomach turn flips. "Definitely time for me to go."

Mom and Grandma Rose hadn't gotten home yet, so I headed upstairs. My phone showed multiple text notifications from Bryce.

The curse-filled rants nauseated me. He offered no apology, only excuses and blame. I hit Delete. Twisting my hair into a messy bun, I plopped on the bed and grabbed my journal.

When the pen touched the paper, my hand started scribbling words as fast as I could keep up. The words flowed from me like I had turned on a faucet.

If I had any doubts about Bryce being abusive, they are gone now. When he showed up at lunch without telling me, I couldn't believe it. Who does that? And how could Sam have allowed that? Bryce walked up to me with that pitiful look of his. How did I fall for his fake apologies all those times before? It was so obvious he was trying to play me, to make me feel sorry for him, to make me forgive him, and hope I'd forget what he did. Of course, it wasn't long until Bryce's true colors showed up. He started yelling. He got so angry and called me stupid. Any other time I would have allowed the name-calling and begged him to forgive me, but not today. Today, I spoke back to him. I told Bryce I wasn't stupid. I actually said it. And that look of shock on his face! Wow! It was priceless. Of course, he yelled some more and even grabbed my wrist. I knew then he has it in him to be physically violent! And Sam saw it too. Now she can't deny Bryce is abusive. When Drew showed up, I was so thankful cause Bryce really had me scared—more scared than ever before. With Drew there I felt really brave. Actually, I felt brave enough to tell Bryce we were done. I couldn't believe I said the words till I heard them come from my mouth. By the look on Bryce's face, he couldn't believe it either, but he knew I meant it. The only reason I found the strength to say it was because of Drew. Him being there made me feel safe. Like I had my own guardian or protector. No telling what would've happened if he hadn't shown up when he did.

I closed the journal and threw it on the floor, then grabbed my phone and texted Drew.

Me: Hey…
Drew: Hey!
Me: Thanks again for being there

Drew: Always 🙂
Me: How's your mouth?
Drew: I told you it's nothing.
Had much worse
Me: Good 🙂
Drew: How bout you?
Me: idk
Drew: Wanna talk?

What am I doing? Drew didn't need to be dragged into my problems with Bryce any more than he had been. I closed my eyes and let myself just breathe. The vibration of the phone startled me. There were four messages from Drew.

Drew: Or maybe go for a drive?
Drew: ???
Drew: Hey Zinn, where'd you go?
Drew: I'm coming over
Me: Drew, I'm fine. Don't do that.
You just left my house!
Drew: Too late, driving already.
Be there in 10

I sat in the swing and let the rhythmic movement calm my nerves as I waited on Drew to arrive. When his truck came around the curve, I jumped off the swing and hit the sidewalk. He opened the truck door as I walked toward him.

"There was no reason for you to come."

His arms circled me and the tension left my body. His strong arms held me until the moment I released him. "That's the reason." He motioned to the truck door. "How 'bout a ride?"

I shrugged my shoulders and climbed into the driver's seat, then slid over to the passenger's side as Drew settled behind the wheel. We left my house and drove down the highway. The grayness hovered above the rolling hillside as rays cascaded down on the leafless treetops, brightening the shades of gray in the horizon and signifying cold weather would soon be here.

"I wanna take you somewhere." Drew turned the truck onto a backroad.

"Where is it?"

"It's just up the road," Drew said.

We drove a couple of minutes and then he turned again onto a narrow road. Surrounded by trees on both sides, the road ended at an old, abandoned farmhouse among a level clearing. Drew parked the truck and took my hand. "Follow me." Sliding out of the truck, Drew led me past the house to another wooded area.

"Drew, whose place is this, and why are we here?"

"It's my family's land. And you're about to see why we're here." He led me through a dense, overgrown area. "Just a bit farther and you'll see." We walked a few more steps and I gasped. Surrounded by trees, we stood on a hillside overlooking a creek rippling between the hillside and bluff. Traipsing down the hillside, Drew guided me along a narrow path. At the end, water rushed from the side of the rock wall into a natural basin of water that fed into the creek.

We sat on a rock beside the spring, enjoying the view. I leaned back and propped my arms behind me, inhaling. The clouds shifted in the sky, allowing the sun to warm me.

"You like?" Drew asked.

I nodded and smiled at him. "It's beautiful."

"It's my favorite place. I come here to, you know, get away. Not think so much."

"I see why. It's so serene."

"Serene, that describes it perfectly."

I narrowed my eyes. "Tell me, Drew, why do you need serenity?"

"I don't know. Doesn't everybody at some time or another need to escape stuff?"

"Stuff? What stuff do you wanna escape?"

"Aw, just stupid stuff."

"You don't seem like you would have any stuff, Drew. Let alone stupid stuff."

"Not everything's how it seems."

From my vantage point, Drew had everything going just right. Not like me, who was a total mess. Drew picked up a rock and tossed it into the water. Grabbing a handful of rocks, he kept tossing them in. The rocks hitting the water's surface splashed and disrupted the trickling rhythm of the creek.

"Zinn?"

"Hm?"

"You ever wonder why certain things happen?"

"What do you mean?"

"Like us meeting this year?"

Puzzled by Drew's statement, I waited for him to explain further.

"I'm not sure you would've liked me if we'd met before."

I straightened myself to a seated position. "Of course, I would've liked you."

Drew's eyes narrowed and his brow furrowed. "I was very different before we met."

"I doubt you were that different, Drew. People don't change that much."

"I hope that's not true."

"Drew, whatever you did, it's in the past. You obviously aren't that person deep down."

"Maybe," he remarked. "I'm just glad we met now and not then."

"I don't think it would've mattered. I see who you are. That's not something you can fake."

His gaze focused on the water as he threw another pebble. "Just the same. I'm glad we met now." Pushing himself off the rock, he took my hand. "Let's walk some more."

We followed the edge of the meandering creek until we came to a cluster of large rocks where the light streamed through the treetops. Drew jumped onto a rock, reached down his hand, and helped me up. We lounged on the rocks, enjoying the sun, while Drew softly hummed. I closed my eyes and soaked in as much of the moment as I could, reminding myself to keep moving forward.

"You okay in there?" Mom asked, tapping on the bathroom door. "You've been running that water for a long time. Making sure you didn't fall into the sink!"

"Yeah, just splashing some water on my face to wake up. I was up late watching a movie for my econ class," I answered.

"Okay, as long as you don't have a headache! I'm going to leave for church, so I'll see you around noon," she said.

"Nope, no headache!" I called out, glad to have the house to myself for a while. And glad she let me off the hook for church too.

"Love you!" Mom called out. I smiled and repeated the same back to her, then climbed back into my cozy bed.

Closing my eyes, I let my mind wander to being at the creek with Drew. Suddenly, Bryce was in my face yelling insults. My eyes shot open. My Janis Joplin poster on the pale-yellow wall brought me instant relief. *It was just a dream.* My breathing slowly returned to normal, but yesterday's incident with Bryce still loomed. Grabbing my phone to text Drew, the spam of texts from Bryce sickened me. More of the name-calling and cursing tirade filled my screen. I turned off the phone as tears poured from my eyes. Oreo jumped beside me and curled himself under my arm as I drifted in and out of sleep. Oreo's growl woke me, and there was Mom standing beside me, brushing the hair out of my eyes.

"You okay, bug?"

"Yeah." I opened one eye to bring her into view.

She kissed my forehead. "I'm gonna make some lunch. I'll holler when it's ready." When she got to the door, I softly said, "Mom?"

"Yeah?" she replied, smiling.

Tears streamed down my face as the words came flooding out like water rushing from a dam. All the details of Sam and Bryce and the fight shot from my mouth. Mom calmly listened as I told her every-thing that had happened. She let me say it all without getting mad. She didn't cry; she just listened. When I finished, she stood and nodded her head.

"Zinn, I'm trying to stay calm, so give me a minute." Mom paced the floor and wrung her hands, then sat down on the bed and touched my arm. "First, how's your arm?"

"It's fine."

"Okay, good." She walked to the window and then back to the bed, smiling but concerned. "Here's the thing. You are done with Bryce, you understand? No more." I nodded. "And as for Sam, well, I'm still thinking on that." She shook her head and began pacing around my room. "I'm not sure what she was thinking, but knowing Sam, I have to believe Bryce used her to get to you."

I shrugged my shoulders. "Maybe, but Sam was way more worried about Bryce than me. How could she do that? She's supposed to be my best friend."

"I get it. You felt betrayed. Sam wasn't there for you. But give it some time and hear what she has to say."

I crossed my arms in front of my chest. "Well, I'm not ready to talk to her."

"I understand, and you don't have to talk until you're ready." Mom leaned over kissed my forehead. "Just don't be mad too long. Sam may need her best friend soon."

I couldn't argue with her because she was right. I was done with Bryce, but I did need some time before I could hear what Sam had to say.

As she left my room, I grabbed my journal from the floor and read over what I wrote last night. Several phrases jumped out at me, so I copied them on another piece of paper. I fidgeted with the pen while the warmth of the sun through the window drew me to it. The clear sky and bright sunlight called to me. With paper in hand, I picked up my guitar, went downstairs, and headed to the backyard.

Settling myself at the table under the maple tree, I laid the scribbled words in front of me. I strummed the guitar strings and pain shot through my arm. As I straightened my arm to relieve the discomfort, an image of Bryce flinging my arm flashed in my memory. Gritting my teeth, I strummed again. The pain was bearable, but it was also inspiring. As I played the guitar, the pain fueled the words.

I walked up to you and looked you dead in the eyes
Smiled and said we're through and this is goodbye.
Call me cold and heartless, but I've gotta say
That look of shock on your face made my day.
This thing between us, it's so over . . . I'm done.
You used all your chances, now you're down to none.

Humming the melody, glimpses of Bryce's verbal attacks replayed in my mind. Things I wished I'd said to him came pouring from me, filling the paper, and prompting more lyrics. Engrossed in my writing and playing, the tap on my shoulder surprised me. There stood Drew, smiling, quietly watching me.

"Workin' on a new song?"

"Um, yeah." I sat the guitar back on the table. "What're you doing here?"

"Been texting you for like an hour. You never replied, so I decided to take a chance and see if you were home."

"Oh yeah. I turned my phone off."

"Aw, ignoring me, huh?"

"Not at all!"

Drew smiled and sat beside me.

"Wow, your lip! It's hardly noticeable," I said, astonished.

His hand rushed to his mouth. "*Hmph*, must've been the good nursing." Drew smiled and winked.

I leaned closer to Drew. "You don't even look like you got hit."

"You prefer me beat up?" Drew asked.

"No, I'm just shocked is all. There's no swelling or sign of the cut."

"Aw, I'm a fast healer." Drew grabbed the journal and scanned it. "What are you working on?"

"Just some lyrics that came to me."

"Intense," Drew replied.

"That would be a good description."

"Let me hear them."

"Um, still working on the melody."

"What I heard sounded good." Drew placed his hand on the guitar. "You mind?"

"Go ahead. You can't make it sound any worse."

"So, D?" Drew's fingers nimbly picked across the strings of the guitar. "You sing."

I sang the melody, and he hummed some harmony. We piddled with the chords and melody. Drew chimed in a line that prompted me to write another verse. With Drew's help, the song began to take more shape, but it was still missing a chorus. As I made some notes on the page, Drew strummed a rhythmic melody and started humming.

"I think I know that song. What is it?" I asked.

"From the day at the park, 'No Hard Feelings.'"

Drew started singing with the guitar. It had a fantastic melody with bewitching lyrics. I loved Drew's singing, but something about the song haunted me. The lyrics totally drew me in, then they lost me. When the song ended, he gently wiped the tear from my cheek.

"Why so sad?"

"I don't know. The lyrics, they threw me."

Drew raised an eyebrow. "What do you mean?"

"The song speaks to me, but it also confuses me. Like it's missing a piece, and I'm waiting for the rest of the story."

"Interesting," Drew said.

"It's just weird to be so conflicted about a song, you know?"

Drew nodded. "I get it, but maybe don't think about it so much and just enjoy the song."

From the back door Mom interrupted us. "Drew, wanna stay for supper?"

"Thanks, Ms. Erica, but I don't wanna intrude," he replied.

"No intrusion! We've got plenty."

Drew glanced at me with a questioning look. I smiled and then yelled out, "Set another place, Mom! He's gonna stay."

Grandma sat at the dining room table. "Zinnia Rose, who's your friend?"

"This is Drew Behr, Grandma," I replied. "He's a friend from school. Drew, this is my grandma, Rose Goodwin."

"Nice to meet you, Mrs. Goodwin. I see where Zinn gets her pretty eyes."

"Well, aren't you a charmer?" Grandma said with a smirk. "From your looks alone, I would have pegged you for a Behr! You must be related to Earl Behr, yes?"

"Yes, ma'am! He's my grandpa."

"Earl and I were in school together. You favor him quite a bit."

"I get that a lot." A completely relaxed Drew chatted with Grandma.

"How is Earl?"

"A little lonely since my grandma died, but he's doing good."

Mom walked in carrying a platter. "Hope you like pork chops."

Drew stood and took the platter from her hands, then set it on the table. "Love 'em."

Mom smiled. "Thank you, Drew." Looking to me, she said, "Zinn, help me with the rest?"

"Can I help?" Drew asked.

"You've helped enough. Just sit and keep my mother company," Mom said as she and I went into the kitchen. Drew talked with Grandma while Mom and I brought the rest of the food to the dinner table.

Grandma dominated the conversation during dinner as she told stories about herself and Drew's Grandpa Earl. Her eyes lit up as she relived the memories, and Drew listened intently. *Look at him laughing with Grandma . . . He's so sweet.* Drew's eyes cut to me. He flashed that adorable smile as he winked. *And so cute.*

CHAPTER SIXTEEN

An array of reds and yellows painted the sky as Drew and I took Oreo on his walk. I shivered as the temperature dipped with the disappearance of the sun. Drew slid off his sweatshirt and wrapped it around my shoulders.

"You'll get cold in only a T-shirt," I said.

"I'm warm enough." Drew smiled.

"Thanks." Handing him Oreo's leash, I slipped the sweatshirt over my head. The musky, spicy smell of Drew lingered on the material. The shirt completely swallowed me and practically went to my knees. Our hands touched as I took the leash from his hand. I caught him looking at me. He was always looking at me! The intensity of his blue eyes made me feel lightheaded. I bit the corner of my lip. He lightly brushed the hair out of my eyes and touched my cheek.

"It's barely noticeable now. You're almost healed too."

"Um, yeah," I whispered. "Almost."

As the gaze of his blue eyes swallowed me, I held my breath as his weight shifted and he moved closer to me. My chin naturally tilted up to maintain eye contact as he stood over me. The heat from his breath when his lips parted made me swallow hard. As my eyes closed, Oreo started barking aggressively. His leash jerked from my hand as he ran toward a cat down the road.

"Oreo, no! Oreo, come here!" I ran after him as fast as I could while Drew passed me on my right. Oreo moved closer to the intersection, and a car came speeding down the road.

"Oreo!" I screamed as the tires screeched. The car stopped and I halted. Oreo wasn't anywhere to be seen. An older man got out, walked to the front of his car, and looked underneath the vehicle. I stood in the middle of the road with a sick feeling in my stomach. Inhaling deeply, I took off running toward the car.

Please, let Oreo be okay!

The man muttered something to himself and then to Drew, who was standing on the other side of the road with his back to me.

"I'm fine, sir," Drew said.

Drew turned around, and in his arms he held Oreo. The tension escaped my body as my pace slowed. The conversation between the man and Drew became louder the closer I got.

"Did I hit the dog?" the man asked, panicked.

"No, sir, the dog's fine." Drew rubbed Oreo's ears.

The older man looked again under the front of the car and shook his head. "I could've sworn I hit something."

Drew bent down and looked too. "Everything looks fine, sir. Maybe it was a stick."

"*Humph*." The man shook his head and gave Drew a questioning look. "You sure you're fine?"

"Yes, sir. Perfectly."

"Well, if there's no harm, I guess I'll be on my way."

"Have a good evening, sir."

The man climbed back in his car, still dazed. "You too."

As the car pulled away, I had finally made it to the intersection. Drew crossed the road back to me and placed Oreo in my arms. Oreo nuzzled up against me as I checked him for any injuries. He didn't have a scratch on him. Drew was right. Oreo looked fine.

Immediately, I questioned Drew. "What just—" Completely confused, I fumbled with finding the words. "What exactly . . . ? Can you explain what just happened?"

"What do you mean?"

"How?"

"How *what?*" Drew replied casually.

"The car! Oreo! Oreo was—" My head shook. "You were just in front of me, then you were on the other side of the road."

"I'm fast." Drew winked at me.

"But Oreo was running. How did you get to him so fast?"

"I wasn't that far from Oreo. Besides, you froze."

I stood in front of Drew. "I didn't freeze."

"Uh, yeah, you did."

My interrogation proved pointless because Drew clearly had no intention of telling me what had just happened. As I bent down to put Oreo down, some blood puddled on the ground next to Drew.

"Drew, your leg is bleeding!"

He looked at the leg. "Yeah, I had a cut on it. It must've opened up when I was running."

"Your jeans are torn," I retorted.

"Old tear." Drew took the leash from me. "Better get Oreo home."

"But you're bleeding. At least let me look at it." I knelt to look at his leg.

Drew stepped back and shook his head. "It's nothing. Don't worry about it."

"Drew, what's going on? Did you get hit?"

"Zinn, your imagination is running wild. No wonder you're such a good writer." Drew laughed as he stepped farther from me.

"You're avoiding my question."

"No, Zinn, I'm not avoiding anything. There's nothing to tell. Besides, I think Oreo wants to get inside. C'mon, Oreo, let's go." Drew took off in a run with Oreo chasing after him.

"Drew Behr, answer my question!" I yelled.

Running backward, he faced me and laughed. "You're cute, you know that?"

"You can't charm your way out of this."

"Oh, can't I?"

Finally, I dropped it. No point in trying to get Drew to talk right now. Besides, I couldn't prove anything anyway, so I kinda had to trust his story for the moment. Of course, it wouldn't keep me from wondering or even trying to figure it out.

Drew left Oreo and me at the porch. He said goodbye and I went into the house. Mom and Grandma Rose sat in the living room, so I joined them and plopped in a chair.

"Your young man was nice company, Zinnia Rose." Grandma sat in the recliner as she crocheted.

"Um, he's not *my young man*, but yeah, he's nice."

"Well, either way, I approve," Grandma said.

"Zinn, everything all right?" Mom glanced up from the book she was reading.

"Yeah, I'm fine.

Mom went back to her book. I straightened myself in the chair and cleared my throat. "Mom, you ever heard of the Beast?"

"The Beast? The Beast of Bargeston?" Mom closed her book and set it on the table. "That story is still going around, huh?"

"Of course that story is still around. The Beast is a legend," Grandma chimed in.

"You know about the Beast, Grandma?"

"Of course I know about the Beast." Grandma crocheted while she talked. "I saw one once."

"You never told me you saw a Beast," Mom said. "Why didn't you ever tell me?"

"I never told anybody," Grandma retorted.

"You saw a Beast and never told anyone? Why not?" I interjected.

"I suppose I didn't think anyone would believe me."

"What happened?"

"It was a long time ago. I was around ten or eleven years old." Grandma stopped crocheting and stared at me, then her eyes shifted upward as the words flowed from her. "I was walking home from my friend's house around dusk. I had to pass through a wooded area that always made me nervous, but this time I got really scared 'cause I heard some rustling in the woods."

"What was it?" I asked.

"I didn't know, but it scared me enough that I started running. The next thing I know a bobcat emerged from the woods, and I froze.

Then I heard screams and realized it was me. Just as the bobcat came lunging toward me, a hairy creature came from the woods. With his massive arms, he grabbed the bobcat and flung him away from me. Then he and the bobcat started brawling. I stood there and watched the fight in horror. Then another hairy creature picked me up and carried me safely to the nearest house, unharmed. As he carried me, I knew it was a Beast. He looked like a hairy man and had the brightest eyes I'd ever seen. When we got near the house, he set me down under a large tree and ran back toward the fighting. When he left, I stood on my porch, feeling out of breath, questioning how I even got home. *Was I brought there by the Beast?* I kept asking myself. Or was I making up a fantastical story? I caught my breath, went inside, and never spoke about what happened."

"Grandma! You saw two Beasts and you never told anybody?"

"Not til today," Grandma declared.

"I can't believe you never told me." Mom's face revealed a look of shock.

"You never asked," Grandma said nonchalantly as she went back to her crocheting.

Mom stood, stunned, shaking her head, then walked toward the kitchen in a daze. I sat with Grandma, asking for more details. Then I shared my Beast story with her. We talked for a long time, and then Grandma's eyes starting slowly closing. I leaned over and kissed her forehead. "Thanks for the talk, Grandma. I'm going upstairs. Got some homework."

Grandma nodded her head as she began moving her crochet hook again. "Well yes, sweetheart, you go. Don't let an old woman keep you from your studies."

I settled into bed and Oreo curled up beside me and laid his head in my lap. As I rubbed Oreo's soft fur, the image of him running in front of the car came to me. How did Drew manage to get to Oreo in time? There was no way he could run that fast. My head swirled trying to make sense of the whole incident. Drew standing on the other side of the road . . . The man getting out of the car and looking under it . . . wondering what he hit. I wasn't imagining anything. The man definitely hit something. I examined Oreo carefully and found no blood or scratches. He was completely fine! What was Drew not telling me?

As more questions flooded me, I grabbed my computer from the floor to check out the Beast website again. Jake's site had so much information: links to resources, videos of interviews, and photos of sighting spots. While there were no photos of the actual Beast, several accounts had detailed descriptions of what people had seen, some even uploaded drawings of the Beast. People described the Beast as having a massive physique, being somewhat hairy, and capable of super-speed and super-strength. Some depicted the Beast as a "wild man" or an ape-like creature. A couple of the stories told of the Beast being injured but then appeared to heal and recover rapidly. There were posts that included stories of generational sightings dating back over one hundred twenty years. One man's story included his uncle's letter that was dated 1901. It fascinated me.

As I read the stories, I noticed the common denominator was that they felt rescued by the Beast, just like Grandma's story. No one described an attack by the Beast; instead, they described the Beast appearing from nowhere and saving them from some type of harm or threat.

The research overwhelmed me as I thought about what had transpired with Drew and Oreo. Drew's evasion of my questions. The driver thinking he'd hit something. Drew's injured leg. How did Drew end up on the other side of the road holding Oreo? Oreo curled up on his pillow fast asleep didn't stop questions from coming to me. The next time I saw Drew Behr, he wouldn't be able to use his charm to keep me from getting my answers.

My racing thoughts kept going. Drew running toward me the day in the park had some mystery about it. He came from the very same direction that I had come from. How did I not register it that day? His ripped and stretched shirt, which I wrote off as roughhousing in football. His statement about me being scared by what happened, as if he already knew what had happened. All the facts had more questions swirling through my head as I relaxed in the comfort of my bed.

Eager to get to school on Monday, I planned to ask Drew exactly what had happened with Oreo. When I got to econ, Drew was talking to some guys. I settled in my seat and waited for him to come to his desk.

"Mornin', Zinn," Drew said. "Hey, would you feel out my arm?"

"What's wrong with it?" I touched it but was unsure why he asked.

"Oh, nothing. I just wanna tell my friends I've been touched by an angel."

"That's so cheesy," I said.

"The cheesiest," Drew said with a big grin.

Enough distractions, now I would get my answers.

"So, Drew, I have a question."

"Shoot."

"Yesterday, how did you get to Oreo so quickly?"

"I just did," Drew replied.

"Yeah, but he was about to be hit by that car!"

"Zinn, you were scared. You're remembering it incorrectly."

"Drew, I know what I saw," I said loudly, causing several eyes to shoot my way. I lowered my voice. "Just tell me what happened, Drew."

"I really don't know what to tell you, Zinn. I've told you exactly what happened."

"No, you didn't. You're not telling me anything."

He turned and faced me. With sympathetic eyes and kindness in his voice, he said, "Okay, what do you want to know?"

"How did you get on the other side of the road?"

With no hesitation, Drew recalled the moment with complete clarity. "You were yelling for Oreo when he was in the road. You ran for a bit, then you stopped, and I kept running and picked him up."

Throwing more questions at him, he replied with total ease. Frustration grew inside me since my interrogation got me nowhere. My last-ditch effort came when I asked about the man. That's when Drew wasn't so convincing.

"Okay, but how do you explain that man thinking he hit something?"

"I don't know. He was an old guy. He was just confused."

"But your leg? It was bleeding."

"Zinn, my leg is fine. I had a small scratch that opened when I ran, and it bled a little."

"Drew, it wasn't a little blood. There was a pool of blood on the road."

"Wild imagination, girl." Drew shook his head.

Here we go again. Stop trying to distract me.

"I'm not imaging it. Your leg was bleeding."

Drew pulled up his pant leg. "There's nothing wrong with my leg, Zinn. I told you it was just a scratch.

His leg revealed a small scabbed spot. It undoubtably hadn't been hit by anything, especially not a car.

I shook my head. "It doesn't make sense."

"You were really scared about Oreo. And your whole weekend was full of stress. Also, you're still recovering from a concussion."

"That's true." My head shook. *This concussion has rattled my brain, for sure. There's no way what I'm thinking could be true, could it?* "It's just, um, I don't know. I could've sworn you were beside me when the car's tires screeched."

"C'mon, Zinn, don't tell me you can't be wrong. I know you're incredibly amazing and practically perfect, but surely even you've been wrong before?"

"Yes, I've been wrong," I conceded with frustration.

"Good."

"Oh, and why is that good?"

"If you're not so perfect, then maybe I do have a chance," Drew said as he winked at me.

"Um, what?" As the words slipped from my mouth, I tried my best not to show shock.

"A chance. A chance that we can go out?"

"Um, go out?" Another shockwave ran through me.

What is going on? Is Drew asking me out?

"Well, you've had time to consider going with me to Bargeston Day," Drew said. "So how 'bout it?"

Bargeston Day, of course. That glimpse of hope withered away quickly.

"Um . . . Well, I wasn't sure you really wanted to go."

"Not go? You serious? Like Haley said, *It's the best.*"

I offered a weak laugh as the confusion consumed me.

"So how 'bout it? Wanna go with me?"

"Yeah, I'll go with you." I smiled nervously.

"All right! We'll go on Saturday, deal?" Drew stated.

I nodded as I tried to play it cool. *What is going on? Is this a date date or friend date?*

Class ending didn't end my mental torture. Drew explained he had to meet with the counselor, which left me walking to class alone. More time to replay the whole econ conversation.

At the end of the hall, I turned toward the history classroom. A group of football players stood along the wall. Dawson caught my eye and made his way toward me.

"Yo, Zinn! How's it going?"

"Good," I said.

"I heard you took a nasty fall," Dawson said.

"Um, yeah, it wasn't real fun."

"Glad you're back. Missed seeing you and your gorgeous smile."

My eyes widened and my stomach tightened. *Ugh, not in the mood for this!* "Uh, thanks."

Dawson grinned at me. "Keep smiling, Zinn."

The heat rose in my cheeks. I kept walking, and he stayed beside me wearing a smug smile. Finally, we arrived at my classroom door.

"Um, well, I'm here so . . ." I said awkwardly, hoping he'd leave.

"I'll leave you to it then. Catch you later, Zinn." He nodded confidently, as always, then walked across the hall and disappeared into the classroom.

What is going on? First, Drew and the whole Bargeston date-or-not-date thing, now Dawson telling me he missed me. Both of them showering me with attention on the same day. Of course, everything with Drew over the weekend loomed over me. None of this making sense made for a very confusing Monday morning. Then there was the whole Bryce thing. It had ended, but just barely. The emotional overload was almost too much. I needed to distract myself from the craziness of boys. *But how?*

At lunch with Savage, I talked incessantly. In normal fashion, Savage listened attentively. While I chatted away about whatever came into my head, Ashlynn popped down beside me.

"Savage, can I get a ride home today? Car's in the shop." Savage gave a nod as Ashlynn turned her attention to me. "Hey, Zinn, heard about this weekend. Sounded pretty drama-filled. Must've been totally terrifying." Savage cleared his throat, and Ashlynn gave him a look I couldn't translate. They really did have some sort of telepathic thing going on, or at least a silent eye-contact code.

"Sorry, not meaning to be nosy," Ashlynn added.

"It's fine," I said.

"Be honest. How you doing with it all?" Concern filled her eyes.

"For the most part, still processing, you know?"

"Well, yeah, you are. How could you not be? Drew said you handled it amazingly." As Ashlynn kept chattering, I had stalled on her words about Drew. *He thought I handled it amazingly. Didn't Drew see the ball of nerves I was?* He had to know I felt helpless until he showed up.

"Well, I'd better go. Zinn, I'll text you later, 'kay? And Savage, I promise I won't be late."

"Hmm," Savage replied.

No doubt Savage had an interest in Ashlynn's comments, but he wouldn't ask. Instead, he would wait until I wanted to talk. I squirmed in my seat and bounced my leg up and down, then I erupted. "You're probably wondering about this weekend."

"Hmm, not my business."

"You talk to Drew?"

Savage nodded.

"I guess you know Drew and Bryce kinda got into it?"

"Hmm, I heard something about that," Savage said.

"What all did Drew say?"

Savage looked at me and shrugged his shoulders. His only intention was to listen.

"I suppose Drew told you about Bryce grabbing me?"

"Hmm." Savage nodded.

I waited for him to say something, anything. But he didn't, so I did. I rambled on about the horrific event. Savage kept his controlled, calm demeanor, but a few times that fiery glint filled his eyes. "You know, what Bryce did really sucked, but the worst was how Sam responded." I paused for a second and then exploded with more of my frustration. "I don't even know why I'm surprised. She made it pretty obvious she doesn't want to be my friend anymore. She didn't believe me when I told her about Bryce in the first place. And now she's taken Bryce's side."

Savage's eyes bore into mine as his mental wheels churned. "What are you wanting to say, Savage?"

"Hmm, maybe it's not what it seems."

I gave him a defiant stare. "It's totally what it seems. You didn't see Sam. She was more worried and concerned about Bryce. She said nothing loving or supportive to me," I retorted.

"You're upset?"

"Yes, I'm upset. She made her choice, and she chose his side."

"What about Sam's side?" Savage countered.

"Sam's side? This is about me and Bryce."

"Hmm, is it?"

"Ugh, Savage! You're not making any sense. This is about me and Bryce."

"Hmm. Okay then." But he didn't agree with me. That much was clear.

"Sam had no right to get involved. She stuck her nose in something that wasn't her business."

"Hmm."

"Ugh, stop with the *hmm*, would you?" I blurted out loudly. "Why can't you just say what you think?"

"I think you should give Sam a chance to explain." Savage's words pierced my soul. I squirmed in my seat, trying to break eye contact, but it was useless. His eyes remained locked on mine.

I cleared my throat, lifted my head, and straightened my shoulders. "I'm done talking about this." He nodded but didn't seem irritated. *How can that be?* We sat silently for a couple of minutes until I said, "Okay, I'll give her a chance to explain."

Savage's smile didn't lessen my annoyance.

His words echoed through my head as we walked to class. *Give Sam a chance to explain.* The word *chance* stood out, just like Drew's word, *hope*. A quiet stillness came over me as my anger began to extinguish with each breath I took.

Savage looked at me with a heightened level of intensity. Then, he softened a little and gave me an understanding nod paired with his relaxed smile. Without me having to say anything, Savage somehow knew what was going through my mind.

I sighed and whispered, "Chance and hope."

CHAPTER SEVENTEEN

Bargeston Day had arrived, and the distraction of a day with friends had me excited for the first time in a long while, at least partially. The whole Sam thing loomed in the background. A week since the incident at the restaurant, and I still hadn't connected with her, making it that much worse. Anytime I went to text or call her, my stomach got twisted in a knot. While staying in permanent limbo had its appeal, the eventuality of texting her was my reality.

It was only noon—three hours before Drew would be picking me up for the festivities. Restless, I grabbed my phone to help kill the time. Scrolling through the feed, a photo of Sam standing between Bryce and Emma at a party popped up. I clicked on Sam's page. There were no other posts since I had moved, only this one. Most of her other photos were of us. Photo after photo featured the two of us at school, on weekend trips, at ball games, enjoying summers at the pool, and spending holidays together. Any big event where Sam posted a picture, I'd always stood right there with her. Not anymore.

I opened my messages and sent Sam a text.

Me: Hey 🙂

A couple of minutes ticked by, but nothing came. I dropped the phone on the bed and went to my closet. I had plenty of time before I needed to get ready, but choosing an outfit gave me something to do. I threw a pink T-shirt, striped cardigan sweater, and some jeans on the bed, hoping I wouldn't change my mind a hundred times. I didn't have the mental real estate to think about clothes with everything else going on.

I checked my phone, but it showed nothing. I set it on the desk, grabbed my hoodie, and headed downstairs. Grabbing the leash, I called for Oreo. He got up from his doggie bed and walked over to me, eager to go outside. I connected the leash and I took him for a short walk.

The walk did more for Oreo than me. He seemed happier from the fresh air and exercise while I still felt anxious over Sam's unanswered text! The walk gave her more than enough time to respond, but still nothing. Once back inside, I tossed the phone on the bed and grabbed my computer to work on some homework. Thirty minutes into my history assignment about the Great Depression, my phone vibrated. Quickly grabbing it, I hoped to see Sam's name. Instead, Drew's name appeared on the screen.

Drew: Hey, whatcha doin?
Me: Nothing much. You?
Drew: Wondering if you want to go a little early 😄
Me: Sure, what time you thinkin?
Drew: Now
Me: Now? OK. How long til you're here?
Drew: Look outside…

Outside my window, Drew stood in front of his truck. His eyes scanned up to me, and he smiled and waved. I smiled back and pointed at my phone.

Me: Give me 5 to get ready

Drew looked at his phone, looked at me, and nodded yes. He

perched himself on the hood of his trunk and tapped his wrist, implying he'd hold me to the five-minute window to get ready.

"Mom, I'm going to leave earlier for the Bargeston Day thing!" I yelled.

"Okay, when you leaving?"

"In about five minutes."

Her steps across the hardwood floor warned me she was headed my direction. "What do you mean five minutes?" she said, her head peeking into my room.

"Drew asked if I wanted to go now. He's outside waiting."

Shock came across Mom's face as she walked to the window. "He's outside waiting right now?"

"Mom, I kinda need to get ready." *What is wrong with her?*

She looked at me with concern. "Please promise you'll take it easy. The doctor said rest is crucial for a concussion."

"Mom, it's been two weeks. Stop worrying! I'm fine."

"I know, but I'm a mom. We worry."

I gave her a quick peck on the cheek. "I promise I won't overdo it. Now can I get ready? He's waiting!"

She shrugged her shoulders, glanced out the window, and shook her head. As she walked into the hall, she mumbled something under her breath about boys, worry, and keeping her sanity. *It's kinda nice for her to worry about me.*

Walking to the bathroom, I slid my hair out of the ponytail and shook it loose. Spritzing water on my hair relaxed some of the frizz in the curls. I brushed my teeth, dabbed on some blush, and applied the pink gloss. *That should do it!* I liked wearing makeup, but only a little. Most girls wore more than me, but I always looked like I was playing dress-up with heavily lined eyes and loads of mascara, unless it was for a special event. Still in the mood for the pink shirt and jeans, I put on the soft clothes and finalized it with the striped sweater.

I said bye to Mom and went outside to see Drew lounging on the hood of his truck. I wondered if he ever went out at night and sat on it to watch the stars. If he did, would I ever be invited? Pulling myself back to the present moment, he gave me a big smile. He slid his phone in his pocket and jumped off the truck.

"Five minutes and you look that good? I don't think I could handle what ten minutes would do," Drew declared.

Immediately, my cheeks were heat-filled. With no quip to shoot back at him, I just smiled. He'd left me speechless.

"Ready to enjoy your first Bargeston Day?" he said as he opened the passenger door.

"Absolutely!" I hoped my enthusiasm covered up the nervousness.

Drew shut the door and darted around to his side and climbed into the driver's seat. "This being your first Bargeston Day, I figured you needed the whole experience."

"The whole experience?" I gave him a quizzical look.

"Yes, the whole experience." Drew's eyes glinted mischievously.

"Is that all the information I get?"

Drew gave me a look that confirmed he would not give me anymore information. *Looks like I have to wait.*

We drove across town to the fairgrounds. He parked the truck and we walked across the lot to the entrance. When we hit the crowd, Drew slipped his hand in mine and led us through the chaos of parents wrangling with young children. We went up a slight hill and joined the short line to a ticket booth. After a few minutes, Drew had two orange wristbands. He wrapped one around my wrist and then the other around his.

"This baby is for all the rides you can handle." Drew held up a ticket book. "And this is good for any of these things." He pointed to a sign beside the ticket booth that read:

- Camel Rides
- Giant Slide
- Pumpkin Blasters
- Zip-line
- Bargeston Beast Obstacle Course and Maze
- Bargeston Haunted History Hayride

"You've got to be kidding?"

Drew shook his head. "I'm not kidding."

"Aren't we a little old for most of these?"

"Too old? No one's too old for a camel ride!"

I shrugged my shoulders and laughed, ready to go with the flow. He grabbed my hand and pulled me to the line for the camel ride. After that, we made our way down the list of activities, saving the haunted hayride for after dark with our friends. We road several rides, ate an assortment of foods, and even visited the "exotic" petting zoo.

After several hours of engaging in as many activities as possible, we met up with some friends at the carnival rides. Jules, Blake, Haley, and Ryan were there, along with some others. The area began to fill with more teens as the evening arrived. When the sun set, we made our way to the hayride. Finding a seat on the trailer, I leaned over to Drew. "It's after Halloween. Why the haunted hayride?"

"Oh, this isn't a Halloween hayride. It's a Bargeston Haunted History Hayride."

I stared at Drew, puzzled. "What does that mean?"

"Just wait." Drew flashed his mischievous grin.

"Wait and see, huh?"

"Precisely."

With the trailer full, a middle-aged man stepped up and walked past us, greeting everyone. "Welcome to the Bargeston Haunted History Hayride. I'm Edmund, the teller of tales for this evening." He settled at the front end of the trailer and signaled the driver to commence. As the trailer followed the barely lit path, Edmund quizzed the group with questions on the history of Bargeston. Someone in the crowd gave an answer for each of the questions. *Smarty pants!* As we drove, a loud squawking sound came from the woods.

"Did you hear that?" Edmund shined the flashlight toward the noise.

"What was that?" I whispered to Drew.

"Shh, just wait," Drew said.

More waiting?

"Okay, we're heading into the woods now," Edmund said dramatically.

Hoots and hollers came from the others as the trailer headed toward the trees, surrounding us in darkness. Edmund broke into a vivid description of the legendary Beast of Bargeston. His animated storytelling kept the entire group captivated. "Stay alert for any rustling in the trees. You never know what may come!"

On the other side of the trailer, the trees began to rustle. Suddenly, something flew over the top of my head. Ducking, I screamed. Laughter came from the group as Drew covered my head with his arm. Peeking out from under his arm, I leaned into his chest.

"What was that?" I said loudly.

"Oh, that was a Bargeston harbinger bird," Edmund explained.

"A Bargeston harbinger bird? What is that?" I whispered to Drew.

"You'll see." Drew pulled me closer to him.

Ugh! He's killing me with this wait-and-see junk.

The trailer traveled along the narrow path between the trees. Edmund returned to the story and continued to delight the riders with his frivolous tale. More squawking sounded from behind me. I ducked down again to brace myself for a peck on the head.

"Don't be afraid," Edmund said.

"How am I supposed to not be afraid when something just flew over my head?" I laughingly yelled out to Drew over the rowdy crowd.

Drew grinned and pulled me closer to him. The trailer crept along the path. Edmund's captivating storytelling hooked me. He explained the harbinger bird warned people when a Screecher was nearby.

"A Screecher?" I mumbled.

Edmund described it as dangerous and large Raven-like bird that's known to prey upon the town and stalk the local hero known as the Beast. "Now remember, Screechers prey upon fear. So don't be afraid."

"He's got to be kidding." I shook my head. Drew chuckled and gently squeezed my shoulders as his arm tightened around me.

As the trailer crept along the path, shrieking sounds surrounded us and caused me to lean in closer to Drew's arm. Near the left side of the trailer, something came flying toward Julie and Blake. She screamed, then laughter erupted from the others. The flapping wings kept me on high alert as I scanned the area. The crowd laughed whenever anyone was startled by anything. We rode on with wide eyes as these squawking birds flew around the trailer. Edmund carried on with his story—all the while giving warnings of more possible attacks. The trailer slowed as three people came running up to the group. Frantically, they chattered, "Please, help us! We've just been attacked!"

"Attacked?" Edmund asked in mock shock. "By what?"

"We heard this horrible screeching, and then a huge black bird with enormous claws flew toward our trailer," a man said. "We jumped from the trailer and hid in the woods."

"Sounds like you came across a Screecher!" Edmund declared.

"I don't care what it is. I don't wanna see another one. I'm getting outta here!" the older man said. The three of them ran out of the woods toward the clearing.

I whispered to Drew, "This is starting to freak me out. You gotta tell me what's going on."

"I gotcha." Drew grinned as he wrapped both arms around me and pulled me even closer to him.

We kept moving along the trail, and a loud scream came from the left. About twenty feet from us, a woman ran parallel to the trailer, screaming. Something very large flew above her.

Edmund pointed to the sky and yelled frantically, "Look out! It's a Screecher!"

This large, black dragon-bird thing flew toward the woman. Suddenly, she fell and landed on the ground. She screamed as the Screecher lunged at her. From the woods came a growl, and then a hairy creature emerged.

"It's the Beast!" Edmund yelled.

The Beast ran at the Screecher and knocked it to the ground. The trailer riders exploded with clapping and cheering as the Beast and the Screecher fought. The Beast overpowered the Screecher and caused it to fly backward a few feet. The Screecher lunged at the Beast, who, in return, swiped at the Screecher. Another loud shriek and the Screecher darted away. The Beast helped the woman to her feet, then escaped into the thick of the woods. After the "show," the crowd clapped and cheered. Some other people came running toward the woman and led her away from the trailer.

"Amazing! Not only did we see a Beast, but we witnessed him rescue someone from a Screecher. Folks, I think we can all agree this well-loved legend of the Beast as the protector of Bargeston is more than folklore; it's history!" Edmund yelled out with town pride.

When the trailer came to a stop, Edmund said his farewell spiel. "Enjoy the rest of your evening, kids. Just be sure and watch out for those Screechers!"

Just as he finished his last words, a loud shriek came from the woods. I grabbed Drew and hid under his arms from anything flying. Several chuckled and laughed. As we walked back toward the rides, we replayed the events of the hayride and enjoyed another round of laughs about it all.

"So this story . . . Is there really a screeching bird?" I asked Drew.

"Screecher?" Drew shrugged. "That's what they say."

"You ever seen a Screecher?" I asked.

"Of course."

"You have?" My eyes widened as I waited for his recount.

"Yeah, on the hayride."

"Oh, you think you're so funny." I slapped at his arm, and he half-heartedly dodged it.

We fell a few steps behind the rest of the group. Still wondering about Drew's stance on the Beast, I brought up the subject again. "So aside from the hayride, have you ever seen a Screecher? Or maybe a Beast?"

"Zinn, it's just a story," Drew said. "Local legend stuff. Every town has one."

"So the Beast is legend? But do *you* think the Beast is real?"

Drew narrowed his eyes as he gave his response. "The Beast is as real as someone thinks it is. I mean it's fun, like believing in Santa Claus."

"But you think it's not real, like Santa Claus?"

Drew came to a halt. He shook his head and looked a little frustrated. "Woah, Zinn. I'm not saying that."

Immediately, I perked up. "So you do think it's real?"

"Yeah, I think it's real." Drew's eyes danced as he replied with gusto. "I mean, it's Santa Claus. He brings me presents."

Watching the big grin on Drew's face, I ended the conversation. He took my hand, and we quickened our pace to catch up with the others. We enjoyed the remainder of the evening with rides and games until closing. Drew and I left our friends and walked to his truck. With one hand, I held onto the stuffed, neon-pink monkey Drew had won for me. With the other, I held his hand. When we got to his truck, we sat on the tailgate as we waited for the traffic to disperse.

"How's your song going?" Drew asked.

"Not really going. I've not worked on it since you helped me."

"It's a great song. You should finish it. Maybe even sing in the talent show," Drew suggested.

I snarled my nose as I shook my head. "I'm too scared to perform."

"You shouldn't be. You're incredible."

I shrugged my shoulders.

Drew narrowed his eyes, signifying a question was coming. "You're really scared?" He shook his head in confusion. "But you sing in chorus and in front of me all the time."

"That's different. Chorus is a group. And with you . . . Well, that's safe."

Drew slid off the tailgate and stood in front of me. He placed his hands on my shoulders and stared at me. "Zinn, don't let fear stop you. The songs you write, the way you sing, it's all a gift. Think about if John Lennon, Paul Simon, or Dolly Parton hadn't shared their gifts with the world. What if your words are the very words someone else needs to hear?" Drew's eyes locked on mine as I tried to process all he had said. Within a few seconds, that signature flicker lit up his eyes.

"Zinn, think about it. You may have that song that the world needs. I mean, we wouldn't have the greatest song of all time if Dolly hadn't shared it with the world."

Drew knew just where to hit me with my favorite song: Dolly Parton's, "I Will Always Love You."

"Could you imagine the world's confusion not knowing '9 to 5'? We wouldn't know how to make a living."

I glanced sideways at him and smirked. "You've been working on that one a while, huh?"

Snickering, he just shrugged his shoulders as he opened the truck door.

I slid into the seat and glanced at my phone. Still no text from Sam.

I inhaled, trying to escape the disappointment with no luck. Instead, nightmarish thoughts of Bryce bombarded me. Drew's mention of his favorite moments of the day ejected the bad memories. His laughter about the day's antics filled me with calmness. Good memories from a day with friends instead of being engulfed or fixated on the day's drama was a new kind of day for me. Would a regular, nondramatic day like this ever be the norm for me? I could only hope so.

Hmm, that word again . . . hope.

CHAPTER EIGHTEEN

The days of fall flew into the holiday season and semester exams were around the corner. Sam had texted me a few times, but things were different. She didn't text daily, and I hadn't seen her since our Saturday lunch. While I missed her, I didn't miss the drama. It was a nice break not to be bombarded with the flood of turmoil that followed most conversations with her.

Since I wasn't hanging out with Sam, I had more time for my friends in Bargeston. Haley, Julie, and I hung out a few times a week while Ashlynn, Savage, and Drew filled most of my weekends. Even though the changes in my friend group felt less dramatic and overall easier and safer, I didn't have complete confidence that it was long-lasting. Bryce still had a measure of power over me. The impending fear of what he might do to me or my friends in the future kept haunting me. What if he texted or called? What if he showed up on my doorstep? When I passed a car like his, I held my breath until I saw the person driving wasn't him. Of course, it didn't help that Sam posted pictures of her and him with all our friends at Kowinville regularly, which kept the reminder of Bryce fresh in my mind.

Ashlynn, Drew, and I spent the forty-minute drive to Cookeville laughing and singing. I loved spending time with Ashlynn and Drew, so when she invited me to go Christmas shopping and recruited Drew to drive us, I jumped at the chance. During the ride they bickered a lot, but you could see how much they loved each other.

After exiting our second store, Drew left us to go wait in the truck. Ashlynn and I took our time and perused the different shops. When we finished, we headed to the parking lot. As we approached the truck, Drew was reclining in the seat with his eyes closed. Ashlynn slammed her fist on the hood in jest, and Drew's eyes shot open. Laughing as we climbed into the truck, Drew rubbed his eyes and tried to deny he got startled.

"Did the baby not get his nap?" Ashlynn teased.

Drew rolled his eyes and mumbled something under his breath.

"What'd you say, Drew?" Ashlynn taunted.

"If I'd wanted you to hear, I would've said it louder," Drew retorted.

Ashlynn shot an insult back at Drew, and they got into one of their typical cousin squabbles.

Interrupting the back-and-forth trash talk, I asked, "Drew, did you get all your shopping done?"

Drew held up one bag. "All done."

"What do you mean *all done*? You were in the store for ten minutes. No way you're all done," Ashlynn countered.

Drew held up one finger for each explanation of his gifts. "I got my mom perfume, li'l squirt a Barbie, and the rest are gift cards."

Ashlynn muttered something as she rolled her eyes, and Drew retorted a smart remark, reigniting the quarrelling. Now I understood why Savage took on the parental role in this trio. Drew knew how to push Ashlynn's buttons, but it didn't appear that she felt annoyed by it.

"Who's the little squirt?" I asked, in hopes I could redirect the good-natured tiff.

"My little sister," Drew replied.

He has a sister? How did I not know this? "So how old is she?"

"Drew, you've not told Zinn about Avery?"

Drew shrugged his shoulders, implying he didn't see the issue. Ashlynn was apparently aggravated by it and shook her head. "Zinn, Avery is six and she is the cutest little thing."

"Really, she's a drama queen just like her older cousin." Drew looked at me and winked, instigating her again.

"Whatever, Drew." Ashlynn flicked the back of Drew's head.

He cut his eyes to her and snarled. Lacking the ability to control myself, I burst out in laughter. Drew looked at me conspiratorially, then broke into a smile.

After getting some food, we headed out of the restaurant. Walking to the truck, I patted my pockets. Panicking, I said, "Left my phone inside. I'll meet you at the truck."

Drew nodded, and he and Ashlynn casually walked toward his truck. Inside, I asked the host if a red phone had been turned in, and she looked under the stand. Pulling out the phone, she handed it to me. I expressed my thanks and stepped outside.

Drew and Ashlynn lingered midway in the parking lot. As I headed toward them, the familiar dark-blue car pulled into a space not far from me. I gasped when Bryce emerged out of the driver's side. The annoyed impatience on his face I'd seen so many times turned my stomach. He tapped on the hood and yelled, "Come on already!" The passenger door opened, and that's when my heart sank. Sam stepped out from his car. I couldn't move. Drew and Ashlynn were almost to the truck. Sam and Bryce, distracted in conversation, didn't see me. I held my breath, trying to figure out my escape. I waited for a large hole to open up and swallow me; instead, a wave of nausea hit me as I stood frozen. *Do something. Don't just stand here. Holler for your friends. Look away, dummy. Pick up your feet and run toward Drew.* There was no way out of this. Drew and Ashlynn were unaware of what was happening. I picked up my feet to move toward them, but it was too late. Sam saw me.

"Z, hey!" Sam smiled awkwardly. Bryce's jaw clenched as his eyes cut to her and then quickly to me.

I threw up my hand and mumbled, "Hey."

Bryce rolled his eyes and let out a loud sigh. He forcefully grabbed Sam's hand and she miserably obeyed. "Let's go, Sam."

What is going on? Are they on a date? This can't be real. Sam and Bryce? I stood speechless and motionless. Sam's gaze fell to the ground.

"You got a problem, Z?" Bryce pulled Sam's hand, bringing her closer into him.

My heart felt like it could explode from my chest. I couldn't process what I was seeing or hearing.

Sam cleared her throat and started fumbling with her words. "Uh, well . . . You see, Z, I've not really had a chance to tell you."

"I think it's best if I go," I said weakly.

"Yeah, Zinn, leave. That's what you do best, ain't it?" Bryce huffed. "Let's go, Sam."

"Bryce, let me talk to her, please," Sam begged.

"No, Sam. I said let's go." Bryce tugged harder on Sam's hand this time.

Not sure what came over me, but out of nowhere I erupted. "Bryce, just let her talk, okay?"

With a startled look on his face, Bryce yelled, "What did you say?"

Bryce moved toward me, causing me to jump back a step. My breathing shallowed as the space around me seemed to be caving in.

By this time, Drew and Ashlynn were beside me. Drew spoke calmly, trying to deescalate the situation. "Zinn, let's go, okay?"

Sam begged Bryce to leave, and he hatefully retorted. "Shut up, Sam." Bryce's attention turned to me, and he proceeded to yell insults, as usual.

Drew moved toward Bryce, but I reached and took Drew's hand, pulling him back to me. "Drew, please don't. Let's just go."

Bryce flew into a rage as he ranted obscenities. He paused, and I wondered if he'd been drinking. Then he added, "Trying to make me jealous, huh?"

Heat crept through me, and I gave Bryce a venomous stare. "Are you serious?"

"You're all over him, and you're gonna say you're not trying to make me jealous?"

I took a deep breath and gave Bryce a stern look. "This may be hard for you to believe, but not everything is about you, Bryce."

Bryce blurted more crass words about me and my selfishness. I tightly held to Drew's hand to keep him from attacking Bryce.

Obviously, Sam was concerned about the scene getting out of control, so she spoke up. "Can we calm down and the three of us talk about this?"

Bryce jerked his hand away from Sam's. "Shut up, Sam. This is between me and Zinn."

More anger filled me. "No, Bryce, it's not. There's nothing between you and me. Not anymore. But it looks like you and Sam have something."

Bryce's face filled with red-hot anger. "Sam and I are none of your business."

"I'm done." I walked away with Ashlynn and Drew following behind me.

Sam pleaded, "Z, please, just let me explain!"

"Sam, shut up! There's nothing to explain. Just get in car!" Bryce ordered.

Putting one foot in front the other as his words followed me, tears spilled from my eyes. He yelled more obscenities at me until he redirected them at Sam. The whole scene made me nauseous. I climbed into the truck and slammed the door, but it couldn't drown out Bryce's outburst. The slam of a door finally silenced the yelling. The squeal of the tires made the pit in my stomach come into my throat. Opening the door to get some fresh air wasn't enough to stop it. The sickness spewed from my mouth. As I wiped my mouth with the back of my hand, another wave hit me and I heaved again. A couple more small heaves, and it finally stopped. I remained bent over with Drew beside me, holding back my hair.

"Zinn, you okay?" Drew asked.

That's when my crying turned to sobbing. He leaned down and wrapped his arms around me. I fell into his chest and continued sobbing into his shoulder.

When I had somewhat calmed down, he said, "Let's get you in the truck." Directing me to the door, he helped me into the seat.

"Ash, hand me a water," he said as he gently wiped the tears from my cheek.

He opened the bottle of water and handed it to me, asking me multiple times if I was okay. When I finally stopped most of my crying, he climbed into his seat. Drew's fingers lightly touched my hand. He gave me his signature serious look. That same look he had when I cried about Sam not believing me about Bryce. If only she had believed me then, he wouldn't be yelling at her right now. Turning to the window, tears blurred my view as we drove back to Bargeston.

I couldn't get the image of Sam holding hands with Bryce out my mind. Sam's lack of texts, her avoidance of making plans with me, and her limited conversations with me finally made sense. Sam and Bryce were a thing. It tore my heart in two.

When I got home, the heated conversation with Bryce wouldn't stop replaying in my head. All the words he spewed at me turned my stomach. His threatening looks and physical presence scared me just like when we dated, except this time I stood up to him. I had never done that before. Suddenly, my words were on repeat. I grabbed a pen and scribbled the words, *Not everything is about you, Bryce.*

During all my time with Bryce, everything had been about him, but not this time. I finally said to Bryce what I wanted to say so many times: *Not everything is about you*. I threw the paper and pen back on the desk and climbed into my bed.

When I finally got settled, I set the alarm on my phone and a text from Sam popped up. Her text, trying to smooth things over, made me sick. Her excuses for Bryce, her apologizing for him, and her justification for his behavior slapped me in the face. This was exactly what I had done when I dated Bryce. I made excuse after excuse for the things he said and did. Never once did I hold him accountable for any of his wrongdoings. Instead, I allowed him to treat me horribly. I sat in the bed and cried.

Reading through the texts numerous times, her explanation that things between Bryce and her happened after the day at El Rey's offered little comfort. What did Sam dating Bryce mean for Sam and me? How could we be friends now? I typed a response to her text, but instead of sending it, I hit Delete and threw my phone on the bed.

The next morning, I woke up and my mood was no better. The drama with Sam and Bryce still consumed me. Fumbling with some papers on my desk, I found the sheet with the scribbled words, then pulled out my guitar. Strumming it, I hummed and sang the new line. It was good. Actually, it was perfect. The very line I needed for the chorus. A few more lines came, and I finally had a chorus for the song. Reading over the words, I smiled. Taking a clean piece of paper, I rewrote the lyrics, then put the paper into my backpack. Drew would want to read it and maybe help me with the guitar part.

I silently recalled the most important words I'd written that propelled me forward with the song: *Not everything is about you, Bryce. This time, it's about me.*

When I walked into econ on Monday, Drew stood at Malone's desk. I let them be and settled into my seat. Reaching into my backpack, I found the lyric sheet and placed it on my desk. Within a few minutes Drew came to his desk.

"Morning, sunshine."

"Morning, Drew."

"Oh, that's my new favorite sound. My name on your lips." Drew winked.

"Do you ever stop?"

"Not as long as I can make you smile," Drew said.

Fighting the smile from coming to my lips proved impossible. I shook my head to signify my flustered state, but he already knew it. That's why he smiled knowingly.

"I finished the song." I handed him the paper.

"You did?" As he read it, his eyes narrowed while his head moved up and down, then his eyes widened and he smiled. "Chorus is perfect. It's what the verses needed. Connects it all and totally makes the song."

"Thanks." My face filled with heat. "Could you help me with the guitar part?"

"Absolutely! You wanna come to my house after school?"

"Can't today. Car's back in the shop and Mom's got a late meeting."

"Not a problem. I can take you home after."

I shook my head, but Drew didn't let me say anything. "And don't say no 'cause you don't wanna be a problem, okay? Just say yes."

After giving him a look of concession, he returned with an amused look and replied, "Counting down the hours."

After school, I met Drew at his truck. He turned out of the parking lot, driving away from town. We drove several minutes down a long stretch of highway. Sporadic subdivisions of newly constructed homes broke the view of rolling hills and wooded areas. The truck turned left onto a side road from the highway. Driving about a mile, Drew made a right turn onto a road with a dead-end sign. Passing a couple of houses with large lots of land, the truck turned onto a short gravel drive beside a ranch-style brick home.

The modest home sat among some large shade trees and a wooded backyard. Flowers lined the walkway, and the large wrap around porch invited you to sit and relax amidst the cozy furnishings. As Drew climbed out of the truck, a large black-and-tan dog greeted him.

"Cricket!" Drew said as the dog placed his paws on Drew's chest, appearing to give him a hug.

As Drew moved, the dog lowered to all fours and followed behind him. Drew looked at me. "He's scary-looking, but he's just a big teddy bear. Ain't you, Cricket?"

The dog trounced around as Drew played with him. Showing my hand to the dog, I gently lowered it to his nose. He sniffed it for a moment and then gently nudged it.

"Cricket?" I asked. "Where'd that name come from?"

"Jiminy Cricket from *Pinocchio*. It was my favorite movie when I was a kid."

"*Pinocchio*, really? A puppet seems a little calm for you." I patted Cricket's head.

"Excuse me?" Drew's attempt at feeling offended was futile because his eyes sent a different message. They were bright and happy. "I'll have you know that Pinocchio's very cool, and he wasn't just a puppet."

"So sorry. Didn't mean to slur your hero."

Drew cocked an eyebrow, furthering his pursuit of intimidation. "I'll let it slide this time."

I battled against full-on laughter as I played along with Drew's antics.

"How'd *Pinocchio* make you such a fan?"

"Hmm, I think because he wanted to be a real boy."

"Real boy, huh? You seem more the hero type. Like in *Tarzan* or *The Lion King*."

"Being real is pretty heroic." Drew spoke with an unusual heaviness, which matched the solemnness in his eyes. As we went on, his gleefulness returned.

"Hey, squirt," Drew said to a little blonde girl lying on the floor watching TV.

Her chin was propped on her hands, and her eyes didn't stray from the screen. "Shh, it's my favorite part."

I almost laughed but held it in. Apparently, she was really into the show and hardly acknowledged Drew. She even completely ignored him stepping over her. Suddenly, he scooped her in his arms and threw her on top of his shoulders. Tickling her stomach, she kicked her legs and giggled. "Oh, your favorite part, huh? More favorite than the tickle monster?"

"Don't. Stop it, Drew!"

"Oh, don't stop? Okay, I won't!" Drew tickled her more.

"No, Drew, stop." She giggled as she wiggled in his arms.

Drew slid her down his back and gently onto the couch. "Where's Mom?"

"In her office," Avery said as she looked at me. "Who are you?"

"Hey, manners." Drew scowled at her.

She looked sheepishly at him and then returned her attention to me. She climbed off the couch and walked over to me. "I'm Avery," she announced, then flooring me when she held out her hand for it to be shaken.

I honored the request while replying, "Hi, Avery, I'm Zinn. I love your name."

A big grin filled her face and she wrapped her arms around me. "Are you my brother's girlfriend?"

"Hey, squirt! Stop with the questions," Drew interjected quickly.

"I'm your brother's *friend*," I said.

She took my hand. "You're pretty, Zinn. You wanna watch *Beauty and the Beast* with me?"

"Not now, squirt. We got some stuff to do," Drew said.

Avery pouted as she dropped my hand.

I knelt beside her. "Avery, maybe another time, okay?"

Avery smiled big. "Promise?"

"Promise," I affirmed.

Avery pulled on my arm and motioned me to come closer. She leaned into my ear and whispered, "I think my brother likes you. Do you like him?"

I smiled at her and put my finger in front of my lips and mouthed, "Shhh."

Avery put her hands in front of her mouth and giggled.

"Avery, that's enough. We've got things to do. Leave Zinn alone."

"Fine, but next time Zinn comes over, she's gonna watch a movie with me!" Avery declared.

"Yeah, yeah, yeah," Drew said. "When Mom comes out, tell her I'm downstairs."

"Yeah, yeah, yeah," Avery mimicked with little-girl spunk.

Drew rolled his eyes and motioned for me to follow him to the kitchen. "Want some food or a Coke?" He peered in the fridge.

"Water's fine, unless you have Sprite," I said.

Drew pulled out a Sprite and handed it to me. Then he grabbed two cans of Coke, opened a cabinet, and snagged a bag of chips. "Let's go downstairs."

I followed Drew out of the kitchen and down the hallway. He opened a door to the steps, which led to a large room with a sectional couch and TV on one side, a pool table in the middle, and a six-person table next to a shelf full of games on the opposite side. Drew plopped onto the couch and tossed the bag of chips on the coffee table as he opened his drink. Appreciating the cozy vibe, I sat down next to him, grabbed a coaster, and set the soda can on it. *His mom will appreciate the gesture even if Drew doesn't.* Drew opened the chips and grabbed a handful.

"Want some?"

"I'm good," I said, laughing inside at how much athletes love to shove food into their mouths. Crumbs were already scattered all over.

"Let's look at those lyrics," Drew said excitedly.

Pulling the lyrics from my pocket, I unfolded the paper and set it on the table. Drew walked across the room, grabbed a guitar, and came back to the couch. As he strummed the guitar, I hummed the melody and then softly sang the song. We progressed through the verse with success, and Drew continued playing as I fumbled with making the chorus flow. We spent some time finding the right sound for the words and the right melody for the verses, singing the chorus over and over. After what seemed like an hour, footsteps came down the steps, which interrupted our flow and Drew immediately stopped playing.

"Drew, you down here?" a woman asked.

"Yes, ma'am!" Drew replied.

A tall dark-blonde woman appeared. She smiled and casually walked across the room. "Avery said you had some company?" she inquired.

"Yeah, this is Zinn."

"Hi, Zinn, I'm Melissa."

"Nice to meet you," I replied.

"You're working on a song?" Melissa asked.

"Uh, yeah. Zinn wrote it," Drew said proudly. "Good, isn't it?"

"Very good! I'd love to hear more."

"You'll hear it at the talent show," Drew stated.

"Oh, it's far from ready," I said self-consciously and lightly laughed. "And I've not agreed to that."

"You'll hear it at the talent show," Drew repeated.

I turned and gave Drew a look of annoyance.

"Zinn, knowing my son, I think there's a good chance I'm hearing it at the talent show."

"I'm starting to realize that myself," I said.

Melissa laughed as she ruffled Drew's curls. "Well, I'll let you two get back to it. Supper's ready in an hour. Zinn, you're welcome to join us."

I said thanks as Melissa headed up the stairs. Drew returned his attention to the song, drawing me back to it too. The chorus sounded great, especially with Drew's picking pattern, but it still needed something more. I wrote the line, *I never knew your love came with such a price, let me give you one bit of advice.* Tapping the pen on the table, Drew strummed and sang a line scribbled on the edge of the paper: *You've found yourself in the dirt.* I repeated the words to myself while I hummed the tune. *That's it.* I quickly jotted down the words and created the bridge.

> *I never knew your love came with such a price, let me give you one bit of*
> *advice. Now that you've found yourself in the dirt, know it's cuz your*
> *price is more than your worth.*

"How do you do that?" Drew said.

"Do what?"

"Write these lyrics. It's amazing!"

"It's just words," I said.

"No, it's not just words. It's a story."

"It's not just the lyrics that tell the story. It's the music and the melody. I can write lyrics all day, but I can't always get the sound right. That's where the real talent is, and that's what you're so good at."

"Nah, it's your lyrics. Chords aren't a story. The story's in the words, the right words," Drew confirmed.

"Yeah, but the words are just a story. They need the music to become the song."

He shrugged as his fingers flowed over the strings. "Maybe you're right. But I do know one thing." With jovial eyes, he said, "We make a good songwriting team."

"That I can agree with," I confirmed.

We kept talking until little feet trounced down the steps. "Drew, Mom said dinner's ready." Avery jumped from the landing onto the floor. "Zinn, will you sit by me?" Avery asked as she dashed over to me and grabbed my hand.

"Hey, squirt, she'll sit where she wants."

Avery looked at him and stuck out her tongue. He grabbed her and flipped her upside down. "What have I told you about that tongue, li'l lady?" Drew said.

"Keep it in my mouth or you'll pull it out?"

"Exactly!" Drew flipped her into his arms and slung her around his back.

She wrapped her arms around his broad shoulders and said, "Sit by me, Zinn, please."

"Absolutely," I said.

"We'd better get upstairs before the momster comes out," Drew warned playfully.

"You'd better not let Mom hear you saying that, or she'll pull out your tongue."

As we headed upstairs, Drew very loudly said, "I'm not scared of the momster."

"Drew, what have I said about calling me that?" Melissa lightly scolded.

"I told him not to, Mom," Avery said as Drew placed her in a chair.

"What?" Drew walked over to his mom and hugged her. "You're the best momster I've got."

"Can't you act better around company?" Melissa asked playfully.

"I'm on my best behavior," Drew retorted.

I smiled as he squeezed his mom tight and gave her a kiss on her forehead. Melissa slapped him with a potholder as he darted from her reach. He chuckled and she handed him the salad bowl. At the table, Avery patted the spot next to her, signaling for me take a seat.

"Hey, she's my friend, squirt."

"She's my friend too," Avery said, sticking out her tongue.

Drew cocked his eyebrow and gave a low growl. Avery pressed her lips and put her head down.

"Smells fantastic, Mom," Drew announced.

"Thanks, sweetie," Melissa placed a pitcher of tea and a basket of bread on the table. Handing the basket to Drew, she filled the glasses, then sat and passed the serving dish to Drew. "Avery, napkin in your lap," Melissa said.

"Yes, ma'am," Avery's little voice chimed back.

Drew picked up one of the plates stacked in the middle and scooped a portion of ravioli onto the plate and handed it to his mother. He spooned another portion onto another plate and handed it to me and did the same for Avery. With the last plate in his hand, he scooped three spoonfuls onto it. Sitting the plate in front of him, he winked at Avery.

"Drew, bless the food, please," Melissa requested.

"Yes, ma'am."

The politeness around here is outstanding. Mom would probably appreciate more "yes, ma'am" and "no, ma'am" from me. Maybe I should ask her. Actually, I better not, she might say yes.

Avery slipped her hand into mine as Drew led a short but beautiful prayer. When he finished, Melissa passed the salad bowl around the table. As we ate, Avery chattered about her day at school. Drew interjected some silly comments, making her either laugh or scowl at him. When we finished eating, Avery dragged me down the hall to show me her bedroom. She chatted away about having a big-girl bedspread and showed me all the toys, dolls, and trinkets in her room. She handed me a Barbie doll. "You be her."

"Okay, what's her name?"

"Belle," Avery answered.

"Belle like in *Beauty and the Beast*?"

"Yes!" she said. "And I'll be Elsa. They're best friends, like me and you."

Ashlynn was right about this little girl. She was the cutest thing, but also a little chatter bug. I got an earful about each of her Barbies, her friends at school, and her favorite movies and books. When she told me her favorite thing was her weekly trip to the library with Drew, my heart melted.

Drew entered the room. "Hey, squirt! I gotta steal Zinn from you. Gotta get her home."

"But we just started playing," Avery whined.

"I know, but momster said it's bath time."

"Can I have five more minutes, please?" Avery begged.

"Nope, squirt. We gotta go," Drew said. "Now go find Mom."

Avery stood and wrapped her arms around me and said, "Will you come back over soon?"

"That's up to your brother?"

"Bring her back over, Drew," Avery demanded.

"I will if you get in the bath."

"Bye, Zinn." Avery kissed me on the cheek and ran down the hall.

Drew put his hand out to help me off the floor. As I stood, he held on to my hand. Leading me to the front door, he announced, "I'm gonna get Zinn home."

Melissa came around the corner. "Zinn, don't be a stranger." Then she hugged me.

"Thank you," I said.

"Drew, drive safe," Melissa said as she hugged him. "And don't be late."

"Yes, ma'am. Love you. Be back soon."

The sliver of the moon shone bright in the clear, inky-blue sky with the dark-red glow on the horizon touching the treetops. Walking to the truck, Drew said, "Thanks for being so sweet with Avery."

"She's adorable," I said, "Besides, she's my best friend now."

"I heard. You rank pretty high if she let you be Belle."

"Oh?"

"Yeah, she never lets me be Belle." He paused as he looked at his legs, laughing at the muscles and general "non-Belleness" about his frame.

I giggled as he opened the door to the truck. Climbing into the seat, he quickly made his way around the truck, got in, and pulled onto the main road.

"I really like your mom. She's super sweet," I said.

"Thanks. She is pretty great."

"Where's your dad?"

"Work. He's got some construction job at Virginia Beach," Drew said. "He comes home about once a month, maybe."

Turning on the radio, he increased the volume as we drove to my house. The music, instead of talking, filled our ride home. When the truck turned into my neighborhood, Drew lowered the volume of the radio. He cleared his throat as his fingers tapped the top of the steering wheel. "That was fun," Drew said, looking at the dashboard and not at me.

"Yeah, it was. Thanks for your help with the song."

"It's a good song," he said flatly.

What is happening? Suddenly, he looked at me with a sense of urgency, then got flat again. I placed my hand on the door lever. Clearing his throat, he turned off the truck, signaling me to release the handle.

"How many finals you got?" Drew asked.

"Um, one Wednesday morning."

"You wanna hang out after?"

"Um, I've got plans with Haley." *Did I just turn down a hang or a date?*

"How about Friday?"

"Sure." *Again, what did I just agree to?*

"Cool." Drew opened his door.

I followed suit and climbed out the truck. Drew met me on the side and walked me to the porch in an unfamiliar way. Something was off—strained, maybe? I climbed the first couple of steps as he stopped on the bottom. He took my hand and turned me to face him. Trying to suppress my unease, he caught me by surprise yet again and took both my hands in his.

"Zinn, I wanna say something, okay?" Drew said nervously.

"Okay." Nervousness hit me, but in a giddy way. He was holding my hands!

"Remember the day we took Oreo for the walk?"

Remember? It's kinda hard to forget. Gesturing with a head nod that I did, he continued.

"Well, um . . . You know, there was that moment?" Drew said, nearly stumbling over his words. "Uh, when we, uh, almost kissed."

"Yeah," I said shyly, immediately recalling every detail.

"I just wanna say I'm sorry about that. That was not a good idea, you know?"

"Not a good idea?" I bit the corner of my mouth, fighting the tears and dreading the emotional roller coaster that was coming.

"Yeah, that was a mistake. I wasn't thinking," Drew said.

"Oh?" The lump in my throat almost choked out the word.

"This whole flirtation thing we have going on is fun, but that's all it is, right?"

"Uh, yeah, sure. That's all it is," I repeated, knowing I was lying.

"Glad we're clear on that, you know? Thinking about what Avery said, I just didn't want you to be uncomfortable around me. Since we're friends, you know?"

"Oh yeah, I get it." *No! I do not, in fact, "get it."*

Drew wrapped his arms around me for a few seconds, then stepped backward and smiled. "Well, I'd better get going. Text you later?"

"Yeah." I was speechless, shocked I even got that word out.

As he got in the truck, I walked in the house and darted to my room. Shutting the door, I collapsed in grief and confusion on the bed. Finally, I could cry. *How could I think Drew was interested in me?* I can't believe I was so stupid to think he wanted anything more. The day with Drew, the songwriting session, and meeting his mom and sister meant nothing to him, but I let it mean something to me. Placing the pillow over my head, I screamed loudly and ugly. No doubt Drew didn't want to deal with a basket case like me. He was holding out for just the right girl. I just wished that girl was me.

Oreo whined, but I had no tolerance for him right now. "Oreo, hush!" He whimpered and waddled over to his bed, leaving me to drown deeper into this feeling of hopelessness.

CHAPTER NINETEEN

Finishing my final on Wednesday made me ready to take full advantage of Christmas break. Sleeping late, no homework, and watching movies all day held a fantastic appeal. Haley's need to celebrate everything had reared its excited head. She insisted we go to The Slice and do some Christmas shopping to reward ourselves for completing the semester. So I waited in the student lounge while Haley finished her last final.

With only a few people in there, I found my nook on the couch by the window. I pulled my journal out of my backpack, then slid in my earbuds. With the music drowning out all the noise of the room, I grabbed my pen and began writing. Just barely into it, suddenly someone flopped on the couch beside me.

Dawson relaxed himself into the seat and ignored my desire to shut off all distractions. I pulled out the earbuds and conceded to his demand for my attention.

"Zinn, how you doin'?"

"Um, good. You?"

"Real good," Dawson said with that annoying, cocky grin of his. "Especially now."

I fiddled with my earbud case, trying to avoid him and this weird game he liked playing.

"Studying hard?"

"Uh, no, just doing some writing," I said.

"Cool. Done with finals then?"

"Yeah, you?" *Don't ask him questions. If you shut up, he might leave.*

"Chem today."

I gave Dawson a weak nod paired with a straight face, signifying that I barely cared about this conversation. The silence made me squirm but not so much to force me to break it. My leg started nervously shaking, and my stomach tightened into a ball of stress. Still, he stayed fixated on me. *Why?* A table of irritatingly loud girls in the corner immersed in shallow, silly antics cackled. Suddenly, I wished I was there or anywhere but here with Dawson.

"Big plans for break?" Dawson asked.

"Uh, not really. Holidays are a low-key event at my house," I said flatly.

"I feel ya. It's just me, my mom, and my brothers." Clearing his throat, he continued rambling about nothing. "You'll be around during break, huh?"

I offered a quick bob of my head to say yes. *Sheesh, he makes me nervous.* The slight pain of my teeth pressing into the corner of my mouth somehow brought me comfort.

"Cool," Dawson said. "Maybe we can hang out?"

Dawson propped his arm on the back of the couch and leaned closer to me. I leaned back, and he tilted his head and smiled slyly. *What? Like all the girls want you inches away from their face? Maybe so . . .*

"Could be fun," he continued. "You like to have fun, don't you, Zinn?"

"Um, yeah," I replied, so ready for this ego-stroke charade to be over.

"Cool!" He smiled and finally leaned back, but just a little. *Ugh!*

The heat rose up my neck and into my cheeks, and my breathing became shallower the longer he sat there.

"I'll hit you up over break." He handed me his phone. "Sharing that contact would really help me."

Help him? As if on autopilot, I took the phone and typed my name and number into his contacts. *Stop! Do you really think this a good idea?*

Handing the phone back to him, his fingers lightly touched my hand, but I quickly pulled it away. He smirked as if this was some control game that he was winning. *He is not winning. He just doesn't know it yet.*

I gave another awkward nod of my head. The pressure of my teeth on my lip increased. Dawson kept his eyes locked on me. *Why is he staring?* These silent stares had a slight semblance to conversations with Savage, yet they differed greatly. This brought so many levels of uneasiness. With Savage, the silence comforted and relaxed me, but Dawson's silence suffocated me. These stares felt intimidating and manipulative, almost like a trick. All of a sudden, he gave a "kindly" smile, but as quickly as it came, it went back to being a bold, confident smirk.

"Zinn, relax," he said confidently. "Maybe, don't believe everything you hear about me."

"Um, sorry?"

"*Hmph!* Innocence. I like that."

"Excuse me?" I shot back, narrowing my eyes at him.

The slightest bit of a smirk formed on the side of his mouth. This cool vibe he had going on kept him in complete control, showing little if any emotion. But his eyes—they showed something. It was something hidden and completely different than his cocky persona. Those eyes showed a kindness. *Hmm, there's more to this guy than he lets on.* That intrigued me. *Ugh, no! Don't get pulled in.*

He stood up to leave. "Later, Zinn."

A slight nod was all I could afford him.

As he walked away, I sat there digesting what just happened. Dawson's cocky yet suave behavior certainly had an appeal . . . but it was also icky and dark and untrusting. Was it because he made me a nervous wreck, or was it because Drew told me to keep my distance? Drew . . . Ugh! Drew made things very clear where we stood. He was glad we were only friends. If Drew wasn't in the picture, then what about Dawson? He was exceptionally handsome and had my intrigue. Plus, he flirted with me. But something about him threw me. He wasn't like Drew, or even Savage. Dawson lacked . . . humility, maybe? As I sat there playing ping-pong with my thoughts, Ashlynn walked over.

"Hey, Zinn," Ashlynn said.

"Hey, Ash! You just getting here?"

"Yeah, got my calc final." Ashlynn settled beside me and looked at me with concern. "You were talking to Dawson?"

"Yeah, about finals and break stuff, you know?" *Not completely true.*

Ashlynn's squint had me readying myself for something serious, but she said nothing. Instead, she rattled about her calculus final and cramming all night. Ashlynn, now her bright, bouncy self, had moved on. But I couldn't shake the seriousness she'd laid on me. Why did she care about me talking to Dawson? Did this have anything to do with Drew? *Geesh! Drew again.*

"Zinn, did you hear me?" Ashlynn asked.

"I'm sorry. What?"

"I asked if you wanna come over Saturday?"

"Uh, yeah. Sounds fun!"

We talked about the weekend plans, then the bell rang. Ashlynn grabbed her stuff and said goodbye as I shoved my things into my backpack and headed outside to meet Haley.

My "friends" conversation with Drew ran through my mind again. Weird how nothing with him had changed. We texted daily and still hung out. If only I could stop thinking about him being anything more than a friend, maybe I could open myself up to someone else.

CHAPTER TWENTY

I had a couple of hours before Drew arrived, so I grabbed the stashed presents from my closet. Rifling through the bags, I pulled out the gifts and laid them on my bed. Shoving my hand in the last bag to find the sweater and earrings, I placed them next to the other gifts. I scrambled to find my phone, which was buried among the empty shopping bags. Today was December 20. Tomorrow was "our" Christmas—December 21. I had almost forgotten. I texted Sam, hoping it was the olive branch our relationship needed.

Me: Hey, Sammy! 😊
Sam: Hey Z
Me: What time tomorrow?
Sam: Sorry, can't do tomorrow
Me: What?! But it's Dec 21
Sam: Tomorrow doesn't work
Me: How bout after Christmas?
Sam: I'll let you know. Gotta go…
Me: Okay. Merry Christmas!!!
Sam: Merry Christmas 😊

I folded the sweater and placed it in a bag and set the earrings on top of it. I stuffed some green, red, and white tissue paper into the bag, then set it in my closet on a shelf. I couldn't look at it. *Who knows when I'd see Sam to give her the Christmas gift. Never?* I let my tears run free. December 21 had been "Sam and Z's Christmas Exchange" for the last eight years. Nothing ever came in the way of this tradition. Our families even scheduled around this day. It was our thing. I let out a scream as I slammed the closet door as hard as I could. Exhausted, I collapsed onto the bed, sunk my face into a pillow, and cried.

When I had finally cried most of the tears out, I got up from the bed and went to the bathroom. I splashed cold water on my face. *Get yourself together, Zinn. Everything's gonna be okay.* I took a deep breath and went back to my room. I changed my clothes and slipped on my boots. Grabbing the other presents, I headed downstairs. When I finished arranging the presents under the tree, the doorbell rang. I opened it and there stood Drew and Avery. She squealed when she saw me and wrapped her little arms around me.

"Zinn, can we watch *Beauty and the Beast* today?"

"I can't wait!" I said.

"Told ya!" Avery said as she turned to Drew.

"Watch it, squirt," Drew playfully warned.

"Let's go, Zinn! Drew's gonna take us to lunch." She took my hand in a possessively sweet way.

"Avery, chill. Give Zinn some room." Drew tried to act like a firm parent, but he was smitten with her.

"Okay." Avery dropped my hand and moved closer to Drew and whispered, "Can she sit by me in the back seat?"

"I already told you no," Drew said. "She's up front with me."

I whispered to Drew, "It's fine. I'll sit with her."

"Nope," he said with a smile. "I've already given in on the movie thing. If it were up to me, we'd be watching a thriller—alone!" He gave Avery a smile, indicating he was only joking.

"You don't watch thrillers, Drew!" Avery chimed in. "You watch my movies. I think you like fairy-tale love stories." She gave me a look that said her brother wasn't as tough as he acted, and I winked back my understanding.

Drew opened the truck door and swung Avery by her arms into the back seat.

"Buckle up, squirt," Drew instructed.

"I know," Avery quipped back, sliding into the middle seat.

Avery chattered on about all the things she wanted us to do.

"Where you wanna eat, Zinn?" Drew asked.

"I want Jack's!" Avery announced.

"Avery! Manners!" Drew lightly chided. "It's Zinn's choice."

"Jack's sounds perfect," I said, smiling at Avery.

Drew cut his eyes toward me and smirked. "I guess it's Jack's then."

At Jack's we enjoyed burgers, fries, and shakes, then we headed to Drew's house. We pulled into the driveway beside a black car, one I hadn't seen when I was over the other day.

"Daddy's home!" Avery said as she unbuckled her seatbelt, opened the door, and jumped out of the truck.

"Easy, squirt," Drew said.

As Avery ran toward the house, a dark-haired man stepped onto the porch. "Daddy!" she cried out, and he swooped her up in his arms and hugged her. Drew and I walked toward them.

"Drew, who is your friend?"

"This is Zinn, sir," Drew responded rather formally.

"I see," the man said.

"Zinn, this is my father."

The man nodded. "Zinn, nice to meet you. Name's Tim Behr. My son obviously doesn't remember how to do a proper introduction."

"Hello, Mr. Behr," I greeted.

"Um, sorry, my bad. Uh, I mean, yes, sir." Drew fumbled with his words as his eyes darted all over the place while rubbing the back of his head. Lighthearted, fun-loving Drew had been replaced by this awkward, nervous guy. *What is going on?*

"Drew, I'm sure Zinn is getting cold standing outside."

"Um, yeah! Let's get inside, Zinn." He moved past his father to open the door.

As I walked past Mr. Behr, he said, "Be patient with him, Zinn. Drew's a work in progress."

I sheepishly smiled and stepped inside the house, unsure of how to respond.

"Sorry about this," Drew whispered as we walked into the living room.

"It's fine," I replied and gave him a smile. I didn't want him to sense my disappointment of this uncharacteristically dark mood, so different than when I was here before.

Drew's eyes were veiled by darkness and his sparkle had gone. He looked almost lost. Avery's chatter filled the room as she fell into her father's arms. Tim—or rather, Mr. Behr, as I felt like calling him—only gave Avery a brief hug, then placed her feet on the floor and directed her to play in her room. *Oh wow! My dad was never like that!*

"Zinn, may I get you something to drink?"

"No, thank you," I said.

He returned to the living room with a glass of water in each hand. He handed Drew one of the glasses as he settled into a chair. "Drew, invite your guest to have a seat," Mr. Behr instructed. *Um, I'm right here, mister! You can talk to me!*

"Um, yeah. Zinn, sit anywhere," Drew said flatly.

"Zinn, please have a seat wherever you wish," Mr. Behr repeated as if Drew had said nothing.

"Um, sorry." Drew's gaze dropped.

"So, what are your plans today, Drew?" his dad questioned.

"Um, not much. Just went to lunch. Probably going over to Savage's in a bit." Drew cut his eyes toward me, letting me know our plans had taken a complete left turn without my input. But I didn't feel hurt, only curious about this whole scene. *Something's off.*

"I see," Mr. Behr said, seemingly uninterested, at least uninterested in me! "Well, tell me about school."

"It's good. All As and one B," Drew replied.

"You got a B, huh?"

"Yes, sir. In English."

"I'm assuming you'll finish the year with all As?"

I couldn't believe what I heard. This man's presence and his pressure were ridiculous, but it wasn't just about grades. He drilled Drew about his workouts, training schedule, sleeping, and eating habits. My whole body tightened just listening to the demands put on Drew.

"I'll do better, sir."

"That's what I like to hear!" He then directed his attention to me. "Zinn, forgive us. Please, tell me about yourself. Who is your family?"

Ha! After ten minutes you finally ask me a question? Nice . . .

"Um, it's just me and my mom. We moved from Kowinville and live with my grandma, Rose Goodwin," I responded as flatly as Drew. I couldn't help it. It was contagious or something.

"Goodwin? Any relation to Hank Goodwin?" Mr. Behr asked.

"Yes, sir. He's my uncle."

"Well, tell me how is Hank? If I remember correctly, he got recruited to play football for Duke?"

"Yes, sir. I think he played a couple of years until he messed up his shoulder."

"What a shame. People thought he might go pro," Mr. Behr said. "Just like we hope for Drew here. That is, if he'll follow the trainer's plan exactly. Isn't that right, Drew?"

Drew gave his dad an affirmative head nod. Mr. Behr returned with somewhat of a scowl that he appeared to be trying to conceal. Drew fidgeted in his seat. "Zinn, we'd better head on." Drew stood to go.

"Uh, okay," I replied, wondering if Avery was getting the movie ready.

What's she going to think with me missing the movie again?

"Drew, don't be late," Mr. Behr stated, his attention on the paper.

"Yes, sir."

"Zinn, pleasure meeting you. And tell old Hank that Tim Behr said hello," Mr. Behr said, glancing up for a few seconds.

"Yes, sir. Nice meeting you," I replied.

"I'm gonna tell Avery bye," Drew said to his father.

Mr. Behr nodded with a grunt as he continued reading the paper. Drew's gaze fell downward as he walked toward Avery's bedroom. Avery sat on the floor circled by dolls and stuffed animals. When she saw us, she jumped up from the floor and bounded over to me.

"Ready to watch the movie?"

"Um, well . . ." I said.

"Hey, Avery, I'm thinking maybe the movie can wait for another day," Drew said as he went down on his knees.

"But you promised we could watch it today."

"I know I did. But we didn't know Dad would be home." Drew took Avery's hand. "And he's only here a few days."

"Yeah, I know," Avery said, her eyes losing all their spark and life.

"I bet Dad would love to read you your new book," Drew offered.

Avery lifted her chin and looked wide-eyed at Drew. "You think so?"

"I think so," Drew confirmed. Avery wrapped her arms around Drew's neck. Drew stood and lifted her from the floor, hugging her tightly in return. She then released her arms from Drew, leaned over to me, and wrapped her arms around me while planting a big kiss on my cheek.

"Zinn, I'm sorry we can't watch the movie today," Avery said, sounding old beyond her years in this moment.

"Oh, sweetie, that's okay."

"You'll come over again and we can watch it, 'kay?" Avery questioned.

"Absolutely," I promised—and meant it.

Drew placed Avery back on the floor. "Now let's find that book and ask Dad to read it."

Stepping to the bookshelf, Avery pulled the book from the shelf and headed down the hall. In a singsong manner, she said, "Daddy can you read me my new book?" She continued chattering about the story as her voice trailed off and mixed with inaudible sounds from Mr. Behr.

"You ready?" Drew forced a smile.

"You sure you don't wanna stay here since your dad's home?"

"Nah, it's all good. Better if we go." Drew's words hung in the air, begging me not to respond further. He motioned toward the door. "Let's go."

We walked to the front door and Mr. Behr's voice trailed from the living room.

"Drew, make sure you're home before dinner is on the table."

"Yes, sir," Drew replied.

"Daddy, keep reading. Clara's just about to go through the secret door," Avery said excitedly.

Drew opened the door and we stepped outside. The brightness of the sun couldn't counteract the cool breeze that engulfed me. I shivered as the wind blew around me. Drew slid out of his jacket and draped it over my shoulders as we walked to his truck. Thankful to have the extra layer of Drew's jacket around me, I slid my arms into it.

"We're going to Savage's?" I asked.

"Um, I don't know, maybe," Drew said. "We don't have to. I just needed to get outta there, you know?"

"Yeah," I lied. His dad was home. He kinda seemed like a drag, but it was his dad. I didn't get why he wasn't spending time with him. I'd give anything to hang with my dad right now.

Drew's normal chattiness was absent. Instead, the only noise was the vehicle on the road. *Should I say something?* He kept his eyes on the road, never once looking at me.

Finally, I cleared my throat. "Drew, you all right?"

His eyes met mine and he said flatly, "Yeah, I'm fine." He said nothing more as he forced out a smile. We drove in silence. *What's the deal with Drew and his dad?* As much as I wanted to figure it out, I couldn't. Drew would have to tell me himself when he was ready.

We rode a few more minutes and then we were back in town. He drove past the school, turned off the main road, and then onto a side street that was hidden from the main road.

"Where are we going?" I asked.

"Here," Drew replied. *A man of many words tonight.*

We came to a small lake nestled in a wooded area. The road ended into a small parking area overlooking the lake. Drew parked the car and turned on the radio at a low volume. He sat silent for several minutes. The oddness of the silence surrounding Drew had me without words. Not sure what to do, I just waited. Drew twisted in his seat to face me, and he finally spoke.

"Sorry about the change of plans."

"It's fine," I replied, hoping he knew I was okay with it all.

"I didn't know my dad would be home today."

"It's okay, really. And I'm fine if you take me home so you can spend time with him."

"Nah, I'd rather just hang with you." Drew smiled at me, but there was a lot still unspoken.

I offered him a sweet smile, assuring him I was happy to be here too.

"Just being here, you know. There's no pressure." He looked into my eyes. The sparkle in his eyes was still gone but the bright-blue color was returning slightly.

The music lightly playing and the serene setting had a calming effect. The lake, the woods, and the quiet all combined brought a bit of solitude and contentment. With nothing to deal with except just being in the moment, I chilled. A buzz from Drew's phone interrupted the tranquility, which I must say irritated me.

Suddenly he let out an aggressive sigh. "Perfect."

"Everything okay?"

"Yeah, just my dad." Drew tossed his phone on the seat.

He increased the volume on the radio and flung his head back on the seat. His head bobbed to the music with his eyes closed for a while. I left him alone since it seemed his way of processing whatever had gotten him upset.

"I like this song."

"Yeah, it's good," he said matter-of-factly.

Drew's quiet moodiness threw me. Unsure of what to do, I contemplated saying something else. Bryce and his silent moods crept into my mind. *No, better to leave him alone. I don't want to trigger a blow-up*. An uneasy feeling came over me. The music pounding through the speakers couldn't deafen the silence or the fear. My face felt flush, and my pulse quickened. I took a slow, deep breath, but it offered no relief. The heaviness of my chest became unbearable. I opened the door and stepped outside.

"Zinn!" Drew said as I walked toward the bench. "You sick?" I could barely make out the words he said. He sounded like he was talking through a muffled pillow from twenty feet away. My vision blurred, and my head began to spin. *Am I going to pass out?*

I nodded and weakly said, "I need some air."

My muscles were like noodles, and I could barely walk to the bench. I willed myself there, taking awkward steps and stumbling. When I made it, I felt like I had conquered the biggest quest. The coolness of the metal bench eased the heat radiating from all parts of me.

Drew settled next to me. "What's wrong?" he asked worriedly.

"Just got hot and the music was a little loud."

"Sorry, I guess I wasn't thinking."

"You're fine. It's just the moment. Kinda triggered a bad memory," I confessed.

"Bad meaning Bryce?"

I didn't respond.

"Wow! I'm some kind of jerk."

"Drew, stop! You're not a jerk."

Drew stared at me for a few seconds and then said, "I never wanna make you feel anything like how Bryce made you feel. I'm sorry I've been so stupid. I let my dad get to me and then it hurt you."

I shook my head. "You don't need to apologize. You didn't—"

"Shh." Drew put his finger to my lips. "I don't ever want to be the reason you feel bad, okay? So let me apologize for this."

I nodded. He stood and took my hand and led me to the truck.

"I'm hungry. How about we get some food?"

I shrugged. "Don't you need to get home?"

"I'm not worried about that."

"But your dad—"

"Shh, I don't wanna think about him. I just want pie."

For some reason, I didn't argue with Drew. I just let it go. As the truck traveled down the highway, he bragged about the pie at this diner. He pulled into the roadside diner parking lot with a "Mildred's Pie House" sign in large neon letters out front.

"You're about to have the best pie in the world."

"Wow, the best? Really?" My words dripped with sarcasm.

"Hands down," he said with a wink.

We stepped through the door and an eccentric lady stood behind the counter.

"Well, hello, handsome. It's been a minute!"

"Hey, Mildred," Drew said with a smile.

"How's that old pa of yours? He'd better come see me soon," Mildred said.

"Yes, ma'am. I'll tell him."

"Grab a seat and I'll grab the pot," she said.

"Table or counter?" Drew asked me.

"Um, by the window," I replied. Part of me still waited for Bryce to follow me, so I wanted to be aware of who was coming and going.

At the table, Drew flipped over the coffee cup in front of him with the skill of a bartender. Well . . . based on the bartenders I'd seen in movies at least—not in person. Mom always went on about Humphrey Bogart in *Casablanca*, and I'd seen scenes with deft moves, tosses, and catches. I'm guessing Drew got his skill from tossing the football.

"Coffee?" he asked. I nodded and he spun my mug with a quick snap of his wrist, smiling. It landed perfectly in his hand after it circled in the air a few times.

I clapped. "You sure college is where you want to go and not bartending school?"

"What? No! Definitely college. You know, football and all? This is just to impress the ladies, especially a little six-year-old." He chuckled as he flipped the mug again. "Avery gets a kick out of the tricks. It helps fill the gaps of time when our dad's gone, at least for her. Personally, I'm fine when he's gone." A somber look came over his face, but then he flashed a bright smile. "Enough of that! Let's order." He handed me a menu stashed behind the napkin dispenser. "What do you want? I'm getting pie."

"Pie sounds good. What kind do they have?"

"You name it," he said, turning the menu to the back page.

This place really did have every type of pie I could think of, and some I'd never even heard of.

"Wow! You weren't lying." I read over the choices, overwhelmed. "I can't pick. What's your favorite?"

He shook his head. "Oh, it's not just one. I like pecan, chocolate meringue, fried apple, strawberry, blueberry, sweet potato. Honestly, I could keep naming more."

Shaking my head, I put down the menu. "I can't decide. You'll have to choose."

"You sure?" Drew said with that all-too-familiar look of mischief on his face.

I nodded firmly, indicating I could handle whatever he threw at me. Drew waved the woman over to us.

The quaint lady walked toward us carrying a pot of coffee. "So, handsome, what's your poison?"

"Mildred, I think we're gonna have a pie platter." Drew winked.

"A pie platter, huh? You think she can handle that?"

"I think so," he said.

"If she can't, I know you can." Mildred chuckled. "Taster's Choice or Crazy Eights?"

"Um, Crazy Eights," Drew decided.

"You got it. One Crazy Eights platter coming up." She poured the coffee into our mugs.

I prodded Drew with my eyes, but he didn't flinch. Instead, he just smiled smugly, so I picked up my cup and sipped the coffee. If he could be silent so could I. We sat in complete silence until Mildred returned with a tray of eight pieces of pie.

"Are you kidding me?" I questioned.

"You told me to choose."

I shook my head. "I can't eat this much."

"Now, girlie, this handsome boy here said you were up for the challenge," Mildred said as she winked at Drew.

I grabbed my fork and shrugged my shoulders. "I'll try my best then."

"Handsome, she's a keeper." Mildred gave a hearty chuckle. "You two enjoy."

"Thanks, Mildred!" Drew looked at me. "Ladies first!"

Cocking my eyebrow, I smirked and stuck my fork in the fried apple pie and shoved it into my mouth. Drew followed suit, and we laughed and talked, nibbling on the different pies, downing a few cups of coffee along the way. After most of the pie had disappeared, Drew put his fork down.

"You had enough pie yet?" he asked.

"I can't eat another bite. I'm stuffed."

He smirked. "Let's get outta here." He counted some bills and set them on the table. "Mildred, it was great, as usual."

"Thanks, handsome. Now don't be a stranger, and be sure and bring that pretty girl back."

"Yes, ma'am." He pushed open the door.

The darkness couldn't compete with the brightness of the moon. The large, vivid circle glowed high in the sky . "I love a full moon!"

"It's not a full moon," Drew corrected.

"You sure?" I said, looking up at the sky.

"Yep. Not for another two nights. It's still a waxing gibbous."

"How do you know that?"

"Just do," he replied.

Between vegging out, watching movies, hanging with friends, and the busyness of the holiday gatherings, winter break went by too quickly. After being back at school for a few weeks, Haley asked me to help her with an application for an art competition. Haley and Julie were waiting in the study lounge. I plopped my backpack on the table and fell into the chair.

"Sorry I'm late. I was talking to Drew," I explained.

"And you say you're not going out?" Haley questioned with a sigh.

I shook my head and replied, "We're just friends."

Julie's head came up from her book and she gave me a sheepish look.

"See? Even Jules doesn't believe you," Haley added.

"Can we just get started?" I said dismissively.

With a wary eye in my direction, Haley opened her computer and pulled up the unfinished application. "Zinn, thanks for doing this. My stress level is off the charts. I gotta have this turned in by midnight."

"Haley, you've been talking about this for over a month!" I exclaimed. *Geez, what's wrong with you?* Haley hung her head in embarrassment, but I shrugged it off. "Don't worry. Done the same myself." *Not this important.* "Most of my boxes are still unpacked, remember?"

A smile of relief came over Haley's face. I prodded her on what help she needed exactly. She flooded me with the details and the pressure mounted. I started reviewing her portfolio and essay, and Haley offered little assistance; instead, she had her phone in hand. I accepted the fact that she believed she had done her part, now it was up to me to *fix this mess*, as she had put it. Julie quietly read a book while sitting across from me. Occasionally, I'd catch her casting me a quizzical glance. Obviously, she worried for Haley more than Haley did. *What a good friend!*

I skimmed over the written portion and made some notes. After a few minutes, Haley leaned over to me. "Just tell me it's awful and put me out of my misery."

"It's mostly editing stuff," I said.

She flopped back in the chair. "That's all? What a relief! I was afraid I'd have to rewrite the whole thing." Haley sat up and grabbed the computer. "I almost forgot. Can you help with this stupid part? I don't know how to explain my inspiration for the photos. I just snap what I see."

"Let me see the photo series."

She clicked on an icon and opened a group of shots of the same mountain range during different seasons and weather conditions. Each photo had its unique array of colors that peaked from the mountaintop that overlooked the rippling creek. Each breathtaking photo made me long to sit under the wispy willow tree at the edge of the creek.

"Haley, these are incredible! Where is this?"

"Bargeston Mountain over by Miller's Creek."

"So can you help me write?" Haley's question shot me back to reality.

"Oh, yeah." I gave Haley some ideas on what to write.

Half an hour later, she closed her computer. "Okay, girls, I'm done. It's submitted."

Julie placed her book on the table, walked over to Haley, and wrapped her arms around her. "I'm proud of you." Haley squeezed her in return and smiled warmly.

"Thanks for your help, Zinn." Haley looked at her phone. "Oh, wow! I'd better go. Ryan's done with practice. You need a ride home, Zinn?"

"No, I've got the car."

Haley nodded. "Jules, you ready?" Julie cautiously slid her book into her corduroy tote bag. Haley quickly shoved her computer and papers into her floral-patterned messenger bag. "Zinn, thanks again. You are a lifesaver."

"Happy I could help." I smiled as Haley scurried out the door with Julie following as best as she could. Then I collected my things and headed out the door.

I shot Savage a text saying I'd be at the restaurant in ten minutes. Outside, the chill of the air hit me, so I slipped my arms into my sweater. Laughter came from some guys exiting the gym doors. I couldn't make out who they were. I rolled my eyes and kept walking.

I'd stayed so long with Haley and Julie; the parking lot was practically empty now. When I got closer to the car, I stopped unexpectedly. My front tire was completely flat. Scrambling through the backpack for my phone to call Mom, the notification screen showed she'd texted saying she'd be home late. *What am I supposed to do now?* Unlocking the door and throwing my backpack in the seat, I checked for Savage's reply. *Ugh, he hasn't answered yet.* I called him and immediately it went to his voicemail. No other option but to try and change the tire myself. *Great! Hope I can remember what Dad taught me.*

I opened the trunk to all this random stuff stored in there. Within a few minutes, I had the contents of the trunk on the ground around me. *The spare is in here somewhere.* Lifting the mat, I let out a sigh when I caught a glimpse of the tire. Throwing the mat on the ground to reveal the entire tire, I tried to lift it, but it wouldn't budge. *Great. How do I get this thing out?*

"Ugh!" I yelled, then mumbled something under my breath. I tried Savage again but got nothing.

"Zinn!" I turned and walking toward me was Dawson. "Everything okay?" he asked.

I rolled my eyes as I pointed to the front tire. "Stupid flat."

"I gotcha," he said.

"Really? Thank you so much." The stress now lifted just as my nerves took over.

Dawson had the tire and jack removed from the trunk in a matter of seconds. I followed him like a lost puppy to the front of the car. Unsure what to do, I just stood there as he went to work. He looked completely at ease in what he was doing like he had done it a million times.

As he changed the tire, he was surprisingly conversational. Very different than any other time I'd had an interaction with him. He was polite and listened to me instead of talking at me and treating me like eye candy. In a few minutes, he had the flat tire off and was putting on the spare.

"Um, is there anything I can do?"

Shaking his head side to side, a slight dimple formed in his right cheek. He seemed happy to be helping me. He finished up and removed the jack, then placed the flat tire and jack in the trunk.

"I really appreciate this," I said again as I picked up the mat to put back in the trunk.

Dawson took the mat from my hands, set it on top of the tire, and said, "It's no big deal. I like working on cars, even if it's just changing a tire."

Once everything was back in the trunk, we walked around to the front of my car. Unsure of what to say, I nervously bit the corner of my lip. "I feel like I should repay you somehow."

Leaning on the car, Dawson smiled. "Okay, I'll take you up on that offer."

"Um, okay," I said, fumbling through my backpack in the driver's seat. "I think I have some money."

"You're cute!" He chuckled. "No, I'm thinking more like letting me take you out."

"Oh, I don't know . . . I mean—"

"I tell you what. Let's grab a pizza sometime," he interrupted me and confidently pushed himself off the car.

"Well, you see—"

"You like pizza, right?" he cut me off again.

"Yeah," I said, sliding into the front seat.

"Cool!" Dawson placed his hand on my door and leaned in closer to me. "Maybe this weekend?"

I let the words hang in the air a bit too long. "Just consider it?" He cleared his throat in an attempt to regain the composure he'd lost, sensing my hesitancy.

"Okay." I gulped as he leaned even closer.

Backing away, he smiled. "Cool. Text you later?"

"Uh, okay," I said as I tried to force down the lump in my throat. "Um, thanks again for the help."

That cocky smile formed as was his typical demeanor. "Later, Zinn." He patted the door and closed it, not taking his eyes off me. I couldn't break the gaze and had no thought of what to do next. Cocking his brow, one side of his mouth formed a smirky smile. He turned and walked toward his car. I quickly started my car, put it in reverse, and backed out of the parking space, hands shaking.

As I drove, thoughts swirled through my head. *Who was that guy? Is that the same overly confident Dawson who roamed the halls of school every day?* He had me totally confused. *Is Dawson really a nice guy?* Maybe I had been wrong about him. I had been wrong about Drew. And I had myself convinced Bryce was a great guy. *Maybe I'm not the best judge of character.* Unsure what to make of all this, I turned the knob on the radio to blare the music. Hopefully, that would get my thoughts off all boys for a moment.

I pulled in the parking lot with Savage waiting outside, as usual. I hopped out of the car and started rambling. "I'm so sorry I'm late. Have you been waiting forever? I had a flat tire. I hope you've not been here long."

He stared at me as I continued to rattle on about the incident in the parking lot. When I finally stopped talking, he calmly said, "Breathe." His words made me aware of my shallow breaths, so I inhaled and exhaled deeply a few times.

Savage spoke again. "We have plenty of time. Let's just get inside."

We walked into the restaurant and settled at the booth by the window. As we ate, I explained to him all about the flat and Dawson helping me. Savage's eye filled with concern.

"Dawson? Hmm . . ." Savage said.

"Yeah, I mean I was sorta stranded and didn't have a clue what to do."

"Hmm, I get it."

"So what about Dawson? You and Drew have both said things, but you've said nothing really. What's the deal with you three?" I asked.

"No deal with me."

"Okay, so it's with Drew?"

"That's Drew, not me."

"Oh, c'mon Savage! You know everything about Drew."

"Hmm, maybe. But his story isn't mine to tell."

I rolled my eyes and let out a sigh. "I don't get it. Dawson seems decent. He stopped and helped me with my tire."

"Hmm, okay."

"What does that even mean?"

Savage shook his head and looked at me expressionless.

"Fine, don't tell me," I said. Savage's expression didn't change.

Obviously, the whole Drew and Dawson drama was in place before I came along. Haley said once that Drew and Dawson got in a fight freshmen year after Drew took Dawson's position. Was this all about football? It didn't really seem like a possibility, but then again, boys do get mad about sports stuff. Bryce always had animosity with team-mates who he saw as a threat. Maybe that was it. Whatever it was, I wasn't gonna let it affect me. They could fight about whatever they wanted, but I didn't have to take a side. Besides, Drew had made it pretty clear he only wanted to be friends. Why not Dawson? He's the only boy showing any clear interest in me, so maybe I should consider his invite. How could getting pizza hurt anything anyway?

White flakes swirling in the darkness caused some slick spots on the paved lot and prompted Savage to walk me to my car. His eyes looked to the road and then to my tire.

"Something wrong?"

"Hmm," Savage said, studying the tire. He knelt beside the tire while examining it closer. "How about I drop you home?"

"I'll be fine."

"Still, with that tire and the slick roads . . ."

"Savage, I'll be extra careful," I said, slipping into the seat and flashing him a smile of overconfidence. "See you tomorrow."

He nodded gingerly. His eyes locked on me as I backed out of the parking spot. I waved as I turned left and headed down the road, blaring the radio and singing loudly. Not two minutes later, things took a bad turn.

I hit a slick spot and the steering wheel pulled to my left. Fighting for control, I jerked hard to the right and my car careened off the road. Quickly turning the wheel back to the left, I lost control and then everything went dark.

My eyes fought to open. *Where am I?* The car . . . I was in the car. *Where's my phone?* I fumbled around in the seat and found nothing. I started feeling dizzy, so I let my head rest on the seat. I reached for the handle and pushed on the door. It didn't budge. Outside, the car was surrounded by tree limbs pressed against the windows. I unfastened the seatbelt and tried to push on the door again. It wasn't moving. Still fumbling around for my phone, a loud thump on the top of my car startled me. My heart pounded. All of a sudden, the driver's door jerked open. I froze, feeling like I was in a dream, still not fully alert from the wreck while this hairy ape-like creature stood there staring at me, holding my car door in his hand. The creature flung the door to the ground and leaned in closer to me. I screamed, then things went black.

CHAPTER TWENTY-ONE

The snowflakes captivated me as they swirled around the amber lights of the tow truck. A large man dressed in coveralls secured chains to the back of the vehicle. I sat in the back of the ambulance, parked on the shoulder of the road, and shivered from the shock combined with the cold night air. An officer directing traffic into one lane had caused a line of cars to form. As vehicles slowly passed the scene, passengers peeked out their windows, trying to get a better view of what caused the delay. My teeth chattered, and one of the paramedics placed a Mylar blanket over my shoulders.

"How you feeling? Any nausea, headache? And you don't remember hitting your head?"

Shaking my head side to side, I took hold of the blanket and held it firmly around my shoulders. "I didn't hit my head. I just passed out when I saw—" I stopped midsentence and dropped my gaze to the ground.

"It happens. Shock of an accident and everything." She smiled at me and patted me softly on the back. "Talked to your mom. She's on her way."

"Thank you."

She reached into her pocket and held out my phone. "Found this under the seat. I'm guessing it's yours?"

Taking the phone, I nodded. "Yeah, thanks."

"You need me, I'm right over here." She smiled and then walked over to the policeman. The wind blew, and I couldn't get warm no matter how much I tried. The phone buzzing brought a welcome distraction. I hurriedly checked the text.

Savage: You home yet?

I snapped a picture of the car and sent it to him.

Me: Not yet

Almost immediately the phone rang.

"Hello," I answered meekly.

"What happened? Are you okay? I didn't feel good about you driving." Savage almost tripped over his words. I'd never heard his voice sound so passionate. So intense. So . . . worried about me.

"I hit a slick spot. Completely lost control and rammed into a tree."

"I knew I shoulda taken you home."

"Savage, you offered and I declined. Remember?"

Savage rambled something else about the tire and the snow causing slick patches on the road. The tow truck had my car fully attached and was now pulling it out from the ditch. The scraping of the metal made me cringe. As the car went past me, I shivered at all the damage it actually had. The entire front end was completely smashed, and the hood looked folded in half. I got sick to my stomach at the horrific sight.

"Zinn, you still there?"

"Yeah, sorry. Uh, can I call you later? Not feeling so well."

"Yeah, sure. Glad you are in one piece."

I ended the call and slid the phone in my pocket.

"Zinn, are you okay?" Mom ran to me and wrapped her arms around my head and shoulders. She pulled away slightly and cupped my cheeks. "Did you hit your head?" She studied my face and looked into my eyes.

I shook my head no.

She turned and hollered at the paramedic. "Excuse me! Did you check her for a concussion? She had a concussion a few months back." The paramedic walked over and gave detailed information to my mom. Mom questioned everything. The paramedic patiently responded to every concern while instructing her to talk to the officer before leaving.

"You wanna go sit in the car while I talk to the officer?"

I nodded and she walked me to her car, then walked over to the police car. I relaxed in the seat as the warmth of the heater hugged me. I leaned my head on the seat and closed my eyes. Images of the hairy creature came to my mind. He was massive, and he completely ripped the door from the car. Could it have been the Beast? Is there more than one Beast out there? *How is it possible for me to be rescued by the Beast twice in a matter of months?* My head swirled with all the questions as I drifted in and out of sleep. The door opening shot me out of my groggy state.

"Finally, I can take you home. How you feeling?"

"Fine."

"Let's get you home and into in a nice, hot bath. Sound good?"

"Yeah, that sounds really good."

My phone buzzed, and Drew's name flashed across the screen.

Drew: Savage said you had a wreck. Please tell me U R OK?
Me: Yes…Had a wreck. Relax, I'm good
Drew: What happened?
Me: Hit some ice and lost control
Drew: Savage had me worried
Me: Yeah
Drew: I'm glad you're safe
Me: Thanks, Drew
Drew: See ya tomorrow, Zinn 😄

As I soaked in the tub, I smiled about Drew's concern. I rested my eyes and images flashed of the Beast holding the door with his glowing, almost neon eyes. . . It just didn't seem real. It was like something from a movie. Where did he even come from? How was it possible that I've not even been here a year and I've seen the Beast two times? Why me? Lots of people needed help all the time. I plunged into the hot water wetting my face, hoping to escape the chaos running through my brain, but it didn't work. Instead, more questions arose. Maybe Jake knew something. I would talk to him tomorrow.

"Students, due to the current snowfall and increasing inclement weather forecasted for this afternoon and evening, we will be dismissing school at eleven thirty!" Mrs. Thompson announced over the speaker. "Please begin making your plans to leave and be safe!"

The shouts and claps of the students echoed from various rooms and hallways across the building. Mrs. Simms made sure to give our class ample homework, then let us relax until the bell sounded our freedom.

Dawson and several guys stood in the hall talking.

"Zinn, heard you totaled your car!" Dawson called out when I walked by.

"Yeah, I hit a patch of ice and then rammed into some trees."

"Man, that's rough. Glad you're okay."

Warmed by his concern, I grinned. He smiled sweetly and stepped closer to me just as someone yelled, "Yo, Dawg! Let's go." He gave a side-eyed glance showing his disappointment in the interruption.

"Gotta meet with Coach." He walked backward down the hallway, smiling. "Catch you later, Zinn."

"Bye, Dawson." I wasn't sure about his sincerity today.

I headed toward the parking lot to catch the bus home. As I walked past the row of buses, someone hollered, "Zinn!" Drew waved as he pounded down the steps. "How 'bout a ride?"

"Thanks, but I'll ride the bus."

"You'd rather take the bus?"

"Well, no! You're better than the bus."

"I rank higher than the bus. Wow, I feel so special," Drew said sarcastically.

"Ugh, you!" I slapped at his arm.

Dodging the slap, Drew laughed as he ran slightly ahead of me. "C'mon, Danthes, let me take you home."

I quickened my pace to catch up with him. I enjoyed our normal flirtation as we walked to his truck. Trying to gauge his feelings, as I always did now, he interrupted my spinning thoughts.

"I'm starving. Wanna grab some food?"

"Sure, I could eat."

We drove to Jack's and an almost full parking lot greeted us. Apparently, most kids from school had our same idea. Struggling to find a table, Blake motioned us over to the big booth in the corner that he and Julie had somehow snagged. I stayed close to Drew as he fought the crowd to get over to our friends. I slid into the seat and Drew settled beside me. We ordered food, ate, and hung out for a while, which helped bring me back into normality after last night's traumatic event. Outside, the snow began covering the road.

"I'd better get home. My road will be rough if I wait much longer," Julie said.

"Yeah, better get you home," Blake agreed.

"See ya!" I said.

"Probably need to get you home, huh?" Drew asked.

"Yeah, probably."

We stepped outside and the blanket of white had already covered the vehicles. I walked to the passenger's side, absorbed in thoughts of the Beast, the car wreck, and boys.

"Zinn! Look out!" Drew yelled.

Just as I turned, I got hit smack-dab in the middle of my face with a hard snowball. Across the parking lot stood Sierra, Jordan, and Riley, laughing smugly with Malone and Tristan standing nearby.

"Oh, man! Zinn, I'm so sorry," Malone said as he came running toward me. "That was meant for Bear, not you. Are you okay?"

"Yeah, it's just a snowball." I wiped the icy wetness from my face.

"Malone, what's your deal? Hitting a girl? C'mon, dude!" Drew said angrily.

Malone slumped his shoulders and gave us a sheepish look.

"Really, a girl?"

"Yeah, you don't throw a snowball at a girl."

"You don't?" I scooped some snow from the hood of his truck.

"Zinn, don't. You're just gonna embarrass yourself." Drew backed away slowly.

"Because I'm a girl?"

"No, 'cause you can't hit me," Drew said matter-of-factly.

"Can't hit you? 'Cause I'm a girl?" I drew back my arm.

"Listen, Zinn, I'm serious. Don't throw it. If you do, then it's an all-out war."

"Oh, so it's probably better if I just drop this snowball?" I lowered my hand.

Drew gave me a cocky grin, then he quipped, "That's a good girl."

"Oh, Drew." I clicked my tongue. "I wish you hadn't said that."

"What did I sa—" A face full of snow interrupted Drew's question.

"Zinn! Seriously?" Drew brushed snow off his face. With a mischievous glint in his eye, he said, "I warned you."

Drew scooped up some snow as he came toward me. I turned to run, but Drew's arm lifted me up and dipped me backward. Holding a handful of snow over my face, he said, "You asked for this."

"Drew, please! No! I'm totally sorry," I begged.

"You're sorry?"

"Yeah, I'm really sorry."

Looking satisfied, Drew dropped the snow. Letting me go, he turned from me toward the driver's side. My hand quickly raked across the truck's hood and scooped another fistful of snow.

"Oh, Drew." I laughed and prepared my launch.

As he turned to me, my hand pushed the snow into his face. Darting to the other side of the truck, I screamed as my arm got hit with a tightly packed snowball. Ducking beside the truck door, everyone around the parking lot hollered and laughed. Before long, teens scurried out of the restaurant and barricaded themselves around the cars. I remained hunkered down and hidden beside Drew's truck as snowballs zoomed over my head. Positioning himself at the tailgate, Drew laughed as he attacked some people across the lot.

I held up my hand and hollered, "Truce?"

"Truce!" he called back.

Moving closer to Drew, I stayed low. He stood while pelting balls at people, all the while avoiding any of the white balls of fluff coming toward him. He dodged everything. Jumping up to throw a ball, snowballs came from every direction. Instantly retreating, I wiped off all the snow.

Drew and his belly laugh drew my attention. He dodged every snowball that came near him. *He's right. Nothing can touch him.* I peeked over the truck bed. While everyone else was covered in snow, Drew remained untouched. Evidently, he had these uncanny reflexes. Kneeling beside me, he gave me a sparkling smile as he scooped more snow from the pavement.

"How is it you have no snow on you?" I questioned.

A serious look came across his face and then turned to a slight smile. "Lucky, I guess." He stood and readied himself to throw another winning snowball, but instead got smacked in the face.

"Huh, so I guess you can get hit after all," I said smugly.

He lowered himself as he wiped the snow from his face. Shrugging, he said, "Everyone's luck runs out."

As the snowball battle ended, the crowd dispersed and the cars in the lot began to diminish. Drew and I got in his truck and drove through town to my neighborhood. When we got to my house, Drew got out and walked with me to the door.

"All that back there at Jack's . . . You know you're to blame?" Drew stated.

"Me? How am I to blame?"

"You threw the first snowball."

"Technically, that was Malone."

"True, but that had been resolved," Drew said.

"Possibly, but you did make that sexist comment."

"Sexist comment? More like chivalrous."

"Ah, fine line," I said. "But either way, it antagonized me, so we can conclude you were actually to blame."

Drew's lip curled slightly upward as he nodded. "I'll take the blame, but you have to admit you were a culprit."

My mouth dropped in exaggerative form at the offense of his words. "Whatever! Just let the record show I did hit you, and you implied it was an impossible feat."

Drew narrowed his eyes as he looked to be strongly considering his words. "The record has been noted."

"Next time, don't underestimate me."

"Oh, I never underestimate you," Drew said with a smirk.

With the snow getting heavier, Drew hugged me goodbye. I went inside and dropped my backpack on the floor, which made Oreo bark.

"Zinnia Rose, is that you?" Grandma Rose asked, sitting in the den crocheting.

"Yes, ma'am. School let out early."

"Thought you might get dismissed early. That snow is really coming down. You hungry?"

"No, I got some food with my friends."

"Who brought you home?"

"My friend Drew."

"The Behr boy?"

"Yes, ma'am," I replied, a measure of pride in my voice.

"He seems like a nice boy."

"He is," I said. "He's very nice."

Grandma smiled as she continued crocheting. I went to the kitchen and got a drink. Out the window, the snow blanketed the ground. The neighbor kids played in their backyard. Three little girls spun around in a circle with their tongues sticking out, catching snowflakes. I spied a little boy hiding at the side of his house, bent down and packing snowballs. He stood up and slung one at the little girls who were still spinning and giggling. One girl got hit, screamed, and quickly made a snowball to retaliate the attack. Within a matter of seconds, a snowball fight was underway. Another boy joined the attack against the group of girls, and they continued pelting each other back and forth. I smiled as my snowball fight came to mind. Drew's look when I smacked him in the face with a handful of snow made me snicker. Drew no doubt let me hit him since he easily dodged all the other snowballs coming at him. Of course, he did get pelted that one time by someone else, so maybe avoiding being hit was simply luck. I finished my drink and went to my room, wondering if Avery was soon to be in defense mode for Drew's snowball attacks.

Grabbing my journal from the desk and my fuzzy grey blanket from the floor, I nested myself on the bed. When I got comfortable, I opened my journal and wrote "My First Bargeston Snow Day" and began to fill the page. Oreo snored beside me and barked as the wind howled outside. Rubbing his head to calm him, he cuddled up against me and quieted.

Feeling chilled even with the blanket, I went to the closet and dug through it for my fluffy sweater. Shuffling through the clothes, a bag caught my eye: Sam's gift. It had been weeks since I'd even talked to her. I set it on my desk, grabbed my phone, and called Sam. It went straight to voicemail. "Hey, Sam, it's Zinn. Just calling to say hey and hoping we could hang out soon. Miss you. Call me." I pressed End and tossed the phone on the bed, then flopped in my chair beside the window.

The large, fluffy snowflakes floated down from the sky and blanketed the tree outside my window. Prompted to write about this wintery display, I grabbed my journal and pen. I curled in the chair, ready to write, when my phone rang. Sam's name flashed on the screen.

"Sam, it's been forever," I answered excitedly.

"Yeah, sorry about that, Z. I've been pretty busy."

"Yeah, me too. Things have been crazy. I just found your gift and realized we never did our Christmas thing. Maybe we could get together this weekend and do our Sam and Z Christmas tradition?"

"Uh, well." Sam paused a moment as she fumbled with her words and then cleared her throat. "Um, don't you think we've outgrown that whole Sam and Z Christmas thing? It's just sorta stupid now."

Stupid? But it's our day. "Uh, no. I don't think it's stupid."

"Oh, Z. You know what I mean. It's a kid thing, and . . . Well, we're not kids anymore."

"I know we're not kids anymore," I replied harshly as anger boiled inside me.

"Z, don't be mad. It's about time we move on from all that, don't you think?"

Sam's words weren't making sense to me. It was like she spoke a different language. "Thanks for understanding, Z."

Did I even say anything? Completely frozen, I tried to form words. "I really gotta go, Z. I'll call you soon, okay?" Before I could even respond, she'd ended the call. I slumped in the chair and swaddled myself in the sweater. Things with Sam were never going to be "back to normal." No matter how much I wanted it, no matter what I had hoped, Sam and I would never be the same again.

I shut the light off, done with the day and ready for sleep. I lay there tossing from side to side, trying to fall asleep, but I couldn't because of Sam's call. *Why is she avoiding me? Is it about Bryce?* As much as I didn't want to believe he'd caused it, I couldn't come up with any other rational reason for Sam's lack of interest in our friendship. *Dating my best friend isn't enough for him?* I flopped onto my stomach in frustration and let the pillow absorb my tears. The situation with Sam truly felt hopeless now, especially if Bryce was keeping her from me.

CHAPTER TWENTY-TWO

A buzzing woke me from a deep sleep. My hand fumbled across the floor until it found the phone. I leaned my head over the bed and hit the side button. The phone lit up and showed a text from Dawson. Scooping the phone in my hand, I sat up. A notification from the school popped up: SCHOOL CANCELED WEDNESDAY 2/7. I threw off the covers, climbed out of the bed, and walked over to the window. A white blanket covered the whole neighborhood. I fell back into the bed and opened the text from Dawson.

Dawson: Morning!
Me: You're up early for a snow day
Dawson: No snow day when it comes to workouts
Me: Sounds intense
Dawson: I guess

I typed out something, then deleted it. I had no idea what to say to him. *Ugh, why am I so bad at this?* Another message came before I replied.

Dawson: Any plans today?

Me: Probably just binge some shows
Dawson: Sounds exciting
Me: Not really
Dawson: Wanna know something?
Me: What?
Dawson: I'm really craving pizza…

Oh, that's smooth for sure. I typed something out and then deleted it. *Ugh! I'm so awkward.*

Me: Pizza's always good

That sounds so stupid. Why did I say that? Another message popped up.

Dawson: Ha! You're funny
Me: lol
Dawson: I'm thinking we could grab some at the Slice. Maybe today?

I smiled until I thought of Drew. *How is he gonna feel about this? Why do I care? He only wants to be friends.* I replied quickly before I lost my nerve.

Me: Sounds great!
Dawson: Cool. pick you up @ 11:30?
Me: Sure!

As the doorbell rang, I yelled to Mom, "I'm leaving!"

She stepped out of her room and looked at me a little anxiously. "Be careful. If it starts snowing, please get home."

"Yes, ma'am," I said, reminding myself of Drew with the "yes, ma'am."

I opened the door. Dawson stood with his back to the house. He turned and smiled when he saw me. "You ready?" He had on a black puffy jacket, which reminded me to go get mine. *Where is my brain?*

"Yeah, I'm ready. Just need my coat!" I grabbed it from the chair and slipped one arm through, fighting to get it on straight. Dawson stepped inside. "Let me help." He held the coat straight as he smiled and his brown eyes shimmered.

"Thanks." I smiled nervously as I slipped my arm in the coat.

"Ready for some pizza?"

"Pizza's good." *Again with that stupid line.*

He laughed as he directed me to walk out the door first. We got in the car and made the short drive to The Slice. Inside, we had our choice of tables, so we settled for one in the back. Dawson handed me a menu and asked me about my topping likes and dislikes. When the server came, Dawson ordered a pizza that included my favorites. I gave an appreciative smile.

"Sound good with you?" he asked while the server waited.

I nodded.

"That'll be it," he said and handed her the menus.

As we waited for the food, Dawson and I talked, like for real. At school, Dawson's cool confidence intimidated me, but here he acted different. He talked about moving here when he was in second grade and how scared he was to be in a new town. I totally understood that fear. He shared about his family and losing his uncle, who was more like a dad, six years ago. Another thing I related to. The food came and we kept talking. The server leaving the check didn't distract us from the conversation either.

I told him all my family stuff and about being an only child. I talked a little about music and my plans for college. When he shared about his mom and his brothers, his protectiveness of them was obvious. And as for football . . . Well, he hoped a scholarship would pay for college. The more he talked, I realized how wrong I had been about him.

"Oh wow! It's two o'clock. I can't believe we've been talking this long." I grabbed the ticket.

Shaking his head, Dawson pulled the ticket from my hand. "I got this."

"Uh, but—"

"Nope."

"It's my thank-you for the help with the tire."

"If changing a tire gave me the chance to go out with you, then I'll change as many tires as you need."

All I could do was smile. I grabbed my coat and followed him to the counter as he paid the bill. We spoke to some people from school and then went out to the car.

"Maybe sometime we can catch a movie?" he asked while opening the car door for me.

"Uh, yeah."

"Cool."

The ride back to my house consisted of small talk, occasional silence, and some background music. Basically, a chill fifteen minutes. He walked me to the door, we chatted for a bit longer, and then he left. No overt affection. No pressure. He was actually a gentleman. I went inside and Mom and Grandma greeted me.

"Did you have fun, Zinnia Rose?" Grandma asked.

"Yeah, it was fun."

"Was this a date?" Mom asked.

"No, just pizza." I rolled my eyes, uncomfortable to be discussing my boy situation.

"Wow, three hours to eat pizza. It doesn't take me that long to eat. What about you, Mom?"

Grandma lightly laughed.

"I'm going to my room," I announced, signifying my annoyance.

"Hey, Zinn, tell me the name of that pizza place. I wanna make sure and not go there if it takes so long to get served."

"I'm not listening to you, Mother!" I yelled as I headed up the stairs. No matter how much she annoyed me with her pickiness, I couldn't stop smiling.

Spending the day with Dawson had me almost giddy and wondering why I had been avoiding him all this time. I slipped off my coat and tossed it on the chair. My shoes came next as I kicked them off, wet with slush. I hopped on my bed to catch up with any missed messages that I intentionally avoided while I was with Dawson. Scanning through my texts, the reason for my steering clear of Dawson hit me . . . Drew. *Drew's not interested. Move on already. Dawson's really cute and nice. Most importantly, he's interested.*

A big lump formed in my throat reading Drew's text that came at noon asking if I wanted to hang out. No doubt he wondered why I hadn't texted yet and would likely ask what I had been doing. *I can't lie to him, but I'm not telling him I hung out with Dawson.* I huffed out a big breath and sent a reply.

Me: Hey…What're you doing?
Drew: Hey! Building a snowman with Avery
Me: Fun!
Drew: Yeah, she wanted you to come help
Me: Aw :(tell her sorry
Drew: UR missin out
Me: Wish I was there
Drew: Me too
Me: 🙂
Drew: Gotta go…Avery's whining. Text you later
Me: K…Give Avery a hug
Drew: Can I have a hug too ;)
Me: Hugs!
Drew: 😁

"Hey, Zinn!" Haley said, giving me a hug. "Let's hang out this weekend now that the snow has finally cleared."

"Sounds good!" I replied, then continued on my way to econ class.

"Text you later!" she called out.

As I walked into econ, Drew was talking to Malone. I walked to my desk and took my seat. Within a couple of minutes, Drew sat down with an unusually moody look on his face.

"Morning, Drew." I shot him a smile, and he returned with a somewhat forced one. This was so out of character for Drew that I didn't quite know how to breach the subject of his sulk. I figured it was a dad-related thing for him and best to let it lie.

He'll talk when he's ready.

"Zinn, what'd you do while we were out for snow?"

"Nothing, really. Slept late. Watched some movies."

"Heard you were at The Slice yesterday."

My stomach sank at hearing his words. *Here we go.*

"And you were with Dawson." He actually sounded angry.

I inhaled deeply as my eyes closed. Before I could reply, he pressed further. "Is it true?"

I don't know which irritated me more: his tone, his questions, or his nerve in thinking it was any of his business. "Yeah, so what?"

"So?" He looked taken aback by my statement. Suddenly, he blurted, "Why didn't you tell me?"

The angry words shot from my mouth. "I didn't know I had to tell you when I get pizza with a friend."

"Friends? Since when are you and Dawson friends?"

"Since we are. What's the big deal?"

Letting out a grunt, he turned around in his seat. I sat there and waited for him to respond, but he said nothing. *Is he actually mad at me?* I debated on what to say to him until I decided I didn't want to say anything. Instead, I took out my journal and began feverishly writing. Within a few minutes, Drew twisted sideways in his seat.

"Uh, Zinn?"

"What?"

"Sorry." His eyes filled with sadness. I exhaled as the heaviness lifted from my shoulders. "Hearing you were with Dawson at The Slice . . . Well, it kinda shocked me," Drew confessed. "And what I said to you was outta line."

"It's forgotten." I smiled and shrugged my shoulders.

He smiled back but still looked a little sad. But then he cleared his throat. "Zinn, just watch out for Dawson, okay?"

"Drew, there's nothing to watch out for."

Drew tilted his head and twisted his mouth to one side, letting me know he needed more convincing.

"Look, it was just pizza. A thank-you for his help with my flat tire," I said matter-of-factly. "Now can we drop it?"

"Fine, it's dropped." The intensity on Drew's face intrigued me. Was it a fair warning or jealousy? Honestly, I couldn't tell.

I sighed. "What?"

"Nothing."

Drew stared at me until I caved and broke eye contact. "Stop staring at me?" I said, rolling my eyes.

"Zinn, don't be mad."

"I'm not mad." With Drew's eyes on me, I fought to keep my focus on my journal. I wrote and then frustratingly scribbled out words. Finally, I stopped, but Drew didn't flinch. "Okay, fine! I'm frustrated," I said with an exaggerated sigh.

"Zinn, I'm sorry."

Narrowing my eyes, I raised one eyebrow. "Tell me why you're giving me advice to watch out for Dawson."

The color escaped Drew's face and his bright-blue eyes dimmed. "It's a lot to explain."

I sighed again, then returned to my writing, and this time the words flowed freely. The remainder of class Drew didn't speak. When the bell rang, he walked with me to my next class, but the conversation was less than stellar.

The rest of the day dragged by, and whenever I saw Drew, he stayed quiet. Apparently, he was still upset that I hadn't told him about Dawson. *Why is he so upset about me having pizza with the guy? And what does he mean by telling me to "watch out" for Dawson?* Our talk in econ turned my stomach.

At lunch, I hardly ate any of my food. Savage's concern signified he noticed something was up, but he didn't ask any questions. Drew had told him something. He was being way too cautious with his questions. Plus, he wasn't saying anything about Drew. No doubt Savage knew I'd gone to The Slice with Dawson, but I wasn't mentioning any of it. Really, I didn't even know what to say. None of it made sense to me. Besides, whatever I said, Savage would just side with Drew. He'd let me know his thoughts on Dawson the other day.

When English was finally over, Savage and I talked about surface stuff as we walked to the doorway. Drew would be leaning on the wall as I entered the hall, so I held my breath as I got closer to the door. Oh goodie, another walk with Drew and his somber, quiet mood. I didn't know how much more I could take. I stepped into the hallway, but there was no Drew waiting for me. Savage cleared his throat.

"Just me today. Bear's with Coach," Savage said.

"Oh," I replied, acting like it was no big deal. Weird that Drew didn't say anything to me about that. He typically let me know when he wouldn't be meeting me after class. Savage walked with me most of the way to the science wing, then he headed to his class. As I entered chemistry class and settled at my desk, Jake walked up to me, eager to chat.

"Zinn, heard about the wreck. You all right?"

"Yeah, I'm fine, but the car's totaled."

"That sucks. But glad you're not hurt." He smiled and turned to leave.

"Uh, Jake, wait." He returned to me and I leaned close to him and murmured, "When I wrecked, I saw a Beast."

Jake's eyes widened as a look of surprised elation covered his face. "Really? Another encounter? That's never happened."

"What do you mean?"

"In all the research I've done, no one has ever said they've seen two Beasts." The bell rang, which prompted Jake to ask for a rain check on the conversation before he went to his desk.

When I stepped into the hallway, there stood Drew. I awkwardly smiled when he saw me. Was this gonna be another walk laced with tense silence?

"Uh, Zinn?" Drew pushed off the wall. "Can I say something, please?"

I tightened my grip on the strap of my backpack as I prepared for the worst.

"Say whatever," I replied.

"Well, uh . . . You see . . ." Drew's gaze fell to the floor. "I can't stand you being mad at me. Please, can you forgive me?"

"Drew, I'm not mad at you! I thought you were mad at me."

"Mad at you? Zinn, I'd never be mad at you."

"This morning you seemed pretty mad at me."

"Not at you," he clarified. "I was never mad at you."

Narrowing my eyes at him, I stopped myself from asking more questions.

"Look, I was stupid this morning. Can we just be normal again?" Drew said.

"I don't know, Drew."

Hurt filled his eyes. "You don't know?"

"I mean, that's gonna be hard. How normal are you, really?" I said with a smirk.

"Oh, now that's low, Danthes. I thought you were better than that."

We both laughed and had more quips to swap during our walk. The normalcy with Drew returning brought an instant change to my mood. Drew and I not talking caused me to feel an uneasiness and confusion that I hadn't felt in a long time. Actually, those were feelings I'd only ever had with Bryce, but never with Drew. One thing was for sure, with Bryce the mood never got resolved. His moodiness always loomed over our relationship. But Drew called his mood out, and it fixed things between us. Talking things out was a new thing for me. Maybe "talking things out" could become a new normal. At least, I hoped it could.

CHAPTER TWENTY-THREE

"The sign-up sheets for the upcoming Spirit Week Talent Show are posted on the bulletin board outside the office. All those wishing to participate in the talent show must sign up by next Friday and pick up the information sheet from the office. It will be held the last Friday of Spirit Week. Spirit Week activity sheets will be posted during the next couple of weeks," Mrs. Thompson spoke enthusiastically, causing everyone to chatter excitably.

"So, are we doing this?" Drew asked with a smile.

"No way! The song is nowhere near ready," I said, secretly wanting to say yes.

"You've got two weeks before rehearsals. That's plenty of time. You're a word maestro, so it'll all come to you," Drew encouraged.

"You're not gonna let this go, are you?"

"Not a chance." He gave me a light pat on the shoulder. "But I will give you to the end of the day."

"Fine, I'll sign up," I said with a dramatic sigh. "But at the end of the day."

Although my nerves were ramped up about what I had just committed to, at least yesterday's tension was completely gone. Dawson's name didn't get mentioned, and I planned to keep it that way. If Drew had a problem with Dawson, I would respect that. Besides, Dawson hadn't texted me or mentioned anything else about the movie. Not to mention, I'd seen him talking to Sloan this morning. Apparently, they'd gone out a couple of times, so it was pretty clear he wasn't into me.

Leaving econ, the halls buzzed with talk of Spirit Week activities, especially the talent show. As we walked to second period, Drew mentioned me signing up again, and I quickly reminded him about our deal with me doing it by the end of the day. In between the other classes, he didn't mention signing up for it until after English. As I walked out of the room with Savage, Drew stood, waiting outside the door. He took my hand.

"Time to sign up, my little procrastinator!"

"It's not the end of the day, Drew," I countered. "Savage, tell him."

"Hmm, nope! Not agreeing to that. Sorry, Zinn."

"Drew, I've got to get to chemistry. Savage, help me out?"

"Nope, he's your problem, not mine."

"Ugh."

Savage walked away, chuckling.

"The sign-up sheet is just over there. Now c'mon." Drew pulled me to the bulletin board outside the office.

"You're beginning to annoy me, Drew Behr."

"Am I? 'Cause this is nothing. Trust me, I can get much worse."

Narrowing my eyes, I huffed and took the pen from his hand and wrote, *Zinn Danthes and Drew Behr: singing.*

Drew looked at the page and shook his head side to side. "I'm playing guitar. I'm not singing."

"You're right," I said. "And I wrote you are singing, huh?"

He took the pen from my hand. "Easy enough fix."

I jerked the pen from his hand and stepped away from him. "I don't think so."

"Oh, Zinn! Now you're just being annoying."

"And I can get much worse too."

He raised an eyebrow at me, impressed. "I've underestimated you, Danthes."

Piercing my lips, I gave a firm nod. "Yes, you did."

"Well, it won't happen again. That's for sure."

"*Hmph!* You said that same thing after the snowball fight."

Drew acted confused but nodded anyway. "I did, didn't I? Learned my lesson, but I promise you it won't happen again."

"Don't be so sure," I retorted, confidently stepping away from him.

Chuckling, Drew caught up with me. "You definitely keep me on my toes."

We headed to the chemistry hall and rounded the corner. Dawson and a couple of other guys territorially stood against the wall, reminding me of ravens for some reason. I shook my head to get the vision of heavy-billed dark birds perching on the wall out of my head. Dawson dipped his head and nodded at me with that same arrogance of when I first met him. I offered a weak smile and nodded back. Drew noticed our silent interaction and cut his eyes at Dawson.

Oh boy, something is about to happen . . .

Dawson snickered. "Something you wanna say, Bear?"

Drew stared at him as we kept walking.

Dawson's taunting continued. "You hear anything, boys? 'Cause I sure ain't hearing nothing."

The snickering boys gave Dawson accolades for what they viewed as an apparent burn on Drew. Drew looked at me in a way that said, *Just keep walking.*

"You never disappoint, Bear. Always walking away. Never quite willing to take a real stand, huh."

Drew stopped, turned around, and made a lunge toward Dawson.

"Drew! Don't!" I touched his arm. Drew didn't flinch; he just kept staring at Dawson.

"What, Bear?" Dawson pushed off the wall. Again, I saw him as a bird poised for flight. Maybe I did have a concussion because there was no reason this imagery should be popping up.

"You don't wanna hear what I gotta say," Drew answered.

"I don't have time for this," I mumbled, walking away, frustrated at the games boys play. I thought girls were bad, but I'd rather be reenacting a *Mean Girls* scene right now than have to watch this testosterone stew simmering before me.

"Zinn, wait!" Drew caught up to me as Dawson's boisterous laughter filled the hall.

"Can't hear you, Bear!" Dawson called out, which prompted the other two guys to cackle and give kudos to Dawson for his supposed "win" of something.

"Zinn, please don't."

"Don't what, Drew?"

"Uh, don't get mad?"

"Ugh! Drew, I'm not mad. I'm just not into seeing you and Dawson act like Neanderthals."

He leaned against the wall as he shook his head. "I get it. It's just how Dawson baits me. He knows exactly what buttons to push. You wouldn't understand."

"I don't need to understand. Just don't drag me into it."

"It's gonna be stopped today, okay?"

Exhaling, I said, "Good."

He walked me to the chemistry door and said a quick goodbye. I stood at the door and watched him leave. As Drew moved closer to Dawson, Dawson stood taller and tried to appear threatening. Drew got in Dawson's face and spoke quietly. The obvious heated words exchanged drew several people, no doubt expecting to see fists thrown. I shook my head and escaped into my classroom.

"Zinn, did Drew and Dawson really fight?" Haley ran up to me all worry and drama.

"I don't know," I said coolly.

"*You don't know?*" Haley looked at me in confusion. "Well, did Drew say anything?"

"Nope."

"Really? 'Cause I heard Dawson shoved Drew. And Drew plowed into—"

"I don't want to know."

Haley stared at me in disbelief. "You don't care that Drew was in a fight?"

I shrugged as I shook my head. "Nope, I don't care. I didn't want to see it when it was happening, and I don't want to hear about it now."

"Oh, okay." Haley became timid.

Obviously, my words projecting my frustration about the brutish display by Drew and Dawson hurt her feelings. "Sorry, Haley. I'm just upset about the whole thing."

"It's okay. Let's just forget about stupid guys right now." Haley wrapped her arm around my shoulders and immediately changed the subject to the talent show.

She questioned me about what song I would sing, what I planned to wear, and how I would do my hair. She had more questions than I had answers. I appreciated her bubbly excitement because it distracted me from the chaos of Drew and Dawson.

After school, the whispers followed me as I walked to my locker. Drew and Dawson's names were flying off people's tongues, and I assumed mine was tangled up in that gossip too. I wasn't worried for Drew and the fight, but the issue between them had me concerned. I wanted to understand the truth of the bad vibes that brought a dark cloud over Drew whenever Dawson came near. It was time for me to find out about all this mystery, but the truth was not going to come easily.

I leaned on Drew's truck, waiting for him to exit from the gym. Every time the doors flung open, I perked up, expecting Drew, but other people kept coming and I kept waiting. The door pushed open with an arm holding it wide, and a figure hidden inside the door frame had me curious. Then I lost my breath. Dawson stepped outside and headed to his car. Not slowing when he got to his car, he kept walking—toward me. *Why is he coming over to me? Please, not now.* I wanted to faint.

"Zinn, what's up?"

Shaking my head, I gave him a blank look. My eyes darted to the building, hoping that Drew's delay kept him long enough to miss seeing Dawson here.

"Waiting on Bear?"

"Uh, sorta. I mean, yeah." My lame awkwardness overtook me. *He makes me so nervous.*

"Cool!" He leaned on the hood of the truck and smiled nonchalantly. "So what about that movie? You up for it tonight?"

No. No, I'm not up for it, and I don't think I ever will be! Both Drew and Dawson had me so confused that I had lost my ability to make sound decisions.

My slight hesitation prompted Dawson to say more. "Zinn, I like you. Honestly, I'd really like for us to be friends."

With no good excuse not to go out with him, I answered meekly, "I guess a movie would be okay." *What have I done?*

"Cool." Dawson nodded as he pushed off the vehicle. "Pick you up around six thirty?"

I smiled. Dawson stepped away and I exhaled. *He's leaving. Crisis avoided.* Then the door opened and Drew flew down the stairs and jogged across the lot. My pulse quickened. As Drew passed Dawson, they glared at each other. Drew's gaze broke from Dawson and he smiled when he caught my eye. When Dawson got to his car, he turned to me and loudly said, "See you tonight, Zinn!"

I smiled gawkily, fearing the explosion about to take place with Drew hearing Dawson's intentionally antagonizing words.

"Why did he say, 'See you tonight'?" Drew asked, his eyes fixed on Dawson.

"Um, well, nothing really, just a movie."

"A movie?" he blurted out in surprise.

The tension in my shoulders tightened. *Here we go again.* Drew's irrational outburst caused me to clench my teeth. I took a breath, trying to calm myself.

"Is this like a date?"

"I don't know, Drew. Does it matter if it is?"

"Yeah, it matters," he said as anger filled his eyes.

I shook my head in total confusion. "Why do you care?"

"Because I told him to stay away from you!"

Heat rose into my face and I fired off at him. "You what?" I shook my head, now overwhelmed at Drew's interference without sound reason. "You told Dawson to stay away from me? What gives you the right?"

"I don't know, Zinn!" he yelled. "I just don't want you going out with him."

"Why, Drew? What is it to you?"

"Maybe I care, Zinn! I don't know!" Drew's voice got louder. He breathed in and out and then regained his composure. "And to be honest, I didn't think you were ready."

"What do you mean 'not ready'?"

"I'm not sure what I mean. I just didn't know you wanted to date."

"Why wouldn't I wanna date?"

"I don't know, Zinn. I just thought . . . I'm just surprised is all."

I didn't know what to say. Drew looked so hurt, and I was so confused. First, he said he only wanted to be friends. Then he got mad because I was talking to Dawson. *Does he really think he can control who I spend time with? Ugh, he has some nerve.*

"Can we just go, please?" I pressed.

"Yeah." He unlocked the door, then turned to me with pain-filled eyes and softness in his voice. "You need to trust me about Dawson."

"Drew, I get you don't like him, but that's your issue, not mine."

"Yeah, I don't like him, but it's more than that." The strain on his face was off-putting. Drew was rattled, and I'd never seen him like this. "Dawson is the last person you need to be going out with, Zinn. He's not right for you!"

"Ugh! This is ridiculous. Why do you care who I go out with?"

"Because we're friends."

We're friends, phew. That phrase made anger boil in me. "Exactly, Drew. We're friends. Just friends. Like *you* wanted!" I yelled.

With shock on his face, he stood there. It seemed forever before he spoke. "Zinn, you're right. I said we were friends. It's just that, well . . . I worry about you."

"I don't need you to worry about me," I said bluntly. "And I don't need you telling me who I can be friends with or who I can hang out with." I huffed and walked away.

"Zinn, where are you going?"

"Home."

"Zinn, get in the truck."

"No."

Running toward me, he gently touched my arm. "Zinn, c'mon. It's freezing and you live three miles away."

Shooting my eyes to him, I said, "I'm not cold, and I can walk three miles." The wind blowing chilled me, but I didn't dare show Drew I felt cold.

"Please, Zinn, just get in," Drew said as he edged me to the truck.

Through gritted teeth I said, "Either shut up about Dawson, or tell me why he's not good for me!"

He sighed as he nodded his head.

I walked to his truck and got into the seat. He drove me home and neither of us spoke. Turning to face me every few minutes, he never said a word. When he pulled into my drive, I immediately got out, said a quick thank-you, and shut the door before he could say anything.

I went in the house and walked into the living room. When I peeked out the window, his truck still sat in the drive with his door opened. Finally, he shut it, but almost immediately it opened. He got out of the truck and took a few steps toward the house. He wrung his hands as he talked to himself, shook his head, then he turned and walked back to the truck. He opened the door and stood holding it. Then he slammed the door and took a couple of steps toward the house, stopping once again. He spun back toward the truck, settled in the seat, and shut the door. He backed out of the drive and pulled down the road. *What in the world is so hard to tell me that he chose to put on that back-and-forth pony show in my driveway instead of speaking the truth?*

"Zinnia Rose, is that you?"

"Yes, ma'am, it is," I said as I walked into the sunroom. Grandma Rose and her friend worked on a new puzzle. I gave her a kiss and said hello to our neighbor, Mrs. Roberts.

"Oh, here it is," Mrs. Roberts said as she fit the piece into its rightful spot.

"Oh good, Martha." Grandma looked at me and smiled. "We've been working on this section for an hour. Finally, have it done."

"You're really coming along." I picked up a piece and twirled it between my fingers. "Where's Mom?"

"Cookeville. Showing another house." Grandma's eyes stayed on the remaining puzzle pieces while she inquired about my evening plans. I shared my night's itinerary with her and got her approval. She and Mrs. Roberts celebrated over another found piece, so I left them to it. "I'm gonna go take a shower."

"Okay, sweetheart. Martha and I will keep attacking this puzzle."

"Bye, Zinnia Rose," Mrs. Roberts said with a wave, keeping her eyes on the table.

As I went upstairs to shower, I threw my phone on the bed, ignoring its buzzing. After I cleaned up, I slipped on my robe and wrapped my hair in a towel. Fiddling through my closet for an outfit, I pulled out a sweater dress and some leggings. Tossing them over the chair, I collapsed on the bed and anxiously picked up my phone.

I replied to the texts from Haley, Julie, and Savage. Still fuming over the ride home, I ignored Drew's text. Grabbing my earbuds, I played some music and closed my eyes. A beep interrupted the music. It was Drew. I hit Ignore and went back to my music.

While waiting for Dawson, I sat on the couch with Mom.

"Zinn, quit shaking your leg. You're driving me crazy," Mom said.

"Sorry." I immediately stopped.

"What's making you so nervous?"

"Uh, nothing. Just the wait, I guess."

"Is this a date?"

"No. At least I don't think so. I mean, I don't know. He just asked me if I wanted to catch a movie tonight. It's pretty casual, I think."

"You don't know if this is a date?"

"Mom!" I rolled my eyes. "It's just a movie."

"So is this the same guy where you said it was 'just pizza'?"

I acknowledged with a quick nod, not really giving her much attention since the vehicles traveling down our road held more of my focus. Every time lights flickered in the window as cars drove past, my stomach tightened.

"Well, what's his name?"

"Dawson Gregory."

"So, this Dawson. I've not heard of him before," she said. "Is he friends with Drew and Savage?"

"Um, well, they play football together." The flickers transitioning to beams of light shone into the window, and I stood. "He just pulled in." I leaned over and hugged her. "I won't be late."

"Hey, hold up a minute. Let me meet this boy," she said as she stood.

Rolling my eyes, I sighed. "Okay, but please make it quick."

Mom threw up her hand, letting me know she would oblige my demand. She stood in the archway as I opened the door. Dawson smiled when he saw me.

"You look nice," he complimented.

"Thanks," I said. "Uh, Dawson, this is my mom."

He held out his hand for her to shake. "Nice to meet you, Mrs. Danthes."

"Hello, Dawson. So you're going to the movies?"

"Yes, ma'am. Then we'll get some food. That is, if Zinn wants," he said, looking at me for approval.

"Well, enjoy yourselves," she said. "Zinn, don't be too late."

"I'll have her home before midnight, ma'am."

"Thank you, Dawson. And please, be safe."

"Will do." Dawson smiled. "Nice to meet you."

I gave her a quick hug to show my appreciation. "Love you." She returned the sentiment.

We got in the car and drove the fifteen minutes to the theatre. Dawson kept the music soft as we chatted during the drive. We arrived at the theatre, and Dawson bought our tickets. He ordered two drinks and a large popcorn, and then we found seats in the back row. With only a handful of people sprinkled throughout, we had the back row to ourselves.

The lights went low as trailers filled the next twenty minutes.

Dawson and I munched on the popcorn as we discussed the upcoming features. Finally, the movie started.

I reached for some popcorn and grazed the top of Dawson's hand. Jerking my hand away, I said, "Sorry."

"You're fine."

I sipped on my drink and avoided the popcorn bucket after that. After a few minutes, Dawson leaned the popcorn toward me. "Have some more."

"No thanks."

He leaned over and placed the bucket on the floor. When he sat upright, he took my hand in his. Leaning closer, he said, "Zinn, did I tell you how pretty you look tonight?"

Giving him a quick look, I nodded. "Yeah, you did."

"Well, you deserve to hear it again," he whispered in my ear.

His breath tickled my neck, and I shifted my head over a bit.

Dawson scooted around, putting some space between us, but he held my hand. Uneasiness swooped over me. My questions about this being a date were answered. I wasn't even sure I wanted it to be a date now that I knew it was. I glanced over at Dawson, and he gave me a smile that both confused me and flattered me. Why did this being a date make me feel weird? He was cute, kind, and attentive. He had been totally respectful, but I had this weird feeling about him, and I couldn't get past it. I wasn't even sure what the feeling was, but something didn't feel right. This uneasiness kept me distracted from the movie. What was this disquietude? All at once I became fully aware of what it was: it was Drew. *How dare Drew tell me to watch out for Dawson?* His stupid problem—that he wouldn't be straight with me about Dawson—was causing a problem for me. Dawson had been great the whole night, but I couldn't even enjoy myself because of Drew. *Ugh! Why do I care so much what Drew Behr thinks?* He made it clear that dating me was a mistake. Here I was on a date with a really nice guy, and I kept thinking about Drew. It was so frustrating that I let Drew get in my head and ruin my night. I let out a sigh, which sounded a bit exasperated, and Dawson glanced my way.

"Everything okay?" Dawson asked.

"Yeah," I said, flashing him a forced smile, though I really did want to appear as if I was enjoying myself. Wasn't his fault, after all.

"I like seeing that."

I felt the heat rush to my cheeks.

Dawson shifted his weight and leaned himself closer to me. This time it didn't bother me, and I relaxed myself next to him. We enjoyed the rest of the movie, the heat of his torso radiating onto my shoulder. *Whew! Is this what chemistry feels like?* When the lights filled the room, Dawson held my hand as we left the theater and walked to the car.

When we got to The Slice, the parking lot was packed, as usual. Dawson took my hand and proudly led me through the door. The noisiness of the restaurant softened to a low roar when we entered. With several eyes on us, I did my best to ignore them. Those same heads immediately tilted down to fingers now fixated on rapid-fire texting. The gossip-spreading texts fueled my anxiety because of my likely assumption: it was only a matter of minutes before most of the school knew that Dawson and I were on a date.

Dawson said something about food or ordering or the table. Honestly, I didn't know what he said. I was feeling a little out-of-body at this point. He could have asked me if I wanted a milkshake on the moon and my answer would have been, "Yeah, sure!" I took a few deep breaths and told myself that all was well. *Wasn't it?*

Dawson motioned for the server and ordered us a pizza and some drinks. Waiting for our food, Dawson talked to several people. Not much was said to me, but then again, I didn't know many of Dawson's friends. As he talked to some guy from the basketball team, people trickled in and out of the restaurant. Ashlynn walked in and I waved at her. She smiled and headed toward me, then she abruptly stopped and the smile left her face. I motioned her over. She mouthed, "Maybe later," then turned and walked back out the door.

Dawson asked me a question, but Ashlynn and her instant exit had me distracted, so I mumbled something to him. I guess my answer suited him because he kept rambling about it. The chatter of the restaurant suddenly quieted, but Dawson didn't notice. He continued with the conversation.

"Dawson!" Drew's booming voice filled the restaurant as he walked through the crowd that parted like the Red Sea.

"Bear!" Dawson said calmly but with authority as he leaned back in his chair and put his arm around me. "Need something?"

"Yeah, I do," Drew snapped back. "I need you outside."

"Naw, I'm good right here with Zinn," Dawson said, leaning a little closer to me.

When Drew got to our table, he slammed his fists down and stared intensely at Dawson. "I guess you didn't understand me earlier."

"Naw, dude! I heard you loud and clear. I just don't care what you have to say," Dawson responded casually.

As they exchanged more words, I took a deep breath and chimed in. "Could you please stop your territorial nonsense?" My words didn't stop either of them, so I said it even louder. "Would you both please stop?" Again, I was ignored. As they continued with their rants, I stood up, grabbed my coat from the chair, and took off for the door.

"Zinn, wait!" Drew's voice trailed behind me.

I pushed open the door and stepped outside. Clusters of teens stood around the parking lot.

"Zinn!" came a voice from my left. Haley waved. As I went toward her, someone took hold of my arm.

"Zinn!" Drew said with concern.

"Leave me alone, Drew."

Then Dawson flew out of the restaurant, grabbed Drew's arm, and pulled it off me. "Can't you take a hint? Zinn's not into you."

"Get your hand off me, Dawson!" Drew yelled as he flung out of Dawson's grip.

"Would you both stop?" I yelled.

"Zinn, what's going on?" Haley whispered.

Drew turned me to face him, softly holding my arm. "Zinn, let me take you home."

Dawson grabbed Drew's shoulder this time and jerked him from me. "When Zinn wants to leave, she'll leave with me."

Drew's eyes filled with rage. "Zinn's not going anywhere with you."

"That's not your decision, Drew!"

"You heard her, Bear. It's not your decision."

"Zinn, please just listen to me," Drew begged.

"No, you listen," I said. "Being my friend doesn't give you the right to tell me who I can go out with."

"Uh, I know that, Zinn," Drew started to explain. "It's just—"

"Yo, dude! Stop embarrassing yourself. Just go already. Zinn chose me. Get over it."

"Shut up, Dawson! Just crawl back into your hole and leave Zinn alone. She doesn't know what she's choosing by hanging around you, and you know it."

I stood there as the two of them yelled back and forth. If I tried to say anything, they just ignored me and kept slinging verbal daggers back and forth. They took a step toward each other with each comment and were eventually chest to chest, yelling in each other's face. I'd witnessed this too many times with Bryce. Knowing exactly what was coming next, I huffed and yelled, "I'm done!"

"Zinn!" Drew snapped out of his testosterone trance and looked at me, moving away from Dawson.

"Yo, dude, chill. Zinn's done. Time to go," Dawson said.

Drew's jaw clenched, and he glared at Dawson in a way that didn't signify hatred, but a warning.

"Stop, Drew. I'm done!" I yelled.

He turned back to me with sad eyes. "Zinn, I'm sorry."

Looking to Haley, I asked, "Can you take me home, please?"

"Yo, Zinn, I got you," Dawson said, reclaiming our original date.

Drew darted toward Dawson's face and started yelling again. Dawson came back at him with a shove.

"Haley, I gotta get out of here," I said, briskly walking away.

"Ryan, let's go," Haley said to Ryan, who had been quiet all this time.

The teens scurried past me as I headed toward Ryan's truck. Haley opened the door and I slipped into the back. As Ryan pulled out of the parking lot, I refused to look at the scene unfolding—first the shoves, then the fists. Unless someone stepped in to stop them, it would get bad. I had no desire to watch their Neanderthal behaviors. They could beat each other black and blue as far as I was concerned. As we drove away, silent tears fell down my cheeks.

Haley flooded me with questions. I responded with short answers and told her I didn't want to talk. They dropped me off at home, and I went inside without them, not in the mood to invite them for a hang, obviously. Thankfully, Mom wasn't anywhere to be seen, so I quickly leaped up the stairs, taking them two at a time. As I stepped into my bedroom, Mom opened her door. "Zinn, that you?"

"Yes," I said quietly from my doorway with my back to her.

"Home earlier than I expected you."

"Uh, yeah," I said, keeping my back to her. "Kind of dead tonight, you know?"

"Did you have a good time?"

"Uh, yeah. Movie was good."

"Good! I'm gonna get back to my show."

"Okay, Mom. Night."

"Night, bug." She closed her door, allowing me to escape into mine.

Safe in my room, I let out the tears again. Oreo waddled over to me and put his paws on my leg. I swooped him up in my arms and climbed into the bed. Oreo patiently waited to settle himself as I got comfortable in a sea of pillows and blankets. His sad eyes filled with concern as he cuddled close against me. My phone buzzed every few seconds. Annoyed, I grabbed it and threw it in the corner. Oreo raised his head and whimpered. Rubbing the top of his head, I lay there crying and finally fell asleep.

CHAPTER TWENTY-FOUR

"Zinn, sweetie! Um . . . Drew's outside. Said he needs to talk to you," Mom said awkwardly, aware she was caught up in my drama.

"What?" I sat up, barely awake, trying to register what she'd just said as the sun peeked through the window. The previous evening flashed in my mind, and immediately the stress returned.

"Drew! He's outside. Begging to talk to you," Mom restated, clearly not enjoying the role of mediator.

"Drew?" I echoed, feeling disoriented. "Outside?"

"Wanna tell me why this boy is ringing the bell at eight o'clock on a Saturday morning?"

I shook my head as I sat up. "I don't know." *I knew* . . .

"Okay," she said, leaning on the door frame. "You gonna talk to him?"

"I don't know, I need a minute to think."

Rubbing my eyes, my fingers moved to my temples. Drew waited outside, filled with an urgent need to talk to me that it overrode his ego to remain calm and in control in front of my mom.

"What do I tell him?"

I snapped, "I don't know, Mom. A minute, please?"

"Hey!" she said sternly. "Just the messenger here. Watch that tone."

"Yes, ma'am. I'm sorry. Just trying to think."

She moved toward the bed and stood beside me. Brushing the hair out of my face, she smiled. "When you have a friend knocking on your door, wanting to talk, then maybe you should hear 'em out."

I sighed. "Tell him I'll be right there."

She smiled, then stepped into the hallway and went down the stairs.

My phone vibrated in the corner. I got out of bed and picked it up. I had twenty-three text notifications. A couple of messages from Haley, one from Ashlynn, one from Dawson, and the rest were from Drew. Since he was right outside, I tossed the phone on the bed.

No reason to read it when he can say it in person.

Still in last night's clothes with makeup smudged across my face, I walked to the bathroom to wash up. After wiping my face clean, I pulled my frizzy hair into a messy bun.

Leaning into the mirror, I took a deep breath. *Mom's right. I should hear him out.* I headed down the stairs, ready to hear what Drew had to say. When I hit the bottom step, Mom sat in the living room alone.

"Well, where is he?" I said with annoyance.

Mom shrugged. "Said he'd wait outside."

"It's freezing."

"I told him that. Said he didn't care."

I flung the door open. Drew was perched on the hood of his truck, but upon seeing me, he immediately jumped off and hurried over.

"Zinn, I'm so sorry."

The chill of the wind cut through my coatless frame and caused me to wrap my arms around myself, attempting to rub away the cold. Drew slipped off his coat and wrapped it around my shoulders.

"Here, you're freezing."

A slight redness around his left eye and few small scrapes on his cheek let me know they had swapped some punches, but apparently it didn't get too out of hand.

"What'd you want to tell me, Drew?"

"Did you read my texts?"

Giving him a cold stare, I shook my head, signaling that would be a no.

"Uh, well . . . I just—" he fumbled, and I quickly interrupted.

"Just say it."

"Well, uh . . . coffee!" Turning to the truck, he grabbed the cup and handed it to me. "I have coffee."

"Is that why you're here? To give me coffee?"

A deflated look came over him. "Zinn, can we go for a drive and talk?"

"You got something to say, then say it."

With longing in his eyes, he took my hand, but I quickly jerked it away. His eyes showed defeat as he dropped his gaze. "I really messed up." He shook his head, then his glance met my eyes. "Please, tell me I've not ruined everything?"

I inhaled then exhaled. "What're you talking about?"

"Us, me and you. Please, tell me I've not ruined things."

"Drew, we're not ruined, okay. I mean, yeah! I'm pretty mad at you, but we're still friends. You've just got to understand that you can't tell me who I can date."

He shook his head, implying I wasn't understanding. His hands grasped my shoulders. "You're not getting it. I'm not talking about us. Not the *friends* version of us. I'm talking about the other version of us. *Us*, us."

"Us, *friends*. Us, *us*. You're talking in riddles, Drew."

"Zinn, I'm talking us."

The intensity of his blue eyes made my tummy do that flip-flop thing. The tough facade I had brought with me began to crumble as his grasp on my shoulders turned into a caress down my arms. Quickly, I hardened back up, straightened myself, and took a step back.

"Us, yeah. I get it," I said firmly. "We need some ground rules for our friendship."

Drew rubbed his forehead as if in emotional pain. "You really don't know. How do you not know?"

"Know what, Drew?"

Running his hand through his hair, he sighed. "Zinn, I like you and not just as a friend."

I swallowed and inhaled. "What?" I shook my head in disbelief, hoping he'd clarify things real soon. "What do you mean you *like me*?"

"Zinn, I don't know how to make it any clearer. I like you."

I took a deep breath as my eyes closed. *What is he saying? Am I hearing him right? Drew just said he likes me.* My head began to spin. *Is this real?*

"Zinn?"

"Hold up. Before, you said you only wanted to be friends," I countered.

"Yeah, that was then," he explained, but just barely.

"Now you're saying you like me?"

"Yeah." Drew's eyes danced. "That is exactly what I'm saying."

He took a step closer to me. A lump formed in my throat, knowing this was a pivotal moment. I threw up my hand to stop him from coming any closer.

"What has changed?" I challenged.

With a stunned look he said, "Uh, well . . . When I heard you went out with Dawson, I just—"

"So this is because I went out with Dawson?" I interrupted.

"No." His eyes were full of concern.

"But you just said when you heard I went out with Dawson . . ."

"Well, yeah. I mean, things are different now."

"What's different, Drew? Is it the fact that someone wants to go out with me, or is it the fact that it's Dawson who wants to go out with me?"

Drew's eye widened. "Well, uh, it's—"

"I get it, Drew. It's this stupid vendetta you have with Dawson, and I'm just the latest pawn. I can't believe you. I've liked you for months, and you've shown no interest in me, and now—"

"You've liked me for months?" Drew interrupted.

Nervous, I was unable to answer for a long moment. "Well, uh, yeah. But that's beside the point. Don't interrupt me."

"You like me? Why didn't you tell me?"

Why didn't I tell him? I can't believe him. He's the one who said dating would be a mistake. Has he forgotten that? "That's in the past, Drew. It doesn't matter now."

"What do you mean it doesn't matter now?" Drew said, confused.

"I mean, that's not what this is about. This is about how you decide to tell me you like me after I get asked out by your . . . your enemy! This isn't about you wanting to go out with me. This is about you wanting to beat Dawson. You are unbelievable!" I walked away, feeling both drawn to him and offended at his possible reasons for him stating he liked me.

Before I got to the porch, Drew had me by the hand. "Zinn, this is not about you going out with Dawson. I mean, you going out with him bothers me, but that's not why I'm telling you this."

Turning my head to face him, I said, "Drew, I wish I could believe you, but I don't. Please, just leave." Pulling my hand from his, I opened the door and stepped inside.

"Zinn, wait!" Drew said as I shut the door.

I leaned on the door with my eyes closed.

Mom's voice trailed from the kitchen. "Zinn, everything okay?"

"I don't know."

She walked into the living room and gave me that mom stare. The good, kind, and compassionate one. "Wanna talk about it?"

"Not really. I'm going to my room." I pushed off the door and headed up the stairs.

Oreo lay curled up in the chair, but his head popped up when I came in the room. I flung Drew's coat on the floor as I fell onto the bed. Oreo jumped up beside me and snuggled, knowing he was back on emotional-support pet duty.

Poor guy. He thought he'd just be a regular dog.

My phone annoyingly buzzed again. Ready to toss it to the floor, I read Drew's texts instead. The first few asked me to call him with some sorrys mixed throughout. The last three or four messages gave the explanation of how much he liked me. *Why now?* As I read the texts again, my eyes blurred. Wiping the tears away, I read Dawson's one text.

Dawson: Sorry about Bear 😅
What a loser...
Hang tonight?

He's not much on empathy, huh? The dull pressure of a headache began mounting. No surprise with all the stress and confusion surrounding me. Scanning Dawson's text again, I noticed it was sent at 2:00 a.m. *I left him at 10:30 p.m.* Checking Drew's texts, his first one came at 10:37 p.m. And the last one was sent at 6:30 this morning. He sent at least twenty messages that came throughout the night. Obviously, Drew didn't sleep. My head hurt even more as I tried to force this confusing scenario to make sense. My phone vibrated.

Haley: Zinn, you awake?

Me: Yeah…

Haley: What's going on? Everyone's talking bout the fight

Me: Ugh, it's a lot to go into

Haley: People are saying you were out with Dawson?

Me: Yeah I was 🙁

Immediately, my phone rang.

"Hey, Haley."

"You were out with Dawson? I thought you were with Drew. What's going on? Why were you with Dawson? Is that what they were fighting about?"

"Slow down, Haley. I can only handle one question at a time."

"You were at The Slice with Dawson?"

"Yeah, we'd been to a movie."

"What?" Haley said with complete shock. "I didn't know you were talking to him."

"I'm not. The movie just sorta happened."

"Zinn, Dawson doesn't 'sorta happen.' He's, uh . . . calculated. Very calculated."

What does she mean, calculated? My momentary hesitation prompted her to give a more detailed explanation. "Zinn, Dawson's got a motive for taking you out. The movies didn't just *sorta happen*."

"Trust me. It did," I said, regretting the sharpness of my statement.

"Zinn." Haley spoke with a very uncharacteristic serious tone. "You know about Dawson, right?"

"I know he's popular."

"Yeah, he's popular cause of The Boneyard. Dawson's a top scorer."

A sick feeling came to my stomach. "Haley, are you sure? He's been so nice to me."

"Yeah, Zinn, I'm sure. He's Big Dawg. Everyone knows it." Her tone expressed softness and sensitivity.

How did I miss this? Dawson on The Boneyard? Of course, Dawson Gregory . . . Big Dawg. I was so stupid. Haley's silence let me process the truth of Dawson's reputation. For once, I rambled incessantly as Haley offered words of comfort.

"Oh, Haley! I can't believe I've done this. Drew warned me to stay away from Dawson." My voice cracked. "He knew the truth, but I didn't listen."

"Figures. Drew would know better than anyone how Dawson works."

"How would Drew know better than anyone?"

"Because they started The Boneyard."

Filled with instant regret, I didn't want to hear any more.

Haley, assuming my silence meant I wanted to know more, began to offer more details. "Freshman year, Drew and Dawson were big buds. That's when Dawson got his, um . . . Let's say that's when he got his Top Scorer reputation."

"Okay, but that's not Drew." Annoyance dripped from my words as Haley teased with the details.

"Well, Drew did too."

Shut up! I don't wanna know this. I felt sick to my stomach. I couldn't deal with this news. *Drew on The Boneyard? No way!* This couldn't be true. My instincts couldn't be that wrong about Drew, could they?

"Zinn, you still there?"

"Haley, I'm so . . . How could I have been so wrong about Drew?"

"Oh, Zinn, no!" Haley quickly interjected.

"Haley, this is too much. I can't handle it." My head was now pounding from the shock and disappointment.

"Zinn, you're not wrong about Drew. He's not on The Boneyard anymore. I don't know all the details. But I do know is this . . ."

She proceeded to explain more about Drew and Dawson being friends freshmen year. How the whole Boneyard fiasco began as a chat room and grew to the abhorrent site of bragging rights with coded posts, a point system, and a Top Scorer's section. Dawson's frequent posts pole-vaulted him as leading scorer. As his popularity and reputation elevated, so did the competition. Drew posted a couple of times, tallying some major points. Suddenly, he dropped off the board. My mind trailed to The Boneyard and those posts by Grizzly. *Drew was Grizzly?* "When Drew's posts stopped, he and Dawson stopped being friends."

"No wonder Drew got upset seeing Dawson and me at The Slice. It makes sense now why he was at my house this morning too."

"Who was at your house this morning? Drew or Dawson?" Haley chimed in.

"Drew. He showed up, declaring his feelings for me. Said he likes me, and not just in the friend way."

"Woah, what? Drew told you he likes you? I knew it." Even the phone couldn't conceal her enthusiasm as she squealed. "You've gotta tell me more about this."

"Haley, not now."

"Oh, sorry! Of course, not now!"

I explained to Haley all that Drew said this morning and how I got mad and left him standing in the cold.

"Zinn, you gotta call him."

"I can't call him. What would I even say?"

"Tell him you're sorry. Tell him you didn't know about Dawson. Tell him you are hopelessly in love with him. Just call him and say something. Anything!"

"A phone call? That's so weird." The thought of calling him made my pulse quicken. "I can't say it on the phone."

"Oh, what am I thinking? Of course you can't call him. You've gotta go see him. You've got to tell him in person," Haley said dreamily.

"Haley, I certainly can't do that. Just go over there? No way!"

"Yes, you can, Zinn. You have to. It's you and Drew. You two are fated or something."

"Haley, this is not a fairy tale."

"Zinn, please! Every love story can be a fairy tale."

Taking a deep breath, I said, "Drew didn't say anything about love. He said he liked me. That's a big leap to love."

"Zinn, every love story starts with a *like* story. Besides, a little fantasizing never hurts," she said. "Now stop talking to me and go find Drew."

"No, Haley! I can't do that. Just show up unexpectedly at his door? No!" As I spoke the words, the crumbled mass on the floor caught my eye. *Drew's coat.* I smiled thinking of how he wrapped it around my shoulders this morning. *Hmph, maybe that would work?* "Haley, I have his coat."

Haley squealed and instantly rattled off what I should do. My courage began to grow, and I felt giddy hearing Haley describe the next moments being like a scene from a movie: me frantically driving, then running into Drew's arms, and finally him kissing me. Even though Haley's Oscar-worthy scenario was unlikely, her excitement was contagious. I was pumped!

"Okay, I'm gonna go."

"Oh yay!" Haley's enthusiasm spilled from the phone. "Now go! No second-guessing."

Ending the call, I grabbed his coat and bounded down the steps. "Mom, I'm borrowing the car. Be back in a bit!"

The drive to Drew's house took forever. My fingers frantically tapped the steering wheel when I got behind a slow truck. Finally, it turned, and I hit the gas, speeding down the road. My stomach flipped-flopped when I turned onto his street. *What if he doesn't wanna see me? What if he — Stop it! Haley said not to second-guess.*

Pulling into the driveway made my heart sink. I was here. *Now what?* Drew was pushing Avery on the tire swing and immediately looked at my car. A twinge of excitement and nerves hit me. He stopped the swing and said something to Avery. He shoved his hands in his pockets as he slowly walked toward me. Hesitantly, I opened the door and stepped out. Avery leapt from the swing and bolted for me.

"Zinn!" She wrapped her tiny arms around my waist.

"Hey, sweetie."

"Zinn, you wanna swing with me? Drew can push us both."

"Hey, squirt. Go inside, okay?" Drew said.

"But Zinn wants to swing with me."

"Let's swing in a bit?" I said, trying to convince her to listen to her brother.

"Squirt, inside, 'kay?" Drew placed his hands on her shoulders. "I need to talk to Zinn."

"I don't wanna," Avery whined as she lifted her chin to see Drew.

"Give us a few moments now, and I'll play a game with you later."

"The princess game?"

"Yeah, sure," Drew answered her as he stared at me.

"Can Zinn play too?" Avery continued her negotiations, trying to take advantage of Drew in his weak moment.

"Avery, just go!" The sternness in Drew's voice let Avery know she had pushed her luck too far. Sadly, she meandered to the house.

Drew looked to Avery. "Hey, squirt! Sorry I snapped. We'll play the princess game and the pony one too."

Avery smiled. "Okay, but don't talk too long." She bounced up the steps and my heart ached for her. I didn't want our mess to upset her happy little world.

Drew looked at me flatly. "What're you doing here?"

"Uh, well"—I held out his coat—"I forgot to give you back your coat."

"My coat? That's why you're here?"

"Uh, yeah. I also wanted to talk to you."

Drew inhaled as he stood quietly. My nerves were jumping around, causing me to fidget and sweat. I contemplated my next move. Haley's voice trickled into my mind:

Just say something.

"Um, well . . . You said a lot at my house."

Sadness filled Drew's face, and he looked a little sick. "Yeah, it was stupid."

I shook my head from side to side. "It wasn't stupid, Drew."

Drew's blue eyes shimmered, and he offered a smile that made me feel a little lighter.

"I was a jerk, and I'm sorry about the whole thing with Dawson. Like I said, there are some things you don't know."

"Drew, I know."

His face lost all color as his eyes bugged out. Then his eyes darkened and the sadness returned.

Crud, I'm messing this up!

"Haley told me some stuff about freshmen year. She also gave me the deets on . . ." I paused, agonizing over saying the name. "Well, she told me about The Boneyard." I cringed inside, feeling embarrassed for him and also sad his past was exposed.

"Oh." I didn't think he could look any sadder until his whole persona transformed in front of my eyes. His somber eyes fell to the ground as his shoulders slouched.

I couldn't bear any more, so I babbled, "She told me enough to know that Dawson is bad news and that you—"

"That I am too," he cut in.

"She didn't say that." I slowly shook my head, wondering what to say next.

"Zinn, just say it. We're not friends anymore, right?"

Stunned by his assumption, I went speechless. *Why would he think that?*

His gaze fell to the ground. "I get it, Zinn. You deserve better. I'm sorry for all—"

"Drew, would you shut up for a minute? I don't wanna just be friends with you."

His head shot up enthusiastically. "Are you saying what I think you're saying? Please tell me you're saying it?" He laughed nervously, but I could tell he was getting more confident.

I gave him coy smile. "I am saying it!" And with nothing else to add, I waited. It was his move now.

Briefly, he paused, then he smiled wide. Suddenly, he engulfed me in his arms, picking me up and spinning me around as he yelled, "You're really saying it!" I wrapped my arms tightly around his neck and I held him close. Finally stopping, he placed me on the ground.

His eyes melted into mine. "Zinn, are you sure? 'Cause if you still need time with the whole Bryce thing, then I'll wait."

Totally lost and confused by what he said, I went silent.

"I saw how torn up you got about seeing Bryce and Sam together. That's when I knew you weren't ready."

"Are you talking about Christmas shopping in Cookeville?"

Drew gave a repeated nod with a questionless look on his face.

"I wasn't torn up about Bryce. I was worried about Sam. I've been over Bryce for a while now," I clarified.

A look of frustration filled his eyes. "What? Why didn't you tell me?"

"Because you told me you just wanted to be friends!" I blurted.

Then his sudden exclamation came. "No! I only said that because I didn't want to rush you." He gently brushed the hair from my eyes. "Doesn't matter now. Besides, I'll wait as long as it takes." He touched my cheek lightly, which heightened my senses and got my full attention.

"Drew, there's nothing to wait for!" I declared.

"Zinn, you're everything, and that's worth the wait." His smile was so sincere. How did I ever believe Dawson's manipulative gestures of affection?

Drew gently wiped a tear from my cheek and then drew me into his strong arms. Sighing, I rested my head on his shoulder as he lightly kissed the top of my head.

"Are you done talking yet?" Avery called out from the front door.

Drew released me and smiled at her. "Yeah, squirt! We're done talking."

Avery came running to us. "Zinn, will you play with me?"

"I think I can play one game," I said.

Avery pulled on my hand excitedly. "Let's play the princess game."

Drew picked her up and tickled her sides. "Calm down, squirt. She said she would."

Avery giggled as she twisted in Drew's arms. We walked to the house and she chatted about the game. When we got inside, Avery climbed out of Drew's arms and ran to her room. Within a few minutes, we were on the floor playing the game. Avery was all princess cuteness and drama, and her liveliness entertained me. When the game was over, Drew stood and held out his hand to me.

"Tonight? You have plans?" Drew asked as he helped me stand.

"No," I said.

"How about we go out?"

"Drew Behr, are you asking me out on a date?" I gave him a smirk.

"Yes, ma'am," he replied with a nod.

In a singsong manner, Avery repeated the phrase, "Drew likes Zinn! Drew likes Zinn." Drew just smiled, making no attempt to stop her. Instead, she laughed so hard she choked on her words, which made her finally stop.

"You'd better believe it! Now let's walk Zinn to her car."

That night Drew took me to dinner, and then we hung out at my house. We talked with my mom before cuddling on the couch to watch a movie. It was after midnight before he left. Sunday morning, he picked me up for church, then we went to his house and ate lunch with Avery and his mom. After spending a couple of hours playing with Avery, we headed to the basement and worked on the song for the talent show.

When we were done practicing, Drew went upstairs to grab some food and drinks. I wandered around the room, which proudly displayed pictures of Drew and his family over the years. A bookcase held Drew's football memorabilia from Peewee league to present day. Pictures lined the shelves, chronicling Drew's history. Picking up a team picture from freshmen year, I scanned for Drew. His serious, intimidating look was so out of character that it made me snicker. The snickering stopped and an uneasiness filled me when I recognized Dawson standing beside him.

Drew coming down the steps prompted me to set the photo back on the shelf. I met him at the couch as he placed snacks and drinks on the table. I settled beside him, questions brewing and ready to be released. I took the drink he offered me. "Can I ask you a question?"

Drew opened his drink and tore into the bag of chips. "Shoot."

"Don't get mad, okay?"

"At you, never."

"What about your posts?" I began nervously. "You know, on The Boneyard?"

Drew's jovial eyes turned sad as he stopped eating the chips. I immediately regretted the question. "It's okay, Drew. You don't have to tell me. It's none of my business anyway."

Drew straightened himself on the couch, set the bag of chips on the table, and scooted closer to me. "Zinn, you have every right to know. It's just the past and stuff I don't like to think about now."

His words hit me in the pit of my stomach. "Drew, let's just forget it, okay? I totally understand. Besides, it really doesn't matter to me anyway. Let's leave the past in the past."

Ease came over Drew, and he wrapped his arms around me as we settled back onto the couch. Forgetting the darkness of our pasts, we enjoyed this moment and allowed a spark of hope to ignite within us for something better that lay ahead.

CHAPTER TWENTY-FIVE

The inevitable return to school had reared its ugly head. Just as Drew promised, he pulled in my driveway at 7:40 a.m. When I walked outside, he slipped out of his seat and greeted me with a hug.

"I've missed you."

"It's been ten hours since you left me."

"And that's an eternity." He winked as he opened my door.

The drive to school went by quicker than I wanted. The truck pulled into the parking lot and my stomach turned upside down. I would see Dawson. People would know Drew and I were together. All the potential gossip stressed me out. I wanted so desperately to fade into the background. We got out of the truck, and Drew gently took my hand. The vastness of his hand engulfing mine instantly steadied my nerves and made me smile as we walked across the parking lot.

As we made our way through the crowded sidewalk and up the steps, heads turned. Phones in the hands of chatty students told me that Bargeston High School's population was receiving the updated status of "Drew and Zinn."

We entered the building and silence trickled through the crowd as we passed. I gulped, but Drew didn't seem phased. He confidently walked the hall, holding tight to my hand. He carried on like it was any other day, greeting all the onlookers the same as he always did.

When we turned left at the end of the hall, Drew's demeanor instantly changed. Midway down the hall in the middle of a group of guys, Dawson was caught up in conversation. My stomach rose to my throat. Tristan nudged Dawson on the arm, getting his attention, then motioned toward us. Dawson's gaze resembled two pools of empty darkness, trying to threaten and shame us both. But today, Drew was his main target. Even with the distance of the hall, the clenching of Dawson's jaw was pronounced. Drew pulled me closer and folded my arm under his as we kept walking. The protruding vein beside his right eye caused a heaviness in my chest and quickened my pulse. My mouth started watering as the nausea set in. My eyes scanned around for a life raft anywhere. No escape was nearby. No stairwell door. No talkative Haley. No Coach needing to speak to Drew. We had to pass Dawson openly to get to econ.

I held my breath as we walked. East Hall was coming up. I pulled slightly to the right, but Drew didn't budge. His pace stayed steady as he headed straight toward Dawson. From the East Hall corridor, Savage's voice trailed to us.

"Bear, come here, would ya?"

Without taking his eyes off Dawson, Drew turned right and headed toward Savage. I exhaled a deep breath. The vein had all but disappeared, but the furrowing of his brow remained. Drew's unusual quietness prompted Savage to take the lead in talking. In an uncharacteristic fashion, Savage's arm draped on Drew's shoulders. Drew held on to my hand and extended his arm as Savage pulled him from me slightly. They huddled near the window as Savage whispered to him, preventing me from hearing. Ashlynn seemed to appear out of nowhere.

"Hey, Zinn! I love that top." *Has she been here the whole time?* "Come with me to the girls' room." Grabbing my hand, she pulled me away from Drew, and I lost the grip of his hand. Darting my eyes to him, he winked and gave an affirmative smile. Savage's back was to me as he continued to talk to Drew.

When we entered the bathroom, Ashlynn jabbered about nothing of importance. She busied herself with touching up makeup as I tapped my nails on the sink.

"Hey, Ash, I'd better get back to Drew."

"Um, just give me a minute. Almost done."

"Okay." I sighed as I conceded to her request.

Ashlynn didn't seem to hurry herself at all. I began tapping my toe as she fiddled with her hair.

"Really, Ash. I need to get to class," I said abruptly.

Her eyes cut to me. "Give the guys a minute to talk, okay?" I raised my eyebrow, questioning her serious tone. She smiled and went back to her primping. "I'll just be a sec."

After another couple of minutes, Ashlynn and I finally exited the bathroom. Savage and Drew were waiting where we left them. Ashlynn said her farewell as she left us. Savage stayed beside Drew and me as we made our way to the end of the hall. Drew, holding my hand, had returned to his jovial self. I breathed a little easier but prayed Dawson would be gone when we hit North Hall.

We came to the end of the hall and made the right turn, and there he stood. Dawson was leaning on the windowsill, arms crossed, surrounded by several guys. Savage stepped slightly ahead of Drew and me. Drew gave me a quick wink as he pulled my hand closer to him. When we were about ten feet away, Dawson stood. About six feet from him, he moved toward us. His eyes beamed into us as if they were lasers, attempting to burn our insides. Savage, still slightly ahead of us, nodded to the group as we got closer. Drew kept his eyes on me as we stepped past them. Mumbles from the group followed us.

"Yo, Dawg! You ain't doing nothing?" a voice called out from the group of guys, and more mumbles followed.

I could barely swallow. My mouth had gone dry from the anxiety. I attempted to swallow anyway, but it felt like a mass was stuck in my throat. A deep breath in and out helped a little, but not much. The energy swirling in the hall had *fight* written all over it. *Please don't let Dawson say anything to Drew*, I prayed silently. Just a few more feet to the door and we would be in the clear.

"Zinn!" Dawson yelled. His tone was filled with more arrogance than he'd ever revealed before. Drew's head shot around and his mouth clamped shut, intensifying his defined jawline. Chuckles filled the hallway. Holding my breath, I waited for Drew's reaction, but he didn't do anything. Dawson's eyes zeroed in on Drew, while he spoke to me. "Zinn, how about we hang again tonight? Let's finish what we started Saturday night, you know?" Dawson's cocky grin widened.

Drew growled low and gripped my hand tighter. Savage's hand went to Drew's shoulder.

"Got something to say, Bear?"

Drew loudly exhaled as he faced forward. He quickly jerked his head to the right, cracking his neck for relief as we progressed toward the classroom. The fervency slowly lessened on his face. "I'm fine."

"Really?"

"Absolutely." He sent a gentle smile my way.

We arrived at econ as the bell rang. Savage nodded and darted across the hall into his classroom. Drew and I entered our class and took our seats. When econ finished, the day progressed as normal—except for Drew and me being the central topic of the gossip mill. This created a frenzy of talk as we walked the halls, all reminiscent of my first day here.

Aside from the talk that followed us, the stroll between most classes was uneventful. My nervous anticipation of any exchange with Dawson had yet come to fruition. Any time there was the potential for an interaction with Dawson, Savage magically appeared. Obviously, the boys had planned out the entire day, and part of their plan involved this whole bodyguard spectacle. When I walked the halls with the two of them barricading themselves around me, it felt like I had a secret-service detail. By the time I went to English class, I'd had all I could take.

"You two have got to stop this."

"Stop what?" Drew questioned while cutting his eyes to Savage.

They quickly let me know that denying was going to be their stance. "Stop with the muscle patrol," I said. "I don't need you two protecting me."

Drew gave Savage a mischievous grin. "Savvy, you on muscle patrol?"

"Hmm, can't say that I am," Savage replied, giving a coy smile.

Turning toward me, Drew's impish grin lit up his face. He shook his head and laughed lowly, trying to blow it all off.

"Don't laugh at me." I huffed, crossing my arms over my chest.

Drew laughed more as he tried to release my hand from my crossed arms. Fighting him from taking my hand instigated more of his attention. His hand lightly brushed the hair from my face. "Zinn, we're just walking to class. No different than any other day. Right, Savvy?"

"Hmm." Savage nodded as he stepped into the classroom. "This is all you, buddy."

I grabbed Drew's hand and led him away from the students filtering into English.

"You're kidding, right? This is not like any other day."

"What do you mean? What's different?" He lightly touched my cheek. "I just want you to be okay. Is that so bad?"

"I am okay," I said firmly. "And I don't need you doing this whole territorial thing with me. I've had enough of that with—" I quickly stopped myself from saying anything else.

Hurt filled Drew's face. "You've had enough of that with who?" Drew's pain-filled eyes gutted me, and disagreeing with him proved pointless. I was comparing him to Bryce and he knew it. The wave of familiar sickness came over me. I wasn't sure what to do or say, so I said nothing.

"I gotcha. I'm reminding you of that jerk." Drew threw up his arms and turned away from me. I froze and held my breath. He's gonna hit something. I closed my eyes, waiting to hear his fists slam into the locker or his feet kick the trashcan.

"Zinn."

I opened my eyes. Drew, standing patiently in front of me, said, "I'm sorry I made you feel that way." The hurt in his eyes made tears well up. Drew's hand gently lifted my chin and, meeting my eyes, wiped the tear falling down my cheek.

"Zinn, please don't cry." He wrapped his arms around me and held me. "Listen, Zinn, I need to make sure you're safe, okay? Please, let me do this. Can you go along with my plan, at least for a few days?"

I nodded, even though I wished for something different. Drew brushed the hair from my eyes and walked me to the door. He gave me a soft kiss on my cheek, then he whispered in my ear, "Hope class is good. I'll be waiting right here for you when it's over."

Dawson's presence loomed around every corner like a lion hunting its prey, lurking and waiting for the perfect opportunity to pounce. Being the sought-after prey made me uneasy the whole day. Anytime I heard his name or saw him and his entourage, I got sick to my stomach, even surrounded by my personal convoy.

Drew took seeing Dawson all in stride. He would hold my hand, chat, and smile whenever we passed by him. No doubt Savage's presence allowed Drew to maintain his calmness.

On top of the stress of an altercation with Dawson, the school's obsession with the situation created even more turmoil. Like the weatherman predicting the forecast, teens were making their bets on who would win the fight everyone believed was inevitable.

By the time chorus rolled around, Savage had finally ended his hallway escort duty. Things started to feel somewhat normal. I wasn't constantly looking over my shoulder for the last walk of the day. Drew leaned on the wall as he talked, his hand running through his curls and his eyes dancing.

"Back lot after school, okay?"

"I gotcha! Back lot," I repeated.

"Don't forget." He pushed off the wall.

I smirked and shook my head. "I won't forget."

"Miss you already!" he called out, walking backward. Forming a heart with his fingers, he winked and ran down the hall.

The bell rang as I stepped into the classroom. Immediately I was met by Haley, who flooded me with questions about the whole Dawson drama. To say I wasn't in the mood was an understatement. When Mr. Myers settled at the piano, Haley finally ceased with the inquisition. When the last bell rang, I breathed a sigh of relief as I headed out the door. Haley walked beside me, rattling off about all she had heard, then asked for clarification. We maneuvered through the hallway and out the courtyard doors toward the parking lot. Busy talking, we were halfway across the parking lot when it hit me that Drew was waiting in the back lot. I explained to Haley and took off to meet Drew. Avoiding the crowd around the buses, I steered around them and made my way back to the courtyard. When I got to the stairwell leading up to the courtyard, I walked up a few steps and then stopped.

"Zinn." Dawson stood at the top of the steps. "How ya doin'?"

I took a deep breath before I replied, "I'm okay."

Dawson stood in front of me as if he'd snapped his fingers and instantly transported himself. Gripping the rails, he leaned close to me, urging me to take a step backward.

"Why so nervous, Zinn?" He eased down the stairs while maintaining close proximity.

Shaking my head side to side, I said, "I'm not nervous. Just in a hurry."

"Hurry, huh? Seems you've been in hurry all day." He pressed closer as I took another step. "Or maybe you're avoiding me?"

I finally stopped and straightened my shoulders. "I'm not avoiding you. I just don't have anything to say to you."

"Ouch! And here I thought we were friends."

"I think your definition of friends is much different than mine," I said, looking at him intently.

"*Hmph*! Maybe, and maybe not. You did make your choice though."

My eyes widened and he gave me an obnoxious smirk. He leaned in close enough that I could feel his hair touch my face, which caused me to lose my breath in fear momentarily. "It is a shame." Finally, he backed away.

"What does that mean?" I said as I narrowed my eyes.

"Yeah, it really is a shame." He shook his head side to side, then took a step forward. "Zinn, don't be stranger, 'kay?" And with that, he walked past me.

I exhaled deeply but the tension didn't leave my body. I grabbed the stair rail as the dizziness hit me. My surroundings began to spin. I closed my eyes to steady myself and gripped the rail tighter. Opening my wet, teary eyes, I ran up the steps and headed to the back lot. When I opened the door and entered the hallway, Savage was talking to Malone. His eyes met mine and worry filled his face. I exhaled and walked toward him. He said something to Malone, then headed toward me.

"Zinn, what's wrong?"

Shaking my head, I tried to speak but couldn't say anything.

Savage quietly stood and waited for me to explain. After I caught my breath, I frantically said, "I forgot Drew was picking me up in the back lot."

"Don't worry. He won't leave you."

"I know that," I said emphatically.

Savage kept his eyes locked on mine but said nothing. *Do I tell Savage about Dawson?* He won't do anything except let me vent.

"I ran into Dawson outside." I instantly regretted my choice when Savage's anger turned into a blank stare, almost like he had disappeared. Savage stared at me but wasn't seeing me. Then, in an instant, the life came back into his eyes.

"Savage, are you okay?"

"Yeah, let's find Bear."

When we hit the back lot, Drew jumped off his tailgate and greeted me with a hug. His eyes trailed to Savage and his brow furrowed. Then his eyes cut to me. I held my breath as I waited for the questions. Shockingly, he only smiled and said, "Hey, beautiful."

"Uh, sorry I made you wait."

"No big." He winked and then glanced to Savage as he took my hand. "What brings you here, Savvy?"

"Just here," Savage said.

"Well, it's my doing, actually. I met Savage in the hall."

"Oh?"

"Well, uh, yeah. I forgot and went to the front lot. And, well . . . I sorta ran into Dawson."

Taking in a deep breath, Drew's eyes closed as he paused. Panic came over me and I apologized. "Look, I'm sorry, okay?"

His eyes shot open. "You're sorry? For what?"

"I forgot to meet you here and ran into Dawson because of it. I'm really sorry. Please don't be jealous, okay?"

"Jealous? I'm not jealous. I just wanna know what happened."

"What do you mean, what happened? Nothing happened!" I was completely annoyed. *Does he think I'm a helpless basket case?*

"*Hmph*. Nothing?" Drew asked.

"Yeah, Drew. He didn't do anything. He just said some stuff."

"What kinda stuff?"

"I don't know. It was something about me making my choice and how it was a shame. It was stupid! This whole scene is stupid. If this isn't jealousy, then what is it?"

Drew shook his head. "It's not your problem, okay. I'll take care of it." He opened the door to the passenger's side and tried to be chipper. "Let's get something to eat. I'm starving!"

When he shut the door, he and Savage huddled together for a few minutes. Then Savage gave me a wave and Drew climbed in and started the truck. He immediately started singing with the music.

What's going on? Is he not gonna say anything else?

"Drew, what about Dawson? I can tell you're upset."

Drew calmly answered, "I'm not upset."

"Okay. So what are you gonna do?"

"Nothing."

All day I had been on edge, waiting for any confrontation that could potentially lead to a fight. Now it had happened, and Drew expected me to believe he planned to do nothing. I didn't know what I expected from Drew, but this certainly wasn't it. He just sang along with the radio. The trees scrolled past as the truck moved down the road. Bryce and his outbursts came to my mind. But Drew did nothing of the sort. He wasn't looking for Dawson to fight him. He wasn't yelling. He wasn't interrogating me about what I had said to Dawson. No, he just sang.

The queasiness came as we pulled into Jack's. This whole day had been stress-filled, and now I waited for Drew's anger to spill forth. The anticipation was more than I thought I could take.

When we got out and headed across the parking lot, Drew tugged on my hand. "Hey, what's wrong?"

Shaking my head side to side, I replied, "Nothing."

"Zinn, somethings wrong. What is it?"

Eyes shot our direction from a group a few feet from us.

"Shh." I pulled him back toward the truck.

Drew stared at me. "Zinn, what's wrong?"

"Um, you tell me," I said.

Drew softly chuckled. "I asked you."

With wide eyes, I bit the corner of my lip as I waited for him to tell me more details. He shook his head as if to say, *I got nothing!*

"Zinn, what's going on? You're obviously upset."

"Uh, well, I figured you're kinda mad at me."

His smile faded to a look of concern. "Why would I be mad at you?"

I peered at him but said nothing. He gently took my hand and pulled me toward him. "Zinn, I'm not mad at you, okay?"

"But the thing with Dawson—"

"The thing with Dawson is with Dawson," he said, cutting me off.

"So does that mean you're gonna fight him?"

Drew cocked his brow, offended I assumed fighting was his go-to method. "Not if it can be avoided."

I breathed deep as my eyes closed. Avoided? He actually said *avoided.* Guys like him never avoided a fight. A guy like Jake might, but not Drew. After all that happened today, Drew wanted me to believe that he planned to avoid a fight with Dawson.

Does he think I'm stupid?

"Really? You expect me to believe that?"

Drew smiled and nodded. "Yeah, because it's the truth."

"Do you remember how mad you got with Dawson this morning? And how you didn't leave my side in the halls?" I said frustratingly.

"Yeah, because I know Dawson."

I rolled my eyes to let him know this was getting ridiculous—the vague "I know Dawson" statements. There was something more to it than The Boneyard fiasco.

Fine, if he doesn't want to offer details of the past, that's fine by me . . . except it wasn't really fine.

"Zinn, you don't know Dawson, but I do. And he's not someone I let my guard down with," Drew said. "Now is that what's got you all upset?"

I stepped away from Drew and leaned against the truck. He moved beside me, engulfing me in his arms and pulling me close.

"Beautiful." Drew kissed the top of my head. "Tell me what's bothering you?"

His blue eyes, full of tenderness, pleaded with me. I wanted to tell him everything, but I was scared. Scared about what he would think about me, scared about what he would say, and scared if I told him all my crazy fears, he would stop liking me. I sighed and rested my head on his shoulder.

"Zinn, please talk to me."

I shook my head and replied, "I'm good. Just tired."

Drew removed his arm from around my shoulders, straightened himself, and turned to face me.

"You don't have to pretend with me. You can tell me anything." He brushed the hair out of my eyes.

All the day's stress came pouring out as the words spilled from my mouth. I rambled on about how I'd been nervous all day. The stress of Dawson looming around every corner had kept my stomach in knots. But his stares were worse. The way his eyes followed me made me want to run the other way. Then I told him the panic I felt when I ran into Dawson and how it almost caused me to pass out. The anticipation of the possible fight that might break out between the two of them had me sick with worry. Being the center of gossip all day at school made me want to cry. Drew listened to me rant about it all. He didn't get angry. He didn't tell me I was stupid. He just listened to everything. He let me express all of my racing, anxious thoughts.

"Zinn, I'm gonna take care of you, okay? Don't let this whole Dawson mess make you sick. And who cares about school gossip? Tomorrow, it'll be focused on someone else. Will you let me protect you?"

"I can do that," I said. "Feeling protected is a new thing for me though." And it was. I had never felt safe with Bryce, so I would have to retrain my instincts and . . . trust.

"Good." He gave me a squeeze.

Relaxing in his arms, I'd never felt so safe, so protected, and so accepted. Drew felt too good to be true. Could I let myself believe in something this good? I really hoped so.

CHAPTER TWENTY-SIX

After school on Thursday, Haley and I went shopping for an outfit for the talent show. She was so excited for us to try on all these different styles. It was like a montage scene in one of those teen movies. The only thing missing was the music interlude as we modeled the outfits. After we finished shopping, Haley drove me home.

Haley chattered about her ideas for the Spirit Week yearbook section. Some kids riding their bikes in the road caused her to break unexpectedly, but she gathered her nerves and steadied the car, then rounded the curve. A strange car was parked in my driveway. Haley pulled into the drive. "Looks like you have company." A blonde girl wearing dark sunglasses sat on my porch.

"Hmm. I don't know who that is." I opened the door and the blonde girl stood and waited at the steps.

"You want me to stay for a bit?" Haley asked.

"Naw, I'm good. Thanks for the ride."

"Okay, then. See ya at Jules's house later."

I nodded as I shut the door.

"Hey, Z!" the girl called out.

"Sam? Wow, I didn't recognize you with the blonde hair."

"Yeah, it's different." She flipped her hair as she forced a smile. "I kinda thought I'd give it a try. You know, something new." She laughed nervously.

It wasn't just Sam's hair that looked different. She was much thinner—almost too thin. Also, she was wearing a lot of makeup. Her outfit . . . It was so revealing! I certainly wasn't used to her dressed this way.

"Whatcha doing here?"

Fidgeting with her hands, she cleared her throat. "Um, I, well . . . I just wanted to say hey. And . . . I was close by."

Unlocking the knob, I opened the door and tossed my keys on the entry table.

Greeting Oreo, Sam kneeled to pet him. "Hey, Oreo! Do you miss me, buddy?"

I went to the living room and plopped in the chair. Sam sat on the couch. "Nice car. Birthday present?"

Sam rolled her eyes. "Yeah, from my dad. He's got a new girlfriend, so you know what that means. He's father of the year, at least while she's around."

"And you had a big party?"

Sam's leg shook the whole room as her eyes darted nervously. "Uh, yeah. I mean, it was a surprise party that some of my friends threw for me."

"I see."

"It's been so crazy. It's like I have no time now, especially since Chris—" Sam stopped midsentence. "Um, since especially the new year. There's just no time to do anything, you know? Like our Christmas and how I just kinda bailed on it." Regret dripped from Sam's words as sadness consumed her face. Even with the look on her face, no words came to me. The pause grew to an awkward silence as she twisted in her seat and fidgeted with her hands.

"Z, I really am sorry about that. I was dumb."

"Sam, you're not dumb. And the Christmas thing? It's forgotten."

She smiled. "It's just that so much has happened since . . . Well, you know." Dropping her gaze, she softly said, "I really miss you."

I was stunned. After months of no contact, Sam was apologizing and telling me she missed me. I wasn't even sure what to say to that.

Then Sam perked up. "I just want things between us to be back to normal."

"Really? You think that's possible now?"

Sam looked at me with confusion. "Why not?"

Biting the corner of my mouth, I mustered up some courage. "Um, Bryce?"

"Why do you have to bring Bryce into this?"

My eyes widened. *Did she just ask me that question?* I inhaled deeply. "Because Bryce is the reason that things with us have changed."

"Bryce isn't to blame for any of this. Things have changed because of us."

"Are you for real? You're blaming me and you?"

Sam looked rattled, and then defiance flashed in her eyes. "You know, I think Bryce is right. It's best if I keep my distance from you."

The sting of her words felt like a dagger had been plunged into my heart. No matter how suspicious I'd been that Sam had been avoiding me because of Bryce, nothing could've prepared me for those words coming from her mouth. She stood. "It was a mistake coming here." She went to the door and walked toward her car. I got up and followed after her but halted in my tracks when she stopped. Turning to me, she shot me a look filled with unwarranted disdain.

"You know, Z, you are right. It's not possible for things to be normal between us anymore." She briskly walked to her car and opened the door as if waiting for a final sendoff.

The crushing ache in my heart hurt worse than anything, but I couldn't let things end this way with her. "Sam, no matter what, I'm always here!" I blurted out.

A look of sadness came from her that broke my heart even more. Her eyes fell to the ground, and she said with a cracked voice, "Just let me go, Z."

And with that, she slid into her seat, started the car, and pulled out of the drive.

I walked back into the house and fell on the couch. Sam's last words, "just let me go," rang through my mind. Did she mean forever? Was she telling me we weren't friends anymore? I started crying and couldn't stop.

The doorbell ringing roused me. Disoriented, I got up and opened the door. Drew stood there smiling, holding a flower. Instantly, his smile left. "What's wrong?" I threw my arms around him and sobbed. He hugged me tight. "Zinn, what is it?" I kept crying and he just held me. After the sobbing became light tears, Drew slowly released me. "What are all the tears about?" Using my sleeve to wipe my eyes, I shook my head and more tears started pouring. Drew wrapped his arms around me. "It's okay, Zinn. Whatever it is, it's gonna be okay."

After a few minutes, I had calmed enough to finally invite him in. We went to the living room and sat on the couch. He didn't ask any questions. He just kept telling me everything was gonna be okay and let me cry. When the tears were done, he looked at me with complete tenderness and took my hands in his and lightly kissed them. Trying my best to fight the tears, I smiled.

"There it is. That smile that melts my heart," Drew said. I smiled a little bigger and he winked. "So tell me . . . Who do I have to kill?"

I shot him a glare. He shrugged his shoulders and gave me a somewhat frightened look. "Just kidding. But who made you cry?"

"Sam was here when I got home."

He inhaled deeply and slowly released it. "Just Sam? No one else?"

"Just Sam."

"What happened? Why all the tears?"

The words began flowing from me as I told him all about the conversation. I shared with him that her last words were *just let me go*, which left me questioning what Sam and I were now.

"I knew Bryce was behind her not seeing me."

"Zinn, I know it hurts, but Sam has made her choice."

I nodded reluctantly. "I know you're right, but it doesn't make it any easier."

He pulled me toward him. "You can't fix her, Zinn. Sam is the only one who can fix this. You just have to be there for her when she asks for help."

"When she asks for help? But what if she never does?"

"Sam knows you'll always be there for her," Drew said optimistically.

I hoped he was right and that Sam did know I would always be there for her.

Bryce yelled in my face, and his muffled words became clearer.

"Z, shut up! Why are you lying?"

My breathing was erratic. His voice faded out again. Sam stood beside Bryce wearing fake designer sunglasses, and I grabbed at them, but Sam disappeared before my hands could reach her. More shots came from Bryce as his fist came toward me.

I sat up in bed, transitioning from the nightmare to the reality of my quiet and safe room. Oreo lay beside me, snoring. I exhaled deeply.

"It was just a dream," I said, desperate to hear my own voice.

I kept taking calming breaths before heading downstairs, where the smell of coffee filled the air. Mom's voice trailed from the kitchen as Grandma replied to her about something on the shopping list for dinner tonight. Greeting them, I poured myself a cup of coffee and sipped, waiting for the jolt of caffeine to bring me fully back to this world. I chatted with them a few minutes before heading to the living room and perching on the couch to look out the window. The dream replayed in my mind. Sam hiding behind the knock-off glasses and then disappearing. I shook my head. *It doesn't make sense.* Sam disappearing brought tears to my eyes. Had she disappeared from my life? I couldn't let Sam disappear. She was too important to me, to my history, and we still needed each other. I went upstairs and grabbed my phone.

Me: Sam, if you need me, I'm here

After a few minutes there was still no reply, so I set the phone on the desk and took a shower. Afterward, I lounged in my room, wearing a robe and a towel wrapped around my hair. I didn't feel like clothes just yet. I checked my phone, but she hadn't replied. I read my text again, and the words jumped out at me. I grabbed my journal and wrote down the line, *You need me, I'm here*. I flopped in my chair by the window, and the rest of the words came out effortlessly, though painfully.

You need me, I'm here. The hurt, betrayal, it's all gone.
Friends are more than any wrong. Nothing to lose, nothing to fear.
You need me, you call. Even when things pull us apart.
Nothing will pull you from my heart. Anytime you fall, you need me, you call.
You need me, I'm here. No worries, no sorrys
You need me, it's fine. I promise it's fine.
'Cause friends love at all times, and I'll be near.
You need me, I'm here. No matter all the wrongs
I'll never be gone. Nothing to lose, nothing to fear
You need me, I'm here.

"Zinn, we're leaving!"

Concentrating on the words filling the paper, I nodded without saying anything. Mom cleared her throat and repeated herself. "Zinn, we're leaving."

"Sorry, I'm writing."

"So what time are you leaving?"

"Elevenish."

"It's almost eleven," Mom said.

"Shoot, I didn't realize." I tossed my journal on the bed. As I walked to the bathroom, I gave her a hug and said goodbye. After I finished drying my hair, I went to my room and scanned the closet for an outfit. I tossed the clothes on the bed when the doorbell rang.

"It's open! Come on in!" I yelled down the stairs.

The door opened. "Uh, Zinn, it's Drew."

"Yeah, I'm upstairs. Be down in a minute."

"Yeah, okay."

I quickly changed my clothes. I fiddled with my hair and put on some lip gloss. Then I slipped on my shoes, grabbed my hoodie and journal, and headed down the stairs. When I hit the bottom step, Drew stood by the door, smiling.

"Hey, beautiful."

"Hey, you. Can you hold this, please?" I handed him my journal as I pulled my arms through the hoodie. Drew's eyes scanned the page.

"Hey, nosy!"

"Uh, sorry. Couldn't help myself. New song?"

"No, just words swirling through my head."

"Seems like a song to me." With his phone, he snapped a picture and winked at me before handing the journal back. "I'm gonna play around with some melodies for it."

"It's not a song. Besides, we don't have time to work on another song right now. We've got to get ready for the talent show, and the song we've chosen is far from ready."

Drew draped his arm around me. "Zinn, you worry too much. Your song is great. Besides, you've got plenty of time."

"Excuse me? You realize it's one week before the talent show, right?"

"Do I look worried?"

"No, and that makes me worry all the more."

Drew chuckled. "Trust me, you have nothing to worry about."

Nothing to worry about. Life felt like one big worry. Was it possible not to worry?

I loved the way Drew grabbed my hand. It always gave me a warm, secure feeling. Something about the size and pressure . . . He covered and protected it.

We stepped outside, and the brightness of the sun made me smile. The limbs on the trees were starting to show little bits of green, signifying the first glimpses of spring. White puffs of clouds speckled the blue sky allowing the sun to peek through and charge the day. As we walked to the truck, Drew quietly spoke. His words encouraged me to trust him. I wanted to trust him. The only thing standing in the way at this point was me. I truly hoped I could get over my issues.

We got in the truck and Drew headed toward his house. The music played softly as he chatted. The passing scenery of rolling hills with daffodils peeking their stems out of the ground gave glimpses of spring. In a week, the yellow flowers would be in full bloom. Avery came running to meet us as soon as the truck pulled in the driveway.

Her hyperfocus on her brother was adorable, especially since their dad was rarely home.

She jumped into Drew's arms. "Can I listen to you sing, please?"

"Squirt, I already told you no."

"But I—" she whined.

"No buts."

Avery pouted, and Drew shook his head. "If you don't tuck that lip back in, you know what'll happen?"

"No, Drew!" Avery screamed.

"Too late! He's already here." Drew transformed his hand into a claw and wiggled his fingers menacingly.

Wide-eyed, Avery shook her head. "I won't pout, I promise. Zinn, don't let him get me."

She reached out, and I wrapped my arms around her petite frame as we both stepped away from Drew. "He won't get you, sweetie."

"Oh, you can't stop me." Drew came toward us.

"Run, Avery! He can't get both of us." Avery escaped my embrace and bolted, obviously fine with me taking the hit from "the claw monster." I quietly laughed as she looked for somewhere to hide.

Avery screamed as Drew's footsteps pounded on the concrete. As was his plan, his "claw" hands grabbed me instead of Avery, initiating me into my first experience as Avery watched from behind a tree, screaming in delighted terror. His grip was on my waist, and then he started tickling me. Avery screamed more and ran into the house, slamming the front door. As I twisted to free myself, he stopped and gently pulled me closer to him. Brushing the hair from my face, he stared into my eyes.

"I got you."

"Uh-huh," I replied, weak with adrenaline and laughter.

As he moved closer, I held my breath. His face inches from mine, I closed my eyes and let the moment happen. His lips gently touched mine for a brief moment, then he pulled away.

"Nope," he said softly.

What just happened? Did he say nope? I opened my eyes and offered a look of humorous confusion. *Is he really taking back a kiss?* He leaned toward me again, but just as his lips got close to mine, he shook his head and moved away slightly. *What is a girl to do in this almost-unheard-of situation? Hours of girl talk didn't prepare me for this moment!* My eyes widened as I stood there, embarrassed and greatly bemused.

His lips pressed the top of my head as he wrapped his big arms around me. Breathing in deep, I softened in his arms.

"Zinn, I'll save you!" Avery's shrill voice disrupted the flow of what was happening between us, so I'd have to figure out why he said *nope* to the kiss later. Avery ran out the front door toward Drew and me, but he just shook his head and grinned as he released me.

"You can't save her. She's mine!" He gave me a wink, then added, "And only mine!"

Avery screamed and jumped onto Drew's back. "Run, Zinn! He can't get both of us."

Pulling Avery off Drew's back, I placed her on the ground and took her hand. "Run with me, Avery! If we stay together, we'll be fine."

Drew ran toward us and fell to his knees, reaching out his clawed fingers in defeat. "Noooo, I can't fight you." He wailed in agony and fell forward on his chest.

"I'm so weak . . . My claw!" Holding his clawed hand in the air, he wailed, "You discovered the secret. Oh, I'm so weak. I can't tickle anymore!" His arm fell to the ground. "You beat me. Together, you girls are too strong for my powers. Nothing can harm you now. Nothing!" He collapsed on the ground with his eyes closed and his tongue hanging out the side of his mouth.

Avery giggled. "Let's get him, Zinn." She quickly ran toward him and jumped on his back. I worried he'd get hurt, then remembered all the tackles he'd endured in football. A fifty-pound girl couldn't do anything but offer a back massage as her tiny feet walked along his broad back. Drew let out a big moan and turned around to cradle Avery. Then he stood and lifted Avery over his left shoulder. "Mwah, ha-ha-ha! You're alone now! It's time for the attack of the tickle claw." He tickled her sides with just enough intensity to not overwhelm her. *Nice touch.*

"No, Drew! Zinn, help me!" Laughing and twisting—and still screaming—she stretched her hand out to me. As I reached for her hand, Drew ran backward, putting distance between us. Avery leaned forward and stretched her hand out to me. I kept chasing Drew and Avery until Drew's arms wrapped around me and pulled me to him. Avery then grabbed my hand.

"We're together now. Nothing can get us," she stated proudly.

Drew pulled me closer and looked into my eyes. "That's right, Avery. We're together now. Nothing can get us."

Avery pulled Drew's face toward hers. "Not you, silly. Me and Zinn." Lifting up our clasped hands, she said, "We're together now. *You* can't get us."

He smiled and lowered Avery to the ground. "You're right. I guess I have to let go now. Some bonds are unbreakable, I suppose."

He was right. Some bonds are unbreakable. And some are . . .

The cool breeze blew over me as I sat on the porch, waiting for Drew. Every vehicle approaching the curve brought a bit of hope, but I sunk with disappointment time and again until his red truck finally appeared and pulled in the drive. I stepped off the porch and met him in the yard.

"Okay, now will you tell me what we're doing?"

"Patience, girl. You'll know soon enough."

"You can be infuriating, you know?"

"I know." Drew grinned mischievously and signaled me to get in the truck. Refusing the hand he offered, he rolled his eyes at my tiny sign of defiance, but he chuckled after he shut the door. He climbed in and said nothing as he put the truck in reverse and backed onto the main road. After a few minutes, we pulled onto the familiar dirt road.

"Why couldn't you tell me we were coming to your family's farm?"

Drew said nothing as he pulled into the drive and parked. He took my hand and we both got out on his side of the truck. We walked the path to the house and then headed to the back toward the creek. A picnic table was waiting, elaborately decorated with a tablecloth, candles, place settings for two, a large basket, and an ice bucket with a bottle of something. A few feet from the table, a blanket was draped over a log next to a wood-filled fire pit.

"This is the reason for all the secrecy?"

He winked and led me to the table. Slowly, he lit the candles, then he took the bottle from the ice bucket and filled the red plastic cups.

"Sparkling juice, huh? Very fancy."

"Pretty impressive, huh?"

Next, he opened the basket and pulled out two Styrofoam containers and placed one on my plate. I pressed my lips together before letting the sarcastic word drip from my lips. "Classy."

"You deserve the best," Drew said.

The meal of chicken nuggets and macaroni and cheese was more than perfect. Drew shared that Avery had recommended the entree for the evening. I loved his affection for his little sister. During our dinner conversation, Drew opened up about his family. The joy in his eyes when he talked about his Grandpa Earl teaching his eight-year-old self the guitar made me smile. That look of joy disappeared quickly when the conversation shifted to football.

"The same year I learned the guitar, I started playing football. My dad bribed me into playing by getting me a Nintendo." Drew laughed it off, but you could see the emptiness in his eyes. "Dad had this idea that music wouldn't teach me the discipline I needed. As if video games were a good substitute."

My brow furrowed as I shook my head and gave a questioning look.

"He says music is just a hobby and would never train me for the real world. *And a man needs discipline.*" Drew spoke in an exaggerated, domineering voice, mimicking his dad.

"And football does that?"

Drew stared blankly, likely resembling the way he stared at his dad while enduring his rants. "To my dad it does." Drew brushed the hair out of my face. "Have I told you how beautiful you are?" Heat filled my cheeks as I bit the corner of my mouth. He stood and held out his hand, leading me to the blanket-covered log. He knelt and lit the fire. "Be right back." Drew walked toward the truck and returned with his guitar.

"You'd better not be thinking about rehearsing the song right now," I said. "I don't want this day ruined."

"No rehearsal." He opened the case and removed the guitar. "I wanna play you something."

"Play me something?"

He settled beside me and began strumming the guitar and singing the words from my journal—the entry I had written about Sam. He'd successfully made it into an actual song. It sounded incredible. My eyes watered as Drew's fingers fluidly ran over the strings and his smooth, sultry tenor voice trailed into the air.

As he sang, he breathed life into my words, transforming them from thoughts on paper to an outpouring of the love and friendship I felt for Sam. When he finished, I sat there, speechless. Finally, I formed the only words I could find. "That's beautiful."

Drew set the guitar beside him. "You're beautiful." He leaned close to me and grazed my arm with his hand. His fingers lightly brushed my cheek, and his body leaned close to mine. I swallowed and my stomach did that topsy-turvy thing. The warmth of his breath hit my lips, and I lightly gasped. Then the soft touch of his lips met mine.

Again! Round two! Will this be a success?

As my eyes closed, a soft hum escaped me. Drew's lips parted from mine and my eyes shot open in embarrassment. He raised his eyebrow, then ignored my awkward noise—thankfully—putting his hand around my neck. Gently, he drew me to him, and his lips lightly pressed onto mine again. It was perfection for a few minutes, then he released me from his grip. With his strong arm wrapped around me, I settled into his side as we watched the flames dance in the darkness.

"Perfect. Just what you deserve," Drew whispered.

So that's why he said "nope" to the kiss before. Drew wanted it to be perfect, and that's exactly what he gave me. *He is too good to be true.*

CHAPTER TWENTY-SEVEN

The talent show haunted me all weekend, and Haley's Instagram post of Drew and me rehearsing amplified the pressure. Since the post had basically gone viral amongst the Bargeston population, I couldn't walk the halls without someone mentioning the song. By this point, I'd grown very tired of it—tired of rehearsing it and tired of thinking about it.

With just five days until the talent show, I wanted to back out because I feared our performance wasn't up to speed. But Drew wasn't having it. Instead, he reminded me of the deal we made and told me in no uncertain terms that he was not letting me off the hook. His insistence was hard to resist, especially since he coupled it with constant raving about the song.

Even with all the attention from him and Bargeston supporters, doubts kept creeping in. When Drew and I rehearsed it, I felt out of touch with the song. I couldn't tap into the same emotions of when I wrote it. The song brought feelings up that I couldn't connect with anymore. The anger at Bryce when I wrote it was gone. Honestly, I didn't want to resurrect it again. What I did feel was sadness for Sam, especially after Drew sang that new song to me by the fire. His music was how I felt when I wrote the words, and how I felt now. I knew what I had to do. I just hoped that Drew would agree to it.

Monday, when Drew and I were leaving school, I lowered the volume of the music and cleared my throat.

"I don't wanna do the song for the talent show," I said firmly.

"But we have a deal."

"I know that, but I don't wanna do *that* song."

"Well, that's too bad," Drew said with a cocky smirk. "I'm holding you to our deal."

"I'm not backing out of the deal. I just wanna do a different song."

Drew looked at me with confusion and shook his head. "Okay, then what song?"

"The song you wrote. I mean the one *we wrote*: my words but your music. Whatever, the one about Sam. I want to sing it."

His eyes widened. "Zinn, that's just some chords I fiddled with to show you that your words were a song. I mean, your words are great, but that's not a song . . . yet. Certainly not with that music. It needs a lot of work."

"I disagree, and I want to do that song or—"

"Or what?"

"Or I'm not doing the talent show," I said with all the sternness I could muster.

He fought a smile coming to his lips. Obviously, he liked my challenge. "You wanna sing a song you've never rehearsed at the talent show on Friday? You, who said that four weeks wasn't enough time, but now four days is?"

"Yeah. Is there a problem?" I said, trying my best to appear coy.

"No problem for me, as long as you're happy."

I nodded while giving him a satisfied grin. He took my hand and lightly kissed it.

I climbed in bed that night with Oreo nuzzling up against my side. I stumbled with the melody as I softly sang the words.

"Ugh! This isn't working!" Flopping on my side, my confidence from earlier today was decreasing. I only had four days to learn the new song. What had I done? I would be plagued with stage fright when I got on stage. I was so nervous to sing in front of the whole school, especially after Haley took it upon herself to post a snippet of Drew and me at rehearsal last week. It wasn't even going to be the same song. We were doing the classic bait-and-switch. But I had something better to offer the crowd. Seriously, though, changing the song a few days shy of the show was probably a big mistake. Regret quickly sank in.

On top of my bundle of nerves, Dawson kept me on edge too. Even though he hadn't approached me again, something about him threw me off balance. Every time he got around me, the hairs on the back of my neck stood up. His concentrated glances bored into me, reminding me of Bryce. The weird thing was that Dawson's stares felt even more territorial than Bryce's. And even weirder than that, Dawson didn't scare me like Bryce had. Dawson looked at me like he was drawn to me, as if he had a longing to be close to me. While I couldn't pinpoint exactly what made me uneasy, I wasn't afraid of Dawson doing something erratic or explosive, but I believed Bryce would and still could.

Whatever it was, it didn't matter. My plan was to keep as much distance between Dawson and me as possible. Since Drew had no desire to be near him either, staying away from Dawson was easy. If he would just stop leering at me, then I could put Dawson out of my mind for good.

CHAPTER TWENTY-EIGHT

I stood frozen at the back of the stage. Why did I agree to perform at the talent show? Drew stood next to me, holding his guitar. We'd drawn the last slot of the show, and I prayed there wouldn't be enough time for our song.

Drew tuned his guitar and focused his attention on listening as he adjusted the tension on the strings. He must've sensed me looking at him because he made eye contact and gave a reassuring smile.

"You're gonna be amazing. As amazing as you look, if that's possible."

Smoothing my dress, I glanced in the mirror. Haley had spent the afternoon helping me with my dress, hair, and makeup. The makeup was more than I typically wore, but it had a very natural look—except for the lashes. How she ever convinced me to put on fake lashes is beyond me. Of course, Haley is skilled at persuasion, and she said I needed it for stage presence—whatever that meant. I had to admit the coral baby-doll dress with cream ankle boots was an eye-popping ensemble, but my favorite thing was my hair. The smooth, defined curls cascading around my face and shoulders looked incredible.

Staring at myself, I wanted to see me as Drew saw me. I wanted to believe everything Drew said about me, but I didn't. I didn't know if I ever really could. Taking a deep breath, I stepped away from Drew, gave him an optimistic smile, and walked to the stairwell. After a couple of minutes, Drew's fingers lightly touched my hand.

"Drew, I can't do this."

"Zinn, you can do this." He took both my hands in his and powered me up with his magical eyes.

"I don't think I can."

Drew smiled as he brushed the hair out of my eyes. "Yes, you can. This is no different than you and me singing in the basement any other time."

"You're gonna be right beside me?" I kept breathing deeply, trying to center myself.

"Right beside you because there's nowhere else I wanna be." He kissed my hands.

The dance troupe walked past as the stagehand informed us it was time. I took a big gulp from the water bottle as the emcee announced our names. Drew touched my elbow. "You ready?" I gave a slight nod. He took my hand, and the heat of his grip sent a wave of energy through me. We walked onto the stage and I felt remarkably relaxed.

"Bear!" someone called from the crowd. Drew threw up his hand and smiled. More cheers ensued as we made our way to center stage. Drew handed the guitar to one of the stagehands and took one of the stools from him. He set down the stool and moved me over to it. "Just take a breath and relax." The gentleness of his mesmerizing eyes filled me with more peace. The stagehand placed the mic stand in front of me, and Drew positioned it before taking back his guitar and settling on his stool.

The crowd was a blur of faces from school. On the right side near the back, Mom, Grandma, and Mrs. Roberts waved at me. Savage, Ashlynn, Avery, and Drew's mom sat in the front row. Avery waved as she gleefully chattered to Ashlynn and Drew's mom. Savage gave his signature nod. A few rows behind them sat Haley with Ryan, Jules, and Blake, who all eagerly waved.

Drew leaned over to me. "Ready?"

"I guess so."

My heart raced as Drew leaned into the microphone. "Hello,

Bargeston! Ready for some great music?" The crowd hollered and clapped. "I know you've seen the post of part of Zinn's original song." Whooping from the crowd interrupted Drew. He beamed proudly as he cut his eyes to me, winked, and then focused back on the crowd. "Now y'all settle down. I know you were expecting that amazing song, but we've got an even better one to sing for you today." Boos and hisses from the crowd didn't stop Drew. "I get it, ya'll, but I promise this one won't disappoint you. It's another Zinn original. So sit back, relax, and enjoy."

Drew's fingers nimbly picked over the strings of the guitar. I closed my eyes and readied myself for the opening line. Waiting for my cue, the melancholy sound of the guitar gave me chills. I leaned toward the microphone and let my words drift into the audience. After the first line, a hush came over the crowd.

Finally, my eyes opened. An enchanted audience had replaced the intimidating crowd. Ashlynn and Avery beamed from ear to ear, but Savage shocked me. He smiled bigger than I'd ever seen him smile. Mom stood in the aisle, capturing the performance with her phone in one hand while her other hand wiped her teary eyes.

Drew, his music, my words, and the crowd generated so much energy and excitement, my heart pounded in my chest. Drew and I turned to each other at the same time, as if we had rehearsed it, but we hadn't. The flow of the music and the moment had taken over, and we followed its lead.

Moving into the second verse, the shakiness of my voice was gone. The words, like an extension of my soul, flowed smoothly and passionately. The captivation of the audience fed my confidence and pushed out any remaining nervousness. The relaxing aspect of the music had found me as I finished the song. When I sang the last words, the crowd exploded into applause.

Drew slipped his hand into mine and whispered, "Incredible!"

Grateful for his encouragement, I nodded as everyone cheered. Drew raised our hands in the air as the boisterous applause continued to fill the auditorium. A few students stood up, causing a chain reaction. Drew wrapped his arms around me and squeezed, lifting me off the ground.

The crowd was now on their feet, except Dawson and several of his friends who remained seated. *Who cares? He's got issues.* Even from the stage, the glare in his eyes bore into me. The emcee settled the crowd as Drew led me backstage. Dawson's eyes followed me, his glare growing even more intense, but then he flipped the script and smiled at me.

What?

Losing him as I stepped backstage, I had an uneasy feeling until Drew swooped me up in his strong arms and swung me around. "You were awesome, Zinn! I mean, that was fantastic. Thanks for letting me be a part of this. It was amazing."

"Hey, that was all your idea. You talked me into it."

"Well, you totally rocked." Drew brushed the hair from my face to see me more clearly. My hair had become sticky and clung to my sweaty face. "I just wanna say—"

Haley yelled out and interrupted Drew's moment. "Zinn, you did so great. That song. Just, wow!" Then several people had me surrounded and pulled me away from Drew.

"Thanks, Haley! Can you give me—"

"It was really good," Ryan said. "The lyrics, the guitar part, excellent."

"Um, thanks. The guitar was all Drew." I mouthed to Drew, "*Sorry*."

He leaned against the wall as the crowd pushed us farther apart.

"Very impressive, Zinn. And I'm not easily impressed." Blake chuckled.

Haley slapped his arm. "Shut up, Blake. Like you could do that."

"Hey, I could. I know music," Blake retorted.

"You can bang a drum, Blake, but that's not music." Haley smiled proudly, obviously feeling accomplished with her playful comeback.

"Ryan, you'd better set your woman straight on the necessity of the beat of the drums."

"Sorry, dude. There's no straightening her out. She thinks we're glorified toe-tappers." Ryan's arms went around Haley, pulling her close.

Haley and Blake continued with their tiff as Julie chatted with me. A few people were now talking to Drew, but his eyes stayed locked on me as I continued to get bombarded with people. Finally, we filtered into the hallway to find our families. I couldn't find Mom and Grandma. I checked my phone.

> **Mom:** Bug, you were amazing. So proud of you.
> Sorry I couldn't see you after the show ☹
> Grandma wasn't feeling well. See you at home.
> Love you bunches!!!

Happy tears fell on the phone as I texted a reply. Savage, Ashlynn, Avery, and Drew's mom appeared, offering me greetings, hugs, and compliments. Mrs. Behr and Avery said their goodbyes.

"Zinn, you really wrote that?" Ashlynn said.

"The words only. Drew heard it as a song."

"The words were so gripping," Ashlynn continued. "Wish I could write like that."

"Ash, first you need a brain," Drew quipped.

Ashlynn hit Drew on the arm. "Oh, you're so annoying, Drew." Directing her comments to me, she added, "Please tell me why you are friends with him? He's my cousin, so I can't get rid of him. But, Zinn, you don't have to have this guy in your life. So why do you want to?"

"He's not so bad."

"Oh, I disagree. He's the worst." Ashlynn gave Drew a look of disgust.

"Ash, you know I'm the best." Drew hugged her and spun her around.

She tried fighting against his strong embrace, but he knew how to get to her. "Yeah, the best at annoying me. Now put me down." She slapped at him as he released her. As usual, Savage stood, quietly watching the bickering between his two cousins.

"Hey, anyone up for Jack's?" Drew asked.

"Can't. Mom's waiting." Ashlynn smiled as she gave me a quick embrace. "Great job, Zinn. You blew me away with that song."

"Savvy, what about you?" Drew asked.

"Naw, gotta get home. But hey, good job on the song." He waved and left us.

"See you, Savvy." Drew patted Savage on the shoulder as he slid his hand into mine.

As Drew and I walked to his truck, I thought about how different my life was now. How good it was. I would have never dreamed of singing a song I wrote on stage in front of hundreds of people. Drew kissed my hand as he gazed at me. And I never thought I would have a guy like Drew, one so sweet who made me feel safe and protected. One whom I could one day fully trust. I smiled as I let myself hope.

CHAPTER TWENTY-NINE

On Monday, Drew had morning workouts for baseball, so Mom drove me to school. I went to my locker and unloaded my backpack before heading to the courtyard to meet Drew. I walked through the hall, aware people were staring at me while huddled over their phones. It suddenly got quiet. Obviously, the talent show performance and song still generated a buzz. Clearly, popularity and fame were not my thing, since the attention was giving me that same eerie feeling of my first day at school here. Haley stood in the middle of the hall, staring at her phone. When I reached her, I affectionately bumped her hip. She turned to me and had a strange, troubled look on her face.

"What's up?"

"You've not seen it?"

"Seen what?"

She showed me her phone. "It's all over school."

Big News from The Boneyard.

It seems one big cat came out of hibernation.

Over the weekend, some growling was heard from the cave between one howling bobcat and a little songbird putting him back on the scoreboard after months of being a no-show.

Boneyard Buffs, it seems that Grizzly gets this week's win with the Big Kill of that Little Birdie.

I lost my breath and stood frozen. Haley guided me to the bathroom. Grabbing a paper towel, she turned the water on full blast as she ranted. Her words garbled with the rushing of the water and made no sense. The room began to spin, and my hand pressed against the mirror, appreciating the coolness of the glass.

Somehow, time both rushed past and stood still. I now stood in the courtyard, unsure where Haley was. The stares and laughter of the crowd didn't interest me. Getting to the other side of the courtyard where that bunch of guys roared with laughter held my interest. They sickened me, huddled around Drew—the latest conqueror of The Boneyard. His laughing, likely about me and the post, fueled my anger. It was all a game to him. I was a game to him. A game to beat Dawson. How could I have been so stupid? His laughter bellowed throughout the courtyard.

I marched toward him. He got nudged by Malone and his head twisted toward me. He smiled and winked, then gave a nod to the group and walked toward me. He had some nerve.

"Hey, beautiful." He reached for my hand and I jerked it away. "Are you mad?"

"Am I mad? Are you serious?"

"What's wrong?"

Shaking my head, I blurted, "You wanna know what's wrong? Here!" I threw my phone at him.

With a stunned expression, Drew grabbed my phone from the ground and handed it to me. "Zinn, what's going on?"

"You are unbelievable. You really think I'm stupid?"

"I don't think you're stupid. Just tell me what's wrong."

"Does it feel good to be a winner again?"

"Zinn, you gotta clue me in on what you're talking about because I'm lost."

"Top Scorer on The Boneyard again? Must be real proud."

"The Boneyard? What're you talking about?" Drew pulled his phone from his pocket.

"Oh Drew, don't play dumb. At least respect me enough to be honest after you've been caught in the lie."

Drew looked at his phone and didn't reply. His nonresponse made me angrier by the second. I shook my head. "I'm done." Turning from Drew, I headed toward the building. Savage came down the steps and I went over to him. Drew stood by himself, apparently not caring I had left. I wiped my eyes, trying to stop the tears now flowing.

"Savage, can you get me of out here?"

He didn't say anything. He just walked with me to his car. He opened his car door, and I slipped into the seat.

When he settled in the car, he looked at me. "What's going on, Zinn?"

I shook my head as I fought back tears. In the distance, Drew ran toward us. I swallowed hard and tried to catch my breath. By the time Drew got to my door and opened it, Savage was out of the car and walking toward Drew.

"Zinn, please talk to me."

Drew knelt beside the door while Savage stood beside him. "Bear, maybe not now."

"I need to talk to her," Drew replied, then directed his attention to me. "Zinn, please just listen to me."

I stared straight ahead while trying to tune Drew out, hoping he'd just disappear. Savage placed his hand on Drew's shoulder. "Drew, give her some space."

"No! I gotta talk to her. Just give us a minute, Savage."

Savage stepped toward the driver's side. Drew's eyes filled with tears as he turned to me. "Zinn, please talk to me."

I crossed my arms, communicating that I was not going to budge.

"I'm so sorry. That whole post was a lie."

"I know it was a lie. I was there!"

"No, that's not what I meant. I'm screwing this up. Just let me explain." Drew gently took my hand, but I jerked it from him again.

"I've given you a chance to explain. You've had your minute, now leave me alone."

"Zinn, please give me a chance." His eyes were full of hurt.

"No, I can't. I won't. Just leave me alone." It was painful to look at him. I pulled on the door handle, pushing him to stand.

"Zinn, wait!"

"We shoulda just stayed friends." I forced the words out as I shut the door.

Drew's face lost all color as he stumbled backward. Savage walked over to him, put his arm around Drew's shoulders, and walked him away from the car. Drew looked back, then nodded slowly as Savage patted him on the back.

Savage returned to the car, and we left the parking lot. We rode in silence for several minutes. The buzz of my phone filtered through the car. I flipped over my phone and Drew's name flashed on the screen. I hit Decline.

"Wanna talk?" Savage asked.

"I don't wanna talk or think or anything. I just wanna go away. Just go somewhere away from all this."

"Hmm, okay."

Savage drove down the highway, making several turns. We were miles out of town in an unfamiliar area. The road meandered through a wooded area where there were no houses. He pulled the car onto a dirt road and parked.

Getting out of the car, he walked over to my side and opened the door. We walked the dirt road until we came to a hidden trail through the densely wooded area. He held out his hand and smiled. "Path's kinda rough."

I took Savage's hand and allowed him to lead me along the downward winding dirt path strewn with rocks and limbs until the trees eventually became sparse. We came upon a clearing surrounded by a rock wall and a beautiful creek flowing beside it. As my eyes traveled along the creek, water splashed off the sides of the rocks. I dropped Savage's hand and stepped toward the misty water.

As I moved closer, the entirety of the massive waterfall pounded over the rocks and crashed into the creek. The water created a mist that looked like a floating cloud. It was incredibly breathtaking.

Savage pointed to a massive log under a cluster of trees near the falls. He held out his hand to help me. I took it and stepped on a knotty log and hoisted myself up. Savage stood behind me as I maneuvered myself to a seated position. Savage, with complete ease, popped himself on the log beside me.

The rushing water over the edge, the crashing sounds of the water hitting the rocks, and the serenity of the trees nestled around us was all I needed. Now I could breathe. The sun straight overhead beamed down on me, providing just enough warmth that I didn't shiver from the cool moisture coming off the falls. The intoxicating smell of the clean, crisp air filled my head, eliminating all the recent bad memories. I continued to breathe.

When the clouds covered the sun, a chill caused me to shiver. The heat of Savage's body drew me toward him. I was unaware my head was resting on his shoulder until his arm wrapped around me. His warmness soothed me, and I melted into his side.

The rushing of the falls drowned the chatter in my head. Savage's steady and calm breathing filled the space of his silence. He knew everything I needed to hear. And in that moment, I heard it.

Rustling leaves woke me from my sleep, and I lifted my head from Savage's shoulder. "Sorry. Guess I was tired."

"Hmm."

"Thanks for getting me outta there. I couldn't deal with it all."

"Deal?"

Pulling up the post, I handed Savage my phone. He took the phone and read it. His eyes glinted some anger, but it quickly disappeared. He handed the phone back to me.

"Hmm. Seems Bear's got some explaining to do."

"Oh, you think?" I said with disgust.

"I do."

"And you think I should listen, huh?"

"Maybe?"

I clenched my jaw. Savage, in his typical fashion, waited for me to speak. I threw my hands in the air. "I know I have to talk to him, but I'm not ready. I'm too mad, too hurt . . . Ugh! I'm too everything."

"Hmm. Seemed Bear was pretty hurt too."

"Yeah, well, he's pretty good at pretending."

"Didn't seem to be pretending to me."

I gritted my teeth over Savage's defense of Drew. My silence apparently triggered Savage to continue. "That post and the way he has been treating you . . . They don't really mesh."

"What are you saying, Savage? That Drew didn't post it?"

"Can't say for sure, but I've never known him to do it before."

"Oh, really?" Sarcasm dripped from every part of me. "What about his freshman year?"

"Hmm, freshmen year? You don't know?"

"Yeah, I know." I shook my head in disgust. "Drew and all those other guys posting on that repugnant site. They all make me sick, especially Drew."

"Hmm, you really should talk to Drew."

I cut my eyes to Savage, hoping he could feel every bit of annoyance I had right now.

Talk to Drew? You're crazy.

He jumped off the log and held out his hand. I rolled my eyes and obliged him the moment, but he had another thing coming if he thought I would listen to anything Drew had to say now.

As Savage pulled into the lot, Drew jumped off the tailgate of his truck and shoved his hands in his pockets. *Ugh, he's still here.* Bitterness went through me as Savage went up to Drew. Savage had some nerve. I tried my best to figure out an escape from Drew and this talk. Savage separated from Drew and headed toward me. *Great, here comes the guilt trip.* Savage opened the door and went down on one knee, making himself eye level with me. He was trying to soften me up, no doubt.

"So you think you could hear him out?"

Gritting my teeth, my head moved side to side, denoting my rejection to his request.

"Hmm." Savage paused, then said firmly, "Zinn, you're wrong about Drew. You need to listen to him."

My eyes widened and I lost my breath when I heard the assertive tone of Savage. I wasn't sure whether to fire back at him or cry, but for some unknown reason I nodded my head. I slipped out of the car and followed him over to Drew.

Drew's bloodshot eyes stabbed me in the gut. *Don't fall for his tears.*

Stiffening myself, I was determined to give him only one minute, then I was leaving.

"Zinn, I'm so sorry. You gotta believe me. I didn't post that."

His words made me cringe and I retorted angrily. "Still lying, huh?"

Savage interjected, "Zinn, you need to hear him out."

I narrowed my eyes, now fully annoyed by Savage and his interference.

"Savvy, just go." Drew motioned for him to leave us. I figured he assumed he could use his persuasive, flirtatious charm on me. But Savage's presence infringed on its effectiveness.

Boy is he wrong.

Savage moved over to his car. Drew reached for my hand, but I refused him.

"Zinn, I didn't make that post. I shoulda told you all that happened."

"I don't want to hear the sordid details," I blurted out as I turned from him.

He grabbed my hand firmly and turned me back to him. "Zinn, you gotta listen. I never posted anything on The Boneyard, ever."

"You really expect me to believe that. You told me you posted—"

"No, I didn't," he interrupted. "I never told you anything about the posts."

"What?" I paused as it all swirled through my head. Dawson, Drew, the fight, Haley, and The Boneyard. *Wait! It was Haley.* The only thing I knew about Drew and his Boneyard posts was what Haley had told me. That day when Drew was willing to explain, I stopped Drew from telling me. A wave of sickness came over me. "Drew, I'm so sor—"

He swooped me up and held me close. "Zinn, please never let go."

While a darkness loomed over The Boneyard post, and Drew and I still needed to talk, I didn't want to think about any of that right now. Instead, I shook off the negative feelings and relished in the good feeling of being in Drew's arms.

When he finally released me from his grip, Drew and I walked over to Savage, who was leaning on the back of his car. Drew cut his eyes and gave him a nod. "Thanks for everything, Savvy." Their eyes were momentarily locked, creating an unspoken dialogue. This unspoken language signaled something deep between them. I'd seen this look between them after the whole Bryce thing at my house, and it intrigued me.

The bell forced us back toward the building. We stepped inside as students crowded the hallway, forming lines leading into the cafeteria. As we came to the end of the hall, Haley ran toward us. "Zinn!" She looked at me, then to Drew. "You need to hear this too. I was just in gym and heard them laughing."

"Heard who laughing?" Drew asked.

"Jordan and Riley. They were talking about the post," she said.

"Haley, we're done with the post," I said.

"No!" Haley shook her head. "They were saying Sierra and Dawson—"

"Sierra and Dawson?" Drew yelled angrily.

Haley paused a moment, but her eyes stayed on Drew. "Uh, well, yeah! They said something about Dawson being good since Sierra's post did the job of annihilating Zinn."

Drew rumbled a low growl as he spoke. "That's it. He's done."

Savage placed his hand on Drew's shoulder and shook his head. "Not the time, Bear."

Drew jerked from Savage's hold. "It's past time. I'm ending this now." Drew headed toward the doors leading to the courtyard.

Following behind him, I grabbed his arm. "Drew, please don't."

Loosening from my grip, he hit the door and flung it open. Drew pounded down the steps. I ran after him as he headed into the courtyard. He stopped and looked around the crowd. Dawson sat with a group at a table under the trees. Drew took off toward him as Dawson continued laughing with his friends. Drew made his way through the crowded courtyard with Savage on his heels. Haley and I ran to keep up with them. Savage tried his best to persuade Drew to turn around, but Drew kept moving toward Dawson.

"Dawson!" Drew yelled across the courtyard.

Dawson looked in our direction, seemingly unmoved. He hopped off the table, readying himself for whatever was coming as his eyes locked on Drew. The crowd gathered around the grassy quad, mumbling and nudging each other.

"Problem, Bear?"

"You know my problem." Drew got louder as he got closer.

"Can't say I do." Dawson stepped forward, unfazed by Drew's tone or close proximity.

"You're not doing this again, not with Zinn."

"Aw! Your post. It is getting you some attention." Dawson's eyes cut to me as he smirked. "Little songbird don't like it so much, huh?"

Drew let out a growl and plowed into him. Dawson got knocked back but remained upright.

"You wanna do this? Then let's do it right now!" Dawson cracked his knuckles and bent his neck side to side.

Drew let out another growl and punched him in the face. Dawson fell to the ground but jumped right back up. He swung at Drew, barely missing him. Dawson shook his head and took another swing. Drew dodged it, stepped back, and then charged into Dawson. Tackling him, they wrestled on the ground as low growls sounded. Each took turns overpowering the other. The crowd surrounded the two guys battling on the ground. Shouts came from everywhere. A couple of guys tried to pull them off of each other but with no success. With Drew on top, Savage and a couple of guys were finally strong enough to pull Drew away. Dawson pounced up instantly, then lunged toward Drew and landed a punch across his chin. Drew lunged at Dawson while Savage and the other guys fought to hold Drew back. With Drew restrained, he finally stopped flailing.

"Let me go!" Drew yelled, flinging his arms and trying to escape the grip of the two guys. "I said let me go!" They stepped back from Drew, but not Savage. Savage stayed right beside him.

"Only yourself to blame, Bear. You knew the cost would be the girl," Dawson said as he spit blood on the ground.

Suddenly, Drew slammed into Dawson, taking him to the ground. He punched his face several times until a few guys lifted him off Dawson. As the guys pulled Drew away, Dawson got up and started swinging at Drew. A couple of guys grabbed Dawson's arms to hold him back.

"This ain't over!" Dawson yelled as he lunged toward Drew.

Drew composed himself and spoke with a stern, calm tone. "Never said it was."

"Don't let your guard down, Bear."

"Never do with you, Dawson," Drew said.

"Drew, let's go." Savage grabbed Drew's arm and pulled him away from the crowd.

"Run along, Bear, and do what Savvy says," Dawson quipped.

Drew's eyes locked on Dawson as he backed away. "Like you said, Dawson, this ain't over."

Drew took my hand and we headed to the steps while Dawson kept taunting Drew. Savage's arm around Drew kept him moving forward as he spoke calmly, trying to counter the effects of Dawson's stream of insults. Drew opened the door and tucked me safely into the building. Drew and Savage lingered outside as the door shut. Through the glass, Drew winked at me and held up his finger, indicating one minute. Savage talked and Drew nodded his head. The determined, focused look softened as he smiled at me. Savage patted him on the back. Drew opened the door and they stepped into the hallway. Savage nodded and gave me his signature half smile as Drew took my hand.

"Let's get you and Savage to class," Drew said.

"It's lunch now," I said.

Drew checked his phone and nodded. "Then let's get some food."

The cafeteria greeted us with many stares and whispers. Drew kept me close to his side as we maneuvered through the crowd to a table in the corner. Drew's guard was up, and his talkative, lighthearted self had been sabotaged by the confrontation with Dawson. A couple of guys approached him, asking for details about what went down, but Drew brushed them off while deflecting all attention away from me or the post.

At any other time, Drew's protectiveness would have me feeling relaxed and at ease, but not now. The threat of when Dawson would appear again and what Drew would do when it happened clouded it. This whole mess with him and Dawson was my fault, and Drew was paying the price. I hated being a burden to Drew and that I had put him in this position.

Leaving the cafeteria, I stayed on full alert, waiting for Dawson to come around the corner. He didn't, thankfully. The walks to English and chemistry proved uneventful, but after chemistry told a different story.

When I stepped into the hall, some guys rushed past me as one of them ran his mouth. "They're fighting again." They pushed through bodies huddled at the end of the hall. A sick feeling came over me as I moved closer to the crowd. The hum of the teens couldn't drown out the intense yelling. My heart raced, and I froze as more people moved past me. The next moment I was on the outside of the mass of bodies.

The crowd made it impossible for me to see anything, but the yelling told me everything. Drew and Dawson shouting at each other would soon lead to more punches being swapped. I took some deep breaths and tried to push myself through the horde of people, but I couldn't make it. Mr. Cavers and another teacher pushed through the crowd. After a couple of minutes, the students had dispersed. Mr. Cavers stood with Drew on one side, and the other teacher walked with Dawson. Drew glanced my way and winked. I took a step toward him, but he shook his head no. Mr. Cavers took Drew by the arm and escorted him down the hall. A wave of sickness moved over me. Then, almost like he knew I needed him, Drew looked over his shoulder and mouthed, *"Don't worry."*

Sitting through chorus was torturous. Not knowing what was happening with Drew had my pulse racing. Singing proved difficult with my lack of focus and the shallow breathing from my nervousness. When the bell finally rang, I ran out of class and darted between the swarm of teens as I made my way to the office. Opening the office door, Drew wasn't there, but the side glass of the principal's office door revealed his chestnut curls. The office was growing crowded with bodies, so I opted to wait in the hall.

Outside the office, I leaned on the wall, fidgeting with the strap on my backpack. As the time ticked by, the people shuffling past me lessened until the hall was nearly empty. After a few minutes, I slid down the wall and sat on the floor. I checked my phone, hoping maybe Drew had texted, but there was nothing. The waiting had me on edge. I slid in one earbud and played some music. It annoyed me, so I removed the bud and popped it back in the case. I grabbed my journal but ended up just tracing around the spiral edging. I frustratingly shoved it my backpack.

I glanced down the hall and saw Savage walking toward me. I got on my feet. As soon as he reached me, he put his arm around me, which released the tears I'd been holding back.

It wasn't long until the office door opened and Dawson stepped out. His fiery eyes bore into me as he moved past Savage and me. Just before the door completely shut, it flew back open and Drew glided to me, folding me into his arms. Releasing me, he brushed the hair from my forehead, lightly kissing me there.

I softly touched the gash near his eye. "You got hurt! Are you okay?"

"I'm fine. Let's just go?" Engulfing my hand in his, he gently pulled me to follow him. I didn't argue.

By the time we got to his truck, my patience was gone. "Would you tell me what went down with you and Dawson and what happened with the principal?"

"Zinn, you don't need to worry about this," Drew said.

"Don't need to worry? Are you serious? You're fighting Dawson because of me. You're hurt because of me. And you had to go the principal's office because of me."

"You think this is your fault?" Drew looked stunned. He turned to Savage. "Savage, she thinks she's to blame."

Savage showed little emotion but gave his standard reply. "Hmm."

I stood there in disbelief. Neither of them said anything, so I was forced to respond. "You wouldn't be in any of this mess if it wasn't for me. Of course, I'm to blame."

Sadness fell over Drew's face and his eyes glassed over. "Zinn, this has nothing to do with you at all. Please don't think that. This is all because of me."

The confusion overwhelmed me and left me speechless. Drew wrapped his arms around me, leaned close to my ear, and whispered, "There is some stuff you need to hear."

CHAPTER THIRTY

Drew turned at the road leading to the small lakeside park. He positioned the truck overlooking the lake. He sat quietly, then said, "I know you need to hear this. I just hope it doesn't mess things up for us."

Before I could respond, Drew disclosed everything about Dawson, The Boneyard, and the reason behind all the strife between them.

"It really started during my eighth-grade year. My dad was between jobs and home for several months. Well, you saw how my dad is. His hounding me every day finally got to me. It was too much pressure. I guess you'd say rebellion kicked in pretty hard. Even Savage became someone I avoided. My family has some pretty strict rules, so rebelling doesn't take much. But a little rebellion wasn't enough for me. I wanted to break free of all the family rules, my dad's pressure, the expectations, and the whole feeling of being an outsider. And Dawson was the key to doing just that. His family and my family have some history, so it's always been understood to keep our distance from them. Plus, my dad has it in his mind that I don't need to mix with "the likes of him." It didn't take long to get chummy with Dawson, which quickly became a pretty tight friendship. Starting high school, me and Dawson got even thicker. Since Dawson's older brother, Devin, was popular, well, his cool factor automatically transferred to Dawson, and it also trickled to me. So this popularity led to attention from girls. Dawson took that and ran with it. He was going out with all these different girls and bragging about it in the locker room. Pretty soon, all the guys were shooting off their mouths about any girl who gave them the time of day. One of the guys joked about girls being points. In our chatroom, someone posted this scoreboard thing using our chatroom handles. It was all just a dumb joke, but then somehow it blew up to the whole Boneyard site. They didn't even care what it did to the girls. It was funny to them. All about scoring points and getting the win, whatever that even means."

Drew rested his head on the steering wheel with his eyes closed. I stayed quiet, not sure what to say. Drew straightened himself and turned to me. "I know this is more than you want or need."

"No," I said. "I'm just confused. Why would Dawson post something now? You've not posted on the page for two years, he—"

"Zinn, I told you I never made a post. It was Dawson. He posted that stuff about me."

"Why?" I asked, completely stunned.

Drew shook his head in disgust. "I don't know. Maybe 'cause we were friends and he thought it was funny? I never questioned him. He just did it."

I sat there silently searching for words, then I flooded him with questions. "Dawson made your posts two years ago. And this riff between you two was over until now? When I came to school here? So this is because of me?"

"Zinn." Drew's eyes closed as he shook his head. When he finally looked at me, his eyes were deep pools of sadness. "You are not to blame. This is all my fault."

"But it's—" Drew's finger flew to my lips before I could say another word.

"Yeah, the post is because of you. But it's not what you think." Drew exhaled. "I need some air."

He got out the truck and walked to the water. He scooped up some rocks and skipped one, and the rhythmic dance on the water soothed me momentarily. I climbed out of the truck and slowly made my way to him. As soon as I got there, he squeezed me tightly, nearly taking my breath away. He wouldn't let go, or maybe he couldn't.

When he released me, he lowered himself to the ground. I folded my legs and settled beside him. "Zinn, this Dawson stuff . . . There's a lot. But I need you to know and understand that it is not about you."

I gave him a nod to let him know I understood.

"Dawson always comes after me in any way he can."

"Why?"

"Because I told Dawson to stop the posts about me and Sierra."

"Sierra?"

Drew nodded. "Yeah, me and Sierra. It was short-lived and really nothing. When the first post happened, she didn't mind. I think she may have been flattered. So I let it go. But then Dawson took it too far and humiliated her. Actually, he ruined her."

Haley had said Tristan's post nearly destroyed her. Sierra didn't seem phased in any negative way by attention from The Boneyard group. On the contrary, she appeared to crave it.

"It doesn't seem like a post would bother Sierra," I said.

"Maybe not now, but the post at that time crushed her. I told everyone it wasn't true, but no one believed me. The damage was done. She homeschooled the rest of the semester. It was even rumored she took some pills, but I don't know. When she came back sopho-more year, she was totally different."

His eyes glazed over as he shook his head, and I touched his hand to show him how sorry I was. "Drew, none of that is your fault though."

"But it is. I shoulda stood up to Dawson after the first post. Maybe tried to hack the site or take it down. I don't know. I should have done something. All I did was tell him I was through with him and to leave me alone."

Drew had never looked so broken. Nothing I could say or do could take away his pain. As he shared more details about it, the guilt poured out through his words. Whether I wanted it or not, Drew was giving me the entire history of the events with Dawson—or so I thought. The confessional moment offered something for Drew. Like he was being purged of all the emotions that he'd kept bottled up for the past couple of years.

"Dawson goes after any girl I talk to. He doesn't care about the girls or if they get hurt. He just wants me to pay. The girls are just collateral damage to him."

"So that's why you've never dated?"

Drew narrowed his eyes at me. "How do you know I've never dated?"

"I don't know. Haley might've said something."

"You're cute, you know that?" Heat rose to my cheeks, and his hand lightly touched my face. "Even more adorable when you blush."

His hand slid across my cheek, brushing the hair back, and then his fingers combed through my hair as his hand went to the back of my head. The gentle force that drew me toward him made my heart sink. As his face moved closer to mine, the warmth of his skin and the smell of his cologne intoxicated me. Then the softness of his lips lightly touched mine. His tender touch grew in intensity until I surrendered my lips to his. His arms enclosed me, and I got lost in his embrace even further.

He took his lips off mine and lifted my hand to his lips, softly kissing each finger. His warm breath flowing across my fingers sent shivers down my spine. I leaned into his shoulder and his fingers lightly caressed my arm as I cuddled against his side.

"Zinn, you're the reason. The reason I waited. I just hoped you were out there. So I kept waiting," he whispered.

CHAPTER THIRTY-ONE

The days were getting warmer and the trees were budding. Everything was fully waking from the winter slumber. As Drew and I walked into school, he held tight to my hand. Even though it had been a few weeks since the whole fight with Dawson, Drew's class chaperoning remained on full alert. The few days of the guard entourage had actually become a constant, whether I liked it or not. Drew had said in no uncertain terms that he didn't want to give Dawson or any of his crew any opportunity to harass me. Complaining was pointless. Besides, I didn't really mind it since I preferred keeping my distance from Dawson. His watchful eye seemed to always be there, so having Savage and Drew nearby put me at ease.

As I left history I leaned against the wall and waited for Drew. Suddenly, my phone flashed notifications of Haley's multiple texts.

Haley: You're not gonna believe what just happened…

Haley: Kate Webster is transferring, so I got the music

Haley: Sorry! I meant to text I got the music section on yearbook. I'm so excited!!!

Haley: You know what this means…
I'll be taking your pic when you get the solo!!!

Me: That's so cool. I'm excited for you.

Me: BTW I've still not decided if I'm gonna try out. So you taking my pic is not a done deal

Haley: But Mr. Wyatt has basically said the solo is yours 😕

Drew leaned over my shoulder as he wrapped his arms around my waist. "Hey, beautiful."

"Just a sec. I'm dealing with Haley."

"What's up with your girl?"

"Yearbook stuff."

Drew rested his chin on my shoulder as I replied to Haley. "Solo? You trying out?"

"Mr. Wyatt is wanting me to try out, but I haven't decided."

"Cool. So when are try-outs?" Drew asked.

Pulling myself from his grip, I turned to him. "Do not do this."

"Do not do what?" Drew brushed the hair from my face.

I shook my head as I stepped away from him. His arm came around my back and he pulled me to him, lightly kissing my forehead and holding me in his arms. "Zinn, it's just a try-out." He kissed me softly on my cheek to butter me up. "It's okay to be scared. Just don't let it steal your hope."

"Fine, I'll consider trying out."

"That's my girl." Drew slipped his hand in mine, and we walked down the hall.

I mulled over Drew's words: *don't let it steal your hope.*

Is fear stealing my hope? When I let myself hope for something in the past, I always got hurt. And I'd had enough hurt. Let myself hope? No, I wasn't ready for that. Besides, I buried those feelings when I buried my dad. It was better to avoid any kind of hurt. It was easier to not hope.

Haley was right. She was gonna take my picture for the yearbook. I wasn't sure how she and Drew talked me into trying out, but they had. And to my complete surprise, I had gotten the girls' solo. Of course, the male soloist came as no shock to anyone. Jake had dominated the tryout. He and I were to be spotlighted in the yearbook as the soloists of the spring concert. Haley was elated to be taking our pictures.

She wanted to shoot them at an old bridge that was just a few minutes from her house. Rolling hills and a wooded area surrounded the bridge over the small creek. When we arrived, I understood Haley's insistence on this spot. The serene beauty of the lush-green field next to the dense wooded area provided a perfect backdrop. The covered bridge over the running water looked like a movie set. As I stood on the bridge, Haley positioned me and snapped several pictures. She did the same with Jake, then she took some with the two of us.

Haley scanned through the photos, showing us the different shots. The noise of some cows from across the meadow became annoyingly loud. As the mooing intensified, my eyes wandered to the direction of the noise. A herd of cows seemed unsettled and nervous, which made them bawl even louder.

Something from the wooded area beside the pasture came running toward the cows. The distance was too far to make out what kind of animal, except whatever it was certainly had speed. By this time, Jake and Haley were engrossed in the scene as well. From the direction of the farmhouse, a farmer hollered. The unidentified animal kept its pace as it ran toward the herd of cows. The cows huddled together and continued to sound distressed. Whatever we watched running from the woods, though, was not causing the anguish of the cattle.

"Haley, let me have the camera," Jake said as he took it from her and snapped some photos. "Maybe it's a Beast." Jake handed the camera back to Haley.

We stood in awe as this hairy figure running on two feet headed into the pasture. It was muscular, tall, covered with dark hair, and wearing tattered-and-torn camouflage clothing as it ran into the disheveled herd. Yells from the farmer didn't stop the advancement of the creature. Then the blast of a shotgun fired. The hairy figure suddenly collapsed to the ground in mid-run.

"It's been shot!" Jake yelled, running down the hill toward the fallen creature.

"Jake, stop! You can't go down there. That man is shooting!" I screamed.

"Zinn, it's a Beast. I know it."

Jake kept running down the hill. I hollered more warnings, but he ignored them as he made his way to the clearing where the figure fell. The tall grass shuffled around the spot where the creature dropped, and a head rose slightly above the grass. Then the creature stood up in a semi-upright position but was injuriously bent over. It slowly limped toward the wooded area.

Handing me the camera, Haley said, "Zinn, you're not gonna believe this."

The camera view blurred and then focused on the staggering figure, only now it wasn't hairy. "Haley, is that—?

"I think so," Haley interrupted, too excited for me to finish the sentence.

"Haley, he's hurt. We have to help him!"

I ran down the hill, my brain fast-tracking all the details and all the puzzle pieces. It hadn't been by chance that the Beast had saved me —twice.

Please be okay!

Holding fast to that prayer, I kept running toward the Beast and holding on to hope.

ACKNOWLEDGMENTS

So much to say, so little space. I am blessed beyond measure with a slew of encouragers who have motivated and inspired me to write this story.

First, I want to thank my husband, Joe, who has supported me through it all and made this dream a reality. Because of your patience, love, and plates of food I have this book finished, finally. I love you.

To my children, who make me better. Thank you for all the help, advice, patience, and tolerance. Cecily, you inspired me, encouraged the story, and gave me insight to make the story better. Colton, you've showered me with encouragement, helped me, motivated me, and assisted me. To my bonus children, Parker and Calie, thank you for your encouragement and enthusiasm.

To my parents, thank you for all the years of support, for always being there, and for the prayers. You planted seeds that will forever bear fruit. I love you both.

To Chris, Karen, Caleb, Lexie, Courtney, Chloe Grace, and li'l C., thank you for all the love, for cheering me on, and for always being there.

To Janie, thank you for all you do. Thanks for reading, editing, encouraging, and helping me with whatever I need.

To April and Isabella, thank you for your encouragement and interest and always asking about my book. Isabella, thanks for the inspiration to publish my story.

To my editor, Jenna, you walked me through this process and made me a better writer. Thank you for the help and for your friendship.

Thank you to my Beta Readers and ARC team. I appreciate your encouragement, your support, and your willingness to read my story. You helped me reach this milestone.

To my tribe, thank you for keeping me *hopeful*. Amanda, Todd, David Ray, and Sue Ann, thank you for keeping me excited, motivated, and for challenging me. Wes, thank you for being the first to listen to my pitch, inspiring me to write the story, and for planting the seed to publish. Lisa W., thank you for being there from the first draft, the feedback, and for the excitement. Laura W., thank you for being with me from the story's inception. You've been patiently waiting while encouraging every step. Gina S., thank you for reading, sharing, encouraging, and praying. Thanks for being in the field with me. Susan, Rhett, Paul, and Kat, thank you for doing your part to keep the spark alive in me. I appreciate your excitement. Tangie, thank you for your friendship. You encouraged me from the beginning with my blog. You saw the writer in me and motivated me to stick with it. I am so grateful for you.

Most importantly I want to thank my Father above for the desire, inspiration, time, energy, talent, and the blessings of all the people who have had a hand in this book's creation. I pray the readers will be blessed.

www.ingramcontent.com/pod-product-compliance
Lightning Source LLC
Chambersburg PA
CBHW021439310726
48971CB00005B/1429